READERS TALK ABOUT RICHARD EVANS

Richard Evans' first book, Deceit, is a five-star thriller that brings the Australian political process to life. – GOODREADS

I absolutely loved it, couldn't put it down. I would love to see your book become a movie. – IAN S., MELBOURNE

Rich in ideas and provokes much thought about our parliamentary process, abuses of power, corruption, and the need, at times, for ordinary people to step up and take a stand in the name of honour and professional integrity. – NADINE D., EDITOR

'The Kill Bill has such a fascinating concept at its heart, and you brought the characters to life brilliantly.' – C.dB, EDITOR

This is an outstanding debut from Evans, and this terrific read comes highly recommended.' – GOODREADS

From former Federal MP Richard Evans comes this exceptional political thriller debut, which serves as the first part of his Democracy trilogy.' CANBERRA WEEKLY

I adored Gordon O'Brien. Straight as an arrow amongst those who are only in things for themselves, I couldn't help but cheer him on as he was like a dog with a bone, searching out the truth' BJ'S BOOK BLOG

Just finished reading Deceit and it was gripping; I could not put it down. It was brilliant. I just loved the book and can't wait to read Duplicity.' FORMER CLERK OF VICTORIAN LEGISLATIVE COUNCIL

I thoroughly enjoyed the book and did not want to put the book down, but neither did I want the story to end! Congratulations! – TRINITY MARKETING

ALSO BY RICHARD EVANS

Democracy Trilogy
Deceit
Duplicity
Doomed

Referendum Series
Forgotten People
The Kill Bill

Stand Alone Books
Out of my Hands

Non-Fiction
The Australian Franchising Handbook

EPISODE THREE OF THE DEMOCRACY TRILOGY

POLITICAL AMBITION CAN BE DEADLY

RICHARD EVANS

852
PRESS

852
PRESS

First published in 2021 by 852 Press,
an imprint of Corven Pty. Limited
Suite 208, 5-11 Cole Street, Williamstown Victoria 3016 Australia
www.852Press.com

10 9 8 7 6 5 4 3 2 1

Copyright © RICHARD EVANS 2021

852 Press supports the right to free expression and the value of copyright. The purpose of copyright is to encourage writers and artists to produce creative works that enrich our culture.

The moral right of the author is asserted.

All rights reserved. No part of this book may be reproduced or transmitted in any form or by any means, electronic or mechanical, including photocopying, recording or by any other information storage retrieval system, without prior permission in writing from the publisher.

This book is a work of fiction. Names, characters, and incidents are the products of the writer's imagination or are used fictitiously and are not to be construed as real. Any resemblance to actual events, locales, or persons, living or dead, is coincidental.

National Library of Australia Cataloguing-in-Publication entry:

Author: Evans, Richard
Title: Doomed / by Richard Evans
ISBN: 978-0-6489328-6-4 (Trade paperback)
ISBN: 978-0-6489328-7-1 (ebook)
ISBN: 978-0-6489328-8-8 (hardcover)
Australian fiction.

A catalogue record for this book is available from the National Library of Australia

Cover Design: 852 Press
Internal design: Glenn @www.fiverr.com/sarco2000

For Jill

Friend and colleague dealing with Democracy.
We did it together and enjoyed it. Thank you.

THE MAJOR PLAYERS

GOVERNMENT:

Peter Stanley	Prime Minister
Barton Messenger	Deputy Prime Minister and Treasurer
Christopher Hughes	Manager of Government Business
James Harper	Foreign Minister
Maurice Roussett	Environment Minister
Ginni Stavloukas	Mining Minister
Jack Stevenson	Agriculture Minister
Helen Cavanagh	Finance Minister
Haydon Charlton	Chief Whip
Wilson Campbell	Regional Development Minister

OPPOSITION:

Meredith Bruce	Opposition Leader
Everett Menzies	Manager Opposition Business
Jaya Rukhmani	Independent Member for Melbourne

MEDIA:

Tony Hancock	Proprietor Hancock Media
Peter Cleaver	Hancock Chief of Canberra Bureau
Cassandra Rogers	Hancock political editor
Tamara O'Byrne	Hancock's protégé

OTHERS:

Brian Tucker	Farmer
Sophie Papadopoulos	Bank Manager
Garrick Higgins	Union delegate
Francesque Hughes	Christopher Hughes' spouse

THE STORY SO FAR

Prime Minister Andrew Gerrard has it all. He is at the top of his political game, having led the parliament and the nation with his charismatic style for twenty years. The only thing he doesn't have is enough retirement money.

After a boozy dinner with his friend, the president of Indonesia, Gerrard agrees to fund a deal for offshore immigration detention centres. Gerrard will then take a clip of the payment on the way through as a commission. Retirement sorted.

Tragedy envelopes the parliament before the crucial vote approving the first tranche of financing. A plane crashes, killing all politicians on board. Gerrard now does not have the numbers to get his funding legislation through the House of Representatives.

Using his devious influence on the speaker, Gerrard demands that the legislation for the full amount of funding rushing it through the parliament, ensuring him a forty-million-dollar secret commission.

The clerk of the parliament observes the manipulation of the parliament, forcing the speaker to resign over her indiscretions with the prime minister. The parliament loses confidence in the government during a procedural confusion in the chamber, sending the nation to an immediate federal election.

Gerrard must now win the election to receive his cash.

The Mercantiles, a long-established group of high tax-paying business owners, appoint ruthless political operative Jonathan Wolff to overthrow Gerrard. During the federal election campaign, no one is safe from his line of fire.

Wolff's tactful manipulation and political prowess guides the opposition towards election success. But fearing they will not win; he plans his own strategy to defeat the prime minister.

Investigative journalist Anita Devlin's editor directs her to promote the opposition's campaign. But unknown to her, her publishing owner is a member of the Mercantiles. She soon detects the nefarious Wolff is managing the campaign and endeavours to expose his influence and manipulation.

Now hot on Wolff's trail, Devlin becomes a whistle-blower, working to expose him and the Mercantiles. She soon realises the price of politics is too much for her. She is let down by close friend Barton Messenger, who explains the need for him and the opposition to do whatever it takes to win government.

The election is on a knife edge; Jaya Rukhmani defeats Gerrard in his electorate with a handful of votes and now holds the balance of power. She supports a new prime minister, Peter Stanley. Meanwhile, Devlin exposes the Mercantiles and Wolff. Uncertain about her future, she resigns. She then meets Wolff on an isolated path.

Three years later, the Stanley government is preparing for a looming election.

CHAPTER ONE

Words didn't flow intuitively for her; they never have done. She struggled for most of her career to get them out, but always finished her assigned stories on time. The dread of approaching deadlines often helped, as did the prospect of failing her colleagues. Couple this sense of dread with the anxiety of it being found out she wasn't as good as many thought, and stress grew. Perhaps the hype of being the celebrated political journalist at Hancock Media overstated her reputation and talent. She often wondered about that. Did she have the talent? Or did male patronage advance her career?

During lonesome nights, Cassandra Rogers often pondered whether she had sacrificed too much. Her husband gave her up when story deadlines became too much, so he left, taking the children. He gave her the option: the family or the job. It was the wrong time for him to ask because she chose an exclusive interview with the King. She assumed she could charm her way back. She never did. Her teenage children seldom see her now.

She calculated the sacrifice and tears would pay off once promoted to a long-promised national current affairs hosting role. But right now, her dreamy gaze out of her office window interrupted her writing. She was following the billowing sails out on Sydney Harbour, the stiff breeze challenging the yachts proving too fascinating.

'Not much inspiration out there, I reckon.'

Cass didn't respond. She just glanced over her shoulder, then said, 'Get stuffed, Charlie.'

He laughed. 'You can't say that anymore.'

'Say what?' She swung her seat to face him.

'You can't be using harassing language anymore,' he mocked her. 'Your mob changed that years ago.'

'My mob?'

'The sisters doin' it for themselves were always going to overreach and spoil it for everyone.'

'Not a fan of equality, Charlie? Happy with your privileged patriarchy, are you?'

'You see… we just can't talk anymore without being accused of micro aggressions and slagging off each other.'

Cass sniffed. 'Respect is a virtue we all could learn.'

'Respect means nothing amongst this hustle and bustle. You, more than anyone know that. We all want the front page or the lead story on the news.'

'Hustle and bustle?' Her lips turned into a mocking smile. 'Have you done a creative writing course like everyone else?'

His eyes glazed over, then he sighed. 'You know what I mean. Ambitious people eat each other in the newsroom. They aren't majestic lions. More your snarling hyenas.'

'You blokes have had it too good for too long.'

Charlie scoffed. 'And that there, ladies and gentlemen, is the damn problem. Tagging everyone as a predator. This anti-male thing will wear thin, and the backlash will be dramatic.'

'Rubbish; it's been going on for way too long.' Cass crossed her arms over her chest. 'We never called out the sleazy morons amongst us.'

'Yeah, maybe,' said Charlie, his head nodding over and over. 'But the line has moved to the extremes. Everyone seems on edge these days, not knowing what to say anymore.'

'Rubbish.'

'You reckon it's okay to use abusive language?'

'Oh Charlie, it's not about language, it's about power and its misuse.'

'Yeah right, so why is there an increasing culture of fear in workplaces?' He moved away. 'Let me prophecise for one moment; I reckon workplaces will become separated again as they were hundreds of years ago.'

Cass stood, moving towards him. 'Hey, are you going to editorial?'

'I have nothing to say; I've got nothing. My dry run is making me nervous.'

'Don't worry, you'll get a lead soon enough. You always do.' Cass checked over the cubicle screen to see if others were about, then in a hushed tone asked, 'Do you know why Hancock is coming?'

'Nah.'

'You think he's announcing a certain government appointment?' Cass winked. 'You know what I mean?'

'Harper would never do it. Why would he?'

'Foreign Affairs wants a celebrity in Los Angeles. I suspect Hancock will give them what they want.'

'Those type of consul appointments go to former politicians.'

Cass moved closer. 'I'm looking for a trail.'

'What?' Charlie shook his head. 'Are you mad?' He moved closer. 'Could be a poor career move.'

'Career is going nowhere at the moment.'

'Do a job on Hancock and it'll be over.'

Cass tapped her nose. 'Let's call it karma.'

Charlie moved off. 'I call it madness.'

Cass watched her scruffy colleague wander off before swivelling and returning to her desk, pushing against the chair, and stretching her back. Her camo pants and black t-shirt fitted snuggly as she stretched, touched the toes of her red Dr Martens, and forced her head into her knees before reaching high for the ceiling, then shaking off the movement. She resumed her seat, ignoring the harbour to finish her story for the evening news.

Words now flowed, and thirty minutes later she emailed the editor her revelation of the government's rejection of the United Nations Climate Council demand for greater action in reducing greenhouse gas emissions in Australia.

She quoted Prime Minister Stanley: *Place your enthusiasm towards India and China before coming to the easily bullied fruit like Australia.* She had no wish to frame Stanley as a moron, but mixing metaphors was dangerous when going on the record.

With a few moments to spare before leaving for the editorial meeting, she mulled over her chat with Charlie. They had fumbled a romance years ago and remained close, sharing struggles with her marriage and his addiction to drugs. The point he made about her career was a little too close to the bone. He knew about her brief liaison almost seventeen years ago with the proprietor, Tony Hancock. She never regretted the relationship and never confessed her enthusiastic participation. But now she remained annoyed by the memory, conceding she might have leveraged her career from the dalliance.

He transferred her to the New York office but became mortified when her engineering fiancé dropped everything to move with her. His lasciviousness for his protégé then dropped off. He redirected his leering gaze to junior staff. Although his energy for office romance shifted to others, he did not put an end to directing and boosting her career.

Now she was Hancock Media's political editor for television and the national newspaper, delivering exclusives, uncovering government scandal, and exposing unwelcome publicity to any wayward politician. As soon as Cassandra Rogers strolled into a government media briefing, ministers fretted about what she might know and how she came to know it.

Notwithstanding her fierce reputation for exposing a political story, she sometimes wondered if her acclaimed position stemmed from patronage or talent. Discovering exclusives was no simple task.

She found what she thought was absolute truth was a shade of truth when a story published proved to be wrong. An impeccable source once told her politics was more about perceptions than reality, and the real dark art of government was to manipulate those perceptions, often leaving truth behind. She could either play the game and bear its scars or she could go write restaurant reviews.

She did what they asked of her, working hard, doing whatever it took to get the story. Cass considered herself a serious journalist, the flirtatious fluff of her youth now long gone. She didn't want to be a celebrity; she wanted respect.

Now the pinnacle of her career, to host the national current affairs show, was within reach. She waited for the nod from Hancock, but the sleepless nights and family regrets didn't make the wait any easier.

A little after four, senior Hancock Media editorial staff assembled in the plush board room, its floor-to-ceiling expansive windows providing a stunning outlook over the towering iconic bridge and the opera house.

DOOMED

Whilst Cass enjoyed her own outlook over the harbour five levels down, this view was impressive.

The dishevelled fashion of the assembled editors was typical of the industry, with the solitary necktie worn by an administration manager. The few women who sat around the table were there on merit and wouldn't allow distracting boorish repartee to interfere with their day, let alone their lives. Cass was never comfortable with the shallowness of her male colleagues, detesting their loathsome observations and sarcasm. She sometimes speculated on whether the childish nature ever matured; if this small cabal of colleagues was an example of what women endured in the broader workplace, then there was much work to be done.

She glanced across the table and smiled at Helen Rasminski, raising an eyebrow when loud laughter broke out from the group of blokey colleagues at the other end of the long-polished jarrah table.

Rasminski shook her head, sighing, smirked then asked, 'What's this about, do you know?'

'Not a clue, but it's weird we're all here.'

'Hancock is about to sack us, cut our pay, or maybe announce a new initiative.'

'He's late, as usual,' Cass said, checking the wall clock.

'How's the kids?'

Cass squirmed, shifting in her chair, not wanting to lie. 'They're beaut; I hope to see them next school holidays.'

'Must be hard for you.'

'It's not so bad. I talk to them most days on Zoom.'

'I couldn't do it.'

'Well, I wouldn't be here if I didn't want to be.'

Rasminski smiled, wincing and nodding, then turned away.

The door crashed open, silencing the room, allowing the energy of the charismatic Tony Hancock to sweep in. Editors resumed their seats. He took his place at the head of the table, newspaper staff on one side, television on the other. The most senior closest, with the most junior banished to the opposite end. Cass sat five places down on Hancock's left, facing the enormous windows. He opened his leather folder and lifted several sheets of paper, bouncing them on the table before neatening his stack.

'Gentlemen, thanks for coming up.' Hancock recognised Cass, correcting himself. 'Sorry ladies, thanks as well.'

Cass dismissed it but wondered whether it had been a deliberate slight.

'I've called you here this afternoon because I have a special announcement.' Various colleagues glanced around. 'Yesterday, after thirty-five years, Peter Nicholls paid me a visit and requested he retire.' Hancock chuckled. 'After all this time, an icon of Australian television, greater than Kennedy or Willesee, has requested, and in fact begged, he go enjoy his garden.'

Cass dropped her head, gazing into her interlocked hands, anxious about making eye contact with any colleagues.

'He has agreed to six months' notice, believing I would need all that time to recruit a replacement. He wished us well and hoped our ratings recover.'

A few of the group chuckled.

Hancock waited a few moments, then said, 'We are now in an awkward position of deciding if we have the talent in our newsrooms, or do we go outside, perhaps worldwide, searching for a replacement?'

Anxiety coursing through Cass troubled her breathing as she battled to control her chest, pumping from heavy, rapid breaths. This was it. This was the show she wanted and promised over a decade ago. She sacrificed her marriage and family, but the grand old fart didn't retire when expected, hanging around for another ten miserable years. She peeped at Hancock to read his face and perhaps gain a nod. *Would he now deliver what he guaranteed all those years ago? Had her sacrifice been worth it?*

'We may not take the six months to appoint a new host, but we shall ensure that whoever we select will reflect our values and connect with our audience.' Hancock scanned the room, ignoring Cass. 'Plus, we expect the new host to broaden audience reach and increase revenue. It's our flagship program and we'll ensure we talk to all stakeholders, including you folks.'

Nothing. Cass could read nothing from him, and he didn't cast an eye towards her.

'Questions?'

There was no response. Just a collegiate acceptance of the announcement.

DOOMED

'I'll come see you all, and if you have any recommendations, then I would be happy to receive them. In the meantime, keep doing what you're doing,' Hancock slapped his folder shut, then blurted a little too brashly, 'I'm loving it.'

The grumpy old blokes stood and left with no fuss, while the younger editors had a little chitter-chatter with Hancock on their way out. Cass lingered to share a moment with her boss.

'Cassie, what can I do for you?' Hancock asked. He rocked back in his chair, tapping a pen on his folder.

Cass smiled, stood, and ventured towards him, leaning her weight against the table. 'You recall what you promised?'

'When?'

'You promised me that show.'

Hancock shook his head as if not remembering any conversation.

'You said when Nicholls pulls the pin, you would appoint me to the role.'

'As I just said, Cassie, we will consider all possibles and probables.'

'You said I would be the next host.'

'Not that I recall.'

Cass straightened, glaring at him. 'You promised me.'

Hancock waited a moment, studying her, then said, 'Cassie, we said a lot of things, and we made promises back then. I took you at your word and you changed it by getting married.' He returned her stare.

'You used this job offer to get me into your bed.'

'That's not how I remember it.'

'You bastard,' Cass said, tightening her lips.

'Cassie, I will appoint the position on merit.' Hancock swivelled in his chair, crossing his legs. 'You know it's only ever about merit here.'

'On that basis, announce me as the new host.'

Hancock raised a finger, shaking it. 'Not necessarily.'

Cass shook her head, screwing her face. 'Not happy with my work?'

'Standards have slipped.'

She stepped back, staggered by the comment, gazing out the window to compose herself. 'My standards have slipped?'

'What happened to the skirts?'

She snapped back, facing Hancock. 'Beg your pardon?'

Hancock waved a submissive hand. 'Look, we will treat you just like other candidates, but I can't promise you anything.'

'Will you treat me fairly?'

'Of course. There will be a selection panel appointed.'

Cass stared at him for a moment, her arms crossed. 'What do I have to do to make certain you appoint me?'

Hancock studied her, thinking for a moment. A reflective thin grin crossed his face as he sat forward, then said, 'Just get me political exclusives. You have lost your touch.'

She fisted her hips and stared down at him. 'You want nothing else from me?'

'Noooohoohoohoo,' he said as he smirked and shook his head, crossing his arms tight across his chest. 'Do your job and then we can talk about this gig. You're an important asset to us. You could do the job, but we need to consider the market and what they want.'

'Just make sure it's done under code.'

'Of course, it will be, Cassie. What do you take me for?'

'I know who and what you are, Tony. I just want to make sure I'm not competing with any other… what did you once call me… a distraction?'

'Cassie, it's only ever about merit.'

CHAPTER TWO

This was the best time of the day. Dawning light revealing the rolling hills once rich in pasture. The morning mist clinging to the land before being burnt off by the sun yet to rise. The air still, with only a few early riser birds beginning their morning song. No matter the culture, no matter the spiritual connection with the land, it was always at its finest during predawn light before reality squashed the humility of this shared moment with nature.

Tucker Farm had been the benchmark in agribusiness in the region for almost one hundred years. The family didn't waste time meeting standards for beef and wool production; they set higher measures, and their reputation opened doors for them.

Politicians listened. Banks queued to lend money. The industry revered them, bestowing a leadership status the family never sought. Throughout their history, the Tuckers just wanted a secure, sustainable future. They worked the land to produce that prosperity.

Brian Tucker's father was the first to set up a carbon neutralising agenda in cattle country, increasing vegetation and tree management on the vast farm and counterbalancing the farm's carbon footprint with better farming practices. The industry now taught Tucker's methane gas methods in several agribusiness university courses, attracting international interest. Tucker Farm also developed water management practices, bringing a significant change to the biodiversity along the waterways and around the dams dotted over the vast property.

But that was then; now a five-year drought was shredding the once prosperous farm model apart.

Tucker stepped off the expansive homestead veranda and down the stone steps his grandfather quarried, strolling down the slope towards his cattle pens. Ever-alert kelpies trotted in behind his saunter, eager for a little action to start their day. They responded to his calls when needed, a pedigree-line bred for work, no different from their owners.

The forty-two-thousand-hectare farm survived extended periods of drought, but the meticulous historical records showed this one was the most drastic, even harsher than the twelve-year millennium. Tucker managed the property for drought early, sensing a severe rolling weather event when winter rains didn't overflow his twenty-two dams five years earlier. Over time, he reduced his cattle herd to five hundred head and sold off sixty percent of his flock. His pastures were too sparse for grazing, forcing him to ship in feed every two weeks for the last thirteen months at a whopping cost of eighty-six thousand dollars a month.

Tucker's liquidity was falling, pushing him to sell parcels of prized grazing land six months earlier. His financiers were supporting him, along with other farmers in the district, but a recent audit of his accounts showed he would need to reduce his herd and flock even further if he was to see out the drought. Reducing his total cattle live weight kilos meant a significant financial burden, as recovery to a productive herd would be very costly.

Rumours spread throughout the region that Tucker might have to sell everything.

The metal gate chilled him as he laid his crossed arms along the top. To save costs, he had deferred farm maintenance, resulting in the powder-coated metal now showing signs of ageing, flaking rust. He cocked his boot up onto the second rung, gazing out into the paddock where his award-winning bulls mingled. They settled by the stand of Lombardy poplars he planted twenty years ago, some hundred metres away.

'Come on!' he bellowed, waiting for a reaction. Nothing. This time louder and deeper, 'Come on!'

First one bull responded by looking towards him, reluctant to move. Another now moved, and by the time the third call came, they were ambling towards Tucker.

Once a hefty eight hundred and fifty kilos, the bulls still appeared strong but were closer to six hundred. They moseyed across the paddock, reaching the gate, and waiting a respectful and safe distance, checking the circling dogs and the farmer. Tucker checked his seven prized bulls, looking for any decrease in condition or evidence of salmonellosis diarrhoea. He also studied their eyes, checking for fly infestation and unusual colouring.

Tucker thumbed his hat to the back of his head as he studied his award-winning, money- making machines, speculating when they would be ready for breeding again. He used artificial insemination for his top breeders. His production ratios improved when he kept them apart from the heifers and inseminated at the ripe time. The breeding conversion rate was a significant line of revenue for his farm. With the bulls not producing for the last ten months, it was affecting his income.

'Take 'em back, Blue.'

The older kelpie responded by squeezing under the gate and yapping at the attentive bulls, which pricked their ears and stepped back before turning and trotting to the stand of trees. Blue and his two companions followed, keeping them in order.

Tucker gave a sharp, shrill whistle, scuttling the dogs back to him. He turned away from the gate, tramping to his sheds, jumping into his Mercedes one-tonne pickup. They always left a key in the ignition, and he kicked it into action as his dogs scrambled into the rear tray. Anyone observing the utility could not be sure of the true colour, as the dirt from years of washing neglect caked the duco, making it an unrecognisable red and brown mess.

He gunned the ute uphill towards the dusty dirt road, heading for the sealed bitumen twenty minutes south at Barellan. Once on the bitumen, he mused whether he had time for a hearty breakfast at the Commercial Hotel before tackling the ninety-minute drive to Wagga Wagga. He slowed as he hit the town limits, gliding past the big fourteen-metre tennis racquet statue in honour of Evonne Goolagong, the world champion local tennis player, and then parking outside the pub. He petted his dogs before taking a drinking bucket to the tiny park opposite to fill it with water.

As he placed the bucket in the tray, he snapped a curt instruction to behave, then wandered into the dining room, ordering six sausages with his eggs and hash browns, eating only three and bringing a treat for each of his dogs. It was practically eight o'clock when he hit the road for Wagga.

The Rural Bank had managed the Tucker Farm finances for almost thirty years and promised the family it would never refuse a request when they took the tough decision to shift their accounts. Kevin Tucker wanted a clean break from the big four banks, believing the smaller rural specialists would look after them, and they did. The bank understood the seasonality of farming with the highs and lows of yield and agribusiness demands. It knew the need for fluidity of cash flow. The manager was also aware of the worry and stress of investing capital in farm redevelopment and machinery.

First, Kevin and now Brian valued the bank's understanding of the specifics of cattle and wool production, with its many seasonal variables, and together they forged a solid, rewarding partnership. This partnership helped the Tuckers grow and reject generous offers from large pastoralist companies buying up farms to merge balance sheets of investor companies. The Tuckers were farmers, not business folk. They stuck to what they understood best: cattle and sheep.

Tucker's appointment was for ten o'clock, and he trooped into the Wagga office with fifteen minutes to spare, having had instilled into his life the cliché that if you are five minutes early, you're already five minutes late. Staff directed him to an anteroom, and at a little after ten a woman he hadn't met asked him to join her in her office.

'Where's Jake?'

'Jake?' The woman gestured him to sit as she looped to the other side of the desk. 'Jake retired four weeks ago. They appointed me relief manager and I'm waiting for the announcement of his replacement.'

'He managed our accounts and understood what we could do.'

'What is it you want to do, Mr Tucker?'

Tucker pushed his thumb into the brim of his hat, teasing it back on his head. 'Well, I want rain.'

The woman studied him.

'I'm certain you do; we all do. It would make my job easier, that's for sure.'

Tucker didn't respond straight away, which was his way.

'What's your name?'

'Papadopoulos. Sophie Papadopoulos. I'm managing your account now,' she said, erect in her chair.

Tucker lay back in his seat and crossed his leg, resting his scuffed right boot on his left knee. He removed his hat, draping it on his boot toe. 'What do you know about Tucker Farm?' he asked, unsure why they invited him to Wagga.

'Thanks for coming in. I wanted to meet you,' she said with a broad smile. 'It's rare to meet members of a dynasty.'

Tucker eyed her, waiting.

'Mr Tucker, I can see you are a little nervous. Would you like a drink?'

'I'm not nervous.' Tucker cleared his throat, shifting in his chair, then said, 'Yeah, a tea would be good.'

She picked up the telephone handpiece and pushed a button, making the order.

'Mr Tucker, I have asked you to visit this morning to discuss your intentions and how the bank fits into those plans.'

'Fits into what plans?'

'Your plans.'

'I don't have any plans until rain comes.'

Papadopoulos studied her client, her lips pouting. After a moment, she asked, 'What happens if it doesn't?'

Tucker grimaced.

'If it doesn't rain, Mr Tucker, what are your plans?'

Tucker twirled his hat around his boot, preferring to look at it rather than the bank manager.

'If it doesn't rain soon, Mr Tucker, what do you think we should do with the overdraft we are carrying?'

Tucker glimpsed up. 'Do what you always do.'

'And what's that, Mr Tucker?'

'Add it to our mortgage; we're good for it.'

Papadopoulos waited as a staffer placed a tray of tea on her desk. A cup then poured and passed to Tucker, who took a sip, then another, before placing the cup and saucer on the desk.

'Your mortgage extensions are at capacity.'

'Do whatever you have to do. It'll rain soon.'

'We would like relief on the overdraft and a reduction in the overall debt.'

'What does that mean?'

'We'll keep providing for your family, but the monthly feed cost will need reducing.'

Tucker took in a deep gasp. 'You concede my liquidity is stuffed, don't you?'

'I'm aware.'

'Then why would you ask me to do that?'

'Because my boss in Sydney wants to feel comfortable about the arrangements. A contribution from you may be a shrewd move.'

'Why should he worry? I don't know him.'

'He has bank interests that must be maintained.' She took a sip of tea.

Tucker dropped his head back further, peering down his nose at the manager.

'This drought is placing a lot of pressure on the bank,' she continued. 'Not just you, but most of our rural clients.'

'You are a rural bank and that's expected.'

'Not by our shareholders.'

'I don't understand. What have they got to do with the drought?'

'They lend you the money.'

'You lend me the money.'

'It's shareholder capital we are lending. We are seeing a reduction in our share price, and they aren't thrilled.'

'Everything will be fine when it rains.'

'And if it doesn't?'

'It will. It always does.' Tucker placed his hat back on and shifted from his chair. 'Is that it?'

'No, Mr Tucker, that's not it; please have a seat.'

She opened a leather compendium, tugging a dot-pointed list from her papers and offering it out for him to accept.

'This is a rough estimate of your assets. The second column is a list of your financial obligations to the bank.'

Tucker whistled through his teeth as he studied the list, thumbing his chin.

'We need a reduction in our exposure, and we think you can either sell more property or livestock. The choice is yours.'

Tucker glimpsed up over the paper, frowning at the bank manager.

DOOMED

'You want me to sell?'

'Not everything, just enough to clear a little of the backlog.'

'Are you foreclosing me?'

Papadopoulos smiled. 'No, of course not. We just prefer to reduce our exposure.'

'Your exposure will reduce when it rains.'

'When do you think that might be?'

Tucker screwed the paper into a tight ball without releasing his glare. He lobbed it over to the desk, bouncing it into her lap.

'My family has worked the land for almost a century. Now you want to rip it from us?'

'We don't require your farm, Mr Tucker, we just need our money.'

'You'll get your friggin' money when it rains.'

He stood, towering above her.

'We may need to get it back before then; that's what I'm trying to explain.'

'There's been no problem in the past,' Tucker said.

'The past is the past; a new era exists in banking, which means a different way of doing business.'

'Is that right?' asked Tucker, placing his hands on his hips. 'Well, perhaps I'll take our business someplace else.'

'Yes, please go elsewhere; that would be helpful, but I'm not sure your account risk will be attractive to other banks.'

'You can't treat us like this.'

'You're too geared and we've supported you for too long.'

'Jake would never do this.'

'Could explain his unexpected retirement, don't you think?' Papadopoulos stood, gesturing her hand to the door. 'We want our money and we're happy to discuss better terms with you, but we need to reduce the debt.'

Tucker didn't respond.

'Mr Tucker, please consider what I say. You have two months to decide and make arrangements.'

'Eight weeks? You want your money in eight weeks?'

'It's time to respond or move on to a new venture.'

'You bastard,' Tucker said, frowning.

'Yeah, well...' Papadopoulos said, then sighed. 'If you didn't overcapitalise your herd, you wouldn't be in this position.'

'You gave me the money.'

'Now we want it back.'

CHAPTER THREE

'Okay, the next item on the agenda is the drought. Who's leading the discussion?'

'That would be me, Prime Minister,' Barton Messenger said, closing and pushing away the health brief, then opening the next item file from the pile beside him. 'I've consulted extensively and then briefed Jack on this.' Messenger glanced across to the agriculture minister, receiving slight nods encouraging him to continue. 'As the government, there is not much we can do. The affected regions are sourcing stock feed, and whilst the national herd has reduced, it hasn't impacted trade. A relief fund has been established, and the nation seems to be kicking in support, as they often do.'

'The money never gets to the folks who need it,' Wilson Campbell, the regional development minister, interjected.

Messenger glanced over to him and smiled. 'You're right. I recommend we tighten regulations concerning donations and distribution.'

The prime minister frowned. 'You're not suggesting legislation? We are the party of less government, not more.'

The windowless cabinet room was silent, many of the twenty-three ministers studying Messenger to view his response. There had been unusual tension between the two since the meeting began, with Prime Minister Peter Stanley taking every opportunity to keep his ambitious treasurer in line.

Messenger first glanced at his notes, then frowned at the prime minister. 'No, I'm not suggesting legislation,' he breathed, filling his chest. 'We don't need to over-regulate a severe drought, but we need to act and control the narrative.' He scanned the table, then focused back on Stanley. 'The banks are circling. If one of them gets nervous and moves to foreclose on their loan ledger, then others will come in for the kill. Our farmers will be done over, and communities destroyed.'

'That's an overstatement, wouldn't you say?' the prime minister asked, tossing down his pen and shifting in his chair; he pushed back, crossed his legs, and checked about his ministers for support.

Messenger arched a brow, glancing at his papers, contemplating what he just heard and why Stanley was burning him.

'Prime Minister if I may?' The former leader and foreign minister, James Harper, intervened. 'It seems Bart has the politics right. It frightens folks out on the farms. I suspect city electorates are nervous their country cousins are struggling. Unless we get national leadership on this, it will run out of control in the media.'

'I agree with Jim, Prime Minister,' Christopher Hughes said. 'The media noise will switch to climate change soon. Then the banks. Then it'll move to food security, then water, and then we'll be discussing compensation to the states for desalination plants. If we don't get rain soon, it may shoot our trade balance of payments. This is an enormous political challenge, which may impact the next election.'

'Yeah, and if we lose those regional seats, it stuffs the government, which means the other mob will be back.' Campbell never held back his views. 'Who's to say Gerrard won't stand again and come back as prime minister?'

'He's had enough,' Harper said. 'He lost his seat; he won't be back.'

'He did you over, though, didn't he?' Campbell provoked the former leader.

Harper cleared his throat and shook his head before eyeing Campbell. 'No, you and your mates around this table did that.'

The room fell silent; ministers seemed embarrassed by the claim.

Hughes released a harsh harrumph. 'Look, those things are years ago; no need to go over them now.' He cast a glance towards Harper opposite, smiling.

'We can't afford to lose one seat, otherwise we're back in opposition.' The prime minister joined the discussion. 'What do we do to control the narrative?'

Messenger waited for a response from a colleague. They offered none. He gripped the arms of his leather chair, lifting himself straight, leaning his forearms onto the jarrah table. 'I think we should have a parliamentary inquiry.'

'What's that going to do?' the prime minister asked.

'I'm surprised you asked.' Messenger cocked his head and Stanley squirmed a little. 'It's second to a Royal Commission, more flexible, allowing quick recommendations.'

Messenger's ministerial colleagues said nothing, waiting to hear more.

'We ask stakeholders to provide submissions and call for the major players to present formal evidence. We get stuck into the banks by backgrounding the media. The inquiry then recommends what we want.'

'That'll be too bloody obvious,' Campbell said. 'We need the other side to help us, and they'll never do it.'

Messenger nodded. 'You're right, Wilson, as always. We need the right recommendations, so we need the opposition's support, but we can't make it obvious.'

'That's what I just said.' Campbell tossed up his hands, falling back into his chair.

'I recommend we appoint the independent member for Melbourne to chair the inquiry.'

'Rubbish. That'll never work,' Jack Stevenson, the agriculture minister, interjected.

'Why is that?' Messenger asked, leaning back, rocking his chair backward and forth.

'Oh, let me think… she's a woman.' Stevenson started numbering off his fingers. 'She lives in the city. She's a humanities professor, she hates us, and she's an immigrant from India.'

'And she's black.' Campbell chimed in, causing several colleagues to wince.

Messenger ignored him.

'Look, I know it's difficult for some of you to come to terms with, but that independent member holds the balance of power that delivers us government. She could switch her vote to the opposition, and we would be stuffed,' Messenger paused for a moment, 'so why not give her a parliamentary title and extra salary with a promotion? She has the academic research rigour to get the evidence we need. She does not have a conflict of interest, and she can open doors others can't. Plus, she can give us the narrative we need, getting us off the front page.'

'Interesting.' Hughes nodded, warming to the idea.

Harper responded, 'You think she has the credibility to be the voice we need?'

'I can assure you, she does. Have you not seen her in the chamber?'

'Any bias amongst all that, Bart?' Stanley teased.

Messenger flicked a quick glance his way. 'She was my politics professor.'

'Nothing else?'

'What are you suggesting?'

'Oh, you know, this place is gossip central.'

Messenger bowed his head then looked across the table. 'Other than helping her with electorate matters, there is nothing untoward between us.'

'When do you think we could get started on this?' Harper shifted the direction of the conversation.

Messenger, still distracted by the prime minister's jibe, turned towards Harper, who was sitting next to Stanley.

'Today, or it would be best to make the announcement tomorrow, setting out the terms of reference.'

Stanley considered Messenger, then asked, 'Okay, does anyone else have a view? If not, who agrees we commence a parliamentary inquiry?'

All hands raised with various levels of enthusiasm.

'Done. What's next?' The prime minister referred to his agenda.

Harper cleared his throat with a cough and opened his presentation folder.

'Prime Minister, I am seeking approval to name the new consulate in Los Angeles. We are seeking to install a person who can open doors for us within the digital communication space. Although the office is based in LA, the appointee will work in San Francisco, focusing on Silicon Valley. This is a two-year sunset appointment and I table my recommendation.'

Ministers flicked through papers to briefing notes, scanning the material.

'Why do we need to specialise and why for two years?' Stanley asked.

'APEC appointed the government to set up a digital broadcasting network for the south-east Asian region. We want to move otherwise our licence will be revoked and turned over to the Chinese. We have eighteen months to source network codes, infrastructure, and security protocols. This is an enormous project needing us to move fast if we are to have access to adequate bandwidths and cloud capacity.'

'What the hell did you just say?' Campbell asked.

Messenger chuckled. Harper smiled at the comment. Stanley waited for an answer.

Harper glimpsed at his notes, then said, 'Unless we secure the right partnerships, we lose management of the network. This means we will not influence content as much as we would want.'

Messenger added, 'This is an important project for us within the region. It will allow us to work with our trading partners, closing the door even further on Europe and the US.'

'Why would we want to do that?' Stanley asked.

'India and China are moving on various economic matters, and we need to leverage broadcasting to protect ourselves against their expansion programs,' Harper said.

'So, is this a security issue? I don't understand,' Campbell asked.

'It is a trade issue. Managing the network will open negotiating doors during trading dialogues; but for us, it remains a high security issue.'

'Who have you recommended for the role?' Stanley asked.

Harper drew a deep breath; conscious colleagues might greet his news with contempt. 'I want to send Tony Hancock.'

The prime minister flopped back into the chair, shaking his head, and blowing out a sigh. Others grumbled to a nearby colleague. Only Hughes seemed to support the idea.

'That's a joke, surely?' Stanley said.

'No, I'm serious.'

'Just because he owns most of the media in the country doesn't mean we should hand him Asia. Anyway, what does he know about digital networks?'

'The very fact he is a media mogul will open doors.'

'He knows all the nerds, does he?' Stanley asked, sniggering.

'Very rich nerds, Prime Minister.' Messenger joined in.

Stanley shook his head again and glanced around at his colleagues. 'Does anyone have a view of this?'

Campbell sat forward. 'Well, with Hancock working for us for two years, it might just help at the next election. He won't be able to influence editorials with his cold-hearted black hand.'

Harper rejected the notion. 'It's not always about politics, Wilson; this is an excellent decision. It's short term and performance based, so he will need to get his skates on.'

'Have you spoken to him about it?' Hughes asked.

'Yes, of course,' Harper nodded.

Hughes cocked his head, nodding, leaning back into his chair.

'Can we defer it? I want to think about it,' Stanley asked.

'We need a decision today, Prime Minister.' Messenger sat forward. 'We have appropriated expenditure and settled on accommodation in San Francisco.'

'You what?' Stanley leaned into the table. 'Money approved before coming to cabinet?'

'We have been waiting on your decision for a few weeks now, Prime Minister,' Harper said. 'You asked us to come to this meeting for a final decision.'

'We need a decision, Prime Minister,' Hughes said.

Stanley shut down, folding his arms across his chest, bowing his head.

After a long pause it was too much for Campbell and he exploded, 'Oh for fuck's sake, Peter, make a damn decision, will you, and let's move on.'

Stanley glanced up at Harper. 'What do you wish to do?'

'I want to appoint Hancock.'

'So be it. Let the cabinet minutes record the recommendation and decision.'

Hughes glanced across the table to Harper, arching an eyebrow and blowing out frustration. Other ministers shared the anxiety in various ways, some whispering sarcastic words to one another.

'What's next?' Stanley moved to the next agenda item.

Hughes straightened, sitting taller, flicking open his brief on the application from the Timor-Leste government to allow citizens to work on offshore rigs in the Timor Sea; a complex, contentious issue, which extended to mining sovereignty rights in the rich gas and oil field.

Ginni Stavloukas, the mining minister, was first to speak.

'Prime Minister, I wonder why Christopher has carriage of this brief rather than my department?'

'You've got your hands full with the coal industry. I wanted Chris to manage this as an industrial relations issue.'

Not impressed with the response, Stavloukas continued, 'The unions are giving me hell at the moment. I don't see your man getting involved in that.'

'Got a thing against men, have ya Gin?' Campbell said, prompting a discourteous stare that shut him up, cutting off his smirk.

'Why aren't you consistent with this policy?' Stavloukas asked.

'I thought I was.' Stanley glanced at Hughes for support, who shrugged. 'Chris is across the brief from his time as industry shadow minister, and I hoped I would save you time.'

'Why?'

'Where are you leading with this, Ginni?' Messenger asked.

'Where am I leading with this? What type of question is that?'

'I just meant; do we need to talk about this now?'

'Yes, we need to talk about this now.' Stavloukas raised her voice. 'Allowing international workers onto our rigs will change the dynamic of the mining industry's labour force. It's not just an industrial relations issue, because it sure as hell affects the entire mining industry.'

Stanley wriggled in his seat as he leaned forward to see Stavloukas at the end of the table, tucked away on his side. 'I just wanted to make it easier for you and lighten your load.'

'Why? Because I'm a woman?' The words hung across the table.

Several colleagues fidgeted, shaking heads.

'You think a woman needs to lighten her load? Is that what you think, Prime Minister? You think a man can lighten a woman's load?'

Messenger gasped, then furiously breathed out.

'You can't make that assertion from what he just said.' Harper came to Stanley's defence.

'You're a man. What do you know about discrimination?'

'Settle down, Ginni; this is not a gender thing.' Stevenson joined the discussion.

'What, you think having someone else do your job, a man, is not a gender thing?'

Stanley dropped his head to his hand, trawling his fingers through his hair. 'What do you want me to do?'

'Start communicating with your ministers for a start. You make these captain calls without talking to the relevant minister too damn often.'

Hughes intervened. 'Look, Ginni. I apologise for agreeing to prepare the brief. I'm happy to pass it back should you think it sensible.'

'I appreciate that offer, Christopher, and will accept it.'

'No, hang on,' Stanley said. 'This is my cabinet and I'll distribute work in the manner I see fit.'

'I have just taken back responsibility for the negotiations over international workers working on our rigs, if that is okay with you?' Stavloukas said with snapping tone.

Hughes looked across at her and smiled. 'I'll get my people to talk to your people. Would you prefer me to finish the brief or would you like to do it?'

Stanley began dissenting, but Stavloukas talked over him.

'You do it.'

Hughes waited for concurrence from the prime minister, glancing back to Stanley, who sat with his mouth agape, nodded, then with a flick of his hand waved Hughes on.

'On the assumption the mining minister will agree, the government recommends an extension to the 457 visas to allow workers from Timor-Leste to be employed on the rigs in the Timor Sea. Australian work conditions will apply, but with a significant difference,' he said.

'Instead of Australian award rates, they'll be offered three times the national wage rate of Timor. This will do two things. One is to step up the production capacity on the rigs and allow an increase in the workforce. The other is to give wealth to workers who will commute from their country and not be connected to Australia.'

'How does this help Australia?' Campbell asked.

Harper sat forward to respond. 'It allows the government to have bargaining leverage when negotiating the maritime borders. In short, my advisers think there will be no appeal from Timor concerning the borders if we allow their workers to man the rigs.'

'Seems a fair thing to do.' Stevenson nodded.

Stavloukas interjected. 'What do you guess will happen when the Indians open the coal mine in the Galilee Basin? They'll prefer to bring their workers in if you do this for Timor.'

'Not sure we should open any new coal mines,' Stanley said. 'At least not until we're re-elected.'

The comment stunned Hughes. 'You want to ban coal mining?'

'The Greens are giving us hell. The UN is insisting we comply. And there is a constant stream of abuse hitting our backbench. We have to do something.'

'That's crap!' Campbell said, slapping the table.

'Ease up, Wilson,' Harper counselled. 'Peter is not suggesting that.'

Harper glanced at Stanley for confirmation, but the prime minister just shrugged, flushing a pained look across his face.

'The union will go ballistic if you even suggest closing any mine,' Stavloukas said.

'India would want compensation from us,' said the finance minister, Helen Cavanaugh.

'The Climate Science Board briefed government the other day, suggesting we act and cease all coal mining,' Maurice Roussett, the environment minister said.

'You can't do this; the Indians will be on the warpath,' said Harper, unaware of his faux pas.

'We are not going to ban mining, are we?' Hughes asked the prime minister.

'It's on the table,' Stanley said.

'Not at this table, I can assure you,' Hughes said, prompting nods from colleagues.

'It's a consideration,' the prime minister said.

'Not if we have to pay liability,' Messenger said. Cavanaugh nodded.

The meeting descended into a vitriolic discussion about the rigour of climate change modelling and the dangerous nature of withholding natural resources from the world. One minister, pointing to history, even suggested a country like China would just come and get it if Australia denied them coal. They ignored the agenda. Further discussion halted when one of the prime minister's staff entered, whispering a reminder of a scheduled briefing. The cabinet then broke when the prime minister scurried away.

As Messenger left the room, leaving Harper and Hughes to caucus views about the meeting, he said, 'This government is going nowhere fast with the current leadership structure. Beware the Ides of March, my friends.'

The two ministers watched him go.

'He's right, you know,' Hughes said.

'A little too ambitious, don't you think?'

'Yes, he is, but his analysis is valid. We may need to ditch Pete.'

CHAPTER FOUR

The treasurer concluded his answer to the opposition's question on tax rates, prompting the prime minister to replace him at the despatch box.

'Madam Speaker, after another mighty display of unity and competence, I ask that further questions be placed on the notice paper.'

His announcement triggered the House of Representatives to go about its business. The speaker called for presentation of documents, causing the government leader of the House, Christopher Hughes, to move to the despatch box and table documents, including departmental reports, then moved a motion to accept the material.

Ministers sauntered out of the chamber as government members moved off to their offices or to gossip over a coffee at Aussie's Cafe. Opposition members waited for their leader Meredith Bruce to be called by the speaker to lead the Matter of Public Importance motion, criticising the government's mismanagement of refugee offshore detention centres.

'The question is: that the motion moved by the manager of government business be agreed to; all those of that opinion say aye, the contrary no.'

There was no response from those remaining in the chamber.

'I think the ayes have it,' the speaker said.

Hughes watched the prime minister scurry from the chamber, arms full of files, not wanting to engage in the next debate, and glanced across to James Harper, who was taking his position at the Table of the House and waiting for Bruce.

'I've been thinking about the Ides of March.'

Harper swivelled in his chair, leaning forward to reduce the chance of a curious colleague overhearing.

'What have you come up with?'

The speaker stood, stopping any conversation.

'I have received a letter from the leader of the opposition proposing that a definite Matter of Public Importance be submitted to the House for discussion, namely: the refusal of the government to honour its election promise to stop the people smuggling boats. I call upon those members who approve of the proposed discussion to rise in their places.'

'Hear, hear!' bellowed the opposition backbench as they stood to support their leader.

'I call the leader of the opposition.'

'Maybe we should talk after this,' said Harper, as Bruce stepped to her despatch box.

'Okay, I'll see you at Aussie's for a coffee in half an hour.' Hughes stood and smiled at Bruce as he sauntered out of the chamber.

'Thank you, Madam Speaker, and you will note that those opposite have deserted the government benches for this Matter of Public Importance with even the minister for industrial relations skulking from the chamber too embarrassed to face the truth.'

Hughes turned at the heavy brass and glass door and bowed to the speaker, as was the custom, mouthing a kiss to Bruce.

Harper settled into his seat to listen to Bruce's fifteen minutes; she decried the government's efforts to improve conditions on Ambon following the construction of a detention centre that did not meet Australian standards. She focused on the terrible plight of families with young children and quoted a report from Médecins Sans Frontières suggesting that the mental health of children was at risk. Harper scribbled a few relevant points as Bruce delivered an emotional plea for the government to get active in saving the children. He would have to choose his words thoughtfully in response.

'Finally, Madam Speaker, I ask the minister. What will you do today to save the children? If we have a death, then you will have blood on your hands.'

'Hear, hear.'

'I call the minister for foreign affairs.'

As Harper prepared himself at the despatch box, the chamber

emptied, leaving a low-ranking shadow minister at the Table. He thought it ironic that Bruce would plead with the government and yet not stop to hear its response.

'Madam Speaker, passions run high in this place whenever we talk about the desperate lives of refugees caught up in the vile web of deceit and destruction that is the people smuggling trade. But I notice that the opposition leader is no longer in the chamber, having delivered her passionate speech. No doubt she is excitedly talking to the media as I give the government's response to her questions.'

Harper delivered a well-worn response covering the essential government talking points, ensuring those rare folks who might listen to the parliament that the Stanley government was on track with building the second detention centre.

'The Indonesian government has reassured us they will bring all construction to Australian standards.'

Twenty minutes later Harper was sitting with a latte outside Aussie's Café, gossip central of the parliament and the place to see and be seen by those playing the political game. He waited in line for his coffee, then secured an isolated table by the windows, waiting for his colleague. The wooden floors echoed with the shoe heels of rushing advisers always short of time.

Once settled, Harper cast an eye over the huddled suits at nearby tables to find any potential eavesdroppers. He noted a few backbenchers from both parties in discussion with journalists, and others talking policy with various lobbyists, as they often did outside the indoor café. He checked out the window, wondering who was sitting in the sun-bathed courtyard.

He first came to Canberra as policy adviser to a member of parliament, progressing his ambitious career using his boss's numbers against him, challenging his preselection, and securing the safe seat for himself. He had learnt the lesson well over his twenty years' service: never allow staff to manage branch preselection delegates.

He leaned back in his small wooden chair, checked his watch, crossed his legs, and brushed particles of lint from his knee. The television behind him tuned into the chamber, but the volume turned down, and he couldn't quite hear his colleague ripping into the opposition.

A dawdling Hughes acknowledged Harper with a wave, joining the queue for coffee and soon settling in with his colleague.

'Sorry to have kept you; I got held up by Stavloukas.'

'What did the Greek God want?'

'She's a bully, to be honest.'

Harper guffawed. 'That's a joke, surely?'

Hughes beamed. 'She just won't let this Timor thing go.'

'She's under pressure and reckons shifting the goal posts will focus on you rather than stay on her.'

'She's stuffed this whole mining policy.' Hughes sipped his cappuccino, checking over his shoulder for anyone listening. 'I wish Pete would shift her out of the portfolio.'

'You're asking for a miracle. Peter can never make a decision,' Harper said, peering over his glass as he sipped his coffee.

'I think we made a mistake electing him.'

'Ya think?' Harper was still smarting over the way they had ripped the leadership from him before the last election.

Hughes shifted in his seat, peeking over his shoulder again, then leaned forward. 'Look, I acknowledge we may have made a mistake getting rid of you, but we had no choice. You took a leadership vote when you shouldn't have, and we left Peter with the prize,' he paused for a moment, 'but it doesn't mean we can't ever change our mind.' He sat back.

Harper didn't respond. He checked about him to see who was close. 'Are you suggesting what I think you're suggesting?'

'I don't know, but we need to do something. We're getting murdered by Bruce.'

Harper leaned his elbows on the table, steepling his hands, rasping them together as he thought about his colleague's comment. 'You think she'll win?'

'Looks, legs and language,' said Hughes, causing Harper to chuckle. 'She's all-over social media, and the magazines love her. Her idea of changing the tenor of the parliament was brilliant. And we fell for it; at least, Pete did. We have nothing we can do to hurt her. Did you see that outfit she was wearing on the weekend? The media ran stories for days.'

'Politics is not about who looks good.'

'You are kidding me, Jim?' Hughes shook his head. 'It's about perceptions. Bruce is manipulating those perceptions very well. Just look at her polls. How many cover stories can she do? Geezus Christ, she's in the same league as Meghan.'

Harper arched a brow, nodding; he squeezed out his bottom lip, and he pulled at it.

'We need a circuit breaker to change the narrative. That either means policy, or the prime minister has to go,' Hughes said.

Harper smiled. 'You have a way with words, Chris.'

'Look, Jim,' Hughes sat forward, closer to Harper, 'we have a glamour as our competitor, and we have Peter Frumpton as our leader. He ain't showing me the way.'

Harper didn't respond to the joke.

'And frankly, my guitar is gently weeping.'

Harper scoffed and smiled. 'Nice one.'

'No, seriously Jim, we need to do something otherwise we lose the election.'

'He won us government for the first time in almost twenty years. We can't dump a first term prime minister.'

'A drover's dog would have beaten Gerrard,' Hughes said.

'Fact is, we didn't beat him. If he'd won his seat, he'd still be in government.'

'That's the point.' Hughes thrust a finger at him. 'Stanley should have done better.'

He dropped his head into a hand as he studied Harper. After a few moments he said, 'You would have smashed him.'

'Yeah well, shoulda, coulda, woulda.'

'All I'm saying is that it might be time to think about a strategy for the next election. In the two years we have left, perhaps recast ourselves and focus on policy.'

'Ease up; here comes Rogers.'

The politicians sat back as a beaming Cassandra Rogers sidled up to the table.

'How's it going, boys? Who are you talking about?'

'Hi Cass, what's happening with you?' Hughes smiled. 'Want a seat?'

'Nah, wouldn't be seen dead sitting with a minister in this cesspit of political intrigue,' Cass said as she looked down at them. 'No, I just noticed you were way too serious, which must mean you are about to bone someone.'

'Not really,' Harper said, gazing up at her. 'We're just talking about the next election.'

'You'll be back in opposition so don't worry too much.'

Harper bristled as Hughes lightened the mood. 'You off to military camp or something?'

'Why? You don't think I'm dressed appropriately?' Cass stepped back, looking down at her trousers.

'Well, you're off to camp or you've jumped to the other side,' Hughes said.

'I might as well; not much talent left on this side of the fence.'

'You're yet to have dinner with me,' Hughes said with a boyish grin.

'You're way too old for me, Hughesie. You'd be asleep before the first over.'

'I was a bit of a demon opening bowler once.'

'Yeah, but you're all spin now,' Cass grinned.

'What's happening, Cass?' Harper asked, breaking the banter.

'You tell me. I hear comrade Tony is up for a gig.'

Harper bounced a forefinger off his nose. 'That's news to me.'

'Yeah, I bet. Just fill me in when you decide. That is, if you ever get to make a decision.'

'Fill me in. Yeah, I can do that,' Hughes said.

'You can't say things like that anymore, Chris, you know that.' Cass frowned at him. 'Well, you should know that.'

'Cass, you're old school. So am I.'

'Mate, one day they'll come and get you if you don't modernise yourself. Then your career is dead; trust me.'

Hughes wanted to argue, but a hand resting on his arm from Harper silenced him.

'I could make an announcement soon, so I'll have one of the team call you,' Harper said.

Now uncomfortable with Hughes, Cass stepped away from the table. 'That'll be great. You guys behave now.'

'Sure will,' Hughes said, as she walked away.

'Why do you have to be so provocative?' Harper asked.

'I've fancied her for a long time.'

DOOMED

'You think smart comments like that work for you?'

'Yes.'

Harper raised his eyebrows, wondering if his colleague was serious. He shook his head and smiled. 'You are a dinosaur.'

Hughes watched Cass as she scooted off through the tables and into the corridor leading to the senate side of the building. She was heading off to the press gallery housed on the second floor.

'Yeah, maybe, but she does it for me.'

'Does what?' Harper asked, breaking Hughes' obsessive stare.

'What do you think Messenger is up to?'

'Finish your coffee and let's go ask him,' Harper smiled.

CHAPTER FIVE

Cass dumped her worn leather bag on the workstation she used when in the Canberra bureau before walking around the Hancock press gallery office, searching for one of her colleagues. She found her squirrelled away in a corner, newspapers stacked high and government reports strewn across the floor with little room to move her chair. Stick-on notes decorated the flat-screen computer, and rubbish from lunches and takeaway coffees overflowed the bin.

'Fatwa, my darling.' Cass collapsed into a chair beside her desk. 'How are ya, gorgeous?'

'You realise I hate you calling me that, don't you?' The woman didn't turn from scrutinising the computer screen.

'Yeah, I know, that's why I say it.'

'You're terrible, Muriel,' her colleague using her favourite movie line cliche, then turned, smiling, and shaking a finger at her. 'You know one day, probably at my next dinner party, you'll say that and then cause so much trouble for yourself.'

'Perhaps, but what are they going to do?'

'Declare a fatwa, of course.' Fatima Abbasi laughed.

'So, tell me, oh smart one: why would two senior cabinet ministers be caucusing outside Aussies?'

'When?'

'Just now.'

'Having coffee, I suppose.'

'Yeah, nah, not these two. Something is going on.'

'Did you get to see Harper?' asked Abbasi.

'This is my point; he was a minister having coffee.'

'Who was he with?'

'Ugh, that sleaze bag Christopher Hughes.'

'Interesting. Maybe they were talking policy?'

'They would have had an adviser with them.'

Abbasi frowned. 'They wouldn't be so open if they were plotting something.'

'These guys are super smart. They know if I saw them in each other's office, we would mark them as planning something sinister.'

'So, meet in public and nothing sinister?'

'Just a chance to gossip, but they looked guilty when I approached them.'

'What do you reckon is going on?'

'I have no idea, but keep an eye out,' said Cass. 'Oh, and just by the by. Do I look like a lesbian or something?'

'Why?'

'That snake Hughes suggested I might be. Geezus, what a bastard.'

'Stand up. Let's look at you.'

Cass stood and twirled.

'Well, you could do something a little more feminine with your hair. Your camos are way too tight, and your t-shirt could be nice shirt instead,' said Abbasi, smiling. 'But if you were gay, I would consider turning for you.'

'Doesn't your mob toss them off buildings?'

'Only the boys, sadly.' Abbasi turned away.

'Gee, that's gone dark all of a sudden. I'm sorry.'

'We're not all like each other. You know that, right?'

'Of course, my lovely.' Cass dropped her hand to her colleague's shoulder and squeezed. 'Hey, I'm in town until the end of the week; do you want to catch up for dinner or something?'

'Sure, why not?' Abbasi returned her energy. 'I have a hankering for Thai.'

'Okay, I'll leave you to it.' Cass leaned over and kissed her forehead. 'Let me know if you need any help with any stories, okay?'

'Sure, girlfriend.'

Cass turned away from the workstation. 'And you might want to clean your desk.'

'Yes, boss.'

DOOMED

She could see Peter Cleaver in his office as she strolled to it. She stood in the doorway and tapped.

'Got a sec?'

'Sure, come in.' The editor tugged a rumpled cigarette pack from his shirt pocket, lighting up after trying to straighten it.

As Cass sat, she shook her head. 'Those things will kill you.'

'Devlin scolded me all the time and yet I'm still here.'

'I sort of miss her.'

'You and me both. What can I do for you?'

Cass thumbed her chin as she hesitated to ask for advice. 'I think our boss is about to be appointed the consulate in LA.'

'I heard gossip. What do you know?'

'Harper told me an announcement is imminent. I want to run the story before he announces.'

'Why the hell would you do that?'

'To massage the message and have it favourable for Tony. If we miss the story, and others beat us, he'll be pissed.'

'If we miss the story, will he blame you or me?'

'Well, you're based here, so I think it will be you.'

'But you're the political editor,' countered Cleaver.

'That being the case, I think we should run it in the paper tomorrow and let the television folks respond to what the government says in the morning.'

'Why do you want to do this now?'

'Pete, when the boss says I need stories to get the Nicholls' gig, then I'm going to find stories, no matter where they are.'

'Treat him kind then, otherwise you're stuffed.' Cleaver coughed a smoker's wheeze.

'As I said, those things will kill you,' Cass said as she stood. 'I'll bounce a draft off you if you don't mind?'

The coughing hadn't stopped, and Cleaver waved her away, nodding as he tried to control himself. When he settled, he picked up his phone and jabbed a few numbers, waiting for an answer.

'Boss, your girl is on the job and will have something in tomorrow's rag.'

CHAPTER SIX

'Now, this looks ominous. Should I worry?' Barton Messenger asked as Hughes and Harper wandered into his office and sat at a round meeting table in the corner.

'Youngster, we have come to have a chat about politics,' said Hughes.

'Politics? Hmm, this should be interesting.'

'As the deputy leader, how do you think we're faring?' Harper asked.

'Getting straight to the point.' Messenger joined them. 'I think we're doing okay.'

'That surprises me, given the polls,' Harper said. 'How do you think we're doing in the chamber?'

Messenger sucked his teeth as he considered the question. 'I think the front bench is doing okay. The back bench is rowdy enough and we are getting our legislation through the parliament.'

Hughes leaned into the table. 'How do you think Bruce is travelling?'

'I think she's a bit of a media celebrity, but as deep as a thimble in policy. She plays the crowd with social policies but weak in economics.'

'Do you think we will win the election?'

Messenger sat back from the table, placed his elbows on the arms of the chair, steepling his fingers against his nose. 'Frankly, if we called it tomorrow, we would lose.'

Hughes slapped the table, flamboyantly sitting back in his chair and crossing his legs.

Harper, a little graver, said, 'do you think we should take it up more against her?'

'She is weak in economics, as I said, and I'm chafing at the bit to get at her, but Pete thinks the luvvies in the media protect her too much.'

'She's a danger to us and we need to cut her down a peg or two,' Hughes said.

'But if we do, they will pin us as bullying white blokes, displaying toxic masculinity, and they'll brand us misogynists,' Messenger countered.

'This is what kills us now.' Hughes almost snarled. 'Damn political correctness.'

'It's a little more than that,' Harper said. 'We just have to be careful about how and what we say to expose her.'

'I think I should take her on,' Messenger said.

'Not the prime minister?' asked Harper with a conspiratorial tone, eyeing him.

Messenger paused for a moment, glimpsing at Hughes then back to Harper. 'Hey, wait a minute. You're not suggesting what I think you're suggesting?'

'What do you think we're suggesting?' Hughes asked.

'We've done that before and it never works; you know that?' Messenger flicked his eyes between them, searching for a sign.

'Desperate times call for desperate measures.' Hughes pushed his thumbnail into his front bottom teeth as he studied Messenger.

Messenger dropped his arms, his knuckles almost hitting the floor. 'Seriously? You want to take out Peter?'

'We need to get back in the game.' Harper nodded.

'Yes, but knifing a first term prime minister changes the entire game.'

'Would you be interested?' Hughes asked, checking for a glint of ambition.

'Noooo, fuck off,' Messenger said before pausing for a moment, then adding, 'Listen, I'm happy to take it up to Bruce, but only as treasurer, not as prime minister. What about you?'

Hughes wasn't expecting the question and dithered long enough for the other two to notice.

'I think we should look at Jim.' Hughes waved his hand and pointed to Harper. 'He has the name as leader and can bring esteem back to the job.'

'This is crazy.' Messenger glanced at Harper.

Hughes unhooked his legs and sat closer. 'Bart, Pete is an accidental prime minister. He was never ready for the job and now sleeps in

Yarralumla. It's not about him, it's about politics and getting our ratings up.'

Messenger remained silent, squinting at his colleagues, then dropping his chin to his chest.

'You are deputy leader, Bart; what say you?' Harper asked.

'I say, let us watch the polls. Increase policy announcements like the drought strategy. Get the narrative back to economics, and we might have a chance.'

'And if we don't?'

'Then maybe we should go visit Peter.'

Hughes stood. 'Fair enough.'

Harper also stood, offering his hand. 'Barton, I still would want you as my deputy.'

Barton grasped Harper's hand. 'Not sure I'd be much of a deputy if I knifed my leader.'

'Well, that's up to you to come to terms with, but you are doing an outstanding job and we would not want to lose you.'

'Thanks for your time, young man,' Hughes said as he strode from the office.

As Harper followed, Messenger grabbed him by the arm to slow him.

'You think this is the right thing to do?' Messenger asked.

'Not sure Pete has the numbers anymore. It would be best for us to act, rather than a worried marginal seat member setting the agenda.'

'I see your point.'

'Bart, trust me; everything will be okay.' Harper squeezed his shoulder as he left. 'I'm from the government.'

Once they left, Messenger closed his door and leaned with his back against it, smirking.

'Interesting development.'

CHAPTER SEVEN

The walk to the backbench offices of the House of Representatives from the central ministerial core could be a long one. It was rare for a minister to trudge back through the green carpeted corridors. They left the carpet as their career progressed.

Ministers appointed by the will of the prime minister often neglecting political roots, sometimes overstating their elevated position, forgetting the cliché they were first amongst equals. Many ministers believed they spent far too long on the green carpet lamenting political ambition when Prime Minister Gerrard ruled the parliament like a bully.

Barton Messenger needed to speak to Jaya Rukhmani, the independent member for Melbourne, which meant a lengthy walk to her office. She had become a political celebrity for defeating a sitting prime minister at the election three years ago. Now holding the balance of power in the House, many claim she was the most powerful politician in the parliament. Unless the government maintained her support, then legislation would not pass.

Jaya had been Messenger's postgraduate supervisor for his studies in politics at Melbourne University. She always had a smile for him and considered him her favourite student. Given they were almost the same age, she sometimes wondered if he ever reciprocated her fondness.

Messenger stepped out the side entrance to his suite, beginning the long trek to Jaya's office on the second floor. He scampered along the blue carpet corridors of the ministerial wing, then clopped the wooden floors past the secretive government marginal seats secretariat. He crossed the centre of the Members' Hall with its black marble water feature, ignoring the tourists on the first floor staring over the balcony.

He smiled at staffers heading to the cafeteria for an early dinner, or perhaps more likely a late lunch, pushing open the heavy doors to enter the connecting glass corridor between the wings.

Once on the Representatives' side, he entered the elevator to take him to the second floor. He stepped out of the lift, rounded the corner onto the green carpet and, just a few doors down, pushed open the door of office 96, entering the reception. He politely walked over to the staff office, asking if Jaya was available.

Robert Wong, Jaya's campaign manager and now chief of staff, tapped on her side door and put his head in to tell her that the treasurer had arrived. Jaya came out her main door, greeting Messenger.

'Minister, so nice to see you. Such a long way from home.' Messenger offered his hand, and she took it. 'What? No hugs anymore?'

'Perceptions, professor; it's all about perceptions. You taught me that.'

'Come in. I have much to talk to you about.'

She sat on her couch, patting the leather beside her. Messenger sat in a rigid chair beside the couch.

Jaya shook her head, clicking her tongue against her teeth in disappointment. 'I wanted to ask you about this mess happening in Queensland with the coal mining.'

'Why are you so concerned? It's miles from the issues of Melbourne,' Messenger said, surprised by the comment.

'Well, this is the problem with the government.' Jaya leaned back into the couch, crossing her legs, tugging at her skirt. 'You think my constituents do not hold an opinion on coal mining, and they don't worry about our international relations?'

'Sorry, Jaya. You're right; my bad.' Messenger leaned forward with his forearms on his knees. 'The people of Melbourne who voted for an independent should be very concerned about the issues affecting Queensland. How stupid of me to think they should be more worried about congestion in the city and population.'

'You're sassing me.'

'Well, to be fair,' Messenger sat back, 'you haven't been very supportive of the government, Stanley, or indeed me since your election.'

'What has the government done to build bridges? You're the ones who sacked me from your party for being a racist, remember?'

'That's true, but if we hadn't terminated your candidacy, you would not be in parliament with the balance of power.'

'And you wouldn't be treasurer,' Jaya grinned. 'You'd still be in opposition with Gerrard as prime minister.'

Messenger smiled. 'Yeah, I guess that's right.'

Jaya tossed her hands in the air. 'Finally; truth from a politician.'

He shifted in his chair. 'Okay, so what's worrying you about coal?'

'The fact you're about to ban exporting it.'

'Why is that a concern for you? I would guess the Greenies in your electorate would love banning exports?'

'They do, but it's my people in India who are being denied cheap energy.'

'I assumed you were a proud Australian?'

'I am, very much so; but India needs our support, not our ignorance.'

Her statement intrigued Messenger. 'You have learnt much since you've been here.'

'I watch and listen, especially you.' Jaya smiled, and he blushed.

'Well, ah,' Messenger hesitated a little, 'the only thing I can say to that is to keep learning. You have the theory, now you can apply it. Just win the seat again and don't be a oncer.'

'A oncer?'

'Yeah, a one termer. Make sure you come back.'

'I suspect I won't. The circumstances were different last time, and I received help.'

'Just keep working hard in the electorate and try to raise your profile.'

'The media bombard me every day about my voting intentions. I don't think I need to be increasing my profile.'

'Something to consider, though, is this.' Messenger rested his elbows, leaning forward. 'Your media at the moment is reactive. You're pitching a replica image of the government. Step away from government policy; try becoming the remedy to your constituent issues.'

'That's hard when there is little opportunity in this place, especially for me.'

'Hence the reason I'm here.'

'So, this is not a friendly visit?'

Messenger moved back in his chair and crossed his legs. 'I have a job for you, an important one. The government would like you to chair an inquiry into the drought. We don't consider that a partisan chair would bring the balance needed, so we thought you would be the perfect leader on this important issue.'

'Why doesn't Stanley just act and distribute relief money?'

'Yeah, well, that's the point.' Messenger tugged at his nose. 'We don't know the full picture and we would like to learn more.'

'You are kidding?' Jaya smiled as she shook her head. 'It hasn't rained. Farmers are struggling. What more do you need to know?'

'That's the political point, but the underlying issues are more complex. That's the reason we need a report. We want to learn if banks are mistreating farm investment; if local councils are assisting; if the national flock and herds are in crisis or is it just regional; and whether trade agreements are at threat.'

'What resources will you give me?'

'I'll set out terms of reference for you. You can seek submissions, take evidence in Canberra, then present a report with your recommendations within three months,' said Messenger, crunching his face.

'Three months, is that all?'

'We have farmers and towns struggling. We need this report so we can help them beyond this drought.'

'What's in it for me?'

'Crumbs, you are learning, aren't you?'

'I learnt enough to know that if you don't ask, you don't get.'

'Your salary will have the standard committee chair increase. I could wrangle extra staff for you.'

'Is that it?'

'Yeah, that's about it, unless I am missing something.' Messenger checked his notes in his faux leather folder. 'I suppose I can have you lead the debate on any legislation that may come from it.'

'I have a couple of things I need done.'

'What might they be?'

'I want an appointment to the parliamentary Foreign Affairs and Trade committee.'

'Why?' Messenger arched his brow.

'I want a say on the issues impacting our relationship with India.'

Messenger considered her for a moment, thinking through the process. 'I can't promise anything, but I'll try to get you elected.'

'You saying that means I will be, so thank you.'

'No promises.' Messenger opened his hands in surrender. 'What else do you want?'

'Dinner?'

'Say what?'

'Dinner.' Jaya grinned. 'I want to have dinner with you, in Melbourne.'

'Have you got something going on?' Messenger tapped a finger on his forehead.

'No,' Jaya said, beaming.

'You've been making obscure signs like this since we were at Uni together.'

'You're charming and I'd like to have dinner with you.'

'You think that's wise?'

'What, a single woman can't ask a single man out on a date? You are single, right?'

'It's the treasurer and the independent member of the parliament who holds the balance of power having dinner,' Messenger said.

'Not friends trying to be friendlier?'

'Do you consider it proper?'

'You want this inquiry done?'

Messenger smiled; his brow knitted. 'Such a good learner.' He stood. 'Okay, but it's just business and I get to pick the place.'

'Not the casino, not a café and nowhere near our electorates.'

'Fair enough. I'll be in touch with the terms of reference.'

The treasurer turned and made his way to the door. 'See you,' he said over his shoulder as he took off.

Jaya still sat in on the couch watching him go, nibbling at a nail, then said, 'Well, Jaya, I think that went well, don't you?'

Messenger heard the squealing laugh as he left; he smiled, shaking his head, and strode off on the green carpet.

CHAPTER EIGHT

Cass was on her second glass of chardonnay when her phone buzzed. It was her son calling from Perth, his tone full of misery.

'What's wrong, mate? You sound anxious about something.'

Christian didn't respond, so she encouraged him to speak.

'It's school.'

'What's wrong?'

'I'm in trouble.'

'For what?'

Christian again didn't speak, his heavy breathing worrying Cass as she listened.

'What's up, honey? Please tell me.'

'Mum, I was in a fight, and I hurt another boy. I didn't mean to hurt him, but he was having a go, so I punched him. His parents came to the school, and I guess they may suspend me.'

'What does your dad say?'

'I haven't told him; he won't be happy.'

'How come?'

'It's Terry Randall.'

The news stung Cass. She hadn't met her former husband's partner but knew she had a couple of kids of a similar age to Christian. She had a sip of wine. 'How serious is it?'

'Pretty bad. I think I broke a tooth.'

Cass ran fingers through her hair, wondering what to say. 'What was it about?'

'I don't want to say.'

'Christian, please tell me so I can talk to your father.'

'Mum, please don't force me to tell you.'

Cass drained her glass, stood, and started pacing.

'Sweetie, I can't help you if I don't know what I'm dealing with. Why was he having a go?'

'I can't tell you,' Christian groaned.

'Okay, okay, it's all right; everything will be fine. Are you okay?' Cass imagined her oldest distraught, needing a hug. 'Where is he now?'

'His dad picked him up from school and he hasn't come home yet.'

'Where's your sister?'

'She's at training. Dad will be late home and I expect Diane home any minute. Mummy, I don't know what to do.'

'Do you want me to call your dad?'

'Could you?'

'I think I should, because otherwise your version of the story may get disoriented.'

'Mum, I'm frightened.'

'It'll be okay, Chrissy. Let me talk to your dad. But it would help if I knew what Terry said.'

Christian didn't respond straight away, and Cass could hear soft tears.

'It's okay, sweetie; I love you.'

'Terry said you didn't.'

'Didn't what?'

'He said Dad told him you didn't love me and Stephie.'

The words shoved into her heart like a blade, and she gasped, as if stabbed.

'You don't believe that do you?'

'He called you a loser, and that's when I punched him.'

Cass's pacing increased as she continued to brush her hand through her hair, anxiety rushing through her. She wanted to hold her son.

'He had no right to say that to you, none. It's not true, Chrissie. It's not true, my darling.'

'I know, but he didn't need to say it.'

'Okay, okay.' Cass was still pacing. 'I'm very sure your dad would not have said such a thing. I'll talk to him.'

'Mum, what do I do?' Christian said, whimpering. 'I'm scared, and I want to be with you.'

DOOMED

'It'll all be okay, sweetie, I promise. Just stay in your room until your dad gets home. Go get food and a drink from the fridge. Just play games until Dad's home, okay?'

'Okay.'

'Don't be frightened, sweetie; Mummy is on to it. But I need you to be brave.'

'Shall I lock the door?'

'Get the supplies and then put a note on the door to say that you want to be left alone and lock it, until dad gets home, okay?'

'Yes, Mummy.'

'I'll call your dad now, okay? Everything will be fine, I promise.'

'Love you, Mum.'

'Love you, sweetie.'

Cass dropped the phone onto the dining table after they had said their goodbyes. She bent over with her hands on her knees, then slumped to her haunches, struggling with the ball of emotion rushing through her. She straightened, moving to her couch, curled into a ball and broke down, sobbing out her anxiety.

Once composed, she then spent the next twenty minutes yelling, whimpering, and pleading with her former husband to resolve the dilemma and to step up for a change by fighting for their children. They quarreled and shouted, but he promised to cancel his meeting and go straight home to sort out the potential mess, supporting their son with any punishment from his partner.

Cass had finished her bottle when she picked up a call from her Sydney colleague Helen Rasminski.

'Are you okay? You sound a little stressed.'

'No, I'm okay. It's just been a busy day,' Cass said.

'Well, I may have news for you.'

'Good or bad? Not sure I could take any bad news right now.'

'I don't know if it is one or the other, but I have it from a reliable source that an agreement is about to be made on the Nicholls replacement.'

Cass smiled as she waited for her animated colleague to tell her the news. 'Who is it?'

'You didn't hear it from me, okay?'

'Sure.'

'It's likely to be Tamara O'Byrne,' Rasminski said, speculating on how Cass was taking the news. 'I got the advice from a contact in Hancock's office. It seems she has already tested and has been running through new formats.'

Cass couldn't speak; she just nodded, staring at the floor.

'I've heard she had interviews with various editors,' Rasminski continued. 'It seems she is a shoo-in, which makes a mockery of the process Hancock announced.'

Cass started to say something but couldn't get anything out. She coughed to free her throat. 'How long has she been with us?'

'Three years, I think; maybe a little more.'

'Wasn't she part of the mentor group?'

'Yeah, I think she was in Hancock's group. She's done nothing though and has done little television. Remember when she stuffed up that story about Hancock's private business group?'

'The Mercantiles?'

'Yes, she did a number on one of them and all hell broke loose,' Rasminski said.

'Has there been any formal announcement?'

'None,' Rasminski responded. 'I think they're going through with the charade of considering various candidates, but I reckon it would be a waste of time.'

'Thanks for the call, Helen. I just need to ring my kids; do you mind if I cut you short and talk later, perhaps next week?'

'No worries, girlfriend. Sisters, right?'

'Thanks for letting me know. Talk soon.'

As soon as the call ended, Cass thumbed through her phone for a familiar number.

'Tony Hancock.'

'It's me.' Cass forced herself to smile a greeting. 'Did you like the piece this morning?'

'I loved it, Cass. I have already had a call from the minister's office. I think it might have pushed them over the edge, so I could be on the way to LA. Thanks.'

Cass changed her tone. 'I wouldn't be so confident if I were you.'

Hancock paused for a moment. 'Sounds a little sinister. What do you mean?'

'You promised I would be considered fairly for the show.'

'Yeah, and you will.'

'That's bullshit, and you know it. I've heard you've already appointed your current girlfriend.'

'Who?' Hancock was almost cherub-like with his response.

'There's more than one? You prick,' Cass said, raising her voice. 'You've appointed O'Byrne and I know you already tested her.'

'I have made no decision.'

'You promised me a fair process.'

'It will be, but to be fair, I asked for stories, and other than the story you did on me, there has been none.'

Cass paused for a moment, then said, 'How would it be if I embroiled the government in a sex abuse scandal implicating their new consulate? How do you think that will play out in the community with the current high temperature about the Me-too movement?'

'What's that got to do with me?'

'Maybe those times you took me back to your room could come back to haunt you?'

'You were an enthusiastic partner.'

'Or was I threatened with my job?'

There was no response.

'Would the government like to know you set me up in an apartment in New York to be your floozy on tap?'

'You took your fiancé.'

'Only for protection from a relentless predator.'

Hancock said nothing, but his heavy breathing gave away his anxiety.

'I wonder how many other victims would share their own stories. I wonder if O'Byrne will ever work again when the industry discovers her promotion came because she was providing sexual favours for you.'

'What do you want?' he said.

'I want a fair process; if it is, then I want to be appointed the new host.'

Hancock remained silent.

An emotional wave washed over Cass. 'I haven't sacrificed my marriage to be mistreated like this. I haven't sacrificed my...' It was hard for her to get the words out as she struggled to speak. 'sacrificed my children to be treated like this.' She sniffed, wiping her nose. 'You owe me a fair deal, and if you don't give it to me, I will destroy you… I promise you that.'

They didn't speak. Cass was crying, trying to stifle and hide any noise. Hancock thought through options.

'Just get me the stories.'

CHAPTER NINE

Riding the metro train system travelling into Melbourne's CBD is compulsory to avoid the traffic congestion on roads planned and built for a metropolis when horses dragging heavy loads dominated.

The journey from Sunshine takes thirty minutes. Garrick Higgins couldn't understand why the ambition to live in new suburbs up to seventy minutes away by rail, even longer by car, was still rampant. He paid off his mortgage on his three-bedroom weather-board house, now ready for major building extensions. Yet his mates struggled to meet overblown repayments in the new housing estates, just so they could claim something new.

Higgins finished the short walk from Flagstaff station to the Queen Street head office of the Australian Council of Trade Unions in time to enjoy a coffee before the meeting of trade union delegates for the mining division of the powerful construction union.

The agenda had only one item: foreign workers. The union remained worried members would miss out on work because of the government agreement with Timor-Leste to man offshore drilling rigs, so they wanted to strategise a response.

He finished the morning paper, drained his coffee, and strolled across the road to the building, taking the elevator to the meeting rooms. There were already a few delegates at the table, nodding a welcome before returning to their phones. Others trailed in, then union secretary Lou Mogg took his place at the head of the table, calling the meeting to order.

'Comrades, thanks for coming,' the older man said, gaining immediate attention. 'We need to discuss the government's statement they have signed an accord with Timor to allow workers on our rigs. It is the union's view that we should not allow this to happen.'

'Before discussing this issue, Comrade Secretary, are you able to tell us if the Council of Timor Unions has a position?' a bearded delegate wearing a blue union shirt asked.

'There's been no formal response. Hancock Media quoted them as supporting the government.'

'Hancock?' a cynical Higgins said. 'It'll be fake news.'

'Surely, they would protect us?' the bearded delegate asked.

'One would hope,' said the secretary. 'We are yet to hear from them.'

'What's our plan?' Higgins asked.

The secretary scanned the concerned faces at the table. 'I've spoken to the general secretary, and he is of the view we go to Canberra and protest outside parliament. He thinks he can get his forestry division to blockade the roads, and we rally in the forecourt demanding to be heard.'

The bearded delegate asked, 'What has the minister said?'

'Her response is provocative. She said what is good for Timor is good for us. She suggested we should agree. She then implied that the standard of living in Timor would increase.'

'Bullshit!' Higgins said, others murmured agreement with him.

'It would for those blokes on the rigs,' the bearded delegate suggested.

'That's not our concern. Our concern is using foreign labour on Australian worksites. If we let them get away with this, what will they do on other sites?'

The bearded delegate scratched his chin. 'Not sure they will extend this policy. Timor owns the rig; they're in their waters.'

'Comrade, think.' Higgins glanced about the room. 'If Timor gets away with it, what will happen if India opens a coal mine?'

'I don't understand.'

'They own the land, the mine, the coal, the rail to the ports, the port, and the ships hauling it back to India. They own everything. Australia and our workers have no say.' Higgins paused for a moment, searching around the table, looking for understanding. 'Why would they not argue that they want their own people working the site? A precedent will be set by what we agree with the rigs. They will then negotiate an enterprise agreement under our current laws, excluding Australians and unions.'

He paused again, taking a mouthful of water from his glass. 'Let me also add so long as they appear to pay a living wage in Australia, they'll stop penalties and the benefits we have fought to win at other sites. India does it with their mines here, then what's stopping the entire industry from doing the same thing? We have to stop it, right now.'

'Foreign workers undermine our authority in the workplace. We will become obsolete as we've become in other industries,' the secretary added.

The discussion remained robust over the next hour. The consensus was to fight the government by protesting at parliament when legislation approving the Timor agreement was scheduled for debate.

As the meeting was winding up, the secretary cast an eye over his delegates, preparing to raise a challenging issue. 'What say you about the coal industry being closed?'

A few delegates shifted in their seats, and a silence washed over them.

'It's a good thing,' the bearded delegate responded. 'The climate emergency is real, and we have to protect the planet for our children.'

The only woman at the table said, 'It's the union movement's policy to support renewable energy, and if we are to do that, then we must commit to climate change action.'

The secretary turned to Higgins for his view, raising a querying eyebrow.

'What about my members?' Higgins asked.

'Your members are losing jobs now, so there won't be much to save if we keep going as we are.'

'That's why we should support foreign investment. We need to create jobs, not lose them,' Higgins said, leaning into the table.

'They'll get jobs in renewables, comrade,' the woman said.

Higgins sneered, as if she just farted screwing up his nose then said, 'We've been talking jobs in that sector for decades and they haven't come. Once a panel is facing the sun or they install a windmill, there is little more a miner can do.'

'We need to save the planet,' she said.

'We also have a duty to our members,' Higgins said, taking in deep breaths to calm himself.

An uncomfortable silence clouded the meeting; the secretary shifted in his chair to end the discussion. 'I'll report that the majority support the ACTU position, but we should always put our people first.'

Higgins nodded. 'Fair enough, comrade.'

CHAPTER TEN

Christopher Hughes had enjoyed a successful career as a barrister before entering parliament. He revelled in the notoriety of his successes, taking on the unions in court action over workplace disputes. He adored his early Sydney lifestyle in the eastern suburbs. He married the ambitious architect daughter of a merchant banker, who designed the redevelopment of a house in Manly when the couple moved to the safe seat. A political career would be good for them, he often said privately, and excellent for the country. He just never expected to be in opposition for over twenty years and never entertained the idea he would not be the leader at this stage of his career.

Hughes' wife Frankie was perhaps more ambitious for him than he was. Whilst it prepared him to wait for opportunities, she encouraged him to make things happen in the true Machiavellian way. She wanted the top job and was keen for Christopher to snatch it, now agreeing with her that perhaps with Stanley struggling in the polls, he might never have another opportunity.

'Look Chris, let's face it; the way the government is performing at the moment you won't win the next election, so we may as well retire and go live the good life elsewhere.' Frankie had called to remind him about a charity event the following Saturday. 'If you challenge, then you will be in the history books as a prime minister, and we can have two years in Admiralty House.'

Hughes smiled. 'Not Yarralumla?'

'Ugh, kill me. Canberra would be the death of me.'

'Harbourside mansion or nothing.' He grinned.

'I'd love to get in there and redesign a few things.'

'You know it's a heritage listed property, don't you?'

'Don't sass me, please darling,' she said. 'Since the Gerrards, they have run the place down. Kirribilli next door needs doing over with more office space. The residence is just not up to it.'

Hughes chuckled. 'You think Margaret Gerrard was a little casual with the interiors?'

'Well, what do you expect from a dowdy Melbourne socialite and a Francophile to boot? She spent all her time in Canberra. No wonder the place needs work. We should do it before we move in.'

'Getting a little ahead of yourself?'

'Am I? You can't continue with the West Australian. He is hopeless. Not sure why you didn't stand against him when you dumped Harper.'

'Timing is always important in politics, Frank; you know that.'

'You didn't have the numbers, darling. Admit it.'

'That may be so, but next time I will.'

'Oh yes, and how do you propose to kill off Harper? Surely, he still wants it, if his comments in the paper are to be believed.'

'What did he say?'

'He said he supports the leader,' Frankie shrieked into the phone. When she was calmer, she added, 'That's a dead giveaway that he is manoeuvring.'

Hughes chuckled at his wife's reaction. 'You sure know your politics.'

'Better than you, it seems,' she said, then changed her tone. 'Oh darling, this is your time. This is what we have worked for; don't let Harper or that young dude Messenger get in your way. You deserve it. You've served faithfully and now it's time to lead.'

Hughes enjoyed her enthusiasm. It was always nice to hear his wife say good things about him, but he pursed his lips. 'Yeah, maybe.'

'Oh, for Christ's sake, Chris, get a grip. You are a leader, now make it happen.'

'I'll scout around and get a view.'

'Don't scout, just do the numbers. You know what to do,' she said. 'Now don't forget Saturday; it's important.'

'Okay gorgeous, I'll diarise it now.'

'It's already in there. I did it months ago. Just don't go planning anything else. Not this time.'

'Okay, I promise.'

DOOMED

'It's not you I'm worried about; it's that snivelling little brat you've got working for you.'

'I'll tell him.'

'Please promise.'

'Darling,' Hughes sharpened his tone, 'it's done. Look, I have to go; see you Friday night.'

'Love you darling. I'll plan something special for us. Bye.'

'See you.' Hughes stubbed the call, then shouted, 'Con, are you there?'

Con Krakos was soon at the door. He walked in and sat at the minister's desk.

'What's happening?' Hughes asked.

'Boss, there has been little movement with the Timorese. It seems Harper's office wants to tidy up a few details, so legislation will have to wait a few days. I have heard we can expect a union protest when it gets introduced.'

'How do you know that?'

'This is why you pay me, to know such things.'

'Did the media give it to you?'

Krakos scoffed. 'Shit, no, they don't talk to us. No, it came from a contact in the union.'

'What's a unionist doing talking to you?'

'It's called networking.'

'It's called playing both sides and I would be careful if I were you. What else is happening? How's the government going?'

'Surprised you asked that; you must know,' said Krakos.

'I know we're struggling in the polls, but what's the actual word on the street?'

'The government is stuffed whilst Stanley remains prime minister. It's not that we lose, it's by how much. I'm thinking twenty-five seats will transfer over.'

'Crumbs, if that is the swing then I might be in danger.'

'You'll be okay, but I suspect your preselection may be under threat.'

Hughes fell back in his chair. 'Really? Why?'

'If the government is about to lose, then a few young Turks may consider it time to come in and take control of policy. The Christians are on the move, building numbers in a few branches.'

'Am I under threat?'

'I would think so, but there is a remedy.'

'What's that?'

'Take Stanley down.'

Hughes studied his staffer. Krakos made his mark running a state member's successful campaign. He then came to Hughes when he was promoted to the Industrial Relations portfolio three years ago.

'You think I should shaft my leader?'

'If you don't, others will.'

'Who?'

'Harper is sounding out numbers. He thinks a return to the leadership will save the chairs on a sinking ship. Messenger is sniffing around, but he's considered a lightweight. Stavloukas maybe if they're desperate.'

'I can't challenge Stanley; there's no reason to do that.'

'Then create a reason.'

'Can't we just use the polls and tap him on the shoulder? Do it a little more gentlemanly?'

'Who will put their hand up?' Krakos asked, 'Who will step aside?'

Hughes nodded his understanding.

'Let's destabilise Stanley, then push Harper,' Krakos said, running his tongue over his teeth.

'Harper? I thought we would move to get me over the line?'

'Harper is the patsy.' Krakos broadened a smile when he caught Hughes' reaction. 'We run him, making sure he loses with a result that will be very close, just a few votes in it. We then have Harper not accept the result, which will tarnish his next push. We spill the leadership again, then you reluctantly compete with Harper. And voila, you win.'

Hughes smirked, shaking his head. 'Have you been thinking about this for very long?'

'From day one, but we had to wait for the polls to drop. So now it's time.'

'We kill Stanley?'

'Softly. We prepare the ground and send in Harper for the kill. No one will suspect you. They won't like what will happen to the PM. They will prefer you with no blood on your hands, rather than the bloodied assassin, Harper.'

'Interesting… So how do we destabilise Stanley?'

'We leak stories, backgrounding various journalists about the decisions being made; simple.'

'What do we leak first?'

Krakos grinned. 'Did you know Stanley has not been in his electorate for six months?'

'He lives in Canberra, so I would expect getting back to WA is hard.'

'He's been back to WA many times; his family has moved back.'

Hughes steepled his fingers in front of his face. 'I didn't know that.'

'Although he has been back, he has done no events, no visits or even constituent work in the electorate.'

'Who's been doing it?'

'His chief electorate officer wants to replace him when he retires and does most of his work. She's been working flat out to get endorsed and handle the office, placing herself as the lead representative at every electorate event. Apparently, her personal ratings are going crazy, and she has the numbers to knock him off now.'

'Crumbs, I'm sorry to hear all of that.'

'Stanley works hard as PM, but he is hopeless. He's losing his family because of it.'

Hughes shook his head. 'We shouldn't use travel against him; it always comes back to bite everyone.'

'We should if he is using it and not fulfilling his electorate requirements.'

'Yes, but we could kill her for doing his job.'

'Then so be it for being too ambitious. We have someone else primed for preselection if we can get rid of her as well.'

'Who?'

'One of us.'

'How big is us?'

Krakos smiled, a little embarrassed, and considered a response. 'Let's just say we already have three in the federal parliament, and we are working to have more at the next election.'

The announcement unnerved Hughes. 'Who are we?'

'A group of like-minded people who think you should be prime minister,' Krakos said, smiling across the desk.

Hughes rolled his tongue around his mouth, licking his lips as he watched his staffer, speculating whether he was serious.

'You think you have that much influence?'

'I know we have.' Krakos nodded. 'If you don't want the job, we'll go with someone else.'

'You're dreaming.'

'Am I?' Krakos stood. 'Give a journalist the gift of this information about Stanley and let me get more goss for you.'

'You're an interesting man, Con.'

'And a patriot minister; never forget that,' Krakos said as he left the office.

Hughes stood and walked to a window to look out over the greenery of the well-maintained courtyard. A gardener was raking the luscious green turf, collecting the few scattered leaves. He thought about his wife, then his adviser, and agreed that maybe it was his time.

Returning to his desk, he picked up his phone and swiped through contacts until he found a number he rarely used. Seeing her earlier in the week had piqued his interest.

'Cassandra, it's Christopher Hughes. I wonder if you have a moment we could talk. Are you in Canberra or Sydney?'

The call startled Cass, as it was the first time Hughes had used her mobile number. 'Hello Minister, I'm in Canberra.'

'I wonder if we could catch up for a chat.'

'Sure, fire away.'

'No, it's a little sensitive and I would prefer we meet.'

Journalists knew that when politicians called, they could divulge something, but when they wanted to meet, they had something juicier to gossip about.

'Let's do coffee at Aussies, in say thirty minutes?'

'No, what I have to tell you is a little more covert than gossip central. I can't afford to be seen with you at this stage.'

'That sounds a little weird. What's it about?'

Hughes didn't respond as he considered his options. 'Let's just say it's about the leadership of Australia.'

Cass scratched her cheek before responding. 'Okay, I'm game. Where?'

'What time do you wrap up this evening?'

'I'll finish by nine.'

'Why don't you swing by my place in Griffith for a quick chat? Should take around an hour.'

Cass grimaced. 'Nowhere else?'

'Trust me on this; we can't afford to be seen. Are you driving?'

'Yes.'

'I live at Hann Street. Can I suggest you park in Lockyer, opposite Roe Street? There's a walkway that goes through to Hann. I'm the second house on the right.'

'Is this necessary?'

'I think it will be worth your while. One-hour tops.'

'If you're planning something, I'll scream loud about it and your career is over.'

'Stop fretting, for heaven's sake. You either want this or I can give it to someone else.'

Cass stroked her hand through her hair and looked to the ceiling.

'Okay, I'll be there around nine-thirty.'

'Excellent. I'll get some cheese out if you're hungry. See you then.'

The line went dead. Cass looked at her phone, wondering what it was all about.

CHAPTER ELEVEN

There was little light in the dim walkway as Cass made her way through to Hann Street. The streetlights were no better, with trees blocking any light from filtering to the path. There was a small concrete footpath that was too close to overgrown shrubs, so she stepped out onto the roadway and scanned the area. It seemed like a quiet suburban street, a wealthy street.

She strolled to the driveway of Hughes' house, spying into the windows. Rooms were bright from no curtains or blinds drawn; it looked enormous. She headed up the drive, then over to the front portico before ringing the bell.

An amplified voice came from a speaker. 'Is that you, Cass?'

'Yes, Minister.'

A buzzer released the door.

'Come through. I'm in the kitchen.'

Cass shoved open, then closed the heavy front door.

'Come on down.'

She heard a voice from a dim room ahead and stalked the long wooden hallway, entering a large room with a casual living area, a dining table on which several candles were burning and the minister working at the stove.

'I'm just whipping up a little food for you. I assume you're hungry.'

'You assume wrong,' Cass said, checking around the room.

'It's just pan-fried calamari. I have a couple of fresh oysters if you like them.'

Hughes scooped the food from the skillet onto a white plate, placing a few cos lettuce leaves to garnish and a wedge of lemon.

'Please take a seat and make yourself comfortable,' he said as he placed the plate on the pre-set table. He then rushed to the refrigerator and returned with a plate of shucked oysters. 'Wine?'

'No thanks, water is fine.'

Hughes tugged a bottle of chardonnay from the ice bucket on the bench, splashing a handsome amount into the two crystal glasses. He then grabbed a small bottle of Perrier from the refrigerator and came back to the table, unscrewing the cap as he sat opposite the still standing Cass.

'Sit down, take a load and let's have a chat.'

Cass glanced around the house, checking for outside access; she noticed a cantilevered door was open and there was a lit below-ground pool just outside the doors. She dropped her bag onto the table, taking a seat opposite the minister and pouring a glass of water.

'I'm a little uncomfortable with this scenario,' Cass said, gazing over the glass paused at her lips.

'Relax and have some food,' said Hughes, as he took three of the oysters and placed them on a plate before him. 'Have some squid whilst it's hot; it's my specialty.'

'What did you want to talk about?'

'I wanted to get your view on the government and a few issues we are facing.'

'Your government is stuffed; you know that.' Cass looked across at Hughes, who was slurping in an oyster. 'If that's all you wanted, I may as well go.'

Hughes picked up his glass, swirled the wine and sniffed the aroma. 'This is a good drop. It's from Margaret River. You should try it.' He smiled at the journalist, who slumped in her chair, arms crossed across her chest.

'What do you want, Minister?' she asked.

Hughes took his time, slurping another oyster before he answered. 'I want you to have something to eat, then we can talk about the leadership of the government.' He smirked as he washed the oyster down with wine.

The candid revelation surprised Cass. She contemplated Hughes, wondering what he was up to. The candles, the chilled wine, the prepared food wasn't a business meeting, but news of leadership intrigue sparked her instincts. She picked a piece of calamari from the centre plate and popped it into her mouth.

'Surprisingly good,' she said to a smiling Hughes.

'Try the oysters; they're from Tasmania.'

Cass took an oyster and slurped it. 'So, what's this about leadership?'

'Always keen to talk business. Have a sip of wine,' Hughes said, finishing his last oyster. He rested his arm over the back of the chair, crossing his legs and spinning the glass through his fingers.

Cass took a sip of wine, enjoying the chilled taste, then took a more generous quaff before helping herself to another oyster.

'You will not win if you don't get rid of Stanley,' she said, staring across at the relaxed, almost smug Hughes.

'What do you think we should do?'

'Change leaders.'

'Yes, but to who?' asked Hughes, spooning calamari onto Cass's plate.

'You are very insistent, aren't you?'

'I suspect you're hungry, and something light would stop any peckishness.' Hughes refilled his wine. 'I can assure you I have no other thoughts in my mind.'

Cass picked up a fork and pushed a small piece of food into her mouth. She was indeed a little hungry. She took another bite before raising her glass. 'Cheers.'

Hughes clicked the proffered glass and said, 'I reckon there's a mood building to replace the prime minister.'

'Who is behind it?'

Hughes smiled. 'Let's just say I suspect James Harper will put his hand up.'

Cass stopped with a fork of calamari near her mouth. 'Not you?'

'No, I reckon my time has come and gone. If we lose the next election, I will resign rather than sit through another five years.'

'Can I quote you?'

'Everything is off the record and background here tonight.'

'That's a shame.'

'Play your cards right and you will lead the field with exclusives on this.'

'You want to give me exclusives?'

'Yes, but I need something from you in return.'

Cass held her glass, a little shocked; she had been expecting it, but not so blunt and not so early. She gulped hard. 'And what might that be?'

'I would like you to run several stories about the prime minister, so we can lay the ground for a leadership spill.'

She was a little disillusioned by his response. 'Is that it?'

'Yes, unless you want to offer me something else.'

'No, I was just expecting you to say something else, that's all.'

Hughes laughed. 'More wine?'

Cass held out her glass for him to splash more chardonnay into.

'The first titbit, so to speak, is about Stanley's work in his electorate.'

'What about it?'

'He isn't doing any. In fact, he rarely does anything, and was last seen at an event in Curtin around six months ago.'

Cass tugged a pad and pen from her nearby leather bag, scribbling notes.

'It seems the poor old bugger is living by himself at Yarralumla, seldom staying at Admiralty House in Sydney. His wife moved back to Perth months ago.'

'So, who's looking after the electorate?'

'It seems a Rosemary Mansfield is positioning herself for a tilt at the seat should Stanley resign or retire. She has the numbers to win preselection. It seems it's only a matter of time before she makes her move.'

'Interesting. Surely, she wouldn't take down a sitting prime minister?'

'Stranger things have happened in politics; I can assure you.'

'How certain are you of this information?'

'My dear Cass, if we are to work together then you must learn to trust me,' said Hughes as he loosened his tie, unbuttoning his shirt. 'I'm going to have a swim and then have coffee and dessert. Care to join me?'

Cass scoffed. 'I don't have a costume.'

'Nor do I,' said Hughes, as he stood and ambled to the outside pool, kicking off his shoes and dragging off his shirt.

'Well, that's my cue to leave.'

Hughes stopped and turned, his belt already unbuckled, his trousers slipping.

'Are you sure? The water is heated.'

'Yeah, I'm sure,' said Cass. She scooped her things into her bag, snatched a last piece of calamari, and turned to the minister, who was now naked and diving into the pool. She walked to the door, and when Hughes surfaced, she waved goodbye.

'Thanks for the wine. Let's stay in touch,' she said.

'You're more than welcome, anytime.'

Cass stepped off through the house before she saw anything she would regret. As she scooted through the lane to her car chuckling. She thought her luck might have just secured a solid contact to secure the stories she needed for promotion.

CHAPTER TWELVE

Question time was due to hear the eleventh question as Meredith Bruce stood at the despatch box waiting for the call.

The opposition's strategy every day was to characterise the government as incompetent, reinforcing the perception the government's performance was like watching the Muppet Show. The Conservatives held the government benches because an independent with the balance of power thought it was time for a change of government. The opposition was turning question time into a vaudeville show with wisecracks and noise.

The community image was one of continuing chaos, and now Bruce wanted Peter Stanley to face the fire.

'I call the opposition leader.'

'Thank you, Speaker. I address my question to the prime minister, and I ask him to confirm that all his government members are using their electoral allowance wisely and not placing an unfair burden on the taxpayer.'

The speaker called on Stanley to respond. 'Prime Minister.'

Stanley glanced at his treasurer, Barton Messenger, who shrugged, just as perplexed by the question.

'Madam Speaker, I can assure the honourable leader of the opposition that it is the duty of all members in this place to work hard for their constituents, ensuring they represent their communities and not waste taxpayer funds. Speaker, I am mystified by the question from the opposition leader, because it allows me to speak about the many changes, we have made to make sure members do the right thing when representing their electorates. We have changed member allowances to make sure they are spent in the electorate and not used personally, as several members have done in the past, during the previous Gerrard government.' Stanley looked back to his backbench members and smiled.

'I'm sure all members remember the inappropriate use of a helicopter years ago.' A few shouts in response came from the backbench. 'We can also recall ministers misusing travel entitlements for holidays in Europe during our winter recess. I am looking at several members opposite who would turn up for the spring parliamentary session with a continental tan, courtesy of the taxpayer. And, Speaker, I am sure you will recall the misuse of taxi vouchers from a member opposite, a former minister, when she visited wineries on her weekend stays in Canberra.'

The government backbench howled derogatory comments.

'I can assure the House, and all hardworking Australians, that the government has tightened allowances, as we are financially responsible and concerned about spending taxpayer funds.'

The prime minister resumed his seat, glancing at his leadership team for a view of the strategy the opposition was running. As they huddled, a government member took the call to ask a question of the education minister.

'What's she on about, Bart?'

'I have no idea, but it seems it might build on something.'

'I just wish we would go harder at them,' James Harper said.

'I agree,' said Hughes. 'We need to bring her back a peg or two.'

'If I do that, then the media will kill me for attacking a woman.'

Messenger shook his head. 'That shouldn't stop you.'

'Does anyone know anything about this?' Stanley asked.

Harper shook his head, and Hughes glanced over at Bruce, who was watching, then smiling to the media gallery high above the speaker's chair. He noticed an unassuming wave from Cassandra Rogers.

'Maybe she's going to talk about loose cash management of the government in the MPI the opposition has listed.'

Stanley dropped back into his chair, swivelling away from his colleagues, and gazing over copies of bound Hansards stacked in front of him.

'What are you on about, Meredith?'

Bruce tapped her nose. She'd spoken to Rogers two hours earlier about an electorate with an absent local member.

Cass had considered the information about Stanley, deciding she would not write rumour, but would have the prime minister answer a question on the issue. It would mean she would lose her exclusive, but she would secure a probable reciprocal titbit from Bruce.

Bruce stood waiting for the speaker's call at the despatch box when the education minister had finished his answer.

'My question is to the prime minister and follows his response to my earlier question. Can the prime minister confirm he has not attended one event in his electorate over the last six months?' Bruce delivered her question with authority and aggression, leaning into the box. 'Can the prime minister also confirm he has not met with any constituents of Curtin during that time? Can the prime minister also confirm that a Rosemary Mansfield has been attending functions and events on his behalf? Can the prime minister also confirm that Ms Mansfield has been delivering speeches, which I'm informed are her own words and not those of the prime minister? Can the prime minister explain how Curtin's electoral allowances have been spent, given they do not entitle Ms Mansfield to claim expenses? And can the prime minister confirm the reasons he is absent from his job?'

Bruce resumed her seat with a broad smile, while Hughes, the government leader of the house, sprang nippily to his feet.

'Madam Speaker, I rise on a point of order.'

'Leader of the House.'

'Speaker, I suspect this question is out of order. Question time is for questions of ministers about their portfolios, not the way they manage their electorates. The prime minister has the biggest electorate in the parliament, although the member for Durack may quibble, given she manages most of Western Australia. But I remind the House that the prime minister has responsibility for the nation. Of course, coming from Perth will mean the prime minister will not be as proficient and active in his electorate as he would wish. I also remind you, Speaker, he is the prime minister, and his responsibility is to all Australians and not just those in Curtin. Madam Speaker, I recommend under Standing Order 142, that you rule the question out of order.'

Bruce was just as sharp to the despatch box. 'Speaker, to the point of order. We should consider the question in order, as the standing order to which the honourable member refers suggests that we can ask a question of a minister relating to public affairs; surely, a minister's electorate is public affairs?'

Bruce stood back, opening her arms, and receiving strong vocal support from her colleagues.

'The opposition leader makes a valid point; I will allow the question. I call the prime minister.'

Stanley was slow to stand at the despatch box, preparing to respond. 'I'll take the honourable member's question on notice.'

The chamber exploded with a racket, forcing the speaker to stand and gain immediate silence.

'Question time in this chamber is to ask questions of ministers and to listen to answers. If members dislike answers, then please use the standing orders to give yourself a voice. I remind honourable members to not bring the house into disrepute by yelling and shrieking.'

High in the media gallery, as politicians jousted below, Cass tapped into her laptop. Her story could now show the House of Representatives' chamber as the foundation source for the information rather than use a mysterious government source.

CHAPTER THIRTEEN

Question time had been another brutal hour for the government. Messenger frustrated by the performance visited Hughes to discuss strategy and tactics to improve media reporting during the following parliamentary session.

'The chamber is becoming a losing bear pit for us. The media are killing us.'

'Can't make a silk purse out of a sow's ear, I'm afraid,' Hughes said, agreeing with the treasurer. 'We need Pete performing better. Bruce is caning us.'

'It just seems he's intimidated by her. He just won't attack.'

'It's the misogyny factor. He's loath to criticise her because he doesn't want to be tagged as a bully for spraying a female with micro aggressions.'

'Such a damn gentleman.'

Hughes waited for a moment before asking, 'Where do you think this issue about his electorate came from?'

Messenger shook his head. 'I know he's having problems at home, but I suspect it's bad form to be using it in the House.'

Hughes leaned into his desk and tapped his computer a few times before observing, 'There is already a story on the Hancock site declaring Stanley to be a slacker, taking his seat for granted. They name his staffer as the proxy member. They have a quote from a local resident who says,' he gave a little chortle, 'she always thought Rosemary Mansfield was the local member and quite surprised to learn the prime minister was.'

'Who are these people?'

Hughes tapped a few more keys. 'I suspect, folks who take democracy for granted.'

'Trust Hancock to be out of the barriers first. Who wrote the piece?'

'Cassandra Rogers. Do you know her?'

'I've had a few things to do with her. She always asks the hard questions. She took over most of Anita Devlin's round.'

Hughes looked up and bit his bottom lip, a little embarrassed. 'I'm sorry, Bart. It must still hurt. Sorry for bringing back the memory.'

'It's a long time ago now. I'm over it,' Messenger lied.

'Did they ever catch who did it?'

'No one saw the incident. The folks who were around the area at the time can't remember anyone who hasn't already been checked by the police.'

'Sorry. I didn't mean to jog your memory.'

'That's fine; let's move on.' Messenger wiped his hands along the top of his thighs. 'Do you know Rogers?'

'By reputation, of course,' Hughes said, his political face free of any movement. 'I've bumped into her a few times; she doesn't seem to want to deal in industrial relations policy.'

'Just political scandal, it seems.'

Hughes leaned back in his chair, lazily rocking. 'But of course, she could be handy for us.'

'In what way?'

'Maybe she can lay the groundwork for a leadership spill without wrecking the government.'

Messenger didn't respond at once but thought about Hughes' comment. 'Just a campaign against the prime minister, you mean?' he asked.

'If we ever need to consider a spill, then perhaps we need the right optics already in the electorate.'

Messenger shook his head, disagreeing. 'I reckon we need to change our strategy against Bruce. Let's get her off the magazine covers and back on newspaper front pages, screaming loser.'

'Perhaps we need someone other than the prime minister to attack her?'

'That could work, but we need policy-based attacks.'

'You should put your hand up for that assignment,' Hughes said.

DOOMED

Labelling Messenger with the macho bully tag would be a good get for his plans.

'I don't mind.' Messenger smiled, relishing the idea of having a greater role in the chamber. 'I'll just focus on the economy and smash them with facts.'

'That'll put Bruce back in her box, but I suspect it won't fix the polls.' Hughes looked at a fingernail, scrapping another under to clear the tip. 'We need to get the leader to be doing more.'

'When is the deadline, do you think?'

'What?' Hughes asked, as if not interested. 'To think about a change, do you mean?'

'Yes,' Messenger said, too hastily. 'I would have thought if we go to an election with the current level of support, we have no chance of winning.'

'Two months, I guess, would be a reasonable time frame. The drought could be over by then, and the coal industry announcement would have affected polling. If it doesn't push us up in the polls, then we are dead,' Hughes said, examining his younger colleague and searching him for ambition.

Messenger's face didn't move. 'I'm not sure Jimmy is the guy we should go back to,' he said. 'Punters may know him, but I'm not clear they like him.'

'He's the best chance we have.'

Messenger delayed his response, studying his colleague. 'What about you?'

Hughes wasn't expecting the question. 'Me?' he laughed, shifting in his chair. 'No, I'm not even considering such things.'

Messenger wasn't so sure. 'You've paid your dues; maybe you are an alternative,' he said, trying to gauge his colleague's appetite to run for the leadership.

'Don't be silly, Bart; I'm never going to nominate.'

'Not even if we ask?'

'Now that's a different question.' Hughes pushed his head back, gazing to the ceiling and tightening his mouth. 'I suppose if someone called for me to lead, then I might have to consider it.'

'Of course,' Messenger said, grinning at his colleague.

'I mean, who wouldn't take the role if asked?' Hughes dropped his head, glancing over to Messenger. 'Would you?'

Messenger had been waiting for the question.

'No, I'm nowhere near being ready. I have another ten years at least before I can even think about those things.'

Hughes was not sure he believed his younger colleague, but his answer made sense.

Messenger then said, 'I tell you this, Christopher, I want to stay in government. If I become convinced Pete can't win, then I would shift my support for a change of leadership and damn the consequences; because if we have to do it, then we can only get better and perhaps win.'

'If you can damage Bruce, that would be a good start.'

Messenger smiled. 'I'll take her for a ride through the drought and come back via the economy. She'll be so tied up with facts and figures she won't know what to say, because whatever she says, I will bury.'

'I love the fact you relish taking her down.'

'It's politics, and if you are not up for the bruising, then why bother stepping into the ring?' Messenger stood. 'We have treated her with kid gloves, only lashing her with a wilted lettuce leaf for way too long. I'll take a big stick to her.'

'Mixing metaphors with clichés is always dangerous,' Hughes said. Then he sniffed, flashing a loathsome smile.

'Where I come from, we don't care,' said Messenger as he got up to leave.

'You think we should get Pete to the Press Club?'

'Couldn't do any harm, and he could announce drought policy,' Messenger said by the door. 'I'll organise it. See you.'

CHAPTER FOURTEEN

The parliamentary inquiry into the drought sought submissions from interested companies, farmers, and other stakeholders. Over three hundred overwhelmed the secretariat during the three weeks submissions were open. The inquiry secretary decided early hearings in the affected regions were proper, so arranged for the select parliamentary committee to take evidence in various regional towns. On the Wednesday before parliament was due to resume, the committee met in Griffith.

They gave each witness forty-five minutes to voice concerns and explain how the drought was impacting their farm. The committee, chaired by Jaya Rukhmani, empathised with the cries of desperation from farmers and traders suffering through lack of cash. Evidence about the delivery of livestock feed raised the interest of the parliamentarians, who probed witnesses whether transport companies were profiteering from the crisis. As a pattern of evidence was emerging, rural members of the committee were focusing on transport companies charging enormous fees to run feed to the stricken areas.

Sitting in a back corner listening to every witness, his distinctive hat dangling from the corner of the chair, was Brian Tucker, scribbling notes. When they announced morning tea, Jaya noticed the man acting cautiously, trying to avoid contact. She wandered over to the secretary of the committee and pointed out the fellow.

Steve Follett then sidled over to engage the mysterious man in discussion.

'How do you think the morning is going?'

Tucker didn't respond, as was his way, then said, 'The bankers.'

Follett stooped, struggling to understand. 'I'm sorry, I didn't hear you. What did you say?'

'The bankers,' Tucker said a little louder. 'Are you going to talk to the bankers?'

'Not today. We have submissions from the banks and expect to hear from them in Canberra next week.'

'That'd be right.'

'What do you mean?'

Tucker glanced to the floor, then straightened with a steely gaze. 'They are killing us, and you folks don't care.'

'I'm not sure that's fair. We are hearing from farmers, but few are pointing a finger at the banks.'

'They're too scared. If they do, they can foreclose them. The banks are killing us. We just want a fair go.'

Follett studied the man for a moment, then asked, 'Did you put in a submission?'

Tucker shuffled from side to side. 'You see? This is the problem. We're farmers, not fancy writers.'

'Have you got a story to tell us?'

Tucker's face turned ugly. 'You don't want to hear it.' He took a breath, then said, 'You're providing a protection racket for the banks. Now you're going after the truckies, by the sound of your politicians this morning.'

'That's a little unfair. We have ten of these hearings. Five in Canberra, and the rest out here in the affected areas.'

'You politicians seem more interested in nailing the truckies.'

'The inquiry chair, Ms Rukhmani, is keen to learn the impact on farmers and the community. Would you like to give evidence and tell your story?'

Tucker didn't respond, rubbing his rough hands together. 'S'pose.'

'Look, what's your name?'

'Tucker, Brian Tucker. I own forty-two thousand acres out back,' he said, cocking a thumb over his right shoulder.

'Mr Tucker, I have a slot on the witness list before lunch. Would you like to join us for ten minutes at twelve-thirty?'

Tucker gazed at the floor. 'Sure.'

'Then take a seat and we'll call you when we need you.'

DOOMED

'Sure.' Tucker turned and went back to his corner.

'Please state your name and address for the Hansard record.'

'Brian Tucker. Tucker Farm, Barellan.'

Jaya made a note of the name and glanced up, smiling at the dour, uncertain Tucker.

'Mr Tucker, on behalf of my colleagues, we thank you for coming to see us today. Would you like to make an opening statement before we move to questions?'

Tucker straightened and swiped his hat to the side, so he could stretch his arms towards the microphone on the desk. He leaned closer to make sure they could hear him.

'My family has worked the land for nearly a century. We built our flock and herds to make sure we could compete with bigger corporate operations, which are ruining the tradition of family-owned property. We were the first to reduce our carbon footprint to beyond zero, and we keep an excellent reputation within the industry. We have faced drought before, and we have survived.'

Tucker paused to gain control of his breathing and then stumbled over his words. 'I'm not sure we will survive this one.'

He sat back, wiping his face. He pinched his nose, rubbing the stubble on his chin as his bottom lip wobbled.

Jaya removed her glasses, looking at the troubled man. 'Mr Tucker, when you say you may not survive this drought, what do you mean?'

He glanced up at her. 'We can feed our stock and look after family. We can ship in water, although my dams are almost empty.'

'How many are empty?'

'I have fifteen dry and seven at less than forty percent capacity.'

'How much is feed costing you?'

'Eighty, maybe ninety thousand a month.'

Jaya pursed her lips, nodding, considering the information. 'That is a hefty bill.'

'It's not the truckies' fault; we pay fair rates.'

'Then why are you suggesting you will not survive?' Jaya asked.

'The banks are going to foreclose.'

Jaya sharpened her attention. 'The banks are going to sell you out?'

'Yep, that's what she said.'

'Who's she, Mr Tucker?'

'The local bank manager; she's new... Anyway, she said the shareholders want their money back and unless I sell my land and stock, then they will close me down.' He rubbed the back of his hand against his nose. 'If we don't have land and we've got no stock, then we have nothing, and a hundred years contributing to the wealth of Australia disappears.'

'How much stock do you have?'

'Six hundred head of cattle and around forty percent of my peak flock numbers, which is around twelve thousand head. Now that might sound a lot to you folks from Canberra, but once the breeders are gone, then stock losses will increase and the farm's financial model collapses. The cattle are losing condition, which means live-weight returns are much less.'

'Do you have much in the way of assets?'

'It's all assets and no cash. This is the problem. I need cash for feed, water and my family, but the bank isn't supporting me.'

Jaya slipped her glasses back on and read her prescribed questions, then asked, 'What can the government do for you?'

Tucker stared at her then scanned the other politicians, a few working their iPhone.

'I don't like handouts.'

'Surely helping with your immediate cash needs is not a handout, but a hand up?'

Tucker again surveyed the politicians and didn't see any engagement from many of them.

'I suppose what you politicians can do for me is pay attention. Pay attention to what farmers are saying about the banks. Pay attention to the difficulties we have to feed our stock and our families.' He gained the attention of several committee members, but not all. 'Just pay attention.' He spoke louder and more firmly. Those politicians who weren't now did. 'Stop playing politics with people's lives and speak to the banks to get relief for us.'

Jaya smiled and reassured Tucker. 'I need this committee to report to the government in a few weeks and we shall consider your very important testimony; it has given us much to consider.'

DOOMED

'The bank has given me a few more weeks, so I would appreciate any help you can give to stall them from foreclosing me.'

Jaya nodded, glancing towards Follett, who dropped his eyes, shrugged, and nodded.

'We will try to talk to a few people, but we can't promise anything,' she said.

Tucker screwed his face as if he smelled a pungent odour.

'Typical,' he scowled. 'As I said, I don't rely on government action. I need to do what I can to resolve the problem myself.'

The comment made Jaya feel uncomfortable. 'What does that mean?'

'Unless I get the banks off my back and they show greater support, then I'll have to do what I have to do.'

CHAPTER FIFTEEN

Ministers often trudged to the prestigious National Press Club to deliver a televised address, then allow questions from journalist members. The greater the politician's reputation, the more cramped the journalists at the tables.

Prime Minister Stanley was to speak for thirty minutes, then answer questions, allowing the national broadcaster to screen an entertaining one-hour event.

'Is that the final draft?' Stanley asked his policy adviser, Stephen Newgreen.

Newgreen passed the speech, encased in a plastic sleeve, to him as they waited in an anteroom away from where journalists, government ministers, advisers and other interested parties were eating lunch.

'I've had the minister's office check over the detail and made slight adjustments.'

'Who had the carriage of it in Hughes' office?'

'Krakos.'

'Do we trust him?' Stanley asked.

Newgreen shuffled on his feet. 'He's well connected in the party and his work with Hughes has been good, although he did stuff up the penalty rates legislation.'

'We just have to tighten up.' Stanley sounded exasperated. 'There are too many leaks coming out of the government, and I'm concerned with you not having total control.'

'Stop worrying, Prime Minister; you'll be fine.'

Stanley shook his head, gnawing his bottom lip. 'Why is Rogers here?'

'I suppose she wants national television exposure.' Newgreen crossed his arms, gazing down on the seated prime minister. 'I'm told she is up for a promotion.'

'She's been attacking us a lot, so why wouldn't she want to attack us today?'

'She can't have much,' Newgreen said. 'She's probably run out of leaks.'

Stanley frowned, again shaking his head. 'She's got something.' He combed his hands through his thinning grey hair. 'These leaks have to stop, Stephen, otherwise I may as well give it up.'

The emotional statement unsettled Newgreen. 'Prime Minister, we are going to the next election in government. We will win if we can take the electorate on a journey. This speech is the first step to getting those polls back.'

'I hope you're right.'

It was drawing close to one o'clock, and the host, a leading journalist from the parliamentary media gallery, entered the room and asked the prime minister to follow her to the stage, where they would sit and wait for the television broadcast to begin. When in place, the floor producer nodded to the host. She sounded a ship's bell with a small tool to demand silence and went to the lectern to introduce the prime minister.

Stanley glanced around the assembled audience, seeing familiar faces, but the lighting glare limited his view. During the generous applause, he stood and crossed to his place with a wave, smiling to where he thought they had stationed the cameras.

'Thank you for the opportunity to address you. I hope over the next hour I can tell you about landmark policy the government has completed, and we will announce in parliament later today.'

Stanley then read his speech like any well-trained politician. He measured delivery by glancing down to read a line, then shifted his eyes to the camera to repeat what he had just read. It wasn't easy, but Stanley had practised for many years to get the timing right. Those who might have been viewing the broadcast would have noted a polished politician.

He spoke about his recent trip to Timor-Leste to negotiate satisfactory gas and oil extraction licences; a bilateral agreement benefiting both countries by harnessing technology.

'The relationship we share with Timor is one of respect and

acknowledgment of our own independence. Australia wants these fields of dreams to be developed so the good people of Timor-Leste will have the opportunity to raise their GDP, bringing a standard of living to their people that will help them with their economic challenges, in particular with health and education.

'We want to work with the government to help them grow and prosper; so, I am pleased to announce a labour agreement that will bring significant support to their fledgling industry.'

Cassandra Rogers was following the speech from a copy of a transcript leaked to her, and she made notes as she worked through it. Colleagues seemed curious about how she had secured a copy, while no one offered papers to them.

When Stanley spoke about work arrangements, she made more notes.

'The minister has agreed with Timor to provide jobs needed to extract oil and gas. The government believes we can allow foreigners to work on Australian rigs because the ultimate beneficiary of the extraction is indeed Timor-Leste. We determined that to be fair, we should encourage their workforce to supply the labour.'

Cass stroked red marks through the speech and underlined statements.

'I am advised that the government has agreed with the union representing rig workers to allow foreign workers to operate our property investments. This transition we have negotiated allows Australia to accept foreign labour on these rigs, and only these rigs.'

Stanley glanced up and smiled, then off script said, 'Something I'm sure all Australians would agree is a mature manner in negotiating for our neighbour's future. I wish to thank the union leadership for finalising the agreement.'

Cass flipped open her pad and wrote a question.

The prime minister continued to the agreed time and then opened for questions.

'John O'Brien, the West Australian.'

The first journalist in sequence stood to ask his question.

'Western Australia is very uneasy about the reduction in seabed borders and the constant change to policy. The WA government has developed the offshore gas and oil fields for decades and now troubled about loss of sovereignty. I ask you whether this is the end of policy on the run? And could you tell us when you will enact the foreign labour laws agreement?'

Stanley handled the question with authority, focusing on Australia's interests. 'It's always Australia first, no matter the nation, or indeed the state, that would have us change our view. Australia is first and last on all policies with my government.'

Cass wrote a second question.

'Karen Partrevsky, Sky News.' Stanley nodded acknowledgement. 'Prime Minister, you just told us you have an agreement with the president of Timor-Leste to supply labour to the rigs; is that forty workers per shift? Will there be Australian workers training and managing other assets and procedures on the rigs, such as safety? And will companies be providing training in Australia for these workers?'

'Thank you for your question.' Stanley stalled a moment as he lifted a sheet of paper to read the copy. The watching Hughes knew he didn't know the answer. 'I have requested Timor to train and develop their workforce to Australian standards, and they will man all shifts to make sure safe work practices.' Hughes smirked as Stanley fumbled for the answer. 'The agreement we have with Timor will see their citizens earn a decent wage based upon an enterprise agreement using Australian standards, and the government will make sure, and enforce, if required, Australian work practices.'

A grumbling Partrevsky sat down, frustrated, and disappointed with the prime minister's response.

'Cassandra Rogers, Hancock Television.' Cass smiled like an assassin.

The prime minister frowned when he saw her.

'Just to help you out on those details, Prime Minister; each shift has a company of one hundred and twenty employees. They also have an additional safety team during the transition and six months beyond the commencement, which, according to the agreement, will be staffed by Australians.'

Stanley feigned checking his notes, feeling embarrassed by the disclosure, and wondering why he had wrong information.

'But, to my question,' Cass continued. 'The major contractor with authority on the Timor Sea fields will be CDI Mining.' Stanley's jaw dropped, pushed open by his tongue licking dry lips. 'CDI, as you know, has strong links to the Saudi Royal family and continues to cause environmental incidents throughout the world, on average every three years for the last forty.'

'Is there a question?' Stanley interrupted.

'Who approved the CDI licence? What regulatory authority has been given the task of deciding whether they are a suitable partner? Was Minister Stavloukas involved with the decision-making process? And… should the fact that CDI donated five million dollars to your party's election campaign have any influence on the government's decision?'

Cass resumed her seat, glancing at the camera, now turned on her, and ensuring they broadcast her best serious investigative journalist face as she looked back towards the stage.

'The process to decide management licences was open and transparent, beginning well before the change of government. We should remember that governments are not miners, and we have no proficiency in the day-to-day running of a significant field such as the Timor Sea. We offer licences to those companies who have international experience of managing such complex, dangerous, and hard conditions. They are the experts, after all. Following on from the previous government's work, we set out a transparent tender process, and CDI group was successful. I worked with Minister Stavloukas in setting out the tender requirements, assisting her during the assessment period. I led the discussion in the cabinet. We had a unanimous agreement to award the licence to CDI.'

Stanley paused and took a sip of water. His hand trembled.

'Now to your question about conflict of interest and the possibility of patronage. My government is transparent, and the manner you framed the question implies that CDI, having donated to the party, expected the licence. Your accusation is quite astounding, suggesting this government, and indeed my prime ministership, is compromised by political donations in granting the licence to CDI.'

Stanley almost sneered at Cass as he paused for his coup de grâce.

'You have deliberately, and perhaps wilfully, suggested there has been a deal done to secure the licence for the Timor Sea. I can assure you; we are not a government struck in the same forge as the Gerrard government, and to suggest such a thing is out of order.'

Stanley then pulled a slip of paper from his jacket, provided to him by Barton Messenger earlier, and read from it.

'You are quite correct to identify that CDI donated five million to our successful campaign; this is on the public record. But what you failed to mention is that they also donated eight million dollars to the Gerrard government, of which only six million is declared. My government will never decide in favour of one party over another for the donation of baubles and pieces of silver.'

Cass smiled. She had the answer she wanted, so stood to ask another question.

'Cassandra Rogers, now representing Hancock Newspapers.'

Stanley held up his hand like a traffic cop. 'Wait up, Ms Rogers. You've already asked your question; give someone else a chance.'

'Prime Minister, I'm not surprised you are not across the detail, but the run sheet for questions reads,' Cass held high the list, 'Hancock Television followed by Hancock Newspapers. I am the person representing both those organisations today.' She then glanced at the camera, smiled, and shrugged. 'Cutbacks; go figure.'

Stanley crouched to speak to the president of the Press Club, who seemed to reassure him that what Rogers was saying was correct.

He straightened and said, 'Never let it be said that the prime minister is not a man of integrity and a stickler for the rules. If it lists you, then please ask the question.'

Cass couldn't believe her luck. 'Interesting you would raise integrity because my question goes to that.'

Stanley's political antenna was pinging, speculating what she would ask.

'Prime Minister, CDI shares, before the announcement, had been listed for months at twenty-seven dollars per share. Immediately after the news, they rose and settled around forty-two dollars a share. A significant increase. I am sure it will thrill the shareholders to see their investment increase. You have stated you led the discussion, and the decision was yours... I wonder if your further declaration of transparency and integrity is just political speak...'

Stanley stepped from one foot to the other; he gripped the lectern and nodded, concerned with the question.

'Prime Minister, is it true you have six thousand shares in CDI, and the decision you made, in consultation with your cabinet, has provided you with a windfall of almost a hundred thousand dollars? Were you not conflicted with this policy decision? Did you declare a conflict? And what action have you taken to remedy the conflict?'

The room fell into an uneasy silence.

Stanley gulped water, emptying the small glass, and calming himself as he prepared to answer the question.

'This is a question an investigative phone call could have answered and not in a public forum like this. To go to the crux of the question, I bought shares in CDI thirty-five years ago. Since entering the parliament thirty years ago, I have placed all my shares portfolio in a blind trust. I do not know of my holdings, nor do I have influence on the buying and selling of shares. So, to answer your question directly, no, I did not declare a conflict because I didn't know if indeed, I have one.'

Cass smiled, taking a note, and knowing the story from the Press Club would focus on her questions, with the perception that the prime minister made the decision for personal gain. She didn't care whether or not he had. She just wanted her headline and got it.

On another table, Christopher Hughes held a hand to his mouth to hide a broad smile. The slip up on the figures for rig workers might come back to his office, but Krakos already had answers. What would never come back to his office was the call he had made to Rogers, promising to send a copy of the speech with the correct figures listed. He had mentioned the cabinet discussion, pointing her to the Electoral Commission's listing of campaign donors. He had also pointed her to Hansard to search for a speech Stanley made when he first entered parliament about his share portfolio, announcing he was placing it into a blind trust. Hansard had the perfect memory, and it would have been an easy find for her.

At two o'clock, when the broadcast finished, Stanley left for the parliament, offering a curt goodbye to the president. Cass observed him going, wondering how question time would treat him that day. She swiped through her phone, pushing the call button for Meredith Bruce.

CHAPTER SIXTEEN

The prime minister's car drew into the parliamentary courtyard, a security car close behind. The ride back to the parliament had been silent. Newgreen sat in front, panicked by how the PM might respond to comments. As they walked into the prime minister's suite, Newgreen ventured a question.

'How do you want me to handle this, Prime Minister?'

Stanley strolled to his desk, then glanced back. 'Handle what?'

'The questions from Hancock.'

'Control the controllables, Steve.' Stanley walked to his sideboard and poured a glass of water. 'Is question time at two-thirty or three today?'

'It's at three; we have time to prepare.'

Stanley laughed. 'Prepare for what, exactly? An execution?'

'Our question list focuses on the Timor agreement and the drought. Do you think we should work on something else to kill the headlines from the Press Club?'

'You know what those questions from Hancock tell me?' Stanley asked as he sat at his desk. 'They tell me there is a leadership challenge.'

'It's too early to be talking about that, isn't it?'

'Wrong figures in my speech; how did that happen?'

'Krakos had the last say.'

'He'll have an answer. I'll wager it was a junior staffer who compiled the last draft, and that's where the mistake will have been made. I also wager no-one from my office read it before giving it to me, and that's where the blame will sheet home.'

'I'm not worried about that; it's the conflict issue that will get the headlines,' Newgreen suggested.

'I'm not concerned about it. I wouldn't know if I hold shares or not. That's why I put them into a blind trust.'

'That's not the point. It's the perception that you do.' Newgreen stood to leave. 'Do you want a cuppa?' Stanley nodded. As Newgreen moved away, he asked, 'How would Rogers know you had shares, anyway?'

Stanley shook his head, pursing his lips as if sucking on a lemon.

'Someone knows something about me, which can only mean one of my so-called mates.' He dropped his head into his hand and sighed. 'The question is, who is Brutus?'

'The one wanting your job?'

'Maybe.'

'Harper?'

Stanley shrugged. 'Or more likely someone standing in the shadows waiting for the opportunity to knife me. It's not always the obvious one.'

CHAPTER SEVENTEEN

'Hello, Cassie, nice one at the Press Club; your questions were outstanding.' Hughes smiled into his phone as he picked fluff from his trousers whilst travelling back to the parliament in a white commonwealth car.

'Why are you doing this, Minister?'

'Are you getting cold feet?'

'I'm happy to get information, but I feel uncomfortable about it.'

'I can't talk right now.' Hughes checked the rear vision mirror, engaging the eyes of the driver, who glanced away. 'I have more information for you. If you want it, then perhaps you can come over this evening.'

'I'm not comfortable about that.' Cass squirmed as she waited for a taxi outside the Press Club. 'Can't we meet somewhere else?'

'If this blows up, I want nothing coming back to me, so if I meet you in public then gossip will put us together and I don't want that to happen.'

'What time?'

'The House adjourns at eight; see you at nine?'

Cass was reluctant but remained tempted by the story. 'I'm having dinner with another member, so ten would be better.'

'Will you be wearing your normal fatigues to the dinner?'

'Why would you care what I wear?'

'Oh, don't get me wrong. I'm just interested to know what comrades wear when they go dining with the enemy.'

'How do you know it's the enemy?'

'Cassie, please.' Hughes scoffed. 'The modus operandi of any journalist is to be seen in public with the opposition and privately with ministers. Promote their status with the opposition and hide the source of leaks from the government.'

'I'd rather see you in public.'

'Yeah, that's because you still don't trust me.'

'Ya got that right.'

'Cass, please… We are working together on this. Have a little trust.'

'I trust no one.'

'In politics that's a pretty respectful attitude to have, but not when you want to lead stories about the prime minister.'

'I'll see you at ten.' Cass pushed the end call tab, leaving Hughes surprised and holding his phone to check whether he remained connected.

'Cheeky bitch.'

CHAPTER EIGHTEEN

Politicians cranked the noise level to the extreme during question time, the rowdiness spurred on by the prime minister's response to claims he benefited from a decision of the cabinet. The speaker was up and down like a Yo-Yo, jumping to her feet to stop the rabble-rousing atmosphere. No sooner had she calmed the chamber than another wave of shouting would wash over, demanding she bring order so they could hear ministers. The prime minister was getting bombarded by the opposition, and the heightened agitation was riling the government front bench.

'Do something to help, will you?' the prime minister said to his leadership team as he flopped into his chair after another bumbling answer.

Hughes glanced at Messenger and whispered, 'Nothing much we can do, other than take it.'

'Maybe a few points of order might be helpful to disrupt them a little.'

'Yeah, righto,' Hughes replied. 'They aren't breaching standing orders.'

Messenger scribbled a question and turned to the member behind him, instructing her to ask the next question. When it was the government's turn for a question, she bounced to her feet before the allocated questioner, and the speaker responded to Messenger's nodded direction.

'I call the member for Cowan.'

'Thank you, Speaker, and my question is to the treasurer,' she said, reading the handwritten note. 'Given the questions to the prime minister today concerning alleged conflicts of interest, I wonder if you could report to the House the duty of all members with conflict of interests, and are there any recent examples of breaches of conflict?'

Everett Menzies, the opposition's manager of business, stood at the despatch box. 'Speaker, point of order.'

Menzies, a well-regarded attorney general in the Gerrard government, considered himself above the rough and tumble of political brawling in the chamber; now required to pull up his sleeves and go toe to toe with the government.

'Manager of opposition business on a point of order.'

'Speaker, under Standing Order 144, b, c, d and g, the question should be ruled out of order as it is asking the treasurer to speculate and make inferences and imputations, which could be speculative and hypothetical.'

'Thank you; there is no point of order. The question applies to the questions being asked by the opposition, and therefore I rule the question in order and call the treasurer.'

'Thank you, Speaker.' Messenger came to the despatch box ready for a fight. 'On a day when we have received the best financial figures seen by our prosperous nation for many years; on a day when we should celebrate success by welcoming the long-term strategy of the Stanley government's fiscal responsibility...'

Menzies, standing at the opposition's despatch box, interrupted him. 'Speaker, on a point of order.'

'The treasurer will resume his seat; the manager of opposition business on a point of order?'

'Yes, thank you, Speaker. My point of order goes to Standing Order 145, and relevance. The question asked the treasurer about conflicts of interest and is yet to raise any.'

The speaker smiled. 'I find it ironic you asked for the question to be ruled out of order, and now you want the treasurer to answer it. There is no point of order. Treasurer?'

Menzies was back at the despatch box. 'Speaker, on your ruling, the treasurer has yet to address the substance of the question and I ask you to bring him to order.'

The speaker turned to Menzies and shook her head. 'I warn the honourable member not to continue to test my patience with spurious points of order. The treasurer has yet to answer the question and has only been talking for twenty seconds. I call the treasurer.'

'Thank you, Speaker.' Messenger paused, gazing at Bruce. 'It's no wonder the opposition leader does not want to hear good economic news, because it was the former government, of which she was a senior member, who went on a spending spree, giving away cash for no reason at all. Who can forget Meredith Bruce, the then education minister…'

'Order; members will be known by their correct title.'

'Sorry Speaker.' Messenger bowed. 'The leader of the opposition when education minister was standing side by side with the then prime minister announcing a handout of almost a thousand dollars to every Australian taxpayer and five hundred dollars to every Australian who was not in the tax system. This is what she did.'

Messenger raised his voice, prodding a finger at Bruce, and continued, 'The leader of the opposition was a member of a government who gave away funds in the hope of re-election. Is this a conflict of interest, Speaker? A conflict for which she has taken no responsibility and given no declaration of remorse, no promise not to do it again. Just throwing the government into further debt for which we will all have to pay. Speaker, I can advise that the Stanley government is now reducing that debt.

'These are more than a magnificent set of numbers, Speaker. These financial results show that the prime minister was right when he sent us in a new direction. One of financial responsibility, and one where we do not play favourites. The Stanley government has not done, nor would it ever do, what the former government, led then by Prime Minister Gerrard and the current leader of the opposition, did when they tried to force legislation through this house that was later found to be a loose money transaction and open to corruption.'

Messenger pointed out to the speaker that Menzies was stepping to the despatch box. The speaker waved Menzies away, and he skulked back to his seat.

'These are not my words, Speaker,' Messenger said. 'These are the words of the auditor general, who found that the funding appropriation Prime Minister Gerrard and the current leader of the opposition tried to force through the parliament would have seen sham funds go offshore and never return in kind. You may recall, Speaker, that like every Australian, we were all promised a government cash handout, but like every Australian, we were not told that it tied the cash splash to a fraudulent attempt to transfer money without proper scrutiny. Again, Speaker, not my words, but those of the auditor general.

'You may also recall, Speaker, that the current leader of the opposition was leader of the House at the time and therefore had full responsibility for the carriage of the bogus legislation. It was her plan to amend the legislation in the senate to add the spurious funds for Indonesia. Quite a startling move, given it breached every protocol and convention of this place, and if it was not for the sterling work of Gordon O'Brien, the former clerk of the House, Gerrard and his confederate the leader of the opposition would have carried out this scandalous fraud upon the people of Australia.'

Bruce sat with arms crossed, gazing towards the press gallery, anxious at seeing many of them scribbling notes.

Messenger stood at the despatch box, one hand flat on the lid, the other fisted on his hip as he faced away from the speaker to the backbench, gazing high into the public gallery.

'You might also recall, Speaker, that the leader of the opposition had,' Messenger air quoted his fingers, 'a close relationship with Prime Minister Gerrard; indeed, a very close relationship.'

The opposition benches erupted. Messenger turned to Bruce and smirked.

'We know about the need for equality in this place, but I remain concerned about the equality the then leader of the House wanted from the former prime minister. Did she want equality when she was doing Gerrard's bidding in this place by pushing through legislation? Did she have a conflict of interest? Did she receive a benefit from the former prime minister, and is this the reason she is now leader of her party?

'So rather than cast aspersions about Prime Minister Stanley, the most transparent and honest prime minister we have had in a lifetime, maybe it's time for the leader of the opposition to temper her vitriol towards him and consider her own conflict of interest with the many decisions at the cabinet table in the last government, creating a significant black hole in the budget, one that we are repairing, as figures confirm today. Maybe the leader of the opposition should consider her role in creating that black hole and whether she had a conflict; for if she did, we will find it and name it Bruce's black hole.'

The opposition benches erupted again; Menzies was at the despatch box, but the speaker ignored him.

'The treasurer was using unparliamentary language and I ask him to withdraw.'

Messenger stood at the despatch box. 'Just some help, Speaker; what was unparliamentary?'

'The treasurer will not debate it and will withdraw unconditionally.'

'I withdraw.'

Menzies was still standing at the despatch box, trying to gain the speaker's attention, but she waved him away as she focused on the next member's question.

'The member for Melbourne.'

'Phew, that was tough going, Speaker; a lot to think about in that answer,' Jaya said with a smile.

'The member will come to her question or sit down. You have the privilege to ask a question, so ask it.'

'Sorry, Speaker. Yes, I had better do that as it doesn't happen very often.'

'The member will come to her question.'

'My question is to the treasurer. Treasurer, as you know I am chairing the parliament's select committee into the drought, and we are close to submitting our report to the parliament.'

'The member will ask her question.'

'Yes, thank you, Speaker. Treasurer: are you able to outline to the House the drought funding program the government is considering? What support will you be providing Australian families impacted by the drought? Are you able to provide any advice on how the government will address the banks who are foreclosing on businesses and farms?'

'The treasurer.'

'Thank you, Speaker, and I want to thank the honourable member for her important question. I remind the House it was the member for Melbourne who defeated the former prime minister in his seat, which has saved the country many millions of dollars regarding the alleged attempt to defraud the Australian taxpayer implicating the leader of the opposition.'

Menzies yelled from his seat over the din from his backbench. 'Speaker, come on. This is not appropriate.'

'Order, I call the House to order.'

Jaya Rukhmani was on her feet again.

'The member for Melbourne on a point of order?'

Messenger sat, and the din subsided.

'Speaker, I would like to hear what the treasurer has to say about this important issue, and I remind my fellow members that many Australians' lives are in peril at this very moment; perhaps dignity and respect during this answer would be appropriate.'

'Whilst not a point of order, I welcome your comments and remind the House to listen to the treasurer in silence, so we can hear him, and I ask the treasurer to be relevant to the question. I call the treasurer.'

'Speaker, this drought is becoming one of the biggest challenges for our nation, and we need to address it in a thoughtful and comprehensive manner.'

The chamber was silent during Messenger's response as he outlined the government's plan to establish funding, focusing on water carting and livestock feed distribution. He also spoke about the need to support families, especially farming families, and advised that the government would introduce a food voucher scheme to support struggling families.

As Messenger wound up his answer, he said, 'Speaker, rural Australia is the heart of our nation. It feeds us whilst contributing to the food supply of many other countries, ensuring their prosperity, and allowing us to benefit. Without farmers we are nothing, and I advise the House that the government will make further policy announcements next week once we have received the committee's report.'

Before he sat down, Jaya was fast to her feet. 'Point of order, Speaker. Point of order.'

'Has the treasurer concluded his answer?'

Messenger glanced at Jaya, who shook her head, encouraging him to let her speak. 'No, Speaker, I have not.'

'The member for Melbourne on a point of order.'

'I raise relevance and remind the treasurer of the banks.'

'There is no point of order; I call the treasurer.'

'Yes, thank you Speaker, and I thank the member for reminding me. The banks play a vital role in supporting the regions and our farmers.

DOOMED

They are doing a mighty job in providing funding solutions that will not burden families. I am surprised to hear of impending foreclosures as this is not my advice, and I would request the honourable member to meet with me, or my office, to provide examples where banks are foreclosing. This is a time for all Australians to work together, to be flexible in our farmers' needs, and to pray that it rains.'

As Messenger returned to his seat, Bruce bounced to the despatch box, but the prime minister spoke first.

'I ask that further questions be placed on the notice paper.'

Then, as if a huge pressure release valve loosened, members went about their business, leaving the chamber. Parliamentary proceedings kicked in with Christopher Hughes tabling papers.

Stanley picked up his files and walked out with Messenger. They both turned and bowed to the speaker before passing through the brass glass doors leading to the ministerial wing, which were held open by attendants.

'Thanks for getting stuck in, Bart. I appreciate it.'

'I've decided to take a hatchet to Bruce; hopefully we can reduce her media gloss.'

'That bit about the former prime minister, is that true?'

'Does it need to be?'

Jaya was following the ministers. 'Treasurer, can I have a word?' she called.

Messenger turned as Stanley kept walking across the black marble of the glass tunnel separating the two wings.

'Have you got time for a coffee?'

Messenger checked his watch and nodded. 'Sure, it's that time of day for me.'

'Such a coffee snob.' Jaya smiled as they strolled past the fountain in the Members' Hall, towards Aussies.

'We're both from Melbourne,' Messenger said, chuckling. 'We both should be snobs.'

'Ha, and both from Melbourne Uni, which also adds a touch of snobbery.'

'Professor, you would never call yourself a snob, would you?'

'Hell no, but given my background, I'm lucky to even be here.'

'I've been meaning to ask, has the university held tenure open for you?'

'Great question. They haven't let me know, but I'm thinking I can go back once done here.'

'You aren't standing again?' Messenger glanced at her as they walked.

'Of course, I am, but I'm not likely to win unless I'm from a major party. It was just a quirk of fate last time, as you well know. So, I'm likely to be back teaching when I'm done here, which will give me a different emphasis on the applied modules I teach.'

'Grab a table and I'll get the coffees. Latte, right?'

'I'm a black, baby.' She laughed at her pun. 'Espresso please, good sir.'

Jaya settled into a table by the window, away from the television screening the parliament, and dragged a couple of old documents from the plastic sleeve she was carrying.

Messenger returned with the coffees and slid a sugar stick to her.

'Sweet enough,' Jaya said.

'I find I have to take one with the coffee here, not so much in Melbourne. Maybe it's the water.'

'Bart, I want to raise Tucker Farm in Barellan, just west of Wagga. I had Brian Tucker give evidence the other day, and he was compelling.'

Messenger listened as he sipped his coffee.

'He is spending an enormous amount on feed every month.'

'How much?'

'North of eighty grand.'

Messenger whistled through his teeth. 'That's steep. How's he coping?'

'He's not. The bank is threatening foreclosure.'

'Really?' He shook his head. 'Banks have advised us they are taking no action against farmers.'

Jaya took the shot of coffee with a flick of her head and swallowed it straight down. 'It's what he said at the end of his testimony I'm concerned about.'

Messenger considered her, perceiving she was struggling with the news. 'What did he say?'

'He said that unless the banks back off, they will force him to resolve the situation.'

'Sounds ominous, bordering on threatening. Did he name anyone?'

'What he said was, he doesn't want any government handout, and he wanted the bank to back off and allow him to continue without selling stock or land.'

'Is he in the Farrer electorate?'

'Riverina.'

'Okay, I'll have a chat with Russ and see what he knows about him. It's unusual that he doesn't want any government help.'

'I suspect there is a lot of history associated with that decision. His family has worked the land for almost a century. Maybe he doesn't want to be the first.'

'They all want money, Jaya, and that's what surprises me about this guy.' Messenger finished his coffee and readied himself for a goodbye. 'Is that it?'

'I'm calling my marker for the weekend.' Jaya flashed a smile, rubbed her hands, then rested her chin on them, hiding her laugh at Messenger's discomfort.

'This weekend?' Messenger screwed a face. 'Can we do lunch, maybe?'

'Dinner. Don't try to get out of it because I know you're free.'

Messenger frowned. 'How would you know that?'

'Your office talks to my office all the time. In fact, they share a house together when they're in Canberra. And don't worry, she has told Robert nothing, other than that a diary entry is available. So, I want to call it in.'

Messenger gave in. 'All right, fair enough, but it won't be an all-nighter. Couple of hours at the most.'

'Couple of hours is all I asked for.'

'Let my office know the place and the time and I shall be there.'

Messenger stood to leave. Jaya breathed deep through her nose, watching him, still masking her mouth. 'Can you tell me about Tucker on the weekend?'

'I'll try. See you.'

Jaya studied him walking, taking in his confident swagger and an occasional wave to others. She sighed again, with a deeper breath still, wondering if her reaction was like a teenager, but she was enjoying the distinct tingling that was running through her.

CHAPTER NINETEEN

It wasn't often the public would see the leader of the opposition out in a Canberra restaurant, let alone with a journalist who had a reputation for breaking stories, but Meredith Bruce didn't care. She was enjoying the chat and the laughs two girls usually have when sharing a bottle of chardonnay. It was a mild twilight, and the women sat on the decked veranda of the Boathouse overlooking Lake Burley Griffin, with its stunning view back to the parliament, its flag limp against its massive flagpole. The fixed four course meal had almost beaten them as they toyed with dessert.

'Who would have thought an avocado could be a dessert?' Bruce swooned after spooning meringue into her mouth.

Cassandra Rogers pushed her dessert around her plate with a fork, puffed her cheeks and blew out. 'I think I'm done.' She glanced at Bruce. 'Hey, thanks for asking me to come. It's been fun.'

'No issue; thanks for coming.' Bruce placed her spoon on the plate, wiped her mouth with the linen serviette, and collapsed back into the chair. 'I think you're right. The food has been brilliant.'

Cass gazed over her wineglass, twirling it in her fingers. 'Was Messenger right today?'

'About what?'

Cass finished her wine, smiled, then hesitated for a moment before asking, 'About you and Gerrard?'

'Well,' Bruce drained her wine, 'let's get another bottle and I'll tell you anything you want to know.'

Twenty minutes later, after a few more laughs over coffee and more wine, Cass broached the subject again.

'Political ambition has a harridan standing in the shadows for any woman wanting to reach the top,' said Bruce. She sighed and dropped back in her chair, clutching her glass. 'It's a boys' club. A woman has little chance unless she compromises her values.'

Cass rocked her head in disbelief. 'You're kidding me?'

Bruce took a generous sip of wine. 'What? You haven't done something in your career to get ahead? Somehow, I doubt that.'

Cass mixed a shake of her head with a nod. 'I'm not sure I agree. But I have done things I regret.'

Bruce smiled. 'You're no different from me.'

'So... you had an affair with the prime minister?'

'Let's put it this way...' Bruce finished her glass and gained the attention of a waiter to bring the bill. 'I will do what I have to do to get the outcome I want. It seems I'm close to getting what I want, so it has been worth it.' She studied Cass before asking, 'Will you?'

She didn't respond, turning away as the waiter placed the leather bill folder on the table.

'Cassandra, these things should not surprise you in politics,' Bruce said, signing the account. 'There are one hundred and fifty-five ambitious members of parliament who want the top job, otherwise they wouldn't be there. They'll do whatever they can to have their ambition satisfied.'

She leaned into the table. 'Cross out marginal seat members. Way too busy trying to win their seat. Front bench opportunities open for those who are in safe seats. Choosing ministries then becomes a balance between states and genders. If you are ambitious and want to move forward, you need a patron. They have their own needs. So... give it to them, and in return you can get what you want.'

'If everyone does that, then no leader is secure.'

'That's why a leader demands a good praetorian guard to protect them from the ambitious. A good leader knows who to promote and who to reward.'

'Please don't tell me you allowed yourself to be objectified to get ahead?'

'I regret nothing, and I suspect you are no different to me.'

Cass smiled, then finished her glass. She stood, a little unsteady, to end the conversation.

Bruce looked at her critically. 'Are you okay with driving?'

'Sure.' Cass searched for her keys in her bag.

'One thing I will say to you,' Bruce said as they reached the steps to the path leading to the carpark, where a commonwealth car waited. 'Ambition is not a male thing. Women can be just as conniving as them. We just have something most blokes want; so, it has a price, and they pay. Just make sure you don't discount.'

'Wise advice I'm sure, although I don't agree.'

Bruce stepped in, hugging her and kissing her cheek. 'Thank you so much for the information you have been providing me. I'm sure there is a reason for it, and maybe I'll be forced to repay you. Nonetheless, I'm happy to support whatever you are doing, as it helps me.'

Cass appreciated the hug and kiss, ratifying their friendship.

'Not sure what you mean about all that. I don't have an agenda other than having stories raised in the parliament. I can then write about them using the information I have.'

'Yeah, well, like you, I don't know what you mean. Thanks for coming; I enjoyed it. Let's do it again.'

'I'll keep you to that promise when you get to Yarralumla,' Cass said.

'Well, let's hope we do it before then. See you.'

Cass watched Bruce bounce down the pathway to her waiting car, waved when she turned to get in, and smiled as the car whisked her away. Bruce was right. Perhaps she shouldn't discount her product to get what she wanted.

It was nearing ten when Cass collided with a curb side rubbish wheelie bin, pushing it over and strewing plastic bagged rubbish onto the verge. She misjudged her parking, and as she opened the door, she almost tripped onto the road. She went to the front of the car, dragging the bin clear and shoving bags of rubbish back.

After collecting her things, she staggered off through the lane to Hughes' house. He answered the door in shorts and a polo shirt, and she followed him through to the large family room. She stumbled straight to the couch, flopping in, and dropping her bag to the tiled floor. The leather embraced her as she gazed up at Hughes, who was offering her a glass of wine. She smiled, reaching up and slurping a mouthful before settling into the cushions.

'Dinner was pleasant?'

'Politics is always pleasant; you know that.'

'What did you learn?'

Cass snorted. 'I leant you are all a bunch of pricks.'

Hughes shrugged. 'What else is new?'

'Yes, but I didn't realise what some of you are prepared to do to get what you want.'

'No different to you, I suspect,' Hughes said, as he walked over to the kitchen bench and grabbed the bottle of wine to refresh Cass's glass.

'I'll have you know I have sacrificed a lot to get where I am. I haven't manipulated or lied to get where I have got.' She swayed the glass at Hughes.

'So, the rumours a few years back about you and Hancock are not true?' Hughes queried.

'I regret nothing.'

'Hey, listen. Before we talk, I want to have a swim. Will you be okay?'

'Sure, why do you ask?'

Hughes slipped off his top and tossed it on the dining table.

'Oh, nothing.'

He then moved to the glass cantilevered doors and tugged them open, stepping out onto the patio and kicking out of his sandals. He dropped his shorts, exposing no bathers.

Cass was watching, smiling at the white bottom. 'Hey Hughesie, nice arse.'

Hughes turned and faced her for a moment, then dived into the pool.

Cass drew another satisfied smirk before draining her glass.

Cass became aware, but not clear, where she was before struggling to open her eyes. The sheet on the edge of the bed was damp from dribbling saliva. Her eyes had difficulty focusing. She was looking down, as her head was hanging over the edge of the bed. She saw carpet and an empty large white plastic bowl. She dragged her head back onto the mattress, noticing the stiffness of the white linen sheet. She stretched her head up and saw a pillow further up the bed; the doona was light, white, and crisp upon her. She sensed she was lying on her belly and rolled back into the bed onto more pillows, struggling to pull the doona over her.

DOOMED

She checked under it and saw that she was still in her bra and panties. She didn't know where she was.

'Good morning.'

The sound of the voice was like a cracker in a tin shed. The explosion startled her, and she lifted her head to see what made the noise.

'Sleep well?'

Hughes was standing in the doorway of a bright sunny room, dressed for the day.

'What happened?' she croaked, her mouth caked in dryness; her lips seemed swollen and numb.

'Well, you passed out on the couch and left your dinner on the floor while I was swimming. I cleaned you up, then rinsed and dried your clothes from the dinner stains. They're on the chair in the corner.'

Cass lifted a hand to shield her eyes, so she could see him. 'Who put me to bed?'

'That would be me,' Hughes smiled. 'There's a towel in the bathroom just there.' He pointed to the ensuite. 'A Berocca is waiting for you, so can I suggest you have a shower, get the vitamin B down you and join me for breakfast? A greasy feast will fix you, then I have a tablet for you.'

Cass dropped back as Hughes left, trying to remember what had happened last night. She remembered dinner, and the wheelie bin, groaning at the thought. She recalled Hughes having a swim and perhaps a bit of nudity, but that was it. She trailed her hand down her body, touching herself to feel for sensitivity, but there was none; a bonus, she thought.

It was a struggle, but the shower roused her. The Berocca increased awareness to her lips, and she appreciated the crispness of her clothes. When she entered the living space, she was apologetic.

'Minister, I'm sorry about my behaviour and I want to apologise. Totally unprofessional, and I'm embarrassed.'

'Not to worry. I just need to make sure you're okay?'

'I'm struggling but I'm coming good.' Cass fist pumped with a strained smile, then straddled a stool at the bench.

'Okay, sit down at the table, because this breakfast will fix you.'

Cass glanced at the food, feeling a little queasy, and grimaced. 'No, I couldn't. I should be going.'

'I haven't told you the news.'

Cass sat for a moment, trying to get her thoughts clear from the brain fog. 'Did you say I threw up?'

'All over the floor and across your leather bag, I'm afraid. I cleaned it as best I could, but the stains will remind you of your evening for evermore.'

'Do I need to clean up?'

'I've done most of it. I have cleaners coming in today, so don't worry.' Hughes carried a serving dish of food over to the table. 'Take a seat over here and let's talk.'

'I feel bad about this, and I want to go.'

'Okay, if you feel awful about it, then repay me by giving me a touch of courtesy and having breakfast. Then I'll give you a pill that will fix you.'

Reluctantly, Cass sat at the table. She then took a sliver of bacon, a chipolata and a fried egg from the serving dish and ate. Her trepidation about how it would affect her was unfounded, and she headed back for seconds in no time.

'You see? I told you it would help.'

'I don't eat this crap, but you're right. It tastes good.'

Hughes poured her a tea from a Wedgwood teapot and waved to the milk and sugar. 'Serve yourself.' He smiled, taking a bite from a slice of a fresh baguette, then as he was chewing said, 'I have a new scoop on Stanley.'

Cass drew her fork from her mouth as she studied him. 'Hasn't he been through enough? Why are you doing this?'

'We need to change the prime minister, and it's my task to generate negative media about him.'

'Can't you just ask him to leave?'

'You're not serious?' Hughes asked, shaking his head. 'He will not go if someone asks him. He won the election. Just, I grant you, but nevertheless, he brought us back into government and deserves respect.'

Cass dropped her fork, clattering it on the plate. 'Respect? What respect if you are feeding him to the media?'

'This is the way it works, Cassie; set the scene and then dethrone him. An assassination like this can only work if we have set the scene.'

'You've done enough; the polls are heading south. He'll never turn them around.'

'We just need one more knife.'

'By we, you mean who… Harper?'

'Well, not Messenger.'

'Not you?'

Hughes smiled. 'I've told you before, Cassandra dear, that the game is government, and the best person should lead us into the next election.'

'You reckon that's Harper?'

'The party room reckons it's Harper.'

Cass noted the word play as she sipped her tea. 'What have you got for me this time?'

Hughes poured another cup for himself and topped up his guest's.

'I have footage and photos of Stanley's brother using his allocated car during working hours in clear breach of parliamentary allowances. We frown on such things.' He passed a thick envelope of photos and typed reports to her. 'This has been going on for a while now, as that information will illustrate.'

'If you frown on it, how come your mates keep doing it?'

'Most of them think they are above the regulations and don't consider it will ever happen to them. It's politicians like me who must police them. When they get out of hand, I use a little stick on them.'

'Can I get the footage?'

'You can when I know your television people have approved the story.'

Cass shook her head. 'What… you don't trust me now? What happened to this trust thing you've been talking about?'

'I need to know you'll run it, then I will release it. I don't want it in social media before you do it.'

'All right, I better get onto it.'

'Okay, take this.'

'What is it?' Cass asked as she cupped her hand, reaching across the table.

'The food will fix your guts. This'll fix your head. It's fifty grams of Voltaren. Trust me; it'll take the pain away.'

Cass popped the tablet into her mouth and washed it down with tea. She then retrieved her bag, groaning at the sight of it.

'Look, I am sorry about last night.'

Hughes smirked. 'Did you enjoy the floor show?'

'What floor show?' Cass shook her head, a little bewildered. 'What do you mean?'

'Oh nothing, I just wondered. I suppose that's a good thing. I'll see you at the House,' he said as she slunk along the passage.

When she got to the door, she turned and yelled back down the corridor. 'Hey Minister?'

'Yeah, Cass?'

'I still reckon it's a nice arse.'

She laughed as she slammed the door, bounding off to her car, which wasn't too damaged. Someone had left an unkind note on the windscreen. She jumped in, turned the key, and wound the window down before tearing off the verge, hitting the road hard and shrieking with embarrassment at how the night had turned out.

'You scored a lucky break there, young lady,' she said as she slowed, remembering that she might still be over the alcohol limit. Turning her music up, she chuckled some more before heading for the House and a date with the prime minister, which no doubt he wouldn't be expecting.

CHAPTER TWENTY

The television in the corner of the Hancock Media office in the parliamentary press gallery was blaring with the last question of the day, and the noise from the ruckus caused by the politicians was unrelenting.

'Can we turn the childcare centre down, please?' Cass yelled to no one in particular.

Someone walking past turned the volume down and she heard yelps of appreciation from behind several cubicle screens.

'Thank you,' she said, raising her voice.

She tapped a number into her desk telephone and waited for the prime minister's office to respond. When they did, they transferred her to a political adviser to discuss a story she was running, for which she wanted Stanley's response.

At three fifteen, she collected her bag and began walking to the ministerial wing. As she marched past Peter Cleaver's office, he called her.

'I have the PM at three-thirty, so be quick.'

Cleaver raised his eyebrows. 'The PM? What have you got?'

'A story that could end his leadership.'

'Sex or drugs?'

'Neither. It's about family misusing taxpayer funds,' Cass said, still standing in the doorway.

'The poor bastard. I feel sorry for him.'

Cass shrugged. 'If you play in the big boys' playground, then expect dirt in your face.'

'Huh, that's funny,' said Cleaver, not laughing. 'Whatever you've got, I want it for the lead on television news.'

'I could have footage.'

'That's why I want it on evening news tonight.'

'How did you know I have footage?'

'What?' Cleaver fussed a little, then went for a cigarette from his crumpled packet. 'Oh, I'm guessing, that's all.'

'Do you know something I don't?'

He sucked hard on his cigarette, making a noise as he breathed deep, before blowing hard to relieve his stress.

'I want you to get the recognition from this story, that's all.'

'Why wouldn't I get the recognition? If it runs tonight or tomorrow, who cares so long as it's accurate?'

'I'll run it tonight.'

'I'm the political editor; I say when a story gets broadcast.'

'I'm the bureau chief and I tell you when it runs.'

Cass frowned as she turned and strode to the elevator. The corridor was busy with journalists returning from question time. At the elevator lobby camera tripod stands for television cameras sat on trollies ready to be wheeled out for a media conference or a politician's door stop. Deadlines drove the busyness of the gallery. She knew her story would lead the news bulletin if it was correct.

When she arrived at the prime minister's office, Cass thought that if she was going to end his leadership, she should come through the front door rather than sneaking through the back media door.

There was a security guard behind reinforced glass, and she flashed him her pass. He then checked his list and waved her in; the door released as she dragged it open, and she stepped into the foyer. Stanley's political adviser was lingering and ushered Cass into the office, where the prime minister was sitting behind his desk waiting.

He glanced up and smiled, waving her to the leather lounge as he stood and moved to a nearby lounge chair.

'I hear you had dinner with Meredith Bruce last night,' Stanley said, unsettling her with his opening observation.

'Yes, I did. The evenings are beautiful by the lake.'

'How was it? Did you resolve world peace?'

'Meredith is a good egg; we had fun.'

'Had a wine?'

Cass glanced at the knowing smile of the prime minister. 'As you do. One or two.'

'One or two bottles, I'm reliably informed.'

Cass shifted in her seat, concerned about the discussion.

'You know you shouldn't drive when you've had too much to drink?'

'Ah yes, good point.' Cass wondered how he knew and who the informant was. *Was it Hughes, or was someone watching Bruce? Was she herself being watched?*

'Prime Minister, speaking of cars, I want to talk to you about the use of your government car in your electorate.'

Stanley didn't respond. He steepled his fingers, resting his chin on their tips.

'I have a comprehensive report your brother has used your taxpayer funded car for over six months to further his business interests; would you care to comment?'

'What evidence do you have?'

'Photos and footage, plus a departmental report of kilometres travelled.'

Stanley didn't respond; he just stared at her. Then, after a few moments, he suggested, 'Would you like a cup of tea?' He stood, moving to his desk, tapping numbers into the telephone. 'Could I have a cup of tea, please? Cassandra?'

'No thanks.' She waited until he returned and asked, 'Would you care to comment, Prime Minister?'

'Where are you getting all of this malicious material? Have you bothered to ask me or my office?'

'My job is to keep politicians accountable.'

'Accountable?' Stanley said, scoffing. 'You are part of a campaign of leadership destabilisation. A few sharp heads are using you.'

'Nothing I have raised about you has been wrong, has it?'

'Quite the contrary, actually,' Stanley said.

Cass frowned, moving her head as if she was searching for something.

'You are being used, I'm afraid.'

'You question the facts I have run with?' Cass asked.

'No, but they are trivial in the grand scheme of things running the country.'

'These stories suggest you are not up to it.'

'Gee, you've a view of me, don't you? No wonder they have got you doing their bidding.'

'I'm no one's patsy.' Cass pressed her lips together.

'Then how are you getting this information and why are you using it? Ever considered that?'

'Where I get my material and my sources is between me and them. I don't worry about their motivation, just the story.'

Stanley waved in a staffer, who handed him a tea. 'So, you assume you have a story?'

'With this, yes. No one is entitled to misappropriate funds.'

'You had a story about my work in the electorate?'

'Yes, it was a fair story about what you are not doing and how others are covering up for you.'

'I see, and you think that is fair and robust.' Stanley sipped his tea. 'Just like the implication in what you wrote about my so-called marriage difficulties.'

'People need to appreciate their prime minister. You talk about families so much; they want to know you have a united family.'

'You never considered that these stories may be part of a campaign?'

Cass screwed her face. 'They're legitimate stories as far as I'm concerned.'

'What if I said you were wrong?'

'You can't deny the facts, Prime Minister.'

Stanley sipped his tea, then placed it on the broad arm of the chair.

'Let me tell you that you are wrong. This information being fed to you is a deliberate campaign to undermine me, readying the party for a leadership challenge.'

'Leadership is not the issue here, Prime Minister. It's the way you are managing your personal life, which, if you don't mind me saying, seems out of control. How can you run the nation if you can't run your life?'

Stanley smiled, leaning forward, and resting his elbows on his knees, his hands open.

'Would it make a difference if you learnt that there are personal answers for these transgressions?'

'I wouldn't call them transgressions, Prime Minister.'

Stanley's now sad, tired eyes captured Cass's gaze and didn't let go as he gnawed his bottom lip.

'My wife has brain cancer and not expected to live beyond Christmas.'

Cass' mouth dried, and she swallowed. She licked her lips.

'She was diagnosed around six months ago and decided to live at home in Cottesloe. When I return to Perth, I spend all my time with her.'

'I'm sorry, Prime Minister; I didn't realise.'

'My brother takes her for treatment every day and uses my car as he only has a small sports car, which is too uncomfortable for her.'

Cass gasped a deep breath; her mouth fell open, and she covered it with her hand. Her eyes welled, and she shook her head slightly. 'I didn't know.'

Stanley wiped an eye as he continued to look at Cass, then said, 'No, perhaps you weren't meant to know. You see, with those facts now in front of you, does your story about the car make a difference?'

After leaving the prime minister, Cass entered Peter Cleaver's office. He was deep in editing mode, a red pen flashing across a story. Smoke trailed up from an overfull ashtray. His sleeves rolled up and hair ruffled like anyone under deadline stress.

'I'm dropping the story,' Cass said as she sat at his desk.

'Television or paper?'

'Both.'

Cleaver dropped his pen and fell back in his chair, swinging his hands behind his head. 'Are you sure you want to do that?'

Cass felt anxious, and her stomach tightened. 'There's nothing in it. Why should I have to rethink it? There's no story.'

'You know Hancock is waiting for a piece that sends you over the line.'

'What would you know about a line, Cleave?' Cass frowned, gnawing her bottom lip.

Cleaver leaned further back, rocking his chair.

'I know Hancock wants to appoint you to his flagship. I know he has provided you with an ultimatum.'

'Why would you know these things?'

'Because I do. I want you to rethink your decision.'

Cass stood; leaving the office, she said, 'I have. It's been dumped.'

Cleaver watched her go, tugging a crumpled cigarette from the soft pack. He lit it with a smouldering butt from the ashtray, sucking hard.

'Maybe you'll be as well.'

He forcefully blew out smoke as he picked up the telephone, punching a familiar number.

'Hi, it's me. She won't do it. My suggestion is to send it to Hancock and let him do what he wants with it.'

CHAPTER TWENTY-ONE

Animals can sense when death is near. Fear is stripped from them, and they seem to accept their lot. Even humans, when faced with death, have shown acceptance of what is about to befall them. Fifty head of once prime Angus beef stood in five gnarled ditches, dug deep and without precision to be their last resting place. The kelpies had led them and now squatted as sentinels on the earth mound above the cattle. They seemed to show the sadness of the moment.

Once the cattle were in place, Tucker sat in his vehicle, musing on any alternative options for him. These were the most degraded of the herd. They would fetch no money at market. A tax loss was better than a sale of underweight beef. They could recover and fatten, but no one in the district would take the risk. His only choice was to amplify his losses and recover reasonable value as a tax write-off.

It didn't make it any easier.

He went to the back of his truck, opening a secure aluminium gun case and hauling his favourite rifle, an M1 carbine, from its housing. His father had passed it on to him. He knew little of its source, although the weapon was a standard issue for the Korean and Vietnam wars. The scratched, dented and scoured wood stock had seen a lot of action; but more than anything the rifle was reliable. Firing a 30 calibre round needed to drop a beast. He clipped in a fifteen-round magazine, unlatched the bolt, picked up three more magazines and marched to the edge of the first pit.

He gazed down on his herd, sad at the sight before him. Innocent animals waiting to be slaughtered. Silent, no movement. His dogs scrutinised him as he brought the rifle to his shoulder, aimed for the centre of the head facing him, and squeezed the trigger. The rifle recoiled hard. Smoke blew from the barrel, the casing flicking out from the top of the bolt housing. The cow dropped. The others in the line didn't respond other than to reposition themselves as the beast collapsed. There was no panic, just resignation.

Tucker took a step to his right, raised the rifle and repeated, then again and then again. When done, he moved to the next pit. He shot fifteen times, changed the magazine, and continued the slaughter. The dogs now lowered themselves, but still alert and watchful. The cattle stood like stone statues, with little reaction or flinch as their number dropped.

When he came to the last cow, Tucker gazed down as it raised its head to see him. He bit his lip, aimed the rifle, and squeezed the trigger. Once done, he lowered his head and weapon to his side, then searched to the heavens to say something but only wrinkled his face, dropping his head and massaging the bridge of his nose with a thumb and forefinger.

He was done.

Two hours later, after grading the ditches, he staggered back to the warm kitchen and a cup of tea. His four children scattered throughout the house, and his wife, knowing what he had just done, provided support as best she could.

'Let's hope you don't have to do any more.'

He glanced up and smiled at the stoic nature farmers were born to bestow. 'I'm not so sure I can do anymore; I hate it.'

'Why don't you take a warm bath and I'll bring you a wine?'

'I still need to mend the fence down by the orchard.'

'It can wait until tomorrow; you've done enough.'

He considered his wife, eyes welling, before brushing a trickle away. 'You are too good for me.'

'Yep, I know that.'

'Kids good?'

'Yeah, they're doing homework.' She aired quotation marks around the word. 'Let's chat to them at dinner after your bath. Leave them until then.'

The television in the background showed a glimpse of the prime minister in a story leading the five o'clock news.

'Can you turn that up for a moment please, darling?'

DOOMED

The news item had just begun, with Tamara O'Byrne standing to camera and reporting the prime minister is accused of misusing his electoral allowance; in particular, his brother was using the electorate car to go about his own business. There was footage of the prime minister avoiding cameras and reporters.

'She's a star, I reckon,' Kathy Tucker said.

'Do you think?' Tucker was listening to the story. 'Politicians are bloody useless, aren't they? Always with their nose in the trough.'

'They're only in it for themselves.'

'Especially when there are no promised announcements on drought funding.'

'S'pose you've heard from the Indian lady?' Kathy asked.

'I'll give her a few more days, then I'll call her.'

'What do you reckon the prime minister will do about this?'

'I suspect he may be in a little trouble.'

'Are you getting this?'

Barton Messenger had taken the call from James Harper as he watched the television news report. 'There must be a reasonable explanation,' he said, increasing the volume.

'Yeah, it's called stupidity; we have to move now,' Harper said.

'We can't drag down a first term prime minister.'

'We can if the guy isn't cutting it. And I'm sad to say, Pete is hopeless.'

Messenger paused for a moment to think about what to say; should he encourage or protect Stanley? He was the deputy leader and had a responsibility to defend his leader. 'I don't think we should do anything that drastic.'

'If I don't bring it to a head, then the polls will go further south. Geez, they can't go any lower, can they?'

'Jim, if you are going to challenge then make certain you have the numbers, otherwise you can kiss goodbye to your career.'

'Hughesie is looking after that.'

Messenger paused, distracted by what Tamara O'Byrne was saying. 'She just said his leadership is in crisis. How would she know that?'

'The games afoot, young man. Make sure you're on the right side,' Harper said, laughing as he ended the call.

'You're effing kidding me,' Cass said, staring at the television, face screwed as if in pain. 'I don't believe this.'

'What's up?' Abbasi poked her head over the partition.

'O'Byrne is reporting the story I dumped.'

'You're kidding?'

'I pulled it about an hour ago and here she is doing the piece right now.'

Abbasi moved to the television, standing beside her.

'How would she know about it?'

Cass shook her head. 'I don't have a clue. I spoke to no-one other than Cleave, and he didn't know any details.'

'Who gave it to you?'

'A politician, but the information is a setup.'

'Could it have been the politician?'

Cass couldn't believe it. Why would Hughes play her like that?

'I'll have his balls if it was.'

CHAPTER TWENTY-TWO

Messenger knocked as he poked his head around the office door. Stanley lay collapsed on a couch watching the television with a full glass of ice and what might have been a half glass of malt whiskey resting on the leather arm, his fingers smoothly spinning it.

'Prime Minister? Can I have a word?'

'Sure Bart, come in.' Stanley waved him in, his eyes not leaving the television. 'They're putting effort in to kill off my leadership, aren't they?'

Messenger strolled in, standing by Stanley, and fascinated by the television commentary on the ABC current affairs show. He took a seat, still watching.

'Is the information reported in the Hancock news true?'

Stanley took a side glance at his deputy, raising an eyebrow of suspicion. 'What do you think?'

Messenger didn't like the question. 'Well, they had footage of your brother driving the car.'

'Then I must be guilty, right?'

'It just adds to the other government issues. Now they're talking about you.' Messenger waved to the television.

Stanley took a sip, flushing it over his tongue for effect. 'Do you want a drink? Help yourself if you do.'

'No, I'm good.' Messenger eyed his leader, then added, 'What do you want to do about it?'

'It seems the chattering classes want my scalp.' Stanley held up his glass to the television as if in a toast. 'I don't want to give them the pleasure.'

'Pete, we need to respond.'

'Why? Is anyone moving against me?'

'There's talk around the backbench. Some marginal members are expressing concern.'

'Who's their man? What have you heard?'

'The ministry is solid behind you, but we need to turn the polls.'

'That wasn't the question? Who's likely to challenge?'

'Folks are talking Jim Harper.'

'What's his position?'

Messenger glanced at Stanley, who held his gaze, searching for a sign.

'He's not interested.'

Stanley continued to stare at Messenger, looking for a lie in his face, then turned away, taking another sip of whiskey. 'Someone is leaking this crap, and it's likely a cabinet minister.'

'A staffer?'

'No, it's someone who knows about my wife.'

Messenger paused for a moment, then lowered his voice, asking, 'What's she been doing?'

Stanley smiled and took another sip, before turning to Messenger. 'She has cancer. Not likely to see Christmas, I'm afraid.'

The weight of the announcement flattened Messenger, who flopped into the leather chair and dropped his head back, breathing in and out, before straightening back, 'Are you okay?'

Stanley pouted his bottom lip as if about to cry, nodding. 'It's been tough for us. I have support from my brother, who drives her to treatment every day. We tried to keep it out of the public eye, but now it seems it might be all over the place.'

Messenger now leaned forward to counsel Stanley. 'Pete, you need to go public. The media will back off and then we get back to normal. We can't allow this to continue without letting folks know.'

Stanley sniffed, then nodded. 'Good for the polls, eh?'

'Wouldn't hurt.' Messenger regretted his comment, gnawing his bottom lip.

'Yeah, that's the problem with politics. You can't keep precious secrets because folks will use it against you.'

'You think one of our colleagues knows?'

'Someone leaked it. They may not know about Alison. They certainly know about my brother if they have been filming him.'

'We have to brief the media, otherwise they won't give up looking for dirt.'

Stanley took a larger slug, clinking the ice. 'Let's move the narrative to policy, away from leadership.'

'We need a couple of big announcements; what do you have in mind?'

'Has your mate finished her inquiry?'

'You mean Jaya?'

Stanley nodded.

'First, we aren't mates; and second, she's finished and will present it to parliament next week.'

'No doubt she will want money, so why don't we announce drought relief before she reports? Then we get two whacks at it.'

'We could put something together. What are your thinking?'

'Transport subsidies for feed and water. We can cover state and local government fees such as local rates. An emergency relief fund for families with no income. And probably, funds for health services; I'm thinking about mental health. It must be tough for them.'

'How much?'

'Two bill, give or take a mill or two.'

Messenger whistled through his teeth. 'That's a mighty big whack to the budget.'

'Now's not the time for fiscal responsibility, Bart. We need an immediate injection of funds to do two things.' Stanley pointed up a finger. 'One, our farmers and their communities need help... now! Not next week or next month, right now.' He poked up his second finger to make a V. 'And two, we change the narrative away from navel gazing at ourselves.'

'Fair enough. When do you want to do it?' asked Messenger, thinking through the lengthy process he would need to start.

'Tomorrow.'

CHAPTER TWENTY-THREE

Tony Hancock was still in his office after watching his news and the ABC current affairs show. Pleased with the exclusive, but disappointed, his current affairs show hadn't covered the prime minister's story. Nicholls appeared drab compared to the ABC offering. He contemplated whether he should pension Nicholls off now, before Christmas.

A glass of Penfolds Bin 389 Cabernet Shiraz sat before him, his third. He was enjoying the rich flavour with a thick cigar, feet on his desk and lying back in his green leather chair. He stretched for his phone when it squealed the ring tone of his top political journalist.

'Cassandra, what can I do for you?'

'How is it that a story I killed was on your news bulletin tonight?'

Hancock smiled. 'Was that the one about the prime minister?'

'You know damn well it was.'

'We got exclusive footage and ran it.'

'No thought to check with me first?'

'I trusted the journo on that one.' Hancock turned his head, smiling at Tamara O'Byrne, who toasted him. 'Anything wrong with it?'

'I killed it for a reason. Now it doesn't matter because you have just exposed Stanley's wife.'

Hancock scoffed. 'What's she got to do with it? It's Stanley who's stuffing up. We ran nothing on her… What have you got?'

'She's got brain cancer, and she's not likely to live to the end of the year.'

Hancock kicked off the desk. 'The hell you say.'

'If you want to manage Stanley, I suggest you ring and apologise. I saw him this afternoon and told him he wouldn't have to worry about the story and to trust you.'

Hancock dropped into a soft leather couch, showing with a wave that O'Byrne should join him. 'I'll call him tomorrow.' He drew hard on his cigar and ballooned the smoke high into the ceiling.

O'Byrne picked up the bottle of wine and sashayed across to the lounge, splashing more into Hancock's glass.

'Where did O'Byrne get the footage?' Cass continued.

'She didn't. Someone sent it to me, and I decided to run it.'

'Yeah, that'd be right,' Cass said. 'Does she ever get anything herself?'

'Don't be like that, Cassie. She is very talented.' He winked at O'Byrne, who smiled, snuggling into the couch, and drawing her frock along her thigh to give Hancock an extended view of her long legs.

'You promised me the gig, Tony. Now I hear you're giving it to her.'

He nodded with a pouted smirk as he ogled O'Byrne, who was trailing a foot along her leg.

'I haven't made my mind up yet.'

'Bullshit! Are you banging her?'

'No,' Hancock said, almost spluttering his wine.

'You are, aren't you?'

'Come on, Cassie, you know what it's like,' he replied, blowing smoke to the ceiling. 'It's only ever about merit here.'

O'Byrne placed her glass on a side table and swung around on the couch, her resting hand now on the other side of Hancock.

'You promised me, Tony.'

'Keep getting the stories and you might get the gig. The articles you have been posting have been great, and your performance at the Press Club was terrific. Just keep doing it.'

'So long as it's a fair process, I will. When do you think you'll announce it?'

Hancock gazed at O'Byrne as she came to her knees and ran her nose along his jawline.

'The way things are going…' he said, smiling, 'soon, but not likely until the new year. Look, I have to go. Keep getting the stories.'

He tossed his phone aside and waited for whatever Tamara had in mind.

DOOMED

Cass dropped her phone to the bench then paced around the kitchen. How did Hancock get the footage, when Hughes said it would not be available until editorial deadline?

She turned to the refrigerator and poured a drink from the cask of wine on the top shelf. It was cold and tasty, and she didn't care about quality. She picked up her phone, swiped through a few screens, and prodded the call button. She crossed to the lounge, flopping into a chair, and waiting for an answer.

'Christopher Hughes.'

'Did you give that footage of Stanley to Hancock?'

'Good evening to you, too, Cassie.'

'Well, did you?'

'You told me you would run the story, and then I got a call from Peter Cleaver saying you had killed it.'

'I spoke to Stanley. I had to verify the facts.'

'Why? What shiny more information would you have got that would have changed your mind?'

'Did you know his wife has cancer?'

'What's that got to do with the plan?'

'You know by giving it to Hancock it basically screwed me, don't you?'

Hughes considered a joke but thought better of it.

'I never screwed you, Cassie. It was Hancock who gave it to O'Byrne. I never considered he would do that.'

'He's selecting her to take over from Nicholls.'

'Why would he do that? You're the better talent.'

Cass took a mouthful of wine. 'It's nice of you to say that, but I suspect he's screwing her.'

'What do you need to get the gig?'

'Stories?'

'Do you want the gig?'

'Is the Pope Catholic?'

Hughes smiled, now closing the deal. 'I can help you with stories, if that's what you need; but next time you have to print them.'

'Stanley's brother is using the car to drive his wife for treatment twice a day.'

'Yeah? So what?'

'You're a prick, Hughes.' Cass shook her head.

'Well, if you recall from your long eyeful the other night, you'd have to admit, I'm a fairly big prick.'

'Don't kid yourself.' Cass ended the call, somewhat disgusted with the comment. 'I can't believe he just said that.'

She took a note.

CHAPTER TWENTY-FOUR

Messenger worked most of the night calling in key advisers and treasury officers to put together the drought relief funding. He slept on the office couch when the others disappeared home, then showered in his ensuite before changing into fresh clothes, ready for his seven o'clock briefing with the prime minister. Once treasury arrived, he marched with them to the prime minister's suite, armed with charts and papers supporting the government decision.

By nine, they finished. The prime minister instructed his chief whip to organise a party room meeting for ten o'clock so he could announce the emergency funding package, which would no doubt please his rural and regional members. He then rang the leader of the Country Party, asking him to step into his office for a briefing. Messenger asked if the PM wanted him to stay. Stanley said no. He sent the officials and Messenger on their way; confident they had briefed him well.

Messenger visited Jaya Rukhmani to brief her on the government's initiative.

'Hi Robert, is Jaya in?'

Messenger grinned as the staffer stepped into her office to announce that the treasurer wanted to meet with her. He wasn't laughing for long, as there was no rushed reappearance and he wondered what the hold-up might be. He glanced at the phone unit on a nearby desk and could see no lights. Surely, she didn't have a visitor so early on a parliamentary day. He checked his watch as he took a chair to wait. He then heard plumbing noises from her ensuite and surmised a quick visit might be the reason for the delay.

The silence seal on the central door to the office snapped and Wong stepped out. 'Jaya is ready for you now, Treasurer; sorry to keep you waiting. Would you like a drink of something?'

'Not for me, but if Jaya would like something feel free.' Messenger walked into the office. Jaya was behind her desk; the bright overhead lights were off, and the office was lit by a dull lap on her desk and the window behind her. 'Hey, it looks homey in here.'

'You were in here the other day.'

'Yeah well, now it looks different. Can I sit on the couch?' Messenger asked.

'Sure.'

Jaya stood and stepped towards him as he relaxed on the leather.

Messenger watched her sashay to the lounge, feeling embarrassed and aware that his cheeks were burning.

'You okay? You look a touch flushed.'

'No, I'm fine. I was just admiring your dress.'

'It's a little summery, I know, but I'm sick of dressing to type.'

'Not happy with the dress code?'

'I suspect it's designed for you chaps; you only need a change of tie to look different. We have to lug plenty of outfits to Canberra, as we can't afford to be seen in the same thing too often.'

'I leave three suits here.'

'Let me guess: blue, grey and black,' Jaya laughed. 'It's a little different for the girls, and with my colouring, well,' she chuckled again, 'I need a contrasting colour against the black.'

'Well, it's a nice dress today.'

'Frock, Barton, get it right.'

Messenger chuckled along with her. She had styled her hair back off her face with a bright scarf that matched her frock; she tied it firmly against her head, her hair billowing out into a frizz behind her. Her thickish lips glistened with a hint of burnt orange.

'What are you looking at? Is there something wrong? Have I left breakfast on my face?' Jaya laughed at Messenger's discomfort, touching her face, relishing the impact of her dash to the mirror to do her hair and make-up.

He breathed in, then said, 'Jaya, we are going to make a drought funding announcement later today and I wonder if you want a briefing on it now so you can prepare yourself for any news coming at you.'

Jaya pouted her lips before screwing her face, crossing her legs, and leaning back into the chair. 'A little premature, I would have thought.'

'The PM wants something out today, I'm afraid, so we can't wait for your report.'

'Well, it asks for money, so I guess it hits the head of the nail.'

Messenger smiled.

'Is that funny?'

'What? No… sorry. It's just your turn of phrase, professor; it still pleases me.'

Jaya dismissed him. 'How much?'

Messenger, now refocused, said, 'Two billion.'

'Crumbs, that's more than we were recommending.'

'As I said, the PM wants to show leadership on this, sending a message to our farmers that we have their back.'

'Take me through it.'

Messenger spent the next ten minutes providing highlights of the package as Jaya took notes, nodding in agreement and questioning parts she didn't quite understand. As he was concluding his brief, his pager sparked up. He grabbed a quick glance, then said, 'I have a party room meeting at ten, for which I have to prepare, so are you okay with what we've done?'

'There's something missing.'

Messenger shook his head.

'You haven't mentioned the banks,' Jaya elaborated.

'What about them?'

'I want them to back off and offer relief for the farmers under financial pressure. In other words, stop foreclosing on farms.'

'I'll talk to the PM,' Messenger said as he stood. 'Can't promise anything, but we shall talk to the big ones, and to the Reserve Bank, to get their view.'

'It's important, Bart, so if you can add that into the package that would be great.'

'I'll see what I can do,' Messenger said as he sidled to the door.

'See you on Saturday night?'

Messenger stopped and shook his head as if not knowing what she was talking about. 'Saturday night?'

'Dinner? Promise? Diary?'

He smiled, remembering his commitment. 'Yeah, of course; looking forward to it… See you.'

'I bet you are,' Jaya said as Messenger rushed from the office.

Wong came through the connecting door, asking how the meeting had gone.

'Money and action for farmers, but no action on the banks. I'll just get out of this thing and then I can call Tucker and let him know.'

'Did he like it?'

'Couldn't take his eyes off it.'

'Told you.'

'What would I do without you, Robert?'

'You'd still be marking assignment papers.'

Jaya laughed and went off to her ensuite to step out of her Dior frock.

CHAPTER TWENTY-FIVE

The journey to the party room was quick from Jaya's. A short elevator ride down two floors and a brisk walk past the Country Party's meeting room, to almost at the end of the inner corridor.

Members were arriving, and when Messenger entered the room, he noted that the prime minister was already in place at the table positioned between various Australian flags. He checked the audio-visual equipment to make sure they had cued his presentation ready for his briefing. He then relaxed on a low-rise lounge chair against the side wall, part of a row of similar chairs below the framed photographs of previous party leaders.

He watched as colleagues took their usual assembled seats, preferring to sit in the same position for every meeting. He knew members got precious about the routine of sitting in the same chair.

Now his ministerial colleagues sauntered in, and he observed Hughes and Harper strolling in as a joking, happy couple before taking their seats alongside each other. He smiled and nodded hello, not bothering to engage in chat as he was more interested in reviewing his briefing.

The prime minister cleared the administrative announcements and called upon the whip to advise on the festivities planned for the Christmas sitting period, outlining the usual events that seemed to rush past as the years merged more and more into each other.

Same routine, same people speaking up in the party room, same outcome, which was basically nothing. The executive and cabinet decided most strategic action for the party, providing the backbench only cursory attention.

Stanley called upon Messenger, who provided a forty-minute briefing on the drought relief package, took questions, and answered all queries, which was a surprise given the haste with which he had developed the proposal.

'When was this first proposed for development?' asked Bob Tilley III, the rambunctious northern Queenslander and long-term member for Kennedy.

Stanley spoke over Messenger. 'I have been considering this for months, which is the reason I asked for a parliamentary inquiry. I spoke about it with Barton, and this is the plan we have come up with.'

'Looks like a rushed job to me.' Tilley didn't want to let it go.

'What difference does it make, Junior? This is the proposal, and we are seeking the party room's support,' Messenger said.

'What about the banks?' Tilley almost shouted, in his unique staccato style. 'You've got nothing there to bring the banks to heel.'

Hughes pulled a phone from inside his jacket and sent a text.

'This is a significant package, and we think the banks will join with us to offer relief,' Messenger said.

Tilley was now on his feet, scanning the room. 'My farmers are struggling. Now I know you city folk don't quite understand, but we need water. Not money. What we don't need is the banks getting carried away and foreclosing. If they do, then I reckon the guns will come out.'

The room responded with light-hearted comments, surprised laughter, and in some cases stern warnings about language.

'Ya see, this is the problem. City folks think food comes from the great farming fairy and somehow materialises on their plate. You don't know what farmers go through to get it there.'

'Hear, hear!' The rural members supported their outspoken colleague.

'I don't want to see any gunplay, but I warn youse… if the banks don't back off then we could have a tragedy.'

Stanley took control. 'Thank you, Bob, for your passionate contribution, as always. As it happens, I have formal meetings with the banking association and CEOs from the big four this afternoon to discuss this very issue.'

Tilley hadn't finished. 'Leader, I'm concerned about the mental health of my community. I welcome the financial support to offer more services, but please, I beg you, just make sure there is no bureaucratic crap that blocks good folks from getting help.'

Messenger spoke up. 'These are significant points, Junior, and I thank you for raising them.'

Tilley finished and sat back in his chair. Two members behind him patted his shoulder in support.

'Colleagues, if there are no other questions, I can advise that the prime minister will make this important announcement later today, Messenger said. 'We would be grateful for you to be on the front foot with your local media and your communities.' He scanned about the room. 'This is important and very good news for Australia. This may change the direction of the polls. The Australian people want something done, and we have delivered.'

The room erupted in applause, with Messenger smiling and making a slight gesture of a wave before returning to his seat.

As the room came back to its respectful silence, Stanley was working his phone. He put it to one side and stood to address his colleagues, glancing about the room. Many of them were wondering what the prime minister was about to say.

'Colleagues, the sanctity of the party room should be absolute. Indeed, we should not fear rising to our feet to speak about any issue that is causing concern. We must trust each other and keep confidentiality. If we leak against each other, then we are nothing other than a rabble waiting to return to opposition.' Stanley breathed in deep through his nose. 'I fear there are some in this room who would prefer to destroy the party and humiliate your prime minister.'

Harper got to his feet. 'Leader, this is unnecessary, as we all know the protocols of the party room. I am sure we all adhere to them.'

'Hear, hear.'

'It is unfair for you to suggest that colleagues are leaking against you because of your own actions. It is not the party room that remains active in the personal and private lives of our colleagues.'

'Thank you for your contribution, James.' Stanley moved around the table, now facing his colleagues. 'I was not referring to me per se. I was thinking more of this room, right now.'

Maurice Roussett, the environment minister, stood and said, 'I find that broad generalisation quite offensive, quite frankly. What evidence do you have?'

Stanley stepped back and sat on the edge of the table, reaching for his phone. He swiped the screen a few times before speaking. 'There is a story online at the moment describing the briefing we just had and detailing the discussions since. What is truly galling is that they have quoted Bob, almost word for word. But with a different meaning: *Tilley slams prime minister, defeating him in party room debate.*'

'That's bullshit,' Tilley shouted. 'Who did that?'

Anxious conversations billowed, with members expressing dismay about the news.

'Who wrote it?' asked Ginni Stavloukas.

'Cassandra Rogers, from Hancock Media,' Stanley said, casting an eye towards Messenger.

Jeers came from the back rows. Someone called her heartless. Others looked to the prime minister to respond.

'It obviously came from this room… one of you.' Stanley waved an arm across the meeting. 'So, I wonder if anyone is brave enough to admit to it?' He looked at Harper, who shrugged, shaking his head.

'Here's an idea.' Stanley stood and moved closer to the front row. 'Why don't you hand your phones to the colleague next to you, so you can check their SMS history?'

Tilley was now standing. 'Yeah, good idea, leader.'

Messenger didn't share the enthusiasm and stood to make a comment. 'Pete, I'm happy to share, but this may turn into a witch burning if we are not careful. If we identify someone, what then?'

Hughes gnawed at the back of his thumb as he watched and listened.

'I have nothing to hide,' Roussett said, 'and nor should anyone else.' He pulled his phone from his jacket and passed it to Jack Stevenson, the agriculture minister, who passed his phone to his colleague. 'So, it wasn't Jack.'

'Maurie hasn't texted since yesterday,' Stevenson said.

Members started handing over their phones to their neighbour, some complaining about a breach of privacy, others making a joke about not telling their spouse.

Stanley moved over to the wall of leaders and stood before Harper with his hand out, offering his phone. Harper glanced up, screwed his face, and took it, passing his own to Stanley, who searched the messages. He didn't find what he was expecting to see. Nothing.

Hughes tossed his phone into Messenger's lap and then moved his attention to Stanley.

'This is crazy, Pete. You won't find anything.'

Stanley looked down at him. 'You sound confident.' He looked to Messenger, who glanced up, shaking his head.

'He hasn't used it.'

Stanley returned to the centre of the room, disappointed, and asked if anyone was identified. There was no response.

'That's impossible unless they have a bug in here,' Tilley said.

Stavloukas stood and addressed the room. 'Colleagues, that was embarrassing. Someone is leaking against the leader, but apparently none of us here. The polls are heading south, and there seems no respite from those who want to pull us down. Whoever you are, just stop it.'

Hughes ran a forefinger back and forward through his lips as he studied the anxiety in the room. Stanley returned to sit at the desk, his face tight. He glanced at Messenger, showing that he wanted to talk. Messenger responded and leaned into him for a private counsel.

'What the hell do we do?' Stanley asked.

'End the meeting, have a media conference and announce the funding.'

'This thing about the phones is already out there, no doubt.'

'Just relax, Pete; it's not the time to do anything rash.'

Stanley pushed his head back and glanced at the ceiling, sighing. 'You say that, but I need to end it.'

Messenger's anxiety increased. 'Peter, say nothing you will regret later. Take a few deep breaths and let's get on with running the country.'

'Yeah, thanks Bart.'

Messenger stepped away.

'Is that the end of the meeting?' Tilley asked.

Stanley looked at Tilley, then at the wall of ministers in their lounge chairs, all watching him with narrowed eyes.

The prime minister stood and coughed to clear his throat. 'I declare the leadership of the party open, and I ask the whips to prepare for nominations and an election if required.'

The politicians said nothing.

Harper turned to Hughes, who shrugged. The chief whip, Hayden Charlton, a no nonsense former military man, strode to the front of the room.

'Colleagues, the position of leader of the party, and therefore prime minister, is declared vacant. I am seeking nominations and I propose that self-nomination is in order.'

Messenger jumped to his feet. 'I nominate Peter Stanley.'

'Is the nomination seconded?'

Tilley stood and shouted, 'I second the nomination.'

'Any other nominations?'

The room fell silent as eyes searched for any sign of a challenger.

Harper stood: all eyes now on the former leader. 'I would like to nominate myself.'

'Is the nomination seconded?'

No hands went high. Charlton scanned about the room for a seconder. 'I need a seconder.'

The room was silent; no one dared move. It was a standoff. No one prepared to expose themselves. Harper doubting his action to nominate.

'I second the nomination,' Stanley said from behind the whip. A whispered reaction rushed through the room.

'Whips prepare a ballot,' Charlton said.

The whips sent a pager alert to announce a ballot for the leadership to government members who might have left the room. They also chased down the wooden ballot box and prepared yellow voting slips from the whips' office.

Messenger sidled over to Stanley and sat next to him, placing an empathetic hand on his arm. 'This is a brave thing to be doing, Pete; are you sure about it?'

'Oh look, at least we know who is doing the destabilisation.' Stanley looked over Messenger's shoulder to check Harper and who he was engaging to work on his numbers.

'But you could lose.'

'Then so be it. Don't worry, Bart, your position is safe.' Stanley picked up his phone and swiped a screen. 'Oh look, Rogers is already reporting the spill.'

'You're kidding.'

Stanley stood and addressed the many clumps of members in deep discussion. 'Just to advise you, colleagues. Hancock Media is already reporting the spill.' He smiled, as their attention was now towards him. 'One of you is being very treacherous.' He sat, and the members went back to their discussions.

After ten minutes, Charlton collected the ballots and went off with his team to count the votes. He returned five minutes later with the election result.

'Peter Stanley sixty-three, James Harper thirty-eight, with three abstentions. I declare Peter Stanley leader.'

Harper hurried to his feet. 'Colleagues, it was a very brave thing the leader did. He placed his faith in his colleagues, and they returned that faith with an excellent result. I will now ask that you rally around the leader and let's work hard to turn the polls around. I believe the decisions we have made today will do just that. Congratulations, Peter, and may we now focus on policy and not ourselves.'

Stanley scoffed and smiled at the comments before standing and addressing the room.

'Colleagues, we don't have long before we move into election mode, so let us focus on providing the policy leadership the electorate craves and let these quiet leadership rumblings end. We must stop the bullying and the badgering. We've made a decision, so now let's get on with it.'

As a group, members stood and filed out into the corridors. Those rushing always had a reason, usually to ingratiate themselves with media contacts. Others joked and laughed as if nothing had happened.

Harper and Hughes agreed to a coffee at Aussies after they left the party room, settling in with their lattes to discuss strategy.

'That went well, don't you think?' Harper scoffed.

'Gutsy thing to do, I must admit.'

'Who do you reckon was leaking?'

'Someone with two phones.' Hughes sipped his coffee and checked over his shoulder to see who was about. Clomping stiletto heels echoed through the tables.

'You have two phones.'

'That I do, Jimmy,' Hughes grinned. 'That I do.'

'It was you?'

'Let's put it this way. We primed him to be boned.'

'Even on those numbers?' Harper was sceptical.

'It means there is work to do, but you'll win next time. We'll get the numbers.'

'When do we start the new campaign?'

'On the weekend.' Hughes looked over his glass. 'You resign and speak out on policy issues that concern you. Important issues such as trade and foreign investment.'

'Resign?' Harper hadn't considered it.

'You want the job?'

'You know I do.'

'Then trust me.' Hughes replaced the finished glass to the saucer and smiled, gazing into Harper's eyes. 'You do trust me, don't you?'

CHAPTER TWENTY-SIX

The white commonwealth car glided to a stop outside Cochin restaurant in Richmond, an inner-city suburb of Melbourne and the hub of Vietnamese cuisine. Messenger lived over the West Gate Bridge in Williamstown and seldom came to the busy congested side of town, preferring to stay in his bayside village, but a deal was a deal, requiring dinner with Jaya Rukhmani, his university professor and now the independent member for Melbourne.

'Can we just get our timing right, Guy?' Messenger said to his assigned driver before getting out of the limousine. 'Let's just say I will be ready for you at nine-thirty, but if I'm not out by then, call me, and that will give me a reason to leave.'

'Rightio, sir.'

'Somehow, I suspect Ms Rukhmani may prefer a long evening, but I need to get away early.'

'I'll be here, sir.' Guy smiled as Messenger left the vehicle.

The hostess welcomed him as he stepped into the restaurant, confirming that his dinner guest was yet to arrive. She encouraged him to sit at the bar, allowing her to prepare a pre-dinner cocktail. He was a little miffed by Jaya's tardiness, so he ordered a vodka martini, a little dirty, to change his attitude. It was the perfect mix when he sipped it, and he complimented the hostess on her skills.

'What's your name?'

'Sonja.'

'Mine's Bart.' He formed his re-election smile. 'What's a European doing in a Vietnamese restaurant?'

'Good question,' Sonja said. 'My partner and I have lived in Vietnam and enjoyed the street vendors and market foods, so we wanted to bring that style and flavour to Melbourne… This is it.'

'Is your partner Vietnamese?'

'No, he's French.'

'Nice one, so what's your specialty?' Messenger took a bigger swig of his cocktail.

'We have shared plates with most things in French Asian style. We have a traditional chateaubriand. We cater for any taste. Our specialty this weekend is our crab and mussel feast. You should try it, you'll love it.'

'Messy?'

'We give you an apron and a finger bowl… even a hand bowl if you need it,' Sonja joked, as she moved onto another guest.

Messenger watched her go, admiring her tanned legs. He checked around the restaurant, which was half full; he relaxed when he recognised no one. The décor was a mixture, with beautiful framed photographic prints of Vietnamese rural regions and stunning statues. He smiled when he tuned into the background music; Charles Aznavour was singing a duet with Sir Elton John.

Messenger hummed along, even inserting a word or two at the appropriate time.

'Yesterday, when I was young, so many drinking songs played awaiting to be sung…'

He wondered how he could know such things, given he owned none of the music catalogue of either the Frenchman or the English piano player. He chuckled, self-conscious at his disrespect for the internationally acclaimed artists.

As he checked his watch, Messenger glimpsed Jaya pushing open the door, stopping the chitter-chat of guests. She had draped herself in a form-hugging red long-sleeved dress; the hem sitting just above the knee; the neckline plunged. With no jewellery, his professor wouldn't have been out of place at any high fashion event. He shook his head, finding it hard to believe she could transform into a stunning fashion statement. She identified Messenger, flicking her straightened hair backward over her shoulder, sashaying towards him.

'You look different.' Messenger got off his stool and held out his hand.

DOOMED

Jaya brushed it away and moved close for a hug. She stepped back and smiled, flicking her long hair again. 'I'm glad you came; this is my favourite restaurant.'

Messenger was yet to release his gaze from her black eyes.

'It's a little French and a little Vietnamese, and I love it,' she said, as she checked about then settled her glance back on Messenger. 'Do you want to stay at the bar for a drink or shall we sit?'

'I reckon sitting would be great.'

Sonja led them to a side table, away from the front door. Messenger pulled the table forward so Jaya could slip onto the bench seat with its red leather padding. He took the wooden rattan chair opposite. Jaya ordered champagne; Messenger asked for water.

'So, Treasurer, tell me, are we here as friends, or do we work?'

'What would you like to do?'

'I think we can do both, don't you?' She clasped her hands together, resting them against her face, gazing at the nervous man.

'Can I ask you a question?' Messenger thumbed his lip.

'Sure, shoot.' She sat back and flicked the white cloth napkin across her lap.

'Do you usually dress like this for dinner, or did you go the extra mile for me?'

'The extra mile for you?' She smiled, resting back on the bench. 'Interesting question.'

'I mean, are you trying to send a message? Because if you are, then I've got it.'

Jaya bristled a little, shifting in her seat. 'Not sure what you mean by that comment.'

Messenger blushed. 'I'm sorry, it's just that I never saw you...'

Jaya interrupted. 'As a woman?'

'Well, yes, quite frankly. You've been my professor, always wearing black clothes. And as a politician wearing boring suits, and now...?'

'Paris Hilton once said about fashion: the only rule is to be never boring, and dress cute wherever you go. I've decided life is way too short to be boring.'

'You look fabulous.'

'Why thank you, Treasurer,' Jaya said, raising her shoulder and tucking her face into it. 'The fact is, my life has been harsh, difficult, but at other times, rewarding. I kinda figure it's my time now.'

'Not sure many politicians look like you, Jaya,' Messenger said into the napkin as he straightened it, placing it over his lap as the drinks arrived.

'Here's cheers to you, Bart, my best student.' She held her glass for a toast. Messenger clinked the glass.

'That sounds creepy, doesn't it?'

'You were. No matter that you're almost my age.'

Messenger sat back, watching the confident woman before him. She was such a contrast from when they first met, when she had been a nervous politics lecturer.

'What do you think you'll have?' he said as he opened the menu.

'Do you want to share plates?'

'I'd rather do that than have the crab feast.'

Jaya smiled. 'Yes, too messy for me, especially in this thing.'

'It looks great.'

'I got the red because it really brings contrast to the black, don't you think?'

'Fabulous.' Messenger continued scanning the menu. 'Would you like a wine?'

'Yes, and why don't we have the nem nuong, the coconut chicken, and maybe the soft-shell crab?'

Messenger glanced up at the proficient server who had taken the notes. 'We'll have a bottle of the Kientzler Pinot Gris, please.'

The server nodded, took the menus, and left.

'So, what work do you want to talk about?' Messenger asked.

'Ah, you politicians are all the same. Work, work, bloody work.'

'I thought we should clear off any business, allowing us to respond honestly if they ever asked us about this dinner. We can tell the truth.'

Jaya laughed, staring into her champagne, then became a little more serious. 'I had a call from Brian Tucker today.'

'The farmer?'

Jaya nodded. 'He isn't pleased with your announcement.'

'The most generous relief package ever in our history, and he isn't happy?'

'He was expecting more from you. Not you per se,' Jaya corrected herself, 'but the government.'

'Farmers are never satisfied.' Messenger shook his head. 'What else could we have done?'

'He wants the banks to stop their push to close farms.'

'Was there much evidence they are?'

'This is the point. There is little evidence from anyone to suggest the banks are moving to foreclose. Tucker thinks the banks will move on him and he will lose his farm, which has been in his family for over a hundred years.'

Messenger studied Jaya, thinking through a response.

'He keeps ringing me; I can't get him to back off.'

'What's he been saying?' Messenger noticed her worried expression.

'Nothing nasty. I would expect nasty from a man in trouble with the drought.' Jaya looked about the restaurant. 'This chap is more annoying than that. He's dark; I think he might do something stupid if the bank moves on him.'

'We can only recommend; we can't stop them.'

Jaya stretched her arm to the table and picked up her champagne, taking a sip, then still holding the glass across her waist, said, 'I reckon this guy is in the twilight zone of trouble. Nothing I tell him will help.' She swallowed another mouthful, draining the glass. 'He just never gives up.'

Messenger could see her concern. 'Do you want me to talk to him?'

Jaya shook her head as a no, then glimpsed at him. 'Would you? That would be great if you could; it would help me.'

Messenger pulled out his phone, tapping in a note to call Tucker, then sent it to his personal assistant. 'Done.'

'Brilliant.' She flashed her teeth in a broad smile, wriggling forward to the table. 'Okay, now that we're done with the drought, what's next?'

'You realise we shouldn't be negotiating like this, don't you?'

'Oh, I don't know, Bart. There are a lot of other things we could talk about.'

Messenger felt a sudden flush thrust through him as she smiled and winked at him.

'What legislation have you got that needs to pass through without complaint from Meredith and her mob?'

'Meredith?' he asked, pleased to have a change of topic. 'Seems you might be on friendly terms with Madam Bruce?'

'She is the alternative prime minister, is she not?'

'She is likely to run a candidate in your seat.' Messenger smiled. 'No doubt you realise we will as well. All of which is likely to see your promising political career come to a thumping end. Unless of course you finish second in the primaries again.'

'That would be okay. No problems with me.' Jaya said, smiling. 'Honestly, this entire experience has been great. We can structure an additional stream of study at the university. I've already spoken to the dean, and it's likely we'll offer an applied politics stream within the curriculum.'

'Something to improve the standard of politicians coming into the game?'

'Exactly, and from what I've seen in your leadership group, I suspect Australia will do better once we have graduates coming through.' She laughed.

Messenger raised his eyebrows, turning down the corners of his mouth like an amateur De Niro. 'I'm surprised to hear that. We're doing a superb job.'

'You're my most enthusiastic student. The rest of your group need vitality. A solid rocket up their arse would help.'

'Sssshhh.' Messenger gulped in his surprise, peeking over his shoulder.

'Let's face it, Bart, the entire leadership thing the other day was a joke.'

'Why do you think it was a joke?' Messenger shifted in his chair. 'It was a strong result for the prime minister.'

'He called on a leadership spill for no reason, just to stop the leaks and quieten the media.'

'The result will do that.'

'I've always counselled you as a student to study history, in particular political history.'

'What does history tell you about the vote?'

'History says this is just the start of the leadership challenge. Your party will now be unstable until there is a change of leader.'

'He won easily.'

'Someone always toppled every leader in Australian politics who forced the first vote within six to twelve months,' Jaya smiled. 'Stanley will be gone soon. The question is… will you replace him?'

Messenger shrugged, shaking his head. 'No, I'll not be.'

'I reckon you would beat Hughes.'

'Hughes is not running; he is behind Harper.'

Jaya laughed. 'Yes, of course he is.'

Messenger couldn't help himself, laughing at the cynical observation and falling back in his chair as they served the food.

The politicians worked their way through a tasty meal, joking and laughing through their recollections of embarrassing moments between them at university, and sharing their observations of colleagues and other politicians with a maniacal approach towards ego. At one stage, Messenger was gasping for breath from his laughter as Jaya described the bumbling attempts of a mayor she had just met at a formal dinner; the man had squeezed her knee under the table, and her response was a good kick in the shins. The idea of someone groping his professor irritated Messenger, even though she laughed it off.

When they had almost finished another bottle and were settling into coffee, Jaya looked at Messenger, then asked, 'Bart, do you recall, I asked you about the Foreign Affairs Committee?'

'Vaguely.' He glanced away to check if there was anyone close.

'You said you would get me on as a member.'

'I asked Harper; he mentioned the prescribed numbers restricted him and it would need someone to come off the committee.'

'Needs the votes, you mean?' Jaya smirked.

'This is the problem with an independent member. They just don't get what they call for all the time.'

'I want to get onto that committee, and you have to help me.'

Messenger fell back into his chair, concerned with the tone of the conversation. 'Why do I need to do that?'

'Two reasons.'

'Oh yes, and what are they?'

'I'm concerned about the various rumblings in foreign policy towards India. I'm worried we're about to make decisions which will affect them.'

'I thought you were against the abuse of the student visas by Indians secretly wanting to enter Australia.'

'I am... very much so. But I'm more concerned with the free trade agreement and the debate surrounding coal mining.'

'There is no debate around coal mining.'

'That's not what I hear.'

Messenger cocked an eyebrow. 'What do you hear?'

'Coal is our highest export, yet most Australians hate it. I understand the government is about to make an announcement.'

'What announcement?' Messenger asked, a finger trailing along his chin.

'Not sure, but it may affect India's power supply, and that concerns me.'

Messenger didn't reply, just rubbing the tips of his fingers under his lip against new beard growth. 'I'm not confident this is true; can you quote a source?'

'The embassy.'

This response bothered Messenger as he speculated why she was privy to embassy briefings. If the Indians were worried, then perhaps he should be. He had heard nothing from the prime minister, or even from Harper.

'I'll talk to Harper again on Monday and try to get you on. You know, of course, that what you hear on that committee can't go anywhere?'

'What?' Jaya grinned. 'You think I'm a spy?'

Messenger blushed. 'I know it goes without saying, but politicians need reassurance all the time.'

'I can reassure you, Barton Messenger,' Jaya leaned forward, 'you can trust me.'

He shifted and searched for Sonja to bring the bill. Once they had completed the account settlement, they stood outside to say goodbye.

Jaya held out her hand and Messenger took it, leaning in for the obligatory kiss on the cheek. Jaya leaned against him as he kissed her soft face, breathing her in before pulling away.

Still holding her hand, he asked, 'How are you getting home? Did you book a car?'

Jaya pulled back from him, as if in retreat, dropping his hand. 'I came by tram, so I'm jumping on the next one at the stop just down the road.'

'Tram?' Messenger tugged at his ear. 'At this time?'
'No issue; it's safe.'
'Yeah, nah. I'm taking you home.' He tugged open the back door of the waiting limousine. 'Hop in and let's go.'
Jaya didn't hesitate, cupping his face with her fingers as she brushed past and sliding into the soft leather seat, but only halfway. She jerked her seat belt, clipping it in as Messenger got in, surprised to feel her so close.
'Thanks for dinner. It was lovely,' he said, as he clipped his seatbelt. 'Excellent suggestion. Actually, it wasn't a suggestion, more like an instruction.'
Jaya grabbed the back of his hand resting on his thigh and threaded her fingers through his. 'It wasn't what I expected.'
Messenger fisted his hand, squeezing her fingers, and smiled. 'Nor I.'
Jaya returned his smile, turning away to watch the passing traffic. Their hands didn't move for the fifteen-minute journey to her apartment on the corner of Rathdowne and Queensbury Streets, opposite the heritage listed Exhibition Building.
As the car stopped in the driveway, Messenger unclipped his seatbelt, opened the door, and assisted Jaya from the car. He was up against the open door as she came out and she gazed at him, smiled, and then placed a hand on his chest above his heart.
'Thanks for a wonderful evening, Barton.'
Messenger smiled, feeling the need to kiss her. She responded, and he wrapped her in an embrace, feeling her softness against him.
After a few moments, she stepped back. 'Do you want to come upstairs?'
He didn't respond, then began gnawing his bottom lip as if in turmoil. 'Yes, but no.'
'I understand.'
'It's nothing to do with you or me, nor politics for that matter.'
Jaya shook her head, as if considering his dilemma. 'We know each other. There've been sparks since we first met, but I understand.'
'Do you? I don't think you do.'
'Tell me then.'
Messenger couldn't say anything.
'I get it; wrong colour.'

Messenger responded. 'That's not it. Don't be stupid.'

'Then what?'

Messenger fumbled with his lip, gnawing again, before saying, 'It's respect.'

'Respect?'

'Yes, I respect you too much.'

'Isn't that my decision?'

'I guess it is, but I would like you to think about the implications if we did.'

Jaya leaned back, considering him down her nose for a moment, then smiled. 'You are one crazy politician, Barton, that's for damn sure. When I decide in the clear light of day without the haze of alcohol and the allure of romance, I'll let you know.' She moved forward and pecked him. Before he could respond, she placed a finger on his lips. 'Good night, handsome.'

Messenger watched her go. When she was inside, he slid back into the back seat.

'She's a nice one, that one, Minister.'

'That she is Guy, that she is.'

Messenger showered when he arrived home. He plonked himself onto a leather couch, watching CNN and sipping on a whiskey, thinking about the complications of getting involved with the independent member for Melbourne.

A sudden, unexpected knock on the front door startled him. He checked his phone for the time. Early morning visits only meant serious business for politicians, so he wrapped his silk robe tighter, padding along the wooden floorboards to answer the persistent knock.

He was gob smacked to greet Jaya standing before him in a white trench coat.

'I thought about what you said, and I made a decision,' Jaya said, unbuttoning her coat. 'I respect the fact you respect me.' She bit her pillar-box red bottom lip as she smiled, dropped her hands into her pockets and waved open her coat. 'But if you are going to respect me, you may as well respect all of me.'

Nothing but her red stilettos were under the coat.

CHAPTER TWENTY-SEVEN

The queue at the front entrance of Parliament House was long and slow, stalled by the need to pass security. It was early, well before the tourist rush. Garrick Higgins found himself behind other lobbyists and trade union members he knew. The minister for mines, Ginni Stavloukas, agreed to meet the union delegates to discuss various labour issues within the industry; in particular, coal mines in the Galilee Basin in Queensland. Three colleagues joined Higgins for the meeting. They were keen to make sure that the government supported employing his members rather than increasing the employment of 457-visas workers, which was now growing in the mining industry, especially at offshore sites.

The delegation was yet to enter the security process and stood looking out across the vast forecourt. Down the hill was the old parliament. The view progressed to the war memorial.

'It's a marvellous view, isn't it, Higgo?' a colleague commented.

'It is, comrade, but I'm sure it loses its significance for the folks who work in here. My dad Ralph would have said they are all a bunch of self-interested morons.'

After another twenty minutes, the delegation made it to the security room. They placed shoes, belts, hats, jewellery, phones, bags, and folders on the conveyor belt to be scrutinised. Each visitor then waited to cross through the metal detector, hoping the buzzer didn't beep for further scrutiny. Once through, they collected their things, donning their items before stepping out into the grand marble foyer of the parliament.

Once Higgins signed in his colleagues, he led them off to the minister's office, the whole exercise taking fifty-seven minutes since their arrival by taxi. They headed to the House of Representatives' side of the lobby, progressing through another security door, and entering onto a jarrah floor that echoed from their steps. The delegation took in the displayed artworks, and when they reached the Members' Hall at the centre of the building, they stood for a few moments gazing up into the atrium and the flag mast.

They circled the portraits of former prime ministers, stopping by the portrait of Julia Gillard, the first woman to be elected to lead the country. Higgins checked his watch and led them off for the 10 a.m. appointment with the minister. Staff directed the delegation to wait a few moments before being led into a small meeting room, which had a metal water jug and glasses in the centre of the table. Higgins poured water as they settled in to wait.

'Sorry to have kept you waiting, gentlemen,' Minister Stavloukas said as she strode into the room ten minutes later, taking a position at the head of the table, near the door. 'I have been looking forward to meeting you and discussing the issues with you.'

Higgins smirked like a boxer at the start of round one. 'What issues might they be, Minister?'

Stavloukas dropped her smile and leaned forward, realising that this might not be a friendly visit. 'I suspect you want reassurance from the government about the use of 457s being restricted to the Timor Sea.'

'The only issue we have with the Timor Sea is the extension of the policy to the mainland. In particular, the new Kirkpatrick mine in Queensland.'

'The Indians want to use local labour if they can,' Stavloukas said. 'They have advised the government that we can expect twenty-five hundred of your members to be hired.'

This news impressed Higgins. 'So, when you say my members, this will be a union site?'

Stavloukas laughed. 'No, sorry, I misspoke. I meant Australians to be employed, sorry.'

'This comment saddens me. I would have thought the government would be keen to make sure reliable labour with little industrial conflict.'

Stavloukas tilted her head. 'You think there will be industrial action?'

'There always is on sites we cannot control.'

'By control you mean what, exactly?'

'Safety for starters. We don't have confidence that labour hire firms will provide a safe worksite. We can.'

'Safety?' the minister scoffed.

'You have a problem with safety, Minister?'

'I have a problem when the union movement uses safety as a disguise to increase wages and conditions, having already signed off on an agreement.'

This time it was Higgins who scoffed. 'That's a typical response from someone who doesn't understand the complexity and conditions on an industrial site.'

The minister bristled at the feedback. 'By typical, you mean a woman. Why wouldn't a woman know what it's like on an industrial site?'

'It wouldn't matter if you were a woman or a man, or a friggin' gender bender. You do not appreciate what it's like to work on a construction site, and the conditions my members have to work.'

'How many women do you have as members?'

Higgins frowned as his face winced. 'What?'

'How many women work in the mining sector and how many are in your union?'

'You must know there are around a hundred and twenty thousand people working in the industry, and around seventeen thousand are chicks.'

'Chicks?' Stavloukas asked.

'You know what I mean,' Higgins said.

'Yes, I know what you mean,' Stavloukas said through gritted teeth. 'Your misogyny is typical and awash throughout the sector.'

Higgins turned to query his colleagues. They shrugged or shook a head. 'Are you feeling all right, Minister?'

'Why? Should I not feel alright?' Stavloukas said, now breathing deep, seeming enraged, as if the discussion had slighted her. Her fingers clenched, then unclenched, then clenched again. 'Why should a woman not be okay in your presence?'

Higgins glanced at her adviser for help, but he remained indifferent.

'Minister, rather than talk about this sudden rush of aggressive feminism, I have come to meet with you to talk about jobs. We want to get an assurance that you will approve the Kirkpatrick mine, and you and the government will deliver jobs for Australians, as promised.'

'What?' She seemed dazed.

'Minister, I'm a little uncomfortable with this meeting.' Higgins glanced at the ministerial adviser, who shrugged; he then paused for a moment, twirling his thumbs. 'We are here to receive your reassurance that 457s will not be used at the Kirkpatrick mine, and the mine will begin operations, as announced by you and the government.'

The minister wiped her mouth as she gathered herself, then smiled. 'Of course, the mine will go ahead as planned, and yes, there will be no 457s offered whilst I am minister.'

'Then let me reassure you, Minister; my union will support you.' Higgins moved to stand, and as he straightened, he paused, leaning in on his hands to face her. 'If you don't do what you promised here today, then you'll have more to worry about than workplace safety.'

Stavloukas waved him away and the delegation left.

As they assembled outside the office, they paused to review the meeting.

'How weird was that?'

Higgins scratched his head. 'That's the first time anything like that has happened to me.'

'Can we believe her, comrade?'

'I recorded her.' Higgins tapped a pocket of his jacket. 'I suppose if she ever denies saying it, we can call her a liar and end her career.'

'That wouldn't stop her from shutting the mine down though, would it?'

'Comrade, they won't shut the mine down; India is too important to them.'

CHAPTER TWENTY-EIGHT

'Thank you for coming. I wish to make an announcement before taking questions.' James Harper fiddled with papers as he waited for latecomers to the media conference to settle. 'Determining the leadership of our party is never easy. I understand many people would question the stability of the government considering the constant uncertainty of who is best placed to lead the country.

'It would be silly to ignore the discontent within the community regarding the leadership and policy direction of the country. Although I supported a ballot for a leadership change, and was a candidate, the cold hard facts are that I lost the ballot. I'm therefore forced to review my position.

'It is vital the government improves and carries out policies that reflect the needs of the community. I am not sure we can continue with our current direction, which may deliver Meredith Bruce as prime minister, and that will be a complete disaster.'

Christopher Hughes smiled as he watched his office television with his advisor, Con Krakos, taking notes beside him.

'I think our boy is doing very well.' Hughes chortled as he leaned his head on his hand, elbow resting on the wooden arm of a visitor's chair.

Krakos smirked, perched like a giant Komodo considering its prey.

'It's an impressive speech, Con, well done.'

'A good start, but he hasn't finished yet.'

'Whilst I lost the ballot, I still believe I am the best person for the job of leading Australia. Therefore, out of respect for the prime minister, I have advised him I can no longer serve as his foreign minister. Twenty minutes ago, I tendered my resignation.' Harper finished reading. 'I am happy to take questions.'

Cassandra Rogers was first to her feet and called to Harper. He responded by nodding for her to ask a question, his anxiety increasing as Cass read her notes.

'Mr Harper, are you still doing the numbers for a second challenge?'

Harper demurred, shaking his head. 'I need to continue to consult with my colleagues. We need to talk about options to defeat Meredith Bruce at the next election.'

'Do you think you're in the best position to make sure that happens?'

'Yes, I do.'

'Are you working the phones?'

'Of course, I am. I'm speaking to colleagues about many issues that concern them and their electorates.'

'That's a brave thing for him to say.' Krakos sneered. 'But brilliant for us.'

'It also means the media will either bash him or promote him, so I'd better increase the leaks.' Hughes stroked his chin and jaw, thinking through strategy. 'I just need to be careful with what and how I leak.'

'Why not set someone up?'

'A colleague?'

Hughes looked at Krakos, who nodded confirmation.

'Who do we need to put to the sword?'

Krakos thought through an answer, his head back and gazing at the ceiling. 'I think we need to shaft an ambitious pain in the arse… so why not the mad Greek?'

'Which one? You're all mad.'

Krakos laughed at the joke, before saying in a high-pitched voice. 'I'm offended.'

'Oh, you mean Stavloukas?' Hughes licked his bottom lip as he glanced back at the ceiling. He did not consider her a threat to his ambition. 'You don't think we should do Messenger?'

'Messenger needs to stay clean. The Greek is such a moron and creates too much trouble with her equality crap.'

'What? You think providing equality amongst the genders is crap?'

'I do,' Krakos said.

'Then why are we pushing this gender pay gap thing?'

'Votes.'

Hughes shook his head. 'You are a devious bastard, aren't you?'

'I'm not here for your thanks Minister; just remember that.'

Hughes felt a little uncomfortable with the conversation, standing, then moving to his desk.

'We have issues for which this government needs to provide leadership. Issues like the environment and the uncertainty for investment, with us dragging our tail on climate change. Our mining industry needs certainty for the many Australians employed within it. We have power prices skyrocketing, yet the government seems incapable of leading in policy or ideas to bring relief to working families.

'As we have done with food, my plan is that we can offer relief by taking the GST off all transactions within the power industry. This will mean the consumer will have an immediate reduction in their power bill of around ten dollars a week. This can make a difference to household budgets. It could be the difference for older Australians turning on the lights, the heater, or indeed cooking food.' Harper gazed out to the calling media, nodding to another journalist to ask another question.

'Mr Harper, what is your view of the Kirkpatrick coal mine? Should the government push ahead to approve it, against the loud voices of the community seeking a ban on all coal exports?'

'This is an interesting question. On the one hand, we have loud folks with a superior living standard demanding the government ban coal exports to nations such as India; and we have the citizens of India needing to have power so they can see in their shanties or their dingy rooms after dark. They need to feed themselves with the electricity coal can produce. To have refrigeration, to have power so their community can prosper in the future, like our economy has done in the past.

'I favour providing India coal energy, so they can raise their standard of living, and by doing so, reduce the carbon footprint from their use of wood and biomass. Who are we to deny others in the world what we have?'

Cass took notes, admiring Harper's courage for speaking out.

Harper eyed the cameras. 'Let me be very clear. I believe in climate change, but I am an adaptationist, not an abolitionist. I will not tremble before social media, because I know that raising living standards in the developing world will do more to reduce atmospheric carbon than banning coal exports or placing a tax on carbon. So, to be clear… I support the Kirkpatrick mine.'

'That's perfect,' said Krakos, slapping the arm of his chair.

'Such a devious political operator,' said Hughes as he dragged a bottle of whiskey from his bottom drawer. With it, two tumblers. 'Want a splash?'

Krakos glanced over. 'Yeah, why not?'

Hughes twisted the wax-covered cork from the distinctive black bottle and splashed handsome portions into the tumblers as Krakos joined him at his desk.

'Harper has done very well for us today.'

'Yes, he has,' Krakos said, twirling the deep copper liquid about the tumbler and sniffing in its aroma. 'This smells sweet; what is it?'

'It's from Queensland, up north. It's a single malt. I think it's a single barrel as well. Costs a damn fortune; they presented me with a case when I visited the company about twelve months ago.'

'What's a fortune?'

Hughes sniffed his tumbler, waiting a moment before responding, 'A little over five hundred a bottle.'

The look of amused shock on Krakos' face prompted Hughes to chuckle.

'Did you declare it?'

'I declared the case of whiskey, but not the price. They have a cheaper version, so I left it up to the department to figure it out.'

'Could be dangerous if it gets out.'

'Con, if it gets out, then I will know who opened the gate.' Hughes wasn't subtle with his glare at his staffer. He took a sip and flushed it over his tongue, enjoying the vanilla aftertaste.

Krakos knocked off his draught in one mouthful, keen to get moving.

'Geez, that's got a kick to it,' he said as he slid the glass back across the desk. 'What's it called?'

'Well,' Hughes scoffed. 'That's its problem.' He lugged the bottle from the drawer, showing the image of a big black rooster on the label. 'Let's put it this way; it's not called Big Black Rooster.'

'They can't do that.'

'Yeah, they can do whatever they want if folks want to pay a fortune for a bottle.'

'A tad racist, I would have thought.'

'Maybe, but once you've had the black, you don't go back.' Hughes took another sip.

Krakos stepped off. 'Be careful with your language, Minister.'

Hughes waved him away. 'It's called black, for heaven's sake.'

'Doesn't matter,' Krakos warned with a sharp expression. 'You can't say things like that anymore.'

Hughes watched him go. 'Just get me something we can use on the Greek.'

'I'll check the files we have on Harper.'

'Not Stanley?'

'Nah, he's already gone. We need to work on Harper.'

Hughes smiled into his tumbler as Krakos left the office. 'Devious little bastard.'

CHAPTER TWENTY-NINE

As James Harper left the media conference, striding to his office to help with the relocation from the ministerial wing, Cassandra Rogers ran to catch up, then broke into a brisk pace with him.

'Jim, just between you and me,' she smiled, trying her luck, 'when do you think the next challenge will be?'

The question miffed Harper. 'I have always served at the privilege of my peers, so the party room will decide if there will be another challenge, not me.' He stepped out quicker.

Cass almost lost her bag as she tried to keep up, swinging it back on her shoulder. 'Just one last question. Did you leak to the media during the last election?'

Harper stopped, catching Cass off guard. 'What are you saying?'

'I have a source who tells me you may have leaked against the leader during the election campaign three years ago.'

'That's a ridiculous suggestion. Who said that?'

Cass was out of breath, sucking in deep before responding, 'You know I can't tell you that, but I know you did.'

Harper glanced around to see if ears were nearby. 'What do you want?'

'I need to know if you are going to challenge. If you do, I prefer to know when?'

Harper glared into her eyes. 'I will run again, and you'll be the first to know.'

'That's all I wanted to know; thank you.'

Harper waited a moment, still engaging his killer stare, then turned, marching off.

Cass took out her phone and pinged a message to Christopher Hughes.

> **Thank U. Harper just confirmed**
> **Dinner?**

Cass crossed her legs as she leaned against a wall and thought about an answer.

> **Rain Check**
> **Always welcome. Bring your togs.**

'Not likely, Mr Hughes,' she said, dropping her phone back into her pocket and setting off to Aussies for a coffee.

Her red Doc Martens didn't clomp on the wooden floor in the way most other shoes did. Cass saw Jaya Rukhmani sitting by herself at a window and approached her to ask her about the Harper resignation.

'Hi Jaya,' Cass smiled as Jaya glanced up. 'Can I join you?'

Jaya darted her eyes about, as this was the first time the journalist had ever approached her. 'Ah, sure. I'm just checking Hansard for a recent meeting.'

'The drought committee?'

'Yes, as it happens,' Jaya said, concerned that she was not across something.

'Would you like another coffee?' asked Cass as she placed her bag on the chair opposite.

'Thank you; you're so kind. A latte, please.'

'Won't be long.'

Jaya watched her go and when she entered the café, texted Barton Messenger.

> **Rogers wants a coffee. What does she want?**

It was a few moments before Messenger responded.

> **Relax. Stop worrying.**
> **Not sure I should have come over.**
> **Too late now. Relax.**
> **What can I say if she raises it?**
> **She won't, no one knows, relax.**

Jaya dropped the phone onto her pile of papers as Cass arrived with the coffees.

'It's nice of you to catch up. I've been meaning to drop by for a while now; how are you enjoying it?'

'It took a while to get used to the place.' Jaya nodded a thank you as she dragged the coffee towards her. 'So much rubbish, but then, fantastic policy work.'

'What have you been working on?' Cass asked as she dipped a half teaspoon of sugar into her glass and stirred. 'How is the drought inquiry going?'

'The government has stuffed the entire thing.' Jaya took a sip of coffee. 'They made the announcement last week and we are yet to report. They hit a few key spots, but there is nothing to bring the banks to heel.'

'Surely the money will be good for the farmers?'

'It is, but it's useless if the banks foreclose.'

'Do you have evidence of banks' foreclosing?'

'I have one farmer in particular who is very concerned.' Jaya took another sip of coffee and glanced out into the sunny courtyard. 'He keeps calling me, trying to get me to stop the bank from foreclosing, but I can't do a thing. I mentioned it to the treasurer. He said he will try to get an outcome.'

'And has he?'

'Not that he has mentioned.'

'How often do you talk to him?'

'The farmer rings my office almost every day.'

'No, I meant the treasurer.'

Jaya froze, not wanting to give any sign to Cass.

'What's wrong?'

'Why would you ask me a question like that?' She was a little flummoxed, shifting in her chair. 'I only get to see him in question time, so I talk to him then.'

Cass suspected there was more to the response than what she had just heard, but let it slide to be queried later when she talked to Hughes again.

'What do you think of the Harper resignation?'

'The only view I have is that he is supportive of the Kirkpatrick mine, which is a good thing.'

'You don't care about the environment?'

The aggressive question had Jaya squirming. 'Of course, I do,' she took another sip of coffee, 'but I'm conscious the developing world needs power to increase living standards, and by denying it to them we are making a shameless judgement upon them.'

'Interesting perspective.'

'Don't get me wrong, climate change is real but to respond by denying a power source to others is just wrong.'

'Will you support Harper if he challenges Stanley and becomes prime minister?'

'In my view, one's as bad as the other.'

'Then why not support the opposition?'

Jaya finished her coffee before responding. 'I'm what you call a rare bird in this political cesspit. I keep my word. I promised to support the government. Who their leader is doesn't matter, so long as they keep their promises.'

'If they change their promises, you will reconsider?'

'Let's put it this way... if they continue to keep their promises, they have my vote.'

'What should they be doing right now?'

'Getting the banks off the farmers' backs should be a priority.'

Cass drained her coffee, then lifted her bag from the floor, moving to rise from the table. 'Thanks for talking to me. Is there anything else you would like to add?'

Jaya looked quizzical before shaking her head. 'No. Thanks for the coffee; it was nice meeting you.'

Cass nodded and moved off. She slipped her hand into her bag and turned off the recording device, mumbling, 'She needs to learn about media protocols, poor thing.'

CHAPTER THIRTY

The prime minister was almost asleep; the papers he was reviewing had already slid to the floor, his head had fallen back, and his mouth dangled open. If he had been on his leather couch, he would be snoring, but he was resisting stretching out and preferred a quick nap. It happened more often these days, after four in the afternoon, usually after a rigorous question time.

A staffer entered and cleared her throat. The prime minister's neck jarred as he regained consciousness. It was sore from the prolonged strain.

'Mr Hughes is here to see you, Prime Minister.'

'Show him in.' Stanley collected himself, picking up his papers and returning to his desk, then flicking the television remote on to hear the five o'clock news headlines. He ignored Hughes, walking to the sideboard, and pouring himself a whiskey before turning and offering one to his colleague, who nodded as the distinct music of the news report began introducing the headlines.

'Foreign Minister James Harper resigns, causing panic in the government as a renewed leadership challenge is expected as early as this week,' a male voice announced. 'Gang violence extends to the Sydney CBD. Aged Care costs increase, forcing many pensioners out onto the street. The Health Department has recorded harmful exposure to lead in Brisbane primary schools, and the Socceroos qualify for the World Cup. This is National One News with Sylvia Burns.'

'Good afternoon. Foreign minister James Harper has challenged the prime minister's authority by resigning today and announcing he his plans for a better government. This follows last week's leadership spill when the prime minister won a party room vote. Reporting from parliament house is Hancock Media's chief political editor, Cassandra Rogers.'

Cass was standing in the forecourt of the parliament

'In what we can only describe as chaos within government, James Harper, the former leader, resigned his commission as foreign minister, and by doing so declared he was a candidate for any future leadership challenge.'

Stanley stretched for the remote and muted the television, then lay back in his leather chair, rocking it. He picked up his crystal tumbler, washing a sip of whiskey over his tongue, squinting as he swallowed the burn.

'Has he got the numbers?' he asked Hughes.

'I wouldn't have thought so, but he will work on it.'

'Slimy bastard.'

'Pete, Jimmy is only reacting to the polls.'

'They aren't that bad.'

Hughes took a quaff of whiskey before answering, leaning back in his seat, and putting a foot on the vacant chair next to him. 'We lost the last twenty-five, so they aren't great.'

'I'm still well ahead in the preferred prime minister figures.'

'It's the primary vote that is worrying us; it's still below thirty-five.'

'It'll come back once we get closer to an election.'

Hughes didn't respond as he eyed his friend.

'I need something that gets us back,' Stanley said.

'I thought that was the plan with the drought relief?'

'Never satisfied.' Stanley drained his glass. 'It doesn't rain; they complain. It rains too much; they complain about flooding. They complain about the dollar, they complain about free trade, they complain about the banks…'

'They may have a point about the banks.'

'Yeah, no they don't. They just over capitalise and don't put money away for rainy days.' Hughes scoffed at his pun. 'They complain about every-damn-thing. Never satisfied.'

'Well, the drought has got the greenies going, linking it to climate change.'

'Weather has nothing to do with climate change.'

'You know that; I know that... most scientists know that; but the great unwashed don't and they think it's our fault.'

Stanley walked over to the sideboard and brought his Chivas Regal bottle back, pouring another handsome dram into his glass and offering another splash to Hughes, who sat forward proffering his glass.

'Where do you reckon Rogers is getting her information?' Stanley was peering at the silent television, watching her complete her report.

'Beats me.' Hughes tried hard to suppress a smile.

The prime minister gazed at the ceiling, his head resting on the chair. 'Someone's got it in for me, and I don't think it's Jim,' he said, letting out a sigh.

Hughes changed position in his chair. 'What does Messenger have to say?'

'He can't identify who it might be and tells me not much is happening.'

'Well, he could be right, but I wouldn't trust him if I were you.'

'I don't; believe me. But I don't think he can do any damage.'

'Then, if it's not Jimmy, and Messenger reckons nothing is going on, who could it be?'

'Oh, look, it could be anyone in the cabinet harbouring a death wish to help Jim. Maybe they assume he can do a better job.'

Hughes sipped his drink and waited for a moment.

'I think you should get tougher.'

'In what way?'

'Start making decisions. You know what to do, so do it.'

'I seek consensus; that's my style.'

'It's killing your leadership, Pete, and the media are arcing up. Just look at Rogers and her stories against you.'

'She promised me not to run the story about Alison, but it still got out.'

'You think someone who knows about her leaked it?'

'Maybe, but I don't understand why.'

'Look, Pete, we need to get on the front foot. We need a big splash announcement, and we need it within a few days, before the end of this sitting week if we can.'

'Like what?'

'Do something in foreign affairs, challenging Jimmy's poor handing of the portfolio.'

Stanley shook his head, smirking a face of frustration. 'Like what?'

'I don't know, but if it was me, I'd be looking to dump on foreign affairs to the get the red necks on side. Then do more on the environment to get the liberals kicking your way.' Hughes knew what the prime minister should do, hoping he could lead him there.

'The drought package didn't get the leverage we were hoping,' Stanley said.

'Politics is all about timing; maybe we went too early.'

'Yeah, thanks for that.'

'Mate, it was your idea.'

Stanley smiled, then took another generous swallow of the whiskey. 'Perhaps we should have waited for Messenger's girl to table her committee's report.'

'No, you did the right thing. You were decisive.'

'Yeah, but Rogers killed it reporting that it was a smokescreen for my leadership troubles.'

'Just think about doing something big,' Hughes encouraged him. 'What does Stavloukas have to say about the unions?'

'I took a call from the ACTU after question time, abusing me over a meeting she had with the mining union.'

'What did they say?'

'They said she was crazy, demanding more female participation in the sector.'

'She's been going on about that a lot.' Hughes shoved the knife in her back, then twisted it. 'Maybe she has an agenda for the leadership?'

'She wouldn't have any numbers.' Stanley stifled a yawn. 'She may say all the right things, and the girls might love her, but when the crunch comes, she hasn't got the numbers.'

'She does if she takes you out of the mix; the leaks must come from somewhere.'

Stanley studied Hughes for a moment. 'What do you think I should do?'

'Take them all on, the entire negative nellies we have in the party room. Take them on.' Hughes delivered the advice with a fist shake. 'Make decisions. Be assertive. Show them you're the boss.'

'It's supposed to be collegiate.'

'Bugger that, Pete.' Hughes finished his whiskey, managing its burn. 'Lead on the climate. Lead on immigration. Lead on mining. Set the policy debate for the next election. You are the prime minister, so make your own decisions. We will back you.' Hughes knew very well the party room would revolt if Stanley started making policy on the run.

A staffer came into the room, motioning to the prime minister, who acknowledged the gesture with a nod.

'I have to go, but as always I appreciate your counsel.'

'Prime Minister,' Hughes stood and bowed, with a cheesy smile, 'I am your humble servant.'

As his colleague left the office, Stanley reflected on his friend's comments, suspecting there was a touch of self interest in the advice he provided. There always was with Christopher.

CHAPTER THIRTY-ONE

The warmth of the kitchen at Yarralumla was never stifling but always cosy no matter the season. They redeveloped it to former Prime Minister Gerrard's specifications after he banished the governor general to a much smaller residence in an obscure Canberra suburb. The enormous kitchen catered for banquets and other events the former prime minister hosted to honour visiting dignitaries.

Gerrard had a penchant for spending government funds on himself, with the wine cellar full of vintage wines, a fromagerie for his taste in French cheese, and an instruction that all food, including bakery and pastries, was to be prepared daily.

It did not surprise Stanley when his house staff explained the many details of Gerrard's extravagance; he was yet to partake in any of the grandeur himself, although he invited his cabinet to dinner every month, and backbench members to a social event twice a year. He still preferred his bowl of cereal with a cup of tea early each morning at the stone kitchen bench, enjoying the cosiness.

'Come in, Bart. Do you want a cup of tea?'

Messenger responded to the prime minister's invitation for an early morning meeting, strolling into the kitchen after being directed by the housekeeper.

'No, I'm good.'

'Thanks for dropping by; have you seen the Hancock media this morning?'

'I've taken a call on it, but I'm yet to read it.'

'Why would your mate be getting stuck into us like that?'

Messenger thought about a response, keen to defuse any link to Jaya.

'First, she's not my mate; and second, I reckon this is a hatchet job by Rogers.'

'The headline is brutal.' The prime minister slid his copy of the paper across the bench. 'It's an attack against me.'

Messenger stopped the paper, spinning it to read the headline: Banks to Ruin Farmers. He then opened it out and looked at the second and third stories, which had similar headlines criticising the government.

'She's implicated you,' Stanley said.

Messenger glanced up, querying with his hands. 'What has she said?'

'Rukhmani is quoted as saying she has asked you to intervene, and neither she, nor the farmer in question, has heard from you. Is that true?'

'It's on my list.'

'Rogers then links this to leadership and Harper's comments about doing more for communities hit by the drought. Which is ironic, given we just announced a huge compensation package.'

'What's this story about India?'

'Another leadership swipe.' Stanley took a sip of tea. 'Harper supports the Kirkpatrick, and Rukhmani has linked the lack of government approval for the mine to an attack on the living standards in India. I thought she had renounced her citizenship rights?'

'She has, but this issue is a concern for her community in Melbourne.'

'She says, the leadership group… meaning you and me, are wasting time and we must act to offer certainty to the industry. She says we are discriminating against the Indians.'

'The rednecks will love that.'

'We can't be bullied into approving the mine because the Indians need to power their lifestyle.'

'Pete, you need to calm down on this.' Messenger now concerned about Stanley's increasing anxiety. 'We must frame these articles as a commentary on the leadership.'

'Christopher reckons Stavloukas is driving it.'

'She doesn't have the political smarts to organise this. It's someone else.'

'From within the party, or outside?'

'It wouldn't surprise me if it's both.'

'Harper obviously. Maybe Stavloukas is his helper.'

DOOMED

'I think you're jumping at shadows.'

Stanley took another sip of tea, then another. 'Stavloukas rang me last night asking for the foreign minister's job.'

Messenger choked a response. 'You're kidding?'

'She threatened me, saying it was time for a woman to be promoted to the role. It's been too long, she said.' Stanley smiled.

Messenger shook his head, thinking through the information. 'We need to have a circuit breaker. Make an announcement of some sort.'

'That's what Hughesie suggested. What would you recommend?'

'Forget the Indians and foreign workers; that'll blow over. We are still weak with women, as Stavloukas suggests, so maybe a statement about domestic violence or more money for women researchers.'

'Such a cynical thing to do.'

'Climate change just keeps hanging around.' Messenger steepled his fingers in front of his face, resting his chin on his thumbs as he thought through options.

'And yet the more we do, the more the public wants. They just don't understand the issues,' Stanley said, pouring himself another cup from the Wedgwood pot. He splashed a touch of milk from a small jug, dropped in a half teaspoon of sugar, then stirred. 'Maybe we should revisit the drought.'

'We haven't got the money.'

The politicians sat on their wooden stools for a while, talking strategy. Messenger read an article by Rogers claiming Rukhmani would switch her vote to the opposition if government did not keep its promises.

'This piece on Jaya has been over the top. She has never mentioned to me supporting Meredith Bruce. This balance of power thing is now coming into leadership calculations.'

'I won the ballot last week, for Christ's sake.'

CHAPTER THIRTY-TWO

The purpose-built television studios in the Canberra press gallery were small, with little room for more than two people, a production assistant and an interviewee. Cassandra Rogers was waiting to be introduced by the national breakfast morning show team, based in Hancock Media's Channel One Melbourne studios, to report on politics. Her phone buzzed.

The caller ID identified the number as that of Tony Hancock. She thought about whether she had enough time.

'Hello, Cass Rogers.'

'Cassie, it's Tony.'

'I'm just about to go to air, so be quick.'

'Congratulations on your pieces in the press this morning. Well done.'

'Good enough to get the gig you promised?'

'You're getting there, but I need more.'

Cass's voice rose. 'What do you mean, you need more?'

'I need Stanley gone.'

'That's not up to me.'

'It is now. If you facilitate it, I guarantee the seat is yours.'

Cass switched her phone to record.

'Are you there?' Hancock asked.

'Yes, I was just thinking about what you told me. If I get rid of Stanley, I get the show.'

'Virtually.'

'So, not yes?'

'Look, go on air, but if Stanley goes, then you take the gig.'

'Why the sudden pressure?'

'He's stuffing around with my appointment as consulate.'

'Who promised you, Harper or Hughes?'

'Stanley has, but he's yet to sign off on it. A metaphor for his government's inaction on everything. You nailed it in this morning's paper.'

'Who do the Mercantiles want as prime minister?'

'It doesn't matter; Stanley has to go.'

'I have to go, but I'm onto it.' Cass switched off her phone, then focused on her notes, waiting to be counted into the broadcast.

The voice of a presenter came through her headphones. 'We now cross to our political editor, Cassandra Rogers. Good morning, Cass. What's happening in Canberra? Is the prime minister safe?'

'Good morning, Donnie. I can tell you Prime Minister Stanley's position is unclear and there continue to be rumblings throughout the party that another leadership challenge is imminent.' Cass would not admit it, but the telephone call had motivated her to step up the assault. 'Sources high in government have suggested to me that the Stanley leadership is now, and I'll use the actual quote, dead man walking.' She didn't enjoy lying. 'This couples with the astonishing news yesterday that the independent member for Melbourne, Jaya Rukhmani, said she may switch her vote to the opposition. This would lead to a vote of no confidence, providing opposition leader Meredith Bruce the keys to Yarralumla and the government benches.'

'Wow, amazing stuff. How confident are you of this leadership challenge happening?'

'I expect they may take the vote as early as this week, if not the next sitting fortnight, which will allow leading contenders to seek support from their colleagues.'

'Who do you think will put their hand up?'

'James Harper, of course. He is the former leader of the party, rolled late at night by Stanley a little over three years ago. Another name I'm hearing who has support in the party room is the mining minister, Ginni Stavloukas.' Cass remained grateful for the lead from Hughes. 'This will mean we could have women as prime minister and opposition leader at the same time for the first time in Australia's political history.'

'What do you think the prime minister will do?'

'I'm a little unsure at the moment; there is no news coming from his office. This is not unexpected, as we all know it's hard getting any government decisions on policy from his office.' Cass checked her notes. 'A cabinet source tells me there is too much delay with decisions and the office is like a black hole. Papers for signing go in; nothing ever comes out.'

'Is the government in crisis, Cass?'

'Very much so. The prime minister needs to pull a rabbit out of the hat if he is to survive this one.'

'We shall just have to wait and see how much of a magician the prime minister is. That's Cassandra Rogers reporting from Canberra.'

Christopher Hughes was watching the breakfast show from his ministerial office and smiled as he switched off the remote, leaning back in his chair and rocking it. He wondered why Cass had become more aggressive but considered everything was falling into place. His phone sparked up, and he checked the caller ID, then answered.

'Good morning, James. How is your morning?'

'I'm worried this plan we have is getting out of control.'

'What's troubling you?'

'The Hancock media and Rogers' appearance on the breakfast show.'

'She is driving our agenda; what do you care?' Hughes examined his fingertips, checking out his nails and searching for any grime he might need to clean.

'She is also damaging the government; she says the Indian will support Bruce.'

'We'll tighten her to us, but we need to first establish the battleground.'

'Rogers identified several potential battles; which should we focus on?'

'I want the Kirkpatrick mine to be the tipping point,' Hughes said. 'Therefore, Stavloukas is important.'

'She's no threat, surely?'

'She'll struggle to get her own vote,' Hughes said. 'But she needs to lead the charge on the mine.'

'Not the drought?'

'It could rain tomorrow. No, we need the unions to be making a noise.'

Harper paused before his response. 'When do you think we should go for him?'

'When we come back from the break. My preference is the second week, which allows us to get the support we need the first week back.' Hughes waved in his staffer, Con Krakos.

'Okay, Chris. Thanks for your support.'

'Just let me choose my ministry.'

'You get me over the line, and you can do whatever you want.'

'See you.' Hughes dropped his phone, steepling his fingers in front of his face and giving Krakos a devious smile.

'Did you arrange for Rogers to go hard?' Krakos asked as he sat at the desk.

Hughes glared at him, hoping that his eyes were not flickering. 'Of course.'

'She did well for us today. Whoever gave her the Indian was a genius. She has done considerable damage to Stanley.'

'Rogers is ambitious to get the stories, so we should keep feeding her.'

'I have a travel rort against the Greek.'

'What's the fool done?'

'She's claimed travel to the Gold Coast the same weekend she bought a condo.'

Hughes clicked his tongue. 'Will they never learn?' He leaned back in his chair with a broad grin, placing his hands behind his head. He sang to himself, 'It's beginning to sound a lot like Christmas.'

CHAPTER THIRTY-THREE

Cass was working through her emails and texts. She had changed from her on-air clothes and was prioritising her morning contacts when a dark shape loomed in the periphery of her sight, scaring her. Jaya Rukhmani stood at the opening to her workstation.

'I wondered when I would hear from you. What can I do for you?' Cass continued checking emails.

'You did me over.'

Cass carried on working. 'Did I misquote you?'

'That's not the point.'

She stopped working the screen and turned to face Jaya. 'What is the point?'

'We were just having a chat. Two girls having a friendly coffee.'

'Did you not say these things to me?'

'You should have said you would use them.'

'I asked you if you wanted to say anything.'

Cass picked up the recorder from her desk, squealing the tape fast forward through the conversation. She then stopped it, allowing Jaya to hear the question and her response.

'That was the time to tell me you were off the record or giving me background.' She flicked stop on the tape and smiled at Jaya. 'You said important things, because, whether or not you like it, you play an important role in this place, so I reported it.'

'You could have told me.'

'Maybe, but I was just doing my job.'

'It's no wonder they have not promoted you, if that's what you think your job is.' Jaya retreated.

Cass froze, thinking about Jaya's comment. She ran her tongue over the front of her teeth, making a sucking noise. Maybe she agreed. She cast a thought to her children and checked the wall clock, deciding it was too early to call. Brushing her cheek, she scooted back into her desk to get back to her work.

CHAPTER THIRTY-FOUR

Brian Tucker collected his mail, purchased several items his wife had requested from the greengrocer and settled in for a coffee to review the Weekly Times, his go-to source for farming news. He enjoyed reading the stock report and figuring the approximate worth of his stock. In better times, he was always smiling as he watched prices going up, but now there was seldom good news for him. The café had the smell of fresh bread, and the black coffee was better now since the new owner had brought an espresso machine to town. He was on his second cup when he opened the front page of the Hancock national paper.

Politics was not Tucker's favourite topic. He knew little about the process and the politicians involved, but he believed the government should always look after rural communities, no matter which side of the argument they belonged. There was something reverential about the bush and its people. It was the paddock-to-plate logic that city folks recognised was in their best interests to protect. He remained confident governments would help when needed, now more than ever. His family needed them to survive this drought.

He flicked open the broadsheet and his mouth gaped as he checked the headline: Banks to Ruin Farmers. He couldn't move his eyes from the words. A moment later, his head throbbed, his mouth was dry, and he struggled to swallow. His hand gripped the paper, crunching into a fist, then he smashed the other hand onto the table, sending the cup and sugar bowl scattering across the floor. Others in the café glanced over.

'Are you okay, Brian?'

Tucker glanced at the café owner, his eyes inflamed, his face scowling like a disturbed alien. He stood, peeled off a twenty from a roll he tugged from his pocket and tossed it on the table.

'Sorry.'

The owner stood aside as Tucker strode to the door, bursting through without worrying to close it. It alerted the dogs in the back of his truck as he tramped towards them, and they fretted when he ignored them. Tucker gunned the truck and sped from town, heading for his bank.

CHAPTER THIRTY-FIVE

Robert Wong struggled to shove open the door to Jaya's office, a large cardboard box under his arm proving difficult to manage. It was heavy, and Wong worried that the weight might split the bottom as he wriggled his way through the door.

'What's all this?' Jaya asked, putting down a briefing paper she was reading.

'A special courier delivered it just now. It's from New South Wales.'

'A special courier?'

'Yes, a refrigerated van.'

'Is it food?'

'I'm thinking it might be perishable, so you had better open it.'

Jaya circled her desk, picking up a letter opener and hacking at the sealing tape. 'I wonder what it is?'

'Too heavy for a cake,' said Wong as he peered over her shoulder.

'Oh look, a note,' she said, as she flipped open the box to find a thick black plastic bag tied with a colourful ribbon with a note attached. *"I have a hundred and fifty-five, so I thought I would share one with you. Enjoy."'* Jaya read. 'How thoughtful; I wonder who sent it? Was there no confirmation of the sender?'

'A company in rural New South Wales is the only detail I have.'

'Maybe it's a gift for the outstanding work we did on the inquiry?'

'I suppose so,' Wong said, now rustling his feet. 'Is it just a coincidence there are the same number of members of parliament in the lower house?'

'Coincidence, no doubt. Pass me the scissors.'

Jaya hacked at the tied opening to the bag, cutting it off at the ribbon. She then tugged away the bag to reveal its contents.

'Oh, Geezus.' She stepped back, her hand rushing to her mouth.

Wong stepped forward to check in the bag, then recoiled, shocked by the sight of a bloodied sheep's head, eyes aglow in fear, a kitchen knife shoved in a socket close to the snout. Its tongue was dangling from its mouth below a piece of cloth shoved hard into the opening.

Jaya, shaken by what she saw, took a seat on a couch away from her desk.

'What the hell is going on? Is it some sort of joke?' Wong asked as he sat next to her.

Jaya just sat, keeping her eyes locked in on the box. 'Call the Feds.'

'A little overreaction, don't you think?' Wong said, taking her hand to steady her on the edge of the couch.

'It's a warning.'

'Warning? What warning?'

'Tucker is sending me a message.'

'Tucker? Who's Tucker?'

'The farmer who may lose his farm.'

'More like losing his mind if he thinks this is normal.'

'Slow down. I can't hear you,' Messenger said into his phone. 'What's happened?'

He couldn't get anything from a babbling, distraught Jaya as she mumbled a stream of words. He could not calm her.

Jaya wiped her eyes with the heel of her hand as she thought about what to say. 'Um, Brian Tucker sent me a message today.'

'The guy from Tucker farm?'

Her lip wobbled as she worked to control her anxiety. 'Yes.'

'What did he have to say?'

She was almost whispering. 'He said that we are all sheep in the parliament and unless we do something we will be exterminated.'

'He said that?' Messenger was doubtful.

'Not in so many words.'

'What did he say, precisely?'

Jaya shuddered a sigh then whispered, 'He sent me the severed head of a sheep.'

Messenger's mouth dropped open, his tongue working the corner of his mouth, eyes agog. 'Are you okay?'

'Do I sound okay?'

'Have you called the police?'

'Yes, and I gave them a statement. They reassured me they will speak to him and determine the threat value… the fucking threat value… and report back.'

'Were they helpful?'

'No.'

'What would you like me to do?'

'Did you speak to him?'

'I'm taking the PM out to the region in a few days, so we can assess the drought relief.'

'So, you haven't spoken to him?'

Messenger was reluctant to respond.

'He has an issue with the banks and that falls under your responsibility.'

'You're right. I'm yet to talk to him, but I will try to get a hold of him today.'

Jaya didn't reply. She just held her head back, shaking it as if she couldn't believe what she had just heard. A tear trickled from the corner of her eye.

'This guy has been doing these sorts of scary things since he gave evidence; now this.'

Messenger considered what to do. 'Do you want me to come over?'

Jaya tightened her lips, gnawing at the bottom one. 'No.'

CHAPTER THIRTY-SIX

'Prime Minister, let me introduce you to Brian Tucker.' Messenger guided Stanley to the farmer, who removed his oversized hat and held out his hand. 'Tucker Farm is an exemplar in farming practice, having a zero-carbon footprint and allowing neighbours to benefit from his carbon credits.' Messenger smiled, hoping for a positive response.

'Oh, well done.' Stanley gripped Tucker's hand, shaking it with vigour. 'You must be well prepared for these troubling times, then?'

'The drought, do you mean, or your government?'

Stanley stopped in his tracks, uncertain what to say in response. He tried to figure out if the man with the steely look before him was joking or not.

Tucker squeezed the prime minister's hand. 'What are you going to do about the thieving banks? Or will you never make a decision?'

Messenger stepped forward, trying with little success to avert Tucker's stare as the farmer focused it on the prime minister.

'Mr Tucker, we've already had our chat. Let the prime minister do his job and I'll do mine.' Messenger stifled a nervous chuckle, hoping to ease the tension. 'Please, Brian.'

Tucker dropped the hand and stepped back. He replaced his hat, pushing it back. 'We don't need your money, although we are grateful. We just need the banks off our backs. Your treasurer has made a few commitments to me, and I hope, for his sake, he does as he says he will.'

'I'm sure Bart will do whatever is necessary to get the outcome you want. Nice meeting you.' Stanley turned on his heel and tracked away, searching for another farmer who might be a little friendlier.

Messenger raised his eyebrows as he considered Tucker, who shrugged.

'Just do what you say you are going to do, and we shall be fine,' Tucker said.

'I'll do my best to meet your expectations, but I can't promise anything.'

'Your best is not good enough, Treasurer. I need more than that, otherwise things will happen.'

'What type of things?'

Tucker smiled and tapped his nose.

'A few more heads, is that it?'

Tucker's face wrinkled with disdain. 'You know what it's like to kill something, Mr Messenger? To kill something, then dismember it?'

Messenger shook his head, his lips pouting. 'No.'

'It can devastate you, but I suspect boning a politician would be much easier.'

He sucked his teeth as he stepped off, leaving Messenger wondering what to do.

Cassandra Rogers watched the exchange as she stood by the linen-covered trestle table weighed down with morning tea cupcakes and sandwiches. She placed a tinned asparagus sandwich on her plate, collected her tea and circled the room, wanting to bump into the hard man from the land she had observed confronting the politicians. She monitored him as she passed a few chubby women in their Sunday best and was careful not to spill her tea as she squeezed through the rolls of fat. She ensured that her red Docs didn't create a scene by stepping on any toes shoved into tight shoes.

The Country Women's Association's morning tea was a prized social event for the region, with most locals crammed into the timber hall that served as the local Catholic church every Sunday.

Tucker had settled in a corner, standing away from the loud crowd keen to discuss the prime minister's speech and his assurances about providing federal funds to support those in trouble with the drought.

DOOMED

'Hello there,' a cheery Cass said as she approached Tucker.

The farmer eyed her as if wondering what she wanted and didn't respond.

Cass felt uncomfortable and tried again. 'My name is Cassandra and I wonder if I could ask you a few questions?'

Tucker considered the question, wrinkling his nose. He sucked his teeth, rubbing the stubble on his chin as he studied her.

'I just wanted to know what you thought of the prime minister's speech?'

Tucker thumbed his hat back, smiling a grimace with a shake of his head. 'Are you a reporter?'

'Journalist, yes.'

'What do you write about?'

'Politics.' Cass smiled, unsure about the conversation.

'You don't write rural?'

'No.'

'Well, best you move on then.'

His comment surprised Cass. Most people talked to her; many were keen to do so. 'That's why I'm asking about what you thought of the prime minister.'

'Just another blah blah bloke with little understanding of the constant risks of being a farmer.'

'Can I quote you?'

Tucker smiled and shook his head. 'You can do whatever you want, just tell the truth.'

'And what's that?'

'The banks are a pack of mongrels.' Tucker almost spat the words. 'They are about to begin foreclosure on plenty of farms around these parts.'

'Do you have trouble?'

'You could say that.'

'And what's the treasurer said to you?'

'He told me what the head offices of the banks are telling him, which is there will be no foreclosures. That's not the message out here on the front line. Ambitious bank managers keen to get back to the city are winding good people up.'

'So, what the banks are saying is not the practice?'

'That's what I keep telling Messenger, but he has his head up his arse and can't hear a damn thing.'

'What's the prime minister got to say to you?'

'Nothing, as usual… the bloke can't make a decision.'

'Are you under threat?'

Tucker glanced over her head to check if anyone was in earshot. 'They have threatened me.'

'What was your response?'

'I threatened them.' Tucker locked eyes with Cass, narrowed his stare and didn't let go.

She felt uneasy and tried to squeeze a gulp. 'Not sure you should do that.'

'That so?'

'Surely the government can resolve this for you?'

'Talk, talk, talk. That's all they do. They don't care. It's a safe seat. Why would they care?'

'Can I call you to learn your views on further government action when it happens?'

'I wouldn't waste ya time.'

'Isn't that for me to decide?'

Tucker considered the answer for a moment and squeezed the tip of his nose before giving it a quick rub. 'If I have anything to say I'll get hold of you.'

'Do you want my card?'

'Nope. I'll find you.'

Cass placed her plate on top of her cup and held out her hand. 'Cassandra Rogers, and you are?'

Tucker was reluctant to grab her hand, but eventually did. 'Brian Tucker.'

'Thank you, sir. I'll be in touch.'

'Not if I can help it.'

Cass stepped back and walked away; she placed her crockery on a sideboard and squeezed her way to the door and fresh air. Once outside, the lilting breeze cooled her face, and she went down the half-dozen wooden stairs out onto the street. She looked around at the cars and the folks standing outside, smoking, smiling, and chatting. She could see that the hall was uphill from the township, so she set off towards the main street, looking for a bank.

'Cleave, this drought thing is creating a potential holocaust out bush.' Cass had settled into a teahouse in the main street to call the Canberra political editor. 'I have a feeling the government is getting snowed by the banks.'

'What's the word on the street?'

'It seems local bank managers are acting in line with policy and getting zero direction from head office; they've dropped the ball.'

'Hearsay or evidence?'

'I have it on the record from a cheerful chap at a local bank here. He tells me he has eight foreclosures he can move on, but he is waiting until he gets pressure to do so from head office. He knows of two major farms that are under immediate threat from other banks. He mentioned one farm struggling big time.'

'How would he know that?'

'They've applied to refinance and got nowhere with him; he told me he couldn't risk it.'

'What line do you want to follow?'

Cass stroked her fingers along her forehead as she rested her head in her hand. 'I think we should go hard on Stanley and ride him for a better deal for the farmers.'

'Is there a story there? It could rain tomorrow.'

'The story is beyond the drought, although that's the human aspect to it.'

'You can't think this is a leadership issue?'

Cass hesitated, knowing that to declare her angle might have it commandeered by others. She didn't trust Cleaver. 'I think we should see everything at the moment through the lens of leadership.'

'Can you add local colour, a farmer maybe?'

'I need to speak to Messenger, but I reckon there's one other bloke who can give us the colour and quotes we need.'

'Okay, do your thing.'

CHAPTER THIRTY-SEVEN

Former Prime Minister Gerrard had forced the governor general from his Sydney residence up the Parramatta River to an obscure clinker brick three-bedroom home soon after the failed republican referendum. He wanted to send a message to monarchists who dared vote against Australia becoming a republic. Voters humiliated Gerrard, and he transferred his rage into the eviction of the governor from Admiralty House, the Sydney harbourside residence with panoramic views of the opera house and the bridge. The result: a grand mansion befitting any head of state, which Gerrard thought he was until his eviction from the job at the last federal election.

Prime Minister Stanley seldom used the residence, preferring Yarralumla in Canberra, or returning to his home in Perth. When he stayed at the Sydney residence, it delighted him to sit out under the veranda for a quiet cup of early morning tea. Today his senior staffer, Stephen Newgreen, joined him to toss around ideas about seizing political momentum.

'Feedback from your visit to drought-stricken regions of New South Wales has played out well in the media.' Newgreen was scanning through clippings from earlier in the week. 'The only issue we have is the continued attacks from Hancock Media.'

'She's like a dog with a bone.' Stanley dropped his hands, and the broadsheet he was reading crumpled into his lap. 'Even today she has another attack editorial against me.'

'What's she said?'

Stanley picked up the paper. 'She quotes a farmer and says he is about to go under, suggesting it will be my fault if he does.' He glanced out onto the harbour. 'Christ, I wish it would rain.'

'Don't we all.'

'Apparently this farmer threatened the local bank manager and could be linked to the severed sheep's head Rukhmani received.'

'Why aren't the federal police doing something with him?' Newgreen asked.

'I spoke to the commander before you arrived. He advised they have little criminal activity from the man, other than chest beating. They had a chat with him and told him to pull his head in.'

'What's his issue?'

'The bank wants to foreclose him.' Stanley dropped his paper from his left hand and picked up his tea, taking a sip, then another. He glanced out onto the harbour, taking another sip before replacing the cup. 'Nice day to be out on the water.'

Newgreen squinted out on the harbour, then glanced back to the prime minister. 'Is there anything you want me to do for him?'

'Messenger tells me he is handling it, reassured by the farmer's bank that all is okay. I met the guy earlier this week.'

'What did he say?'

'He was a touch severe; I can tell you. He told me to make a decision and protect farmers.'

Newgreen put aside his clippings. 'Maybe he's right.'

Stanley glanced over at him. 'What do you mean?'

'Let's shift the entire political discussion away from the troubles of the drought and the drilling platforms in the Timor Sea.'

'Stavloukas says we are making a mistake with the 457s for the rigs.'

'She doesn't know what she wants,' Newgreen said, frowning. 'She says she wants the union to approve agreements on the rigs, then denies them a seat at the negotiation table with the Indians in Queensland.'

'How close are we to a deal with the Kirkpatrick mine?'

'We maybe have a three-month window to complete the deal. The environmentalists are up in arms; they have protests planned in every state over the next few weeks.'

'What? What do these folks want, for Christ's sake?'

'They want us out of coal,' Newgreen said.

'We can't do that; the economy would buckle if we did.'

'The climate groups are all over it wanting us to stop exporting.'

'What?' Stanley frowned. 'So, they protect their standard of living and deny the third world an opportunity to improve theirs?'

'They do not grasp rational thinking in politics these days, boss; you know that.'

'Once politicians got involved with this climate nonsense, we lost all rational debate.' Stanley folded his paper, bringing his tea towards him and resting the saucer on his thigh, his hand steadying it. 'What ideas do you have about controlling the media narrative?'

'We make a grand announcement?'

Stanley drained the lukewarm tea, replacing the cup and saucer on the side table. 'A social policy announcement?'

'I'm thinking something about health, maybe a new research project or even a cancer centre.'

'What about something we can deliver to middle-aged women? My figures with them have collapsed.'

'We could offer them a dollar-for-dollar superannuation contribution.'

'Where did you get that nonsense?' Stanley queried.

'Stavloukas has been getting traction with the idea.'

'What does Hughes think about that? He would hate that idea going into employment awards.' Stanley laughed. 'No, we need something that affects everyone.'

'Tax?'

'Maybe. Messenger seems to think there could be room for a cut.'

'Do you think he's doing the numbers against you?'

'I can only take him at his word, and he says he will stick,' said Stanley.

'Who do you think is working with Harper?'

'No idea. Hughesie reckons he is working the phones himself.' Stanley crossed his arms, taking in a deep breath through his nose and gazing out onto the harbour.

'Not sure the party room will go back to him,' Newgreen said.

'To be honest, I don't know. My man says we're safe, so I must trust him, which is the worst thing to do in this business.'

'When do you reckon Harper will make a move?'

'Christopher seems to think next week when we're all back in Canberra.'

'I'll sound out a few offices,' Newgreen said.

'Good lad, but let's try to get our heads around an announcement. I think we should do something before we go back, which only leaves tomorrow or the weekend.'

'Maybe we can go to war with Indonesia because they cancelled the detention centres?'

'Don't even joke about those things; context is everything, but if that got into the media the entire government would be dead.'

Stanley was entering his office at the converted Kirribilli House next door to the Sydney residence when he advised by an agitated staffer that a call was waiting from Minister Stavloukas.

'Oh, Geezus, what does she want?' He dropped his briefcase on his desk.

'She says it's urgent and demands to speak to you and won't take no for an answer.'

Stanley moved around his desk, picking up the receiver and prodding the flashing button. 'Ginni, hi. Sorry to keep you waiting.'

'I'll just put you through, Prime Minister,' Stavloukas' staffer said.

Stanley shook his head, massaging his temple as he held the phone to his ear.

'Prime Minister?'

He didn't respond.

'Prime Minister, are you there?' Stavloukas pleaded, then her voice changed to a screech. 'I thought you fucking told me he was on the line?'

'I'm here,' he whispered. 'What can I help you with?'

'Yes, hilarious,' Stavloukas said. 'I just wanted to know if you have decided about foreign affairs?'

'Not yet.'

'This is typical,' she said, raising her voice. 'This is the reason you are under threat; you can never make a decision.'

'Ginni, when I decide you will be one of the first to know.'

'That sounds like you are considering someone else for the role.'

'Why aren't you focused on getting the Kirkpatrick through the mountains of delays?'

'I am focused.' She calmed her tone. 'It's the Indians and their constant demands.'

'What do they want?'

'They want jobs for their people.'

'Not going to happen. You can see the crap we are going through with Timor on the rigs.'

'Harper screwed it up when he said they could have key engineers on site, so it's his fault.'

'Never yours.'

'What's that mean?'

Stanley lay back in his seat, placing a foot on this desk. 'It means you don't have the ticker to be prime minister.'

'Why? Because I'm not a bloke?'

'You don't get it, do you?' Stanley checked his fingernails.

'Get what?'

'The reason you never get what you want in this business is not that you are a woman.' The prime minister delayed his further response for just a moment. 'It's because no one likes you. If you run against me, you'll only get a handful of votes, if that.'

There was no immediate response from the other end of the phone.

'If I don't get the foreign affairs portfolio, I will convince those numbers I do have not to vote for you.'

'And there you have the reason you'll never be a senior minister in my government.' Stanley sat up, dropping the phone into its cradle.

CHAPTER THIRTY-EIGHT

The Bower Street property in Manly, overlooking secluded Shelley Beach, was a little tired. Christopher Hughes' family had enjoyed it for many years, but the Tudor-style house needed to be pushed over and a more stylish house built to replace the quaint, but small, home. The deck faced the coastline to the north, also providing an expansive view of the Pacific.

His parents had moved to their holiday home on the beach in Byron Bay, claiming the weather was much better there. Hughes then moved in with his young family. Although he treasured the homely nature and its memories, his wife Francesca had been encouraging him to redevelop the site. His children were yet to move on; why would they? He questioned whether it would be better to leave the redevelopment to one of them.

James Harper had accepted the invitation to dinner, and the two politicians escaped to the outside stone-tiled snug on a patio high above the stone cliffs. They stretched out on the rattan amongst the soft cushions, admiring the vista, talking politics.

Harper flushed a sip of bourbon across his tongue and smiled. 'This view isn't too bad, but the Gold Coast offers a better lifestyle.'

'You wish.' Hughes chuckled as he sipped his drink.

Harper wanted to get to the reason he had accepted the invitation. 'What's the plan?'

Hughes drained his glass, leaning forward and placing it on the small glass-topped matching table. 'I think we should go hard next week. Give us the weekend to sort out the final numbers and bring it home the following Tuesday at the party room meeting.'

'How much more damage do we need to do?' Harper looked over to his friend. 'I mean, honestly, hasn't he gone through enough?'

'We just need to push the knife in to the hilt.'

'Can he save himself by pulling something out of his arse?'

'No, he's too far off the pace now,' Hughes said, studying his colleague.

'No other challengers?'

'We need to kill off Stavloukas, but we still need to use her as the provocation point for the challenge.'

Harper clicked his tongue. 'That'll be tricky; no one takes her seriously.'

'They will once Rogers does a number on her, talking up her credentials.'

Harper nodded, pouting. 'Does Messenger pose a threat?' he asked.

'He's young and knows he has plenty of time.'

'Will he support us?'

'He needs to be seen to support Pete, and I'll give him a little sage advice to do so.'

Frankie Hughes leaned over the wrought-iron fence above them, calling them for dinner. They clambered out of the cushions and Harper drained his glass, tossing the ice onto the nearby lawn.

'This is what the party needs, isn't it?' he asked as they climbed the stone steps.

'We should have stuck with you before the last election.' Hughes draped his arm around his friend's shoulders. 'If we did, we wouldn't be in this mess.'

'I just feel sorry for Pete.'

Hughes stifled a smile, trying to be serious for a moment. 'Yes, it will be sad for him, but we have to move on from him.'

'Hmm, the king is dead, long live the king.'

'He's not dead yet, but soon will be.' Hughes dropped his arm and watched Harper move in front of him. He smiled. 'Then we will crown you.'

'Let's hope it's not with thorns.'

Hughes broadened his smile, knowing there would never be a crown for James Harper.

DOOMED

As Hughes closed the front door, waving off his friend, his wife moved up behind him, slipping her arms around him and cupping his chest, her head resting between his shoulders.

'Will it be long now, darling?'

Hughes spun around, drawing his wife to him, and kissing her.

'It's almost done. We set it up this week, then the following Tuesday you will be selecting colour schemes.'

'What needs to be done?'

'I just need to get Stanley fighting for his job, set the Greek up, and have Harper call for a ballot.'

'That doesn't sound too difficult for you?'

'Harper will make sure we have a ballot, and I will be the compromise candidate.'

'All the little ducks in a row.' Frankie dropped her head to his shoulder as they strolled to the lounge. 'Do you have the support of the media?' She lay back on the soft cushioned couch, yanking Hughes towards her.

'I think I have them on side.'

She tugged at his shirt as he shifted his weight. 'I want to live at Admiralty House, darling. Give me what I want, and you will never regret it.' She gasped, dragging him over her.

'It's tricky, but I reckon we are close.'

'Do whatever you have to do,' she whispered. 'I won't come to Canberra this week until they choose you. Do what you must do. Make it happen, darling.'

Hughes loved his wife. He loved her aspiration even more.

CHAPTER THIRTY-NINE

The reconfigured prime ministerial office at parliament house provided formal office space and a private lounge where Prime Minister Gerrard entertained. Entertained was the euphemism to describe the covert, hushed up stories of sexual exploitation. Tales of Gerrard seducing young politicians remain infamous, but no one was prepared to go on the record. His incendiary political payback for those who crossed him was fearsome and legendary. No one crossed him without ever regretting doing so.

Christopher Hughes slouched back into a soft leather couch with a glass of chilled chardonnay dangling in his hand. He trickled his finger along the leather cushions, wondering what stories they could tell.

The prime minister was in a rigid chair opposite a glass of chilled mineral water with a slice of lime on the marble table before him. Hughes came to discuss party room tactics for the week. Stanley needed to appease the backbench from moving against his leadership.

'You need to make an announcement; I keep telling you that.'

'My team has been considering tax breaks,' Stanley replied.

Hughes raised his eyebrows, shaking his head in the negative.

His response disappointed Stanley. 'I considered a social policy announcement. Maybe more funds for domestic violence.'

'They already expect that type of thing from us; you need to go much bigger.'

'Okay, wise guy. What would you suggest?'

Hughes sipped his wine to mask his pleasure at the question. 'Oh, I don't know.' He knew but played the game a little longer. 'If we could have a climate change announcement of some sort, we would create a massive response from the lefties.'

'We can't put any more money into renewables; it's killing us for so little return,' Stanley said

'I was thinking you could make a statement of intent.'

'Like what?'

'Uranium.'

Stanley eyed his friend. 'You think announcing a nuclear power plant will do it?'

'No, I'm not suggesting that.' Hughes took another sip. 'Look, India wants our coal for power. So why not give them uranium instead?'

'They're an aggressive nuclear threat to the region.'

'So what?'

'We can't give it to them without restrictions.'

'You will not give it to them; you just say you are.'

Stanley scoffed at the idea as he picked up his drink, careful not to let any condensation droplets dribble onto his trousers.

'You announce you'll begin negotiations with their PM. This will send the media into a frenzy, getting you back onto the front pages looking like a new era leader focused on climate change. I mean, if the rest of the world can build nuclear power plants with zero emissions, why should we deny the Indians that opportunity?'

The prime minister shook his head as he thought through the idea. 'I'm not convinced.'

'It'll take over two years to get done, and after the next election talks will break down and we have five more years.'

Stanley wiped his glass of cascading drips with a paper serviette. 'I see what you mean.'

'Look, Pete, the electorate is crying out for leadership on climate change. They want it so badly they will accept any new direction, rewarding the party that does it… let's give them something to look forward to. The other mob is invested in coal for India and the electorate hates it.'

Stanley leaned forward, resting his elbows on his knees.

Hughes drained his glass before standing. 'I have to go. I have to prepare for a dinner date… Think about an announcement for tomorrow and let's talk further.' He headed for the door, leaving the prime minister with head bowed, deep in thought. 'We've got this.' He fist-pumped as he hauled the door open and left.

Stanley waited for a few moments, then straightened. 'Stevie?' he bellowed to the open door, and Newgreen entered. 'We need to prepare a ministerial statement for tomorrow at the start of parliament. I think I have an idea.'

CHAPTER FORTY

It was just after nine-thirty when Hughes opened his front door, stepping aside and allowing Cassandra Rogers to walk through to the living room. She dropped her leather bag on a seat at the kitchen bench and straddled another.

'Wine?' Hughes asked as he opened the refrigerator, waiting for a response.

'What have you got?'

'Champagne, or something a little woody from Margaret River.'

'If it's a Chardonnay, then I'll have that,' Cass said with a smile, thinking that maybe she might have already had too much. 'Do you have anything to nibble on?'

'Sure, I have cheese, or would you like me to whip up a plate of calamari for you? I have it marinating.'

'Cheese will be fine.' Cass nodded her head in thanks as Hughes slid a glass to her. 'Why do you think Stanley has called a media conference for the morning?'

Hughes didn't respond, his lips holding back a smile.

'Is he finally going to make a decision on the Kirkpatrick or is it something more sinister, like resigning his position?'

Hughes remained silent as he prepared the cheese.

'What do you think?'

Hughes pushed a platter towards her, along with a plate and a knife. He then drew a cotton serviette from a drawer, placing it before her.

After a moment of studying her as she considered her cheese options, he asked, 'Why are you here?'

Cass glanced up as she shoved a soft milky smudge of Camembert onto a carrot stick, popping it into her mouth and chewing as she eyed Hughes. She smiled as she swallowed, then took a sip of wine.

'I always follow the story. You know that.'

'You've heard the prime minister since the leadership spill. His leadership is back on track, and he is working with the Indian government to increase trade, establishing a new trade agreement. So, no story here.'

'You know, and I know, that's bullshit.'

Hughes smiled, taking a mouthful of wine before stepping around the bench and sitting in the corner opposite Cass.

'So why are you here?'

'I want the true story.' Cass felt anxious and exposed, so avoided Hughes' gaze by sipping her wine, scanning about the room. 'Does Mrs Hughes ever come to Canberra to stay with you?'

'Often, as you well know.' Hughes took a swig of wine. 'She prefers Sydney but said she might be here next week.'

'Any reason she would come next week?'

Hughes cocked his head, pausing for a moment. 'Why are you here?'

'I'm here for the story, and I reckon you know what's going on,' Cass said, taking another stick and cheese, scooping up her wine then sauntering over to the lounge and collapsing into the soft cushions. 'You know, Hughesie, I don't have a lot of time for you.'

'What a surprise.' Hughes stayed at the bench.

'I reckon you're the story.'

'Why do you think I'm the story?'

'I reckon something is afoot with you and Harper. I suspect James is not smart enough to be doing what he's doing by himself.'

'What's he doing?' Hughes replenished his glass, bringing it and the bottle, placing them on the table, dropping into the cushions at the opposite end of the expansive lounge.

'You've always said you need a change of leader. I don't believe any new direction the prime minister will announce tomorrow will save him, so I reckon you're the story.'

'Tell me, Cassie, what do you think?' Hughes said.

She demurred, taking another sip of wine. 'I think there will be another challenge within this next sitting period.'

'And who do you think has the numbers?'

'I don't think Harper does.'

'What about Stavloukas?'

Cass screwed her face at the very mention of the minister's name. 'I wouldn't have thought so.'

'She's very ambitious.' Hughes paused for a moment. 'Just like you, I suspect.'

Cass was about to take another drink but paused the glass at her lips, considering Hughes and wondering how much he knew about her plans.

'For instance, I know you are keen to get your own television show, and you are up for the chance to replace the old fart, Nicholls.'

She shifted in her seat, bringing a leg up under her, sitting straighter.

'I also know that unless you win a few exclusives, you may not get the gig, and a younger, shall we say, more willing journalist may get it.' Hughes smiled as he noticed a look of disdain cross Cass's face. 'What's her name? Good looking thing... I heard she goes off like a rocket. Hancock loves her, I'm told.'

'Tamara O'Byrne,' Cass said.

'That's her.' Hughes grinned. 'She's a shoo-in, I'm told. Unless you can bring major stories to the table.'

Cass glanced away, resting her chin on her thumb for a moment, then draining the glass.

'Why are you here, Cassie? Drinking wine with a politician you don't respect?'

She uncurled herself, stretching for the bottle and emptying the remains into her glass. 'I'm here for the story,' she said again, repositioning herself.

'What's it worth to you?'

She didn't respond; the comment surprised her and wondered what to say. She'd heard the line many times before but hadn't expected it now.

'Relax, Cassie.' Hughes smiled, relishing her discomfort. 'Don't misunderstand me; I'm not looking for a screw. I'm wanting complete loyalty and confidentiality.'

Cass gulped to help breathe before taking a sip of wine, then said, 'Go on, I'm listening.'

Hughes sat forward. 'You're right; there will be a leadership challenge next week and Stanley will be gone. There will be two contenders.'

'Stanley?'

'No, I will make certain he will have to resign.'

'How will you do that?'

'It's a procedural thing with the party. If a petition of two members requests a special meeting to vote on a leadership spill, then the party room must agree. I will have Stanley insist on fifty percent plus one to sign the petition rather than just two. If the expected numbers sign the petition, then this will mean a loss of confidence, forcing him to resign as leader.'

'Who are the candidates?'

'This is what I want you to drive this week.'

'You want me to get involved?'

'Only in a reporting sense,' Hughes reassured her. 'I want you to report that Stavloukas wants the job as foreign minister, and if she doesn't get it, she will challenge the leader.'

'Has she said that?'

'No, but you can write it. She'll own the idea because I will support her push.'

'I can't do that.'

Hughes shook his head. 'You're not listening. If you want the show, then you will write it.'

'Is this Hancock's idea?' Cass sneered.

Hughes shrugged.

'He hasn't got his approval for the LA gig. Harper didn't approve it, so it's sitting with Stanley, and he won't do it.' Cass moved from the couch, pacing back and forward across the room before him. 'But if Harper wins the leadership, then he won't approve Hancock's appointment.'

'Harper will not be leader.' Hughes frowned, nodding.

'Who will be?'

Hughes leaned back into the lounge and smirked, saying nothing.

'You?'

'I need to have Stanley out of the contest, which means Harper is likely to win. But if I get the petition up and get Stanley out of the contest, then Stavloukas will run against Harper. I will reluctantly nominate to stop her bid.'

Cass stopped pacing, gazing out to the lit garden and the steaming pool. 'What do you want from me?'

'I need you to write the story about Stavloukas. It can be a profile piece but put in it her demand for the foreign minister's job. Puff a couple of pars saying she has leadership ambitions.'

'What do you want me to do on Stanley?'

'Write the truth; he will stuff up this announcement tomorrow. I'll make sure he announces the petition by the end of the week. Use words like leadership chaos and turmoil a lot.'

'What do I get?'

'You get direct access to the new prime minister.' Hughes moved to the kitchen to open another bottle. 'You get daily briefings this week about what Stanley is planning, and I suppose you get the first exclusive interview within an hour of me being elected prime minister.'

'Will you sign off Hancock's appointment?'

'I'll sign it off during that interview... just for you.' Hughes refilled his glass.

'Can I use that information to get what I want?'

'You want to negotiate with Hancock?'

'I want the show... he wants the LA gig.' Cass turned, glaring at Hughes. 'If I don't get the show, can you assure me you won't sign his appointment?'

'Sure, what's in it for me?' Hughes returned to the lounge, glass in one hand, bottle in the other, refilling her glass.

Cass clinked his proffered glass, sealing their arrangement with a toast before sipping her wine. She leaned past him, placing her glass on the wooden coffee table. She kicked off her red Docs, dropping her jacket and tugging off her black singlet, exposing her breasts.

Hughes didn't move, wondering what to do.

Cass smiled as she turned away, stepping out of her unbuttoned camos, and moving to the glass door. She slid it open, tiptoeing naked to the pool's edge and dropping into the warm water. When she surfaced, she brushed back her hair, moving to the side of the pool, resting on her arms.

'Bring my wine with you.'

CHAPTER FORTY-ONE

The House of Representatives' chamber was settling in as the speaker finished prayers and the acknowledgment of Country for the daily opening. The speaker waited for a few moments to allow members to reach their designated seat before calling for questions without notice. She sat forward, but before she could ask for questions, the prime minister rose from his chair, standing at the government despatch box, waiting for the call.

'Madam Speaker, I seek leave to make a statement.'

The speaker was a little taken aback by the request, as no one had informed her it was the intention of the prime minister to make a formal statement. 'The prime minister is seeking leave to make a statement; is leave granted?' She looked at Bruce, who nodded agreement. 'Leave is granted; I call the prime minister.'

'Thank you, Speaker.' Stanley removed a clipped wad of papers from his leather folder. 'I wish to make a formal statement about the Kirkpatrick coal mine in Queensland, confirming the government's intention to renegotiate trading arrangements with India.'

Christopher Hughes swung about him, seeking the attention of James Harper, sitting at the back of the chamber. Harper shook his head, surprised by the announcement. As Hughes returned his attention to the prime minister, the mining minister, Ginni Stavloukas, slipped next to him for a chat.

'What's this about?' she whispered.

'I don't know, so let's just enjoy the moment.'

Stavloukas moved past the prime minister to the advisers' box, tucked away near the speaker. She leaned into speak to her staffer.

'Prepare a response to this statement. I don't want to be left swinging in the breeze on this, whatever it is.' Her staffer opened his computer, tapping as the prime minister continued.

'For many months now, uncertainty has riddled the Australian public as to the government's position regarding the Kirkpatrick mine. All necessary approvals are complete and preposterous studies foisted upon the government by special interest groups now settled. It will please members to learn that the grey-chested finch is not at risk. Water catchment was never at risk. Even the northern Australian river system some fifteen hundred kilometres from the mine site is not, and never was, under threat.'

Hughes glanced to the media gallery, spotting Cassandra Rogers tucked away in the third row, glaring down on him with a look saying, *what is happening?* Hughes shrugged, then glanced over to Bruce, who caught him in his by-play with the journalist. She smiled, tapped the tip of her nose, and nodded. An attendant was before him, offering a note. He checked the scribblings. Harper was demanding to know what was going on and if the leadership group knew why the prime minister was making a statement. Hughes peered back and shook his head. He didn't have a clue.

Two hours earlier, once Stanley returned to his office from the uneventful party room meeting, in which they approved various ministerial legislation submissions, Barton Messenger knocked his way into the prime minister's suite.

'Pete, we have to talk.'

'Et tu Brutus?'

'Not at all, and indeed, far from it.'

'Then what do we need to talk about?'

'There's a push for another challenge,' Messenger said, almost matter-of-factly.

'Doesn't surprise me; who's pushing it?'

'There's a push for Harper, with Ginni mentioned in dispatches. I'm uncertain who the overlord is, but the push is gaining momentum.'

'When?'

'This week maybe.'

Stanley rocked his chair back and forward as he considered the news. 'Hughesie thinks I should make a big announcement.'

'Like what?'

'He says to talk about uranium exports and nuclear power.'

'Why would he suggest that?'

'Something big, he said.'

'Nuclear?' Messenger asked.

'We'll never do it, but he said to mention it and set the hares running.'

Messenger didn't respond straight away. He steepled his fingers, cupping his chin and his nose. 'Who do you reckon is leaking to the media? Why is Rogers getting all the good stuff from our cabinet meetings?'

'She's always had her nose close to the ground.'

'Yeah, but not this close.' Messenger paused before he continued. 'Are you briefing her?'

'Don't be ridiculous.'

'Well, if you aren't and I'm not, then who does that leave?' Messenger asked.

'Jim?'

'He hasn't been at the last few meetings, so how would he know what our plans were?'

'Wilson Campbell has always had a loose mouth. I think he is still dirty about losing the deputy position when you took over.'

'Yeah maybe... What about Chris?' Messenger queried.

'Nah, he's been very supportive.'

'Like Brutus?'

Stanley didn't respond. He gazed out the window over the prime minister's courtyard.

'Maybe,' he said, saddened by the idea. 'What can we do?'

'I hear you have an announcement planned?'

'Christ, how do you know that?'

'Your words are leaking like a sieve.'

Stanley shook his head, unnerved by the revelation. 'I was planning a media conference later this afternoon.'

'To discuss what?'

'To announce a new trade proposal with India.'

'Have they agreed?'

'They don't need to know about it.'

'You're going to announce an initiative and the Indians don't know? Do you think that's wise?'

'Hughesie suggests I just announce our intention. He reckons it will shift the national media narrative to focus on strong leadership.'

'Yes, but whose? Yours, or maybe a new leader?'

'If they're coming for me, then I have to do something. I can't just sit and wait for them.'

Messenger felt uncomfortable. 'Maybe you just need to shock everyone and dump everything from the cot.'

'You and your clichés and metaphors… Will you ever get over yourself?'

Messenger shifted in his seat, bristled by the rebuke. 'All I'm saying is this… You can't announce intent. You have got to do something spectacular.'

'Like the dud drought announcement, you suggested?'

'It was the right thing to do; you know that.'

'Maybe, but it didn't impact the polls.'

'Not everything we do is about popularity, Pete.'

'Easy for you to say; you're not the prime minister.'

'Neither will you be unless you respond over the next few days.'

'Tax cut?'

'We can't afford any.' Messenger shook his head.

'Then what, smartarse?'

Messenger leaned forward, resting his arms on his knees, unsettled by the conversation. 'We have drought, the mine, energy prices, a flat economy, workers complaining, so there is plenty to choose from. My only suggestion is to go big.'

Stanley pondered the idea for a moment. 'When?'

'The sooner the better, I would suggest. We need to kill this idea of leadership rumblings.' Messenger stood. 'Just make sure it doesn't come back to bite you.'

'Thanks, Bart.' The prime minister was already deep in thought.

DOOMED

Messenger was paying attention as the prime minister began his statement and wished he had spoken to him about whatever he was about to say. Ignoring the advice of colleagues is never a good idea, and he cast an eye to Hughes, who was scribbling a message, which he thrust to the waiting attendant. As Hughes sat back, he glanced at Messenger and shrugged.

Messenger tracked the attendant, who passed before him before walking behind the government benches via the steps by the advisers' viewing boxes. As he watched, it surprised him to see the attendant pass the note to another attendant, who then walked to the glass and brass doors of the formal entrance to the chamber. The man ducked into the attendants' chamber management studio, with its glass window overlooking the chamber where other parliamentary officers watched the proceedings, sourcing papers for politicians, if required. The attendant wasn't there for long before he returned and walked to another attendant sitting in the corner for the opposition by the water station. He leaned in, whispered something, and passed the note to his colleague, who then stood, poured a glass of water, and walked down the steps to the chamber floor, sidling up to the leader of the opposition, placing the glass on a coaster and passing the note to her.

Bruce read the note, glanced up into the media gallery, then checked Hughes, before standing at the opposition's despatch box.

'Madam Speaker.' Bruce waited a moment for the prime minister to pause. 'I wish to make a point of order.'

'The prime minister will resume his seat. The leader of the opposition on a point of order, which is unusual given that the prime minister is making a statement to the House and leave has been granted.'

'Thank you, Speaker. I refer to House of Representatives' practice, which states that normal consideration of ministerial statements be made at the end of question time. Whilst we granted leave, we were unaware of the subject of the prime minister's statement. We now have cause for concern that he may be in breach of practice. I refer you to the anticipation rule.' Bruce was reading from the note. 'They describe this rule on various pages of practice, but in particular, page 482, where it states that no member may anticipate any subject that appears on the notice paper. Speaker, I refer you to today's notice paper, in particular the matter of public importance and legislation about trading treaties, which is scheduled for discussion later today. With these points in mind, and the prime minister's introduction, is he not anticipating discussion that is listed in the notice paper?'

Bruce resumed her seat as the speaker referred to her copy of parliamentary practice. The clerk clambered the three steps to her side to discuss the point of order. Bruce swung to her frontbench colleagues, whispering a few points before swinging back to the table, crossing her arms, and stealing a glance towards Hughes.

The chamber was silent as the speaker prepared her response. When she was ready, the clerk resumed his seat. The speaker moved to the edge of her large chair, referred to and touched a scribbled note, then said, 'The statement before the house is by the prime minister, who, as defined under standing orders, can make a ministerial statement on any matter. Therefore, the point of order is out of order. I call the prime minister.'

'Speaker, how strange that the opposition leader would think there is something sinister afoot by talking about jobs and growth for regional Australia.' Stanley changed his tone. 'The opposition speaks about the development of regional Australia, but when the government wants to speak about these matters, they don't want to listen.'

Bruce suppressed a shrug towards Hughes as the prime minister continued reading his speech. Messenger scrutinised the by-play between Hughes and Bruce, surmising that there was more going on with the leadership rumours than he figured. *Maybe it was Hughes who was the puppet master, and not Harper.*

With a renewed authority, Stanley straightened, reading with more enthusiasm than when he had started moments earlier. 'Speaker, we as a nation face several significant challenges before us. We are an important nation for the world. We provide resources other nations do not have. We provide food, raw textile materials, such as wool and cotton; we also provide minerals and ore providing wealth for other nations.

'The point I stress for the opposition, and indeed for all Australians to accept, is that our nation's wealth is not generated from the streets of Melbourne or Sydney. The bureaucrats of Canberra do not create wealth; no, Speaker, the hard-working folks who live in the regions create it. They are miners, farmers and the many folks who support them, such as transport and communication workers.

'These are the Australians we need to think about with every decision government makes; but and I say this not to be insensitive, far from it… but we should not be beholden to our regional communities to the extent where it threatens our nation's sovereignty and our wealth. This is the major challenge we face. We have vocal people with vested interests who have an unforgiving attitude towards resolving these challenges their way.

'For instance, we have rabid activists still screaming a climate emergency. They have done so for decades with little action by the world to resolve their hysterical claims.

'We need new thinking.

'We also have old-world unionists, insisting their members are the ones more qualified to do a job in Australia, rather than more highly qualified foreign workers. This is a protection racket, one which is worse than the tariff walls we used to fence our country's prosperity.

'We need new thinking.

'We have banks who lend our farmers money in the good times, then destroy them by foreclosing in the bad times.

'We need new thinking, Madam Speaker.

'We have an energy sector so wedded to coal that they will not even countenance the thought of investing in renewables or even uranium power.'

Messenger liked where Stanley was heading, glancing to Hughes, who smiled. Messenger then glanced to Stavloukas, who curled her lip in response, not happy with what she was hearing.

'Speaker, it's time for new thinking. It's time for new leadership; it's time for this government to step away from the chaos of never making a decision about these issues, and now make one.'

Hughes checked Cassandra Rogers, raising his eyebrows. He knew that the reason the government was not making decisions was because of the prime minister's reluctance to make one. She nodded, stuck the end of her pen in her mouth, and grinned. Messenger saw the by-play as he listened, his legs crossed, hands cupping his knee.

'Effective immediately,' the prime minister paused for a moment, 'my government will approve the Kirkpatrick mine, allowing preparations and construction to begin. The mine will have a mixed workforce, with foreign workers filling the gaps Australians cannot, or will not, fill. We will welcome here these workers under 457 visa arrangements.

'I also announce that the Kirkpatrick mine will be the last mine approved by the Australian government. We will legislate a twenty-year moratorium on approval for any future application for coal mining rights, passing through the parliament within the next two weeks. Australia needs to make a statement on climate policy, and we will lead with this initiative.'

The chamber seemed stunned; not a sound could be heard. Hughes stroked his face as he contemplated the implications.

'The government will now approve the expansion of uranium mining, intending to replace coal exports with an increase in uranium exports. We will seek investment in the provision of uranium-based power plants in Australia. We would hope to approve construction of four uranium power plants within the next two years. We must increase the supply of base-load power, reduce emissions, and decrease the cost of energy for all Australians. We want families to turn on their heaters. My government will make sure they have that choice; with a price I expect to be eighty percent cheaper than current prices.'

Messenger couldn't respond, even though he wanted to. He was in camera shot. Any gesture of surprise would have undermined the prime minister's statement.

'My government will begin negotiations with the Indian government to increase export of uranium. The unambiguous condition of sale is that such imports are to be used for energy creation. We encourage them to raise their population's living standards with cheaper, cleaner energy and reduce fossil emissions.'

Messenger glanced to Jaya, who smiled, raising her thumb.

'To make sure this important legislation is drafted and brought to the parliament within the next two weeks, I have changed ministerial arrangements. The parliament requires us to appointment as a replacement for James Harper as foreign minister, I intend to ask...'

Stavloukas sat eyes agog, waiting for her name.

'Wilson Campbell to take that role.'

'Hear, hear.' The government benches concurred.

'I have asked Maurice Roussett to accept the role of mining minister, to be added to his current environment portfolio. This will be a delicate and important task for Maurice to manage, especially introducing the coal moratorium, but I am sure he is up for the challenge.'

Roussett smiled, as if already briefed, but Messenger noticed a startled stare in his eyes.

'The importance of the drought cannot be understated, and I have appointed Ginni Stavloukas to make sure the funding proposals announced by my government are implemented in full, and that the financial institutions pull back from their aggressive approach to our hard-working farmers affected by the drought. It will be her job to manage the day-to-day queries of our regional and rural populations, to ensure they can survive until the rains return.'

Messenger considered it smart to move Stavloukas sideways, assigning her a public role she could not cope with. All those white male farmers with their misogynist views would drive her crazy. He smirked as he glanced away from her glare.

'Speaker, I will further report to the nation later today, when I will expand upon the government's plans as we bring forward legislation. I thank you for your indulgence, and I move that my statement be agreed to.' Stanley handed a copy of his speech to the clerk, who stamped it before noting it in the official record.

'The motion is that the prime minister's statement be agreed to… All those of that opinion say aye, the contrary no. I think the ayes have it.' The speaker didn't hesitate in declaring the outcome on the voices.

'Questions without notice; are there any questions?'

Stanley moved to the despatch box, shutting question time down. 'I ask that questions be placed on the notice paper.' He collected his files and strode off, leaving through the speaker's door.

The chamber erupted with noise from a rowdy opposition shouting objections. The leader of opposition business rushed to the despatch box, seeking a ruling for the cancellation of question time.

The speaker had no option other than to proceed with the daily program and provided a ruling. 'The prime minister has closed question time, which he may do at any time. There is no obligation to listen to one or twenty questions, as it is a privilege provided by the government. Therefore, the government can cancel questions by calling for them to be placed on the notice paper. I ask the opposition to please consider that alternative, as there will be no question time today. Clerk?'

The clerk stood to read notices, the normal business of the parliament resuming.

CHAPTER FORTY-TWO

'This is perfect for you. You now have a reason to call him out,' Hughes said as he topped up Harper's glass with Chardonnay.

'That rubbish he announced will destroy us.'

'Don't you see? It's a perfect opportunity for you now.'

Harper eyed Hughes for a moment, then sipped his wine as his colleague resumed his seat. 'I thought you said it was us that will strike down his leadership?'

'It is us.' Hughes squeezed a smile. 'Trust me; we need to get rid of him and we need to do it before the end of this sitting fortnight.'

'How do you think we should move?'

Hughes stretched a foot onto his desk. 'I reckon we raise the Greek's leadership ambitions.'

'Does she have any?'

'She doesn't yet know she has, but let's use her to get the discussion going.'

'Then what?' Harper asked.

'You call for a leadership spill, nominating yourself as a candidate, on Friday.'

'Why not next week?'

'Gives us time to get the numbers over the weekend, and to have the media demand a change of leadership.'

'Why would they do that?'

'For the sake of the country for starters, and to calm the relationship with India.' Hughes said.

'We don't have any trouble with India.'

Hughes smiled. 'We will when you point out tomorrow the racist undertones of cutting coal exports to them.'

'He wants to give them uranium.'

'A nuclear weapons threat, and he wants to give uranium to them?'

'I just take the foreign affairs angle?'

'It's important, as are the foreign workers, so it will need a subtle difference.'

'Why don't I just call the entire statement a crazy, chaotic approach to government, with decisions being made on the run?'

'You could do,' Hughes nodded, 'but remember, you were in the cabinet just a week ago, so he could tag you with those decisions.'

Harper sipped his wine, mulling over the plan. 'We call for a spill, then we defeat him. What then?'

'You make immediate decisions about food security, water management, and the value of supporting farmers.'

'We are already doing enough,' Harper said.

'Bash the banks.'

'They are our strongest supporters.'

'They know it's all politics. They know we don't mean what we say about them.'

'I'll think about that,' Harper said

'If you want to be prime minister, I suggest you need the public to hate Pete, thinking he is mad, demanding a change.'

'They have asked me for comment about today's statement.'

'Who asked you?'

'Cassandra Rogers. Any suggestions?'

Hughes chuckled for a moment. 'Don't go swimming with her.'

'Minister, I need a response to an article I am writing about you for tomorrow's national paper,' Cassandra Rogers said.

'What are you writing?' Stavloukas asked, as she straightened, leaning into her desk.

'I'm suggesting you are doing the numbers for a leadership challenge.'

'Well, I'm not.' The suggestion staggered the minister.

'I'm advised of a leadership spill next week, and you'll be a candidate.'

'Who's advising this?' Stavloukas pushed back in her chair.

'I'm also told this strategy is being driven by your demotion today.' Cass read from the notes she had taken when talking to Hughes thirty minutes earlier. 'Would you care to comment?'

Stavloukas stood and began pacing, stretching the telephone cord. 'I'm happy to serve the government in any capacity.'

'Oh, come on, Ginni. That's bullshit, and you know it. You have an opportunity; the door is open, why not step through?'

'Cass, you know I'm not happy with Stanley… this is off the record, by the way.'

'Yes, yes, of course.' Cass said, disappointed with the minister's declaration. 'What do you plan to do, support someone else, or go it alone? If you decide to call out Stanley, I will give you airtime tomorrow night.'

'To talk about what?'

'Alternative policies other than this rubbish announced by the prime minister this afternoon.'

'Why is it rubbish?'

'Aside from you getting sacked?'

'Yes, well, I would have thought the population would welcome the moratorium on coal mining. It's what they've been demanding for years.'

'You don't think by locking up our coal reserves we will not become an international pariah? Our national sovereignty threatened. Banning coal will not make it rain.' Cass referred to her notes.

Stavloukas swung about, leaning against her desk, and swapping the receiver into her other hand. 'Someone is counting numbers for me?'

'I'm surprised you don't know. I'm told you have a firm base of support.'

'Really?' Stavloukas smiled as she gazed at the ceiling. 'Would they choose a woman as leader?'

'Ginni, you are attractive, assertive and accessible. There is no reason you couldn't do the job.' Cass winced. 'I mean, you couldn't do worse than Stanley.'

'I suppose.'

'What can I say about your leadership ambitions for tomorrow?'

'You can say I'm considering my options and talking to key advisers.'

'Nice one. Look out for a page three feature.'

'Really?'

Cass didn't enjoy gilding the lily, but she had got what she wanted. 'This is your time; make the most of it and enjoy.'

Robert Wong struggled through the heavy office door, a piece of toast in his mouth, a file under his arm and two cups of tea clinking in their saucers. Jaya watched him as he made it to her desk, placing first the tea, then the file on it. He sat down, yanking the toast with its lashings of peanut butter from his mouth and biting off a generous mouthful.

Jaya chuckled at her staffer as he settled. 'Before getting into anything you want to talk about, what is your view of the prime minister's statement?' she asked.

Wong swallowed his mouthful. 'I reckon a leadership challenge is being mounted.' He tore off another generous chunk.

Jaya smiled. 'What does that mean for us?'

With a mouthful of toast, Wong said, 'Trouble.'

Jaya's face dropped with surprise. 'How so?'

'We have a change of prime minister; we lose our seat.'

Jaya clasped her hands in front of her face, worried by his response. 'You think we will lose?'

'Only if they change the prime minister.'

Wong finished his toast; he licked his fingertips then opened his file, sifting through papers until he found a list of numbers.

'I organised polling within the electorate; the results are interesting.' He passed a copy of the figures to Jaya, who studied them, paying particular attention to the summary. 'You'll note that if we stay with Stanley, the likelihood of us increasing our primary vote is high if they don't run a candidate against us. You'll also note that if the government runs a candidate against us, we keep that share of the vote of the primary vote. A spectacular result.'

'So, what's the problem?'

'Flip over the sheet.' Wong waited for Jaya to look at the reverse side. 'If they change to anyone else, then our primary vote collapses.'

'Badly?'

'Significantly, and you'll be a oncer.'

Jaya dropped her forehead to her hand, rubbing it with her thumb and forefinger as if relieving a headache. 'A oncer? We don't want that, do we?'

'We just make sure the government doesn't run a candidate against you.'

'Good point; how do we do that?'

'We argue to them it's better to have an independent winning the seat, rather than the progressives, or even the Greens.'

'What do we do?'

'We seek to support a leadership change on condition the government doesn't run a candidate. If they don't do the deal and they move to change the leadership, you threaten them to support the opposition, causing a change of government on the floor of the House.'

'You're kidding? I change sides to the opposition?'

'You only suggest you will change your support to leverage them to agree not to run a candidate against you.'

'So, I become one of them?' The idea did not enamour Jaya.

Wong shifted his glasses higher up his nose before flopping back in his chair. 'You either want to win another term, or you don't.'

Jaya swung her chair away from the desk, leaning back and stretching her arm along the desk, drumming her fingers. 'What do you suggest I do?'

'I think the prime minister's statement gives us plenty to work with.'

'Banning coal mining and depriving India of future coal for their energy network?' Jaya asked.

'Not only that, but banning all exports, which can only mean it will compromise Australia.'

'We lose export revenue?'

'That's one.' Wong slid a tea towards Jaya. 'Second, I reckon the idea of uranium power plants replacing coal-fired plants will not happen. Energy will become a significant cost to the population, killing business advantage. Plus, I reckon appointing Stavloukas to manage the drought is stupid.'

'Tell me what you really think, Robert.'

'We have to move.' Wong hesitated for a moment. 'You need to work Messenger.'

Jaya sighed and turned her head to face Wong. 'That could be difficult.'

'He's your closest contact with the government.'

Jaya tightened her jaw and lips, saying nothing.

Wong gnawed at his bottom lip before speaking. 'No matter what you think you may do together, get an outcome that will save you. All I'm saying is, think about it.'

'Easy for you to say,' Jaya said, smirking and running her forefinger along her lips.

CHAPTER FORTY-THREE

The loud thumping on his front door disturbed Messenger. He slipped on a t-shirt and padded along the duplex's long wooden corridor to answer the repeated early morning thump. He checked his watch as he opened the door and smiled when he recognised Jaya Rukhmani, decked out in sporty gym gear and with a pile of newspapers under her arm.

'I thought we agreed we wouldn't do this in Canberra,' Messenger said, standing aside and allowing Jaya to pass.

'You lot changed the rules yesterday with that stupid prime ministerial statement.'

'Have you eaten?' he asked, following Jaya as she turned into the kitchen.

She placed the newspapers on the bench and turned as Messenger entered. She stood before him, wrapping her arms around him, yanking him for a kiss. 'I've missed you.'

'Ditto, sweetheart,' Messenger whispered as he responded.

Jaya hugged him and placed her head on his chest as he put an arm around her, kissing the mop of curly hair.

'Do you want a coffee?'

'Offering anything else?'

Messenger raised his head, gazing to the ceiling with a sigh and a smile. 'Not at this time.'

'Then coffee will do.' Jaya disengaged and straddled a wooden stool at the bench.

'What brings you here?'

'The papers do.'

'What are they saying? Something complimentary, I hope.'

'Yeah, nah,' Jaya said as she spread the papers, opening Hancock Media's national paper. 'It seems Ginni Stavloukas is about to mount a challenge. Hancock Media are saying she has the numbers.'

'Bullshit.' Messenger stopped his coffee preparations, dragging the paper to him to review the headlines and scan the news. 'Cassandra Rogers wrote it. I reckon it's a setup.'

'She quotes Stavloukas,' Jaya said, pointing to the quote.

'She may have two or three votes; that's about it.'

'The other papers talk about the prime minister. Most are suggesting he is crazy, and the government is in chaos. The cartoonists have gone to town on him.'

Messenger went back to preparing the coffee. 'Doesn't mean a challenge is happening.'

'That's what I want to talk to you about.'

After pushing a few buttons on his espresso machine, Messenger turned to face her, a little alarmed by her comment.

'Why are you so interested in what we do?'

Jaya pouted her lips, then said, 'Well, you'd expect me to be interested in you, wouldn't you?'

Messenger flushed and wiped his face, turning away to retrieve the coffees.

'Frankly, I want to tell you I cannot guarantee supporting the government if they change the prime minister.'

Messenger stopped, his mouth dropping open ready to say something, but he didn't utter a word.

'I promised Stanley I would focus on my electorate first, then the government, treating all legislation on its merits.'

'You've kept your agreement.'

'It was an agreement with Stanley, nobody else.'

Messenger slid the cup to her; he dragged his coffee with him as he straddled a stool next to her. 'Nobody?'

'Well, not that obnoxious goose, Stavloukas.'

'What about Harper?'

Jaya tightened her jaw, screwed her nose, swaying her head. 'Perhaps not.'

'Nobody then?'

DOOMED

Jaya reached out to touch his hand. 'Maybe you, but then, I don't have a deal with you.'

'Political deal, you mean?'

'Is there any other arrangement between us?'

'Not yet.' Messenger laughed.

Jaya first sipped, then swallowed her espresso. She stood, resting her arm on Messenger's shoulder, tracing back a wisp of his hair around his ear with a finger.

'I have to get my morning exercise done, and if the gym isn't open here, I better get going.'

Messenger placed his arm around her. 'I take it the message you want to give me is that we should sort out the leadership.'

'Bart, let me say this clearly. I have a better chance of winning Melbourne if Stanley is leader than I do if someone replaces him.'

'But we could lose government.'

'Not my issue.' Jaya stepped around him. 'You could lose government if I support the opposition on a confidence motion, which I will move if you move against him.'

'That's somewhat provocative.'

'As I said… I want to keep my seat. So, it's in your best interests I do that.' She pecked him on the cheek and began to leave. 'Can we have time together on the weekend? Dinner perhaps?'

Messenger was still considering her comments as he followed her down the passage to the front door. 'Yeah, let's.'

Jaya turned as she reached the front door and they embraced, kissing as passionately as they had when she arrived.

'You feel good,' Messenger said.

Jaya smiled as she stepped back, skipping off the front step and waving goodbye. 'So do you, minister.'

Messenger sighed and closed the door, making his way back to finish his coffee and scan the papers again. He took the television remote from the fruit bowl, flicking on the morning news program just in time to hear the final few moments of an editorial interview with Cassandra Rogers.

'The government remains in chaos after the prime minister's statement in the parliament yesterday. Many ministers tell me he is out of step with government policy. We have not even discussed the decisions he has made in the cabinet. We already have one leadership contender raising her hand, counting numbers. I am told James Harper will issue a media statement later this morning, outlining his concerns with the PM's statement.'

'What is the opposition leader's response, Cass?' Tamara O'Byrne asked, grinning at the camera.

'I'm not sure Meredith Bruce's opinion is relevant right now, given the obvious crisis within the government. Although I have spoken to her about the chaos, her response was muted. Do you have another question?'

O'Byrne sat back in her chair, checking the production sheet but not seeing another question listed.

'Perhaps you could ask what the leadership group of the government is saying?'

There was dead air until O'Byrne realised she should speak. 'What are the other leaders saying?'

'Yeah, good question.' Cass smiled. 'Christopher Hughes has supported the prime minister, as has a spokesperson for the treasurer.'

Messenger cocked an eyebrow, wondering who had said that to her, given he hadn't spoken to her for over a couple of weeks.

'This will be a very interesting few days, as we could have a new prime minister in Australia within the week,' Cass said.

'Thank you, Cassandra Rogers in Canberra.'

'Oh, and before I go, let me tell you that the drought relief package should begin filtering its way through the affected communities this week. As you know, Tam, many of these communities are doing it tough.'

'Yes, indeed, they are. I am sure we will see significant improvement within many regions.'

'Many? Which ones?' Cass asked, holding back a smile.

O'Byrne looked off camera and fumbled with a sheet of paper. She dithered over answering the question before taking instruction from her earpiece and ending the interview. 'Thanks once again. That was Cassandra Rogers in Canberra.'

Messenger thought the by-play between the newscasters was weird, but focused back on the issue at hand… would there be a leadership challenge? He assumed he had better go find out.

CHAPTER FORTY-FOUR

The prime minister was sitting at his desk reading the national Hancock broadsheet, a piece of jam toast in his hand, a cup of tea nearby. He peered over his glasses as Messenger entered and waved him to a seat at the desk. He folded away the newspaper before he spoke.

'What do you reckon is going on?'

'I reckon there is a tonne of white noise about your announcements yesterday, but nothing we can't manage.'

'Any reaction from the financial media?'

'Positive, although cynical about the moratorium on coal.'

'We will pick up the climate change lobby at least.'

'Maybe.' Messenger wasn't so sure. 'I'll be happier once we see the polls.'

'What's Harper doing?'

'Jimmy has revealed little at this stage.' Messenger gnawed the edge of his lower lip. 'I haven't heard of anyone doing numbers.'

'Stavloukas has suggested she is.'

'I wouldn't believe anything she's got to say at the moment. She may resign from cabinet though.'

'This will be a good thing.'

'What is Christopher advising?'

'Nothing.' Stanley popped the last piece of toast in his mouth. 'I haven't reached out to him.'

'Was it his idea to do the statement?' Messenger asked.

'He didn't say not to do it. The uranium deal was his idea. I think I may have told you.'

'Are you sure he's solid?'

'Like concrete.'

Messenger was doubtful. 'I had a chat to Rukhmani this morning.'

'Oh yes,' Stanley smirked.

'She was out jogging when she came past.' Messenger tried to tell the truth. 'She is supporting you.'

'What does that mean?'

'If you go, the government will go, because she will move a motion of no confidence.'

The news surprised Stanley. 'Well, good for her. I should drop her a note.'

'Can't hurt.'

'Should we run someone against her?'

Messenger hesitated for a moment. 'I think we should, no matter what happens.'

'It might send the seat back to the other side.'

'Or we could win it with her preferences.'

Stanley nodded. 'That would be a big win for us.'

'If we run a suitable candidate, we split the vote even further. If we finish second, then we'll win. The Gerrard factor is gone, and we can turn it into a strong Conservative seat.'

'This is your university supervisor for your PhD?'

Messenger shrugged. 'It's politics.'

Thirty minutes later, Messenger wandered into Christopher Hughes' office for a chat. Hughes was just back from his morning swim at the parliamentary gym pool and was still in his gym suit, although he had kicked off his track shoes and was resting his bare feet on his coffee table as he lounged on the leather couch. He was reading a wad of press clippings supplied by the government's media liaison office.

'The prime minister seems to have raised a small fire storm with some in the media,' Hughes said as he straightened, waving Messenger to sit.

'Especially from Rogers.' Messenger searched for a reaction but detected nothing.

'She works hard, that one.'

'Is she right about the Greek?'

Hughes glanced up, smiling like a cheeky boy. 'She could be.'

'Are you setting her up?'

'Who?'

'Both.' Messenger examined Hughes again.

'I may have told a few folks that all politicians are ambitious.'

'Including you?' asked Messenger.

Hughes' face dropped, his lips pursed, eyebrows knotted. 'And you, no doubt?'

'I once had ambitions, but not now. You, on the other hand are coming to the end of a stellar career.'

'Mostly in opposition.'

'Whether it's opposition or government is no matter,' Messenger said. 'What is important is whether you remain a player. I think you do.'

Hughes didn't respond, gazing at Messenger for a few moments, then averting his stare. 'What are you suggesting, Barton?'

'Nothing… other than who stands to gain from a leadership challenge right now?'

'Jimmy, of course. He will make a solid prime minister.'

'You know, and I know, he doesn't have the numbers.'

Hughes eyed his colleague. 'Who does?'

'You do.'

'For the prime minister.'

'If the prime minister was not a candidate in a leadership challenge, what then?'

'Then my numbers can vote for whoever they want.' Hughes bristled. 'But you forget, Pete is my leader, and my numbers support him continuing that job until he deems otherwise.'

Messenger raised his hand to his mouth, poking his thumbnail into the gap in his front bottom teeth. 'Where do I sit amongst all of this?'

'You are the deputy, the future of the party. I wouldn't expect that to change anytime soon.'

'No matter who is the leader?'

'No matter who is the leader,' Hughes said with a sly smile.

Messenger studied Hughes, then said, 'I was talking to the member for Melbourne this morning.'

'I gather there might be something between you two.'

Messenger shifted in his chair, hoping to hide his anxiety. 'I wouldn't believe everything you hear.'

'Comes from the driver pool, actually.'

'As I said, don't believe everything you hear. My job is to secure her vote. I'm doing what I can to make sure she votes with us.'

Hughes smiled a broad cheesy grin, nodding. 'Good boy.'

'Anyway, she tells me she may move a motion of no confidence in the government if we move on Stanley.'

Hughes tensed. 'Say what?'

'She claims she has no deal with anyone other than Peter. If we dump him, there is no reason she couldn't dump us.'

'How serious is she?'

'Very.'

'Does she want anything?'

'Re-election.'

'That ain't going to happen. It'll be us or the other mob at the next election.'

'If we don't run a candidate, what then?'

'We will, I can assure you,' Hughes said.

'Okay.' Messenger felt comfortable with the confirmation. 'My point though, is this… If we need her vote, do we negotiate on not running a candidate against her?'

Hughes sighed. 'Let's hope it doesn't come to that.'

'If it does?'

'Then you had better do whatever you have to do, to make sure she supports us.'

CHAPTER FORTY-FIVE

Cassandra Rogers unclipped her mic and was leaving the Canberra studio when her silenced telephone throbbed. She checked the screen, tapping it to answer.

'You're ringing to tell me I have the job?'

The manner in which she answered his call took Tony Hancock by surprise. 'Well, no, I'm not.'

'Don't tell me, you still think I should get even more exclusive stories?'

'You're doing fine,' Hancock said.

'You know I can get that LA appointment for you, don't you?'

There was no response.

'Tony, did you hear? Once there is a new prime minister, I can guarantee you, you'll get the gig.'

'How do you know that?' Hancock asked.

'I'm very close to the next prime minister. He promised me he will sign the appointment once he knows you have appointed me to host the show.'

Hancock exhaled with force.

'You will not let me down, will you, Tony?'

'This is the reason I called.'

'You've made a decision?' Cass checked about as she stepped out into a corridor.

'You belittle Tamara again on camera, or indeed any time, then you won't be working for Hancock Media in any role, let alone hosting a television show.'

Cass stopped walking, rubbing the back of her head. 'Say what?'

'You embarrass and ridicule a colleague again, and you can walk out the door.'

'Is that you saying this, Tony… or your cock?'

'For heaven's sake, Cass, I'm serious. What you did was cheap. I cannot condone that behaviour, then promote you. You are on thin ice. I have pressure to let you go.'

Cass panted, trying to calm herself. 'I've given you everything. I have sacrificed things that are important to me, for you and the company. You promised this program to me… you promised me.'

'Things change.'

'Well, let me tell you this, Tony,' Cass said, seething the words into the phone. 'Unless you change your view and start treating me with respect, fulfilling your promises, then what I will rain upon you will not be worth the memory of any pleasures you have with that tramp.'

'Are you threatening me?'

'You give me what I want. I will give you what you want, and everyone will be happy.'

'Heed what I say, Rogers. You do what I have asked you to do.'

'No, you listen, Tony.' Cass punched the wall with the heel of her hand. 'If I don't get the promotion you promised me, then you will be exposed to be the lying, sexual abuser and predator you truly are. Your life will never be the privileged dream ever again. So, choose wisely, my friend; choose very wisely.'

'Leave Tamara alone.'

'Your choice.' Cass ended the call.

CHAPTER FORTY-SIX

The audio guys from StageWerks began setting up their equipment on the grassy slope, just down from the forecourt of the federal parliament, soon after dawn. Their client insisted they wanted a sound system good enough for several thousand union protestors expected to hear various speakers at the planned rally. Facing towards the old parliament house, they erected the aluminium stage before 8 a.m., and were now testing the system with sound checks.

Already the slope was attracting various groups who were staking their piece of grass with union flags and protest banners. Buses began pulling up in Federation Mall, spilling out passengers keen to hear union leaders protesting the government. Organisers were stalking through the massing crowd with loud hailers, encouraging comrades to be loud and proud, which was a union code for fighting for their rights… meaning there could be trouble.

The previous afternoon, in a convened national telephone hook-up soon after the prime minister's statement, the national executive agreed on a powerful response to the threat of job losses for Australian workers at mining sites. The outrageous attack by the prime minister, with his threat to close the coal industry and import foreign workers, would undermine the pay and conditions of members, and this shocked the executive.

They agreed to a press release stating that this government attack on workers was not only the unions' fight but should concern every Australian about the callous nature of the prime minister towards working families.

During the two hours of lively discussion, they called a National

Day of Resistance for the following day. They encouraged workers who could get to Canberra to do so. They needed loud, angry voices to send an obvious message of resistance to the government. The union asked each executive member to pledge their membership to the day; there was no hesitation. Once a commitment was made, Unions ACT coordinated arrangements to cater for a large protest. They organised transport, booked flights, hired buses, and established carpools to get union members to Canberra. The response was immediate as workers downed tools and headed to Canberra overnight.

Garrick Higgins had taken the first flight from Melbourne, working on his speech in the hire car he organised at the airport. The formal speeches were due to begin at noon, after those marching from various points around the parliament precinct arrived. He parked near the top of the hill and could see the crowd as protestors began filling up space. He expected five thousand union members to attend, but it already seemed the number was well past that figure.

The early atmosphere of the growing crowd was one of amusement, as sporadic games of cricket were organised, and gas bar-b-ques began smoking from meat on the grill. To add to Higgins's anxiety, he could see tough types knocking back cans of beer. He hoped union marshals would attend to this recklessness and remained concerned the protest could get out of hand.

Nearing noon, Higgins watched as groups chanting anti-government slogans marched in. He estimated the crowd now to be nearing a staggering twenty thousand, which was amazing given the limited time available. He noted an increasing number of vocal students near the front of the stage chanting anti-fascist slogans, likening the government to right-wing demigods keen to harm working Australians. This also alarmed Higgins as he moved closer to the stage, searching for an event organiser so that he could introduce himself and ask for tighter management protocols to be placed upon the students.

After expressing his concerns, he waited for the opening session with other colleagues, all looking forward to their moment to speak to the crowd, although anxious at the growing number of protestors. He took a call from an exasperated colleague, who reported that a group of construction workers were heading in the wrong direction, marching towards the forecourt of the parliament, and being held back by lines of police in riot gear.

'Where are you going, comrade?' someone asked Higgins as he strode off towards the demonstration.

He stopped to respond. 'There's a hiccup at Parliament House. They have called for me to come and sort it out. There is a group of protestors at the wrong place, and they have asked me to convince them to come to Federation Hill.'

'Don't be long; we can't hold your place. We kick off in ten minutes.'

'If I'm not back, then don't wait.'

Higgins hurried away. As he left the organised protest, he recognised the potential trouble brewing in the parliamentary forecourt. He estimated that a thousand unionists were creating a chanting mass. They were by the enormous stone pylons supporting the parliament's veranda at the front entrance.

'The workers, united, will never be defeated. The workers, united, will never be defeated.'

Higgins scouted the edge of the chanting mob, coming to the end of the police line. He explained to a parliamentary security officer who he was, flashing his ID, and what he wanted to do. The officer let him through, and he worked his way to the centre of the action behind a thick line of police in riot gear holding back the surging mob of chanting protestors. He went to a police sergeant who was organising his men and monitoring the action a few metres behind the line.

'I'm here from the major event,' Higgins said, wasting no time with formalities. 'Let me talk to them.'

The sergeant tightened his bottom lip, gnawing it as he considered the offer. 'Sweet; just calm them down if you can.'

Higgins took the microphone from the loud hailer someone had handed him and began speaking in demanding tones to his workers.

'Comrades, listen up,' he bellowed into the microphone. 'Listen up; a bit of shoosh.'

'The workers, united, will never be defeated.'

'Comrades, settle down.'

'Give him a chance,' someone yelled a little way back into the mob.

'The workers, united, will never be defeated.'

'Shut up!' a few more workers screamed.

'The workers, united, will never be defeated.'
'Comrades, this isn't the way.'
'Let's go in! Let's go in!' A new chant started from the back.
'Comrades, we can't do this.'
'The workers, united, will never be defeated.'
'Break the door! Break the door!' Another new chant started.
'Hold them!' yelled the sergeant.
'Comrades, hold back.'
'Shut the fuck up!' an angry tattooed man shouted.
'Steady boys,' the sergeant commanded.
'The workers, united, will never be defeated.'

A group of workers had broken through the weakened line at the edge and were now fighting their way forward against the police line, which began using batons and shields to hold them back.

'The workers, united, will never be defeated.'
'Fall back!' the sergeant cried.

The police line fell away, regrouping four deep in front of the glass and metal front doors of the parliament. A heavy metal stave came crashing down on the police line, hitting helmets and shoulder guards.

Higgins was hard up against the glass door as hands grappled his arms and shoulders, pulling him through to the void between the outer and inner security doors.

'Lock the security doors,' the sergeant barked. 'Can we get the shop locked as well?'

'This is unbelievable,' Higgins said, unaware that a film of rich red blood was covering the left side of his face.

'Friends of yours?' the sergeant asked.
'What do we do?'
'You do nothing. Go through to the foyer; there's a medical triage set up by the great hall doors. Use it.'
'Nothing wrong with me.'
'Comrade, you have blood all over you. I suspect you'll be out like a light soon, so go through, will you, and leave this to us.'
'I just want to talk to them.'
'Mate, nick off, will ya?' The sergeant directed a security guard to lead Higgins away, then spoke on his two-way radio. 'Commander,

we have fifty of ours under direct threat at the doors. I have another hundred in the foyer to hold the line once we give up the outer doors.'

The sergeant listened to instructions, then moved to brief his unit commanders in the foyer, with instructions to let no one through. He spoke into his communication headphone device, advising the line outside the doors to push forward and then wave back through the doors, retreating through the security passageway.

At the directed moment, the police line moved forward, smashing their batons to repel the workers, who collapsed back against the vicious attack. As the workers moved, the police line weakened, with officers funnelling back into the void, then scurrying through the security passageway to reinforce the line forming in the marble foyer. Most of the police outside could make it. Two didn't, falling at the feet of the angry mob, which was pushing into the void unaware that two police officers were lying injured against the heavy metal and thickened glass inner doors.

'The workers, united, will never be defeated. The workers, united, will never be defeated.'

Leading rioters realised they could never get through the reinforced doors, instead making their way to the now locked parliamentary gift shop door. A man smashed a large wrench into the glass, and it fell away, allowing the shouting mob to enter the shop to get into the parliament through another door. Police held the doorway as flaying arms and metal rods came down upon them. The wrench raised again, then thrust down before being blocked by a baton. Another baton smashed the shoulder of the demonstrator wielding the wrench. He dropped it and they kicked away it.

As rioters tried to push their way through the blocked door, others ransacked the gift shop, tossing books and other items at the police line. First one rioter, then another, and then yet another crowd-surfed the blockade, jumping over the police line, only to be brought down by parliamentary security staff, who grappled them to the marble floor, tying their wrists behind them with plastic stays, then flinging them along the tiled floor to the side, by the marble stairs. Those rioters who hadn't made it to the shop now pushed hard against the main doors. The police line linked arms and pushed back against the doors, with staff and others linking in behind the police line to create a greater barricade.

Rioters were now smashing whatever they had against the reinforced glass.

The thumping and screaming attracted a crowd of tourists, parliamentary staff, and political operatives, who were standing back watching; most were on the first-floor balconies, staring down at the mayhem. Parliamentary security staff were yelling instructions, scurrying about the foyer, and keeping the area clear.

Barton Messenger was oblivious to the chaos in the parliament foyer, as were most folks enjoying a late morning latte at Aussie's café. He returned his cup, not wanting to have the gossipers of Parliament House report his poor form, leaving someone else to clear up his mess. He knew that the metaphor could be a critical look for the nation's treasurer.

He stepped out through the security and into the foyer, wanting to cut through to the House of Representatives' wing. He planned to visit Jaya. Nothing important, just a drop-by whilst he had the time. Messenger observed that the security guard was not at his station as he walked out of the secured area. Now conscious of yelling coming from the front entrance, he slowed his walk as he passed the marble stairs, noticing a police contingent outside the main doors in the vestibule trying to stop a noisy mob from coming in. There was a line of police and parliamentary security barricading the main doors. He could see fighting in the vestibule recess as police were filing back through the security passage, coming to reinforce the human barricade.

'Sir?' a parliamentary security officer interrupted. 'Mr Messenger; please, for your own safety, could you move away?'

Messenger mounted the marble stairs, transfixed on the ugliness descending on the entrance. He watched as a female police officer was struck and then collapsed at the front door. He then saw another officer go to her aid, kneeling over her, but they pushed the man down as the mob pressed forward. The officers now caught underfoot, hard against the doors. The commander, who Messenger thought was in charge, barked several orders, and police along with security staff linked arms, pushing into the doors, holding tight. Then another line of security staff, and what seemed to be parliamentary staffers, formed two more lines of human shield, linking into the barricade that was now six deep against the glass front doors. Messenger called his office, reporting the chaos to his staff, insisting they lock the doors and contact other ministerial offices advising the same.

He glanced about the foyer, observing several people with injuries being treated by the doors to the Great Hall. He moved to help the parliamentary nurse.

'Can I help?'

'Mr Messenger, if you want to help, then I suspect you should not be here. You'll only cause a conflict of priorities for the security staff,' the nurse said.

'Messenger?' a voice growled.

Messenger checked about and saw a bloodied man lying on a blanket, resting on his elbow, and gesturing to him.

'This is your fault.'

Messenger moved over, crouching over the man. He didn't recognise him. 'How's this chaos my fault?'

'Your dumb arse prime minister, and his stupid statement yesterday, caused this.'

'Mate, this looks like a rogue union riot to me.'

'We didn't come here to cause this.'

'Yeah, well, who's smashing the doors? Students in hard hats?'

A scream pierced the air as a rioter jumped over the barricade, then was brought down near the stairs by a security officer, smashing his head into the marble floor. Messenger straightened to watch, then returned his attention to the bloodied complainer on the floor.

'Here's a question for you.' Messenger said, shaking his head. 'What were you dropkicks thinking you might do by smashing your way into the parliament? What did you think you would achieve?'

'This is not our riot; this is yours.'

'Yeah, sure mate.' Messenger straightened, moving away. 'You and your mates will cheer this for years, but you'll lose the Australian people because of it.'

'You already lost them, ya prick.'

Messenger turned, walking towards the entrance to the House of Representatives' wing, thinking he now had a reason to check on Jaya.

Garrick Higgins yelled at him as he left, 'Ban coal and we will fight you forever.'

Messenger didn't respond as he strode away, hoping to get away from the chaos. He knew this would help the government but wondered if it would help the prime minister.

'Hold!' the sergeant barked at the human barricade.

More rioters clambering over the police line at the shop entrance were arrested, many with bloodied faces. The rioters pushed hard. The two police officers at the feet of the rioters, against the bottom of the doors, protected themselves as best as they could against the shoving mob.

The chanting stopped, becoming a cacophony of loud yells of effort as the rioters kept shoving at the doors.

The sergeant responded to his radio communication, 'We need you now. Do it now or we are done.'

A solid armoured blue truck jumped the gutter of the forecourt, speeding alongside the concrete retaining wall with siren blaring. The windows were wire-mesh covered, and they plastered the word POLICE along the sides and back. Rioters divided as the truck moved around the edge of the mob. A large nozzle on the roof engaged and a solid spurt of water gushed from it, increasing to a high-pressure jet, which knocked over rioters caught by the stream of water.

The water cannon had an immediate impact, with the mob splintering and dispersing as more riot police arrived, pushing them away from the parliament's doors, away from the forecourt. The water seemed to cool mob aggression; rioters ran away from the parliament, back to the Federation Hill congregation. Within moments, the front doors were clear.

As the rioters dispersed, the sergeant directed six officers to attend to their fallen colleagues, now stretching along the floor in front of the doors. He could see blood from his officer, a colleague jerking off her helmet as willing hands got to them.

CHAPTER FORTY-SEVEN

The parliament fell silent as the speaker stood to address the House before question time to report the riot and its immediate aftermath.

'I'm sure I speak for members on both sides of this House when I say the disgraceful and unjustifiable demonstration that occurred earlier today at the front entrance to Parliament House is one of the most shameful in this nation's history. A protest rally remained peaceful until just before noon, when a group of marchers entered the parliamentary precinct. It was very clear that alcohol affected many of these demonstrators. This group refused to accept police direction and forced a breach in the police lines, running towards the main entrance of Parliament House.

'Police first formed a protective line but then forced back to the main doors. The police line was further withdrawn from this area because of the high level of violence being experienced by officers. An extra line of defence then redeployed to an area inside the front doors with the support of parliamentary security personnel. This deployment stabilised the situation for a short period. However, rioters using increasing force broke through the first line of security doors.

'Rioters then used weapons, including a large hammer, a wheel brace and a stanchion torn from the external doors, to break open the internal doors. Simultaneously, a second group of rioters used other weapons to break into the Parliament House gift shop. Security and police held them at the internal doors. They ransacked the shop with major damage caused.

'Police repelled rioters from Parliament House and driven back onto the forecourt after the police used a water cannon in a coordinated counterattack.

'Shortly afterwards, rioters dispersed, and police controlled the area. So far, about ninety personnel have reported injuries, including lacerations, sprains, and head and eye injuries. I understand one person remains in hospital. The full extent of the looting and criminal damage that resulted from the occupation of the Parliament House gift shop has yet to be determined. They made arrests of fifteen people charged with a variety of offences.

'On behalf of members, I would like to commend Parliament House security staff, Australian Protective Service officers and Australian Federal Police officers for ensuring the building remained secure. I would also like to acknowledge the efforts of several other members of staff called upon to help during the initial stages of the disturbance.

'In particular, I want to pay tribute to the Parliament House nurses. They performed in a most commendable and professional manner, treating forty injured personnel on the floor of the foyer.

'Finally, I wish to apologise most sincerely to the Australian people, and those from overseas visiting Parliament House, who may have been involved, inconvenienced, frightened, or shocked by this deplorable incident. To them I say: what you witnessed here today is not typical of Australia or Australians, and I speak for all my colleagues when I say we hope and pray it never will be.'

'Hear, hear!' members responded.

'I call the prime minister.'

Stanley stood at the despatch box, checking his notes.

'Madam Speaker, on your indulgence, I would like to address the matter that you have just spoken to. On behalf of the government, I want to endorse everything you have said about what happened earlier today. It was very unpleasant, and for the people involved… the Australian Federal Police and Parliament House staff, whose responsibility it was to deal with this incident. A very frightening experience, and not an incident I would want any of them to go through again.

'I have thanked, on behalf of the government, and I now do so on behalf of the people of Australia, all the police officers and Parliament House staff. I had the opportunity of speaking to an assembly of them before question time.

'I would also like to inform the House that I went to Canberra hospital and visited Senior Constable Helen Casperelli, injured during the riot. Several of these shameless rioters kicked her in the head and body. I'm pleased to say she is recovering well and will be out of hospital, I hope, tomorrow.

'Anybody who thinks for a moment that the violent demonstration served any purpose today and that it will intimidate this government into changing its policies on anything is one hundred percent wrong.'

'Hear, hear!' the government members responded.

'I hope the leader of the opposition will disavow, in language as strong as mine, what occurred today, and totally disassociate the party she leads from what occurred. I do not think anybody can for a moment pretend that those who organised today's rally, those who used inflammatory language, those who exceeded reasonable political criticism, can escape responsibility for what occurred.

'Robust political exchange is part and parcel of Australian way of life, and I hope it will always remain a part of Australian life, but thuggery, and behaviour that allows thuggery to occur, is not part of the Australian political scene. I hope an incident like today never occurs again.'

'Hear, hear!' government members responded again as Stanley resumed his seat.

The speaker glanced towards Meredith Bruce, and she nodded, before standing at the despatch box.

'On indulgence, let me say on behalf of the opposition that we condemn the appalling violence that occurred at the doors of Parliament House just a few hours ago. We on this side of the parliament have always believed there is no place for the storming of a parliament or for violence against police. Our sympathy goes out to those police officers and others who suffered injury in the line of duty. We share the disgust that many have expressed at the violence that occurred at the demonstration.'

'Hear, hear!' opposition members responded.

'I want to say that I stood, along with many thousands of others, at the real rally that took place in front of Parliament House at Federation Hill. These were many, many thousands of decent, hardworking Australians. Of course, that rally was well away from the place where a small number took matters into their own hands. Many, many thousands of people took the opportunity to express their views peacefully and properly. At the real rally I, along with many thousands of others, heard a crowd voice a measured anger at yesterday's statement by the prime minister, and what his government wants to inflict on Australian workers by introducing foreign workers to replace Australian workers and by banning coal mining.

'But, as far as the opposition is concerned, we clarify that we condemn acts of violence, destruction of property and attacks on police, attendants, and other staff, and I associate the opposition with those remarks the speaker and the prime minister made. We have always been of the view that violence has no place in the political life of the Australian community.

'We will never defend the actions that took place at the door and inside Parliament House, and we will support you, Speaker, in the plans you have to tighten security. You can be confident you will receive the absolute cooperation of the opposition as we work together to make sure that violence never occurs in this place again. I thank the House.'

As Bruce moved away from the despatch box, Stanley was quick to his feet, reaching across the table to shake hands with her. She stretched to take his hand as the photographers clicked to capture the moment.

Christopher Hughes watched, then retired to the government members' lounge off the chamber. He texted James Harper, asking him to join him. Hughes surmised that question time would focus on the demonstration and the prime minister's statement, and he would not get questions. A perfect moment to have a brief chat with Harper.

Within moments, the two politicians were discussing the events of the day.

'He may have just recovered,' Harper said with a heavy sigh.

Hughes didn't respond as he sat with his fingers steepled before his face, tapping the tips.

'I'm not so sure,' he said. 'His decision yesterday was nuts and can benefit us.'

'Not sure today's events would help that. He'll have wonderful media plastered everywhere from his visit to the hospital. Whoever thought of that for him is a genius.'

'That's why we now have to attack him.'

'For visiting a beaten copper? Give me a break.'

'No,' Hughes said. 'For his idea to deny India a source of coal.'

'It's not just India.'

'We can make it all about India and call it xenophobia.' Hughes smiled.

'Call Pete a racist?' Harper scoffed. 'Not sure that'll go down well.'

'We don't call him a racist. We imply that the decision to ban coal exports to India might be.'

'How is that going to help?'

'You are the former foreign minister; you imply you did not discuss the decision with the prime minister when you were a minister, and the PM is acting on the run, trying to save his leadership.'

Harper nodded.

'You call him out on that,' Hughes continued. 'You call him out on the foreign workers' legislation. And call him out on the drought package as not doing enough for our farmers.'

'But we are.'

'No one knows that, so own the narrative.'

'Then what?'

'You declare that the prime minister should call a party meeting and spill all leadership positions.'

Harper shook his head. 'He'll never do that.'

'He will if I recommend him to do so.' Hughes tapped his nose.

They sat for a moment, a faint sound of yelling coming from the chamber. Harper asked, 'When do you think I should do this?'

'An hour after question time, which gives me enough time to brief the media.'

'Rogers, you mean?'

'She's doing excellent work for us.'

'You finally bed her?'

Hughes smiled. 'Not yet, but it's close. We had a nice nudie swim the other night.'

'You can't help yourself, can you?' Harper laughed. 'This is why you'll never be leader.'

Hughes laughed too, narrowing his eyes, and tapping his hand against the padded arm of the chair. He was just days away from becoming prime minister, and his chuckling mate opposite was going to make it happen for him.

CHAPTER FORTY-EIGHT

Cassandra Rogers' phone pinged a text as she left Christopher Hughes' office. She checked it as she strolled the blue grey carpet of the ministerial wing, surprised to find two texts. One was advising a James Harper media briefing in the courtyard in thirty minutes, and another was from Jaya Rukhmani, asking her to call by for a quick chat. It would be a tight timing squeeze, but she headed off to the independent's office in the furthest point of the House of Representatives' wing.

Cass declined the offer of tea, waiting for Jaya to retrieve information she wanted to discuss. Jaya ignored the separate chair, joining her on the couch.

'I'm sorry Jaya, but I have a media conference to get to.'

Jaya smiled. 'This is background.'

Cass smirked and nodded.

'You have been writing about a possible leadership challenge with the government.'

'I'm doing my job.'

'What they haven't factored into their plans is that I may not support a new leader and could switch to the opposition.'

Cass's hand dropped to her bag, dragging out a notepad and flicking to an open page before taking notes. 'You say you only support Stanley?'

'I'm not being quoted, am I?'

'No, we're fine.'

'I mean, I need to trust you on this.'

'Trust away, as much as anyone in this place.'

'I have certain needs and I want them satisfied.'

Cass was quizzical, a little unsure what Jaya meant.

'I don't want coal exports to stop for India.'

'This a personal thing for you?'

'Personal?' Jaya hesitated. 'No, not at all; but if I know the Indian government, and its people, they will not accept Australia ending their agreement. It would be tragic for the Indian economy, ending any dream of raising its lower caste from the depths of poverty.'

'How is this framed with the chatter around government leadership contests?'

'I will support a prime minister who continues to trade with India.'

'That cuts out Stanley.'

'Maybe so.'

'Just to be clear.' Cass scratched her head. 'Although you have advised the government that you may shift your vote to the opposition if they change leaders, you also want the government to continue to supply India with coal.'

'Yes.'

'Do you see a paradox here? Stanley is not supporting coal.'

'Oh, I think he will, if his leadership depends on it.'

'You think he will back flip?'

'He may very well have to if the rumours you write about are to be believed.'

'Who won't you support?'

'Stavloukas and Hughes.'

'Hughes is not a candidate; he supports the prime minister.'

'Does he, Cass?' Jaya remarked with a smirk. 'Does he?'

Cass felt a flush rush through her and shifted on the couch. She wondered if Jaya knew anything about her association with Hughes.

'Quote me on this.' Jaya smiled. 'I want the farmers to be looked after, and I want the leadership chatter to stop. The farmers deserve better.'

Cass made sure she had the exact quote, and asked, as she finished writing, 'Have you heard from your farmer friend again?'

'Messenger said he was looking after him.'

'I might follow him up.' Cass took a note. 'Who are you talking to in the government about your concerns?'

Jaya avoided a direct answer. 'I speak to them all, but on this issue, I have a direct line to the prime minister.'

Cass chewed the end of her pen. 'Interesting.' She studied what she thought to be a novice politician. She might consider changing her view. 'What's the endgame for you, Jaya?'

Jaya didn't hesitate in answering. 'Re-election.'

'I've called you together to make a statement.' Harper was standing surrounded by over twenty journalists, camera operators, and sound technicians.

'As the former leader of the party for a long time, it concerns me that the government is stagnating in its focus on policy to help growth and prosperity of the Australian economy. I am very concerned that as we stagnate, we give an opportunity for a Bruce government, which would be disastrous for the nation. It is my judgement that I have the experience of leadership to become prime minister and defeat Meredith Bruce. I remain concerned by the prime minister's statement this week, which identified a new direction for the government. A direction which I do not agree.

'I do not have a nasty word to say about Peter Stanley. I worked with him, serving loyally, but now is a time for change. It's not about personalities. For me, it's about policy.

'The prime minister's recent statement, to me, is framed with no thought for the future energy needs of the country. No thought about the economic needs of our trading partners. I would go so far as to suggest that they could consider it xenophobic for a government to deny another country an energy source, based upon a weird notion of moral righteousness.'

Cass was standing at the back of the pack. She shook her head and smirked as Hughes' earlier words came back at her.

'I believe we need a new direction, a new energy on the front bench. We need a new focus on the things that matter to all Australians, such as our security, our welfare, and our prosperity.

'These are not the messages we heard from the prime minister. The message he gave me, and I am sure the people of Australia, is that we have closed our doors to helping our neighbours. We have closed our mind on protecting Australian jobs, and we have declared, by the government's omissions in funding, that our farmers are no longer important. This is in contrast to the financiers and policy flakes, who would have us believe we are under the catastrophic effect of an immediate climate emergency. Therefore, instead of managing our drought, we would rather invest in the hoax industry.

'We cannot continue with this blinkered policy. I am asking the prime minister to declare all leadership positions vacant at the party room meeting next Tuesday. This will allow the party to vote on the future, based upon liberal values, focused on Australia and its people.

'I therefore announce that I will be a candidate in any future leadership vote. I believe that as prime minister, I will withstand the attacks the government is experiencing from within the party, within the mainstream media and within the community. It is vitally important that Meredith Bruce is not elected as prime minister at the next federal election. I believe her policies will be a disaster for this country.'

Harper paused for a moment. A silence descended on the media gathered, as if they were in shock at the announcement. Then the first questions were yelled.

Cass was loudest. 'Do you have the support of your colleagues?'

Harper acknowledged her by nodding, then answered. 'I need to continue to talk to my colleagues. We need to talk about strategies for the nation and ways to beat Meredith Bruce at the next election.'

Cass followed up with a question, shouting above others. 'Are you working the phones to get the numbers?'

'Of course, I am. I'm speaking to my colleagues every day. We need to do whatever it takes to keep Meredith Bruce from being the prime minister of this country. I believe I have the energy and the policy ideas to do so.'

Another journalist asked, 'Are you a puppet of others? In particular, the far-right members such as Christopher Hughes?'

'That's rubbish. I have proven in the past as a leader that I have the skills and policy to lead. I take direction from no one.'

Cass took a note of the comment, sighing; she had heard the answer in Hughes' office earlier.

Another question came. 'Do you support coal mining?'

'Of course, I do. Renewables only provide less than three percent of energy needs. In fifty years, we predict they'll be less than five percent worldwide. It is shameful that a resource-rich country like Australia cannot offer its people and industry cheap power when we have the natural resources to do so. This idea is poor policy and should be rejected.'

'The prime minister announced the idea of importing labour; do you support such measures given the riot this morning?'

'I believe immigration is vital for this country, but we should consider who we bring in and the manner in which we allow them to come. I want new citizens to contribute to the wealth of this nation. Not to take the wealth of this country. I want Australians working, but if there are jobs Australians can't fill, then our immigration system should allow skilled workers to come. I don't consider unskilled workers to be a priority. I want new immigrants to come knowing they have a job, contributing to the nation's growth and prosperity.'

'Would you cut Muslim immigration?'

'No. I don't support any program that favours one group over the other, discriminating against religion, country or skin colour. We want the best people to come. As I always say, keep your culture, but we expect folks to integrate into our society.'

Cass scribbled notes, then shouted a question. 'What do you say to the farmers?'

'We support you. You are vital to the nation. You give us with essential supplies, such as food and water. We know you are struggling and the government, indeed the parliament, will work together under my leadership to bring relief while we wait for rain. There is no reason we cannot support you.'

Cass had enough information for several stories. She placed her notes into her satchel, waiting for the media conference to end. As Harper walked away, she trotted after him, scooting past a staffer to walk beside him.

'Do you think you will have any other candidates?'

Harper snapped her a sharp look. 'I don't expect Ginni to stand if that's who you are referring to?'

'I wasn't, actually.' Cass smiled as they walked together. 'I was wondering… if there was another running, other than the prime minister, could they pull votes away from you?'

'I don't expect anyone else to stand. What have you heard?'

Cass stopped. Harper slowed, then turned.

'I don't think it will be as easy as you are assuming.'

Harper considered the information. 'This will be an easy vote for my colleagues to decide. Stay with Pete and chaos or move back to me, feeling safe and comfortable.'

'Can I quote you?'

Harper turned and walked away. 'Of course, you can't.'

CHAPTER FORTY-NINE

'Cassandra, how can I help you?' Meredith Bruce smiled to hear from the prized Hancock journalist. 'Are you wanting to speak to a leader who is not mad?' She laughed.

'Actually, I was wondering if we could have dinner?'

Bruce turned her head away and cupped the phone, pushing it between her legs to muffle her voice.

'She wants to have dinner. What do you think?'

'Go for it,' her staffer nodded.

Bruce resumed the discussion. 'That would be lovely, Cass; when are you thinking?'

'I would prefer as soon as possible. I'm following a line for a feature on the weekend. I would like your view.'

Thirty minutes later they were clinking glasses of champagne in a quiet corner by a window at the Ottoman in Barton. With an elegantly presented dish of Turkish dips and pide bread, the women began the political dance of trust, sipping French non-vintage and sampling dips.

'What is your view of the prime minister's statement?' Cass asked, moving beyond small talk.

'I thought he was brave.' Bruce smiled, leaning back in her chair. She waved her glass of champagne, settling an elbow on the upholstered arm. 'What do you think?'

'I think he's a dead man walking and will lose the leadership next week.'

Bruce seemed surprised. 'Really? That soon?'

'I think they're worried about the drought. This image of a

do-nothing government is biting. I reckon Stanley believes he is under siege and they're coming for him.'

'Who will win?'

'Who don't you want to win?'

'It doesn't matter; they're all stale, pale and male.'

'Harper is the front runner,' said Cass, studying Bruce for a reaction. 'I suspect he'll beat Stanley this time. They did not organise him last time.'

Bruce drained her glass, then stretched for a morsel of dip. 'Well, Harper is old, and I suspect the electorate wants something different.'

'Someone like you?'

'That's what I'm working on.'

'What about Hughes?' Cass asked.

'That old sleaze bag? What about him?'

'Would he challenge you if he was prime minister?'

'He has such a poor reputation with too many skeletons in the closet to risk being out front.'

'Does he have a reputation with you?'

'He has hit on everyone in the parliament, I'd reckon. You know that.'

Cass shifted in her seat, hoping not to give away any agreement with Hughes. 'He thinks he's a player, but he overstates his abilities,' she said.

'Just like any man. You know the cliché: it's a man's world.'

Cass smiled, bringing the champagne to her lips. 'But,' she paused for a moment, 'it would be worth nothing without a woman.'

Bruce smiled. 'The good thing about the Me-too movement was stopping the incessant sexual innuendo we have to put up with. Thank Christ those days are over.'

'Oh, I don't know.' Cass smirked as she lowered her glass. 'I confess it's worked for me in the past.'

Bruce laughed out loud. 'Yeah, me too.'

They ordered meals from a hovering waiter, including a bottle of Lark Hill Chardonnay, then gossiped about various issues, each aware they would soon come back to politics.

'You know what I think?' Cass asked.

Bruce placed her knife and fork together, pushing the plate away. 'What do you think?'

'I think the patriarchy will never let us achieve our aspirations.'

'Oh, I don't know.' Bruce took up her Chardonnay, relaxing back into her chair. 'I think we do okay.'

'We seem to only have two acceptable aspirations, beauty and motherhood. Men control everything else.'

Bruce considered the comment and shook her head. 'I'm leader and being a woman didn't disrupt my aspiration.'

'Men didn't give it to you?'

'The only man who mentored me was Gerrard, and he's no longer here. I'm pretty sure I'm doing it for myself.'

'Yes, but even saying a man mentored you might suggest you are only in the role because of a man.'

'I wouldn't have thought so,' Bruce said, then smiled. 'Although the great man told me once his political patronage was based upon looks.'

'What did he say?'

'He compared me with a colleague who had greater experience and proficiency within the education portfolio, yet I was his choice as minister. She wasn't photogenic enough compared to me… apparently.'

'Well, there you go.'

'Yeah, but wait up.' Bruce sat forward. 'I'm leader, not because I'm photogenic.'

Cass smiled. 'Maybe, but it just seems to me they only support us if we comply with the patriarchy.'

'If there was a choice between Gerrard and me for the leadership, who do you think would win?'

'That's a little unfair, Meredith.' Cass didn't want to answer. 'It's a hypothetical.'

'There's a reason women don't get the same pay.'

'Why?'

'They don't value themselves and don't ask to be paid on their value.'

'That's my point, though,' Cass said. 'The patriarchy gives us those two aspirations and we fight our sisters seeking crumbs.'

'Sounds like you have personal experience with that.'

Cass hesitated, taking a sip of wine, then said, 'As it happens, I have several challenges at the moment. I'm up for a promotion, but I'm competing with a younger me.'

'Ah, the beauty aspiration,' Bruce suggested, then eyed Cass. 'Do whatever it takes is what I say.'

Cass hesitated. 'I have done.'

Bruce shook her head with a wry smile. 'Yeah, me too.'

The ladies burst into spontaneous raucous laughter at their similar disclosures, as a waiter stepped forward to replenish their glasses. When they settled after ordering coffee, Cass zeroed into the current politics of the leadership disruption.

'You know you could be prime minister next week, don't you?'

Bruce tightened her mouth in doubt, shaking her head, 'Not likely.'

'The member for Melbourne has told me she will not support a change of leader.'

Bruce paused for a moment, her wine glass almost to her lips, cocking her head as the news surprised her. 'She said that?' She lowered her glass without taking a sip.

'I have her quoted. That's the reason I wanted to have dinner with you. I wanted your response.'

'If she doesn't support the government in a no confidence motion, then we either go to an election, or she can support me.'

'Yes, Prime Minister.'

Bruce scoffed a laugh. 'That's crazy.'

'Are you ready?' Cass asked, watching for her reaction.

Bruce twirled the stem of her glass between thumb and forefinger, staring at it.

'Meredith, I thought the news would excite you.'

'Say what?' Bruce glanced up, back into the conversation.

'I thought you would like the news,' Cass repeated. 'What do you reckon you will do?'

'Crumbs.' Bruce paused for a moment. 'I had better get my team together and discuss this news.'

'Are you ready?' Cass pushed her again.

'Of course, I am… we are.'

'Can I quote you?'

'Hell, yeah,' Bruce laughed.

'What's your first move?'

Bruce smiled at the question. 'On the record, we will sit observing the chaos of the government. Off the record, I'll be doing whatever I can to woo the member for Melbourne. Even munch a curry with her if I must,' she chuckled.

Cass noted the slight against Rukhmani.

Bruce continued, 'Wouldn't that be something?'

'What?'

'Shoving a hot iron up the patriarchy that runs this place with two women holding the power.'

'How long would that last? It hasn't in the past,' Cass responded.

'So long as we don't have to bow to the privileged blokes to get what we want, I reckon we could build a culture of equality.'

Cass nodded with a touch of admiration. 'More power to you, girlfriend.'

'That's what I hope to get when I chat with the poppadum.'

Nestled amongst her pillows in her Canberra rental, Cass reflected on the bizarre few days. A prime minister who must know his days were ending, taking tactical advice from a colleague who was going to run against him. A former leader wedging the government on provocative issues like immigration. An independent member with the balance of power prepared to change sides if she didn't get her own way, and an opposition leader who espoused feminism, but was clearly as acrid as any other ambitious male politician.

Her phone buzzed.

'Why are you calling so late?'

'I was just thinking about you,' Tony Hancock said

'So, you thought you'd ring, to say what?'

'I thought I would ring to say I am considering making the announcement about you taking over from Nicholls.'

Cass's chest tightened as she sat up, shoving pillows in behind her.

'I'm almost there in deciding, but I just need to be convinced.'

Cass swallowed hard. 'On what?'

'How much you want it?'

'I've given you exclusives. I'm about to do a couple of stories that will blow the roof off the parliament.'

There was no response from Hancock, but she could hear him breathing.

'Tony, what do you want from me?'

'I want to give you this gig, I really do.' Hancock seemed genuine. 'There are others here who want O'Byrne.'

'You know I deserve this; you promised me.'

'I know. I'm sorry.'

'I have exclusive leadership stories to follow this week.'

'That's great, but I think I need a little more.'

'What do you want?'

'I want us to be friends again.'

'By friends, you mean close friends, don't you?'

Hancock hesitated for a moment. 'I miss you, Cassie.'

Cass screwed her face, shaking her head, her fingers tapping her lips. 'So, what you are saying, is this… if I want the job as host, I will need to submit to your offer.'

'Well, it's not an offer.'

'Have you been drinking?'

'I've just been thinking about you, that's all.'

'You call me late because you've been thinking about me. Then you tell me that for me to be promoted we need to reengage as close friends as you describe it. My work doesn't count, but being your friend does?'

'I wouldn't put it in those terms. Let's have dinner on the weekend.'

Cass fiddled with her hair for a moment before saying, 'Let me think about it.' Then she ended the call, sliding through her phone to her recording app and pushing replay.

Satisfied with the recording, she slid further into her bed, switching off the lamp and smiling as she closed her eyes.

'Me too, Mr Hancock. Me too.'

CHAPTER FIFTY

The sun was yet to rise when Brian Tucker collected his dogs and sped off to resolve the finance challenges of his farm. He was keen to get to Wagga Wagga and confirm with the bank what the government had said: there would be no foreclosures for any farmers stricken with drought. He parked his truck out front, waiting for the bank to open. He wanted an end to the stress and worry dominating his days, but mostly he wanted sleep.

Kathy Tucker had contacted various services seeking support for her husband. She noticed he was changing, becoming darker with his moods and snappy around the children. She sought help from various government agencies, but they turned her away. They were too wealthy to qualify for support. She laughed out loud when the second government officer she spoke with declined her application. They offered them budget management support, but no counselling, certainly no mental health support.

The Tuckers had experienced the vagaries of farming many times. Drought was common in the region, so too flood. Fire had caused various challenges when it ripped through the district twelve years earlier, but this time it was different. No one seemed to care.

Kathy heard him speed up off, and as the sun came up, she checked his secured gun locker for any weapons missing, relieved there were none gone. She then went about her day preparing the kids for school before tending family food plots, repairing, picking, and planting.

She met Brian at college. Although never a farming girl, she got used to the harshness of working the land, enjoying the plentiful rewards it provided when the farm yielded good years. She hoped her husband would overcome his stress, wishing she could be more support for him. Communicating feelings was always tough. In recent weeks, it had been non-existent as he moped about, cranky and stern with the children.

Tucker's phone buzzed at nine o'clock, waking him from a nap. He seemed exhausted these days, putting it down to disturbed sleep, so he took quick naps when he could. A warm cabin in the sun was the perfect nest for him to relax. He didn't bother locking the doors; he never did. The dogs glanced up but seemed settled as he ruffled their ears before strolling to the bank.

'I want to see the manager.'

'Do you have an appointment?'

'I'm the client.'

The staff member behind the security glass left him, going through a door behind the counter. A few moments later she came back, smiled, and said, 'She won't be a moment.'

Tucker stepped back, moving to the side of the room, and checking if his dogs were behaving.

'Mr Tucker,' Sophie Papadopoulos said, with a smile and hand extended. 'Won't you come through?'

Tucker exhaled when he saw her. He hoped they had moved her to the city. He shook her hand with little enthusiasm then trailed after to her through to her office.

'Still the manager, I see.'

'Yes, no decisions yet on my future.'

Tucker settled into a chair, then leaned forward, resting his forearms on his knees. His hands were wringing in front, the newspaper he brought squashed into the chair beside him. He thumbed the brim of his hat back, waiting for the manager to settle herself.

'I've come to confirm we are okay.'

'How do you mean?'

'I want to know if the bank is going to back off from forcing me to sell.'

'Well, as I said a while back,' Papadopoulos tugged a file from a small stack in front of her, 'the bank wants to lessen its exposure and suggested it would help if you reduced the loan.'

Tucker smiled. 'The government has advised it will look after all farmers and no foreclosures will take place.'

'News to me.'

Tucker drew the newspaper from his side, straightened it smoothly out, then tossed it onto her desk. 'The prime minister made the announcement the other day.'

Papadopoulos scanned the headline, skimming through the article. 'This doesn't say there is a guarantee of government funds to secure loans.'

'It's a statement from the prime minister saying that the government will direct banks not to take action. If you read the article, it says the treasurer will pledge help for farmers doing it tough. That would be me.'

'I'm not sure you could describe yourself as doing it tough, considering your assets.'

Tucker gnawed at his bottom lip, irritated by the comment. 'You think I should sell?'

'I have recommended we offer you relief, but you must show us goodwill by reducing your loan.'

'If I sell anything more, we are finished.' Tucker gripped the side of the chair his tone deepening.

'I have to ask you to calm down please, Mr Tucker.' She waved and a male staff member entered the office, standing by the door.

Tucker peeped over his shoulder, feeling intimidated by the move. He realised he was wasting his time. He would not get any support, so he stood, placing everyone in the room on alert for any unexpected movements.

'Mr Tucker, we need a reduction in your debt exposure within the week. If you can do that by close of business Wednesday, that would be terrific.'

'Otherwise?'

'Otherwise, we will be out to conclude the arrangements on your property, which could include taking ownership of the farm.'

Tucker inhaled. 'You come, I'll be ready, and it won't be pretty.'

'Mr Tucker, please.'

Tucker brushed past the man by the door, striding out of the building. He jumped into his truck and sped off.

As Papadopoulos watched him leave, she said, 'This could be trouble next week.'

The male staffer shrugged and went to the kitchenette to make a mug of coffee.

Before leaving the city limits, Tucker pulled over at a rest stop by the bridge crossing the Murrumbidgee River. He reflected on the discussion, thinking through what to do next. It was a two-hour drive to Canberra, which would get him there well before question time. Maybe if he saw the prime minister, he could do something, or even if he saw that backbencher who chaired the inquiry. Or maybe he should go to Sydney, demanding to see the bank manager there. Perhaps something could work out. He checked his wallet, counting out six twenties. Maybe he had enough for fuel. He maxed the credit card out so he might have to risk it with cash, but he also needed supplies for home.

The sun was making him drowsy; his head drooped, and he dozed.

An hour later, his kelpies barking woke him and he sat up with a start, checking the area. He stepped out of the truck. It pleased his dogs to see him, and he accepted their affection as they licked and nuzzled him. Tucker walked away from the truck and whistled a sharp call; they followed him to the slow running river, its bank now exposed from its normal levels. Gingerly, the dogs went to the edge and lapped water before rushing about, enjoying the freedom.

Tucker smiled, watching them chase each other. After twenty minutes, he headed for home, but before he crossed the bridge, as if making a spur-of-the-moment decision, he spun the vehicle around and headed for Canberra. He needed help, and he considered the prime minister to be the only person who could give it.

CHAPTER FIFTY-ONE

The parliamentary press gallery was a hive of activity. The smell of political leadership blood was in the air, and the hyenas were circling for their piece of flesh. Staff members rushing about to meet deadlines. Journalists calling contacts, camera operators waiting for a media conference, sub-editors rushing about snatching draft copy from baskets, and politicians wandering the corridor seeking journalists for a radio or television interview.

The Hancock political media team requisitioned a meeting room, squeezing around a table to discuss the likely scenarios during a day of potential crisis. Several Sydney correspondents travelled to town during the morning, speculating that there could be a new prime minister by the end of the day. Peter Cleaver ignored the moans and complaints of his colleagues as he sucked on a bent cigarette, trying to control the strategy of the meeting.

'Look, we are coming up to question time; does anyone have any suggestions?'

Fatima Abbasi cleared her throat, sitting forward into the table. Cass smiled to reassure her, nodding.

'I think the drought is bigger than what we think it is.'

'No one's interested.' Cleaver coughed as he dismissed her.

She glimpsed across to Cass, who raised her eyebrows before nodding again, encouraging her to keep going.

'I was talking to Rukhmani this morning about her report, which is yet to be tabled.'

'So what?' Cleaver asked.

'She says the banks will foreclose soon.'

'Well, that's agri-business,' a hotshot from Sydney said from the other end of the table, unsettling Fatima as she took a swift glance at him.

'Here's the thing. Stanley promised no foreclosures the other day, but Rukhmani has it on good authority that the banks will ignore him,' she said.

'So what? We're focused on the leadership challenge from Harper. Not farmers over-capitalising,' her colleague persisted.

'Harper has little evidence to base his challenge, right?' Fatima said.

'Yeah, but it has never stopped them in the past.' Cleaver said, dropping his butt into a cup after firing up another fag.

'If we expose the banks as ignoring the prime minister's direction, surely that action is commenting on his leadership and a reason to challenge.'

Cleaver stretched his arms up, linking his hands behind his head. He leaned further back and gazed at the ceiling, the new fag hanging from the corner of his mouth, ash now dropping on his shirt.

'I get your thinking. Maybe there is something in it.' Cleaver dragged from his cigarette without touching the stick of tobacco, blowing smoke to the ceiling. 'If Stanley has lost the banks and the workers, then maybe this will get the government members to act. If we link that angle to unrest in the community, then that might add a nail to his coffin.'

'We don't know that for sure,' Cass responded.

'Yeah, but they don't know that.' Cleaver coughed.

'Are you suggesting we run fake news?' Fatima asked.

'No, I'm not.' Cleaver straightened up and yanked the cigarette from his mouth, coughing again, a little phlegmier this time. 'We could run encouragement for the morons to pull their fingers out and get rid of him.'

'Are we campaigning for a change of prime minister?' Cass asked.

'Hancock's suggestion, yes.'

'He wants Harper?' another journalist asked.

'He wants change.'

Cassandra studied Cleaver, wondering how involved Hancock was, and if this editorial attitude had anything to do with his LA appointment.

Cleaver glanced at Cass. 'What does your source say?'

'Still backing Stanley, publicly. Privately, I suspect they are doing other things.'

'All right, let's get started.' Cleaver wanted to end the chit-chat. 'Fatty, you run down the farmers versus the banks; let's work to get something in the paper tomorrow. Try to score a case study if you can.'

Cass smiled at Fatima, who had a surprised expression all over her face. Cass responded by pointing at her, thumbing her chest and mouthing, 'Me and you.'

'Cass, try to get a story from your source on when it's likely to happen. Television, I want interviews with Harper, Messenger and Stanley, if you can, and…' His assistant pushing into the room interrupted Cleaver. 'What's going on? What's so damn important?'

'Sorry chief, we have just received a notice that former Prime Minister Andrew Gerrard has called a press conference for four o'clock this afternoon.'

Cleaver checked his watch. 'Where?'

'Sydney.'

'Why?'

'He's announcing he is running at the next election, and he'll be pursuing the leadership.'

'What the hell?' Cleaver scratched his head. 'Okay, I want several of you back in Sydney to cover this story. Cass, you had better do it.'

CHAPTER FIFTY-TWO

Tucker parked his truck in the shade in an off-street carpark by the old parliament house. Reassuring his dogs with a ruffle, he set off up the hill, arriving at the Parliament House front door security an hour before question time. He passed through the security metal detectors, stepping out into the marble front hall, in awe of the grandeur. An information officer approached, asking if he could help. Tucker said he wanted to see the prime minister. She directed him to the security kiosk to get a pass.

'I would like to meet with the prime minister, please.'

'Yes sir; do you have an appointment?'

Tucker shook his head. 'No, I don't, but he told me to come by anytime when we met recently.'

'You'll need a confirmed appointment, sir.'

'How do I make one of those?'

'You apply with the prime minister's office, and if approved, they will schedule a time for you.'

'Can't you call them for me?'

'No, I can't, sir.'

'This is important. How do I contact him?'

The security attendant took a sheet off a pad, writing a telephone number. 'Try this, sir.'

Tucker nodded his appreciation, stepping away from the kiosk. He tugged his phone from his jeans and prodded in the number of the prime minister's office.

'Prime Minister Stanley's office; can I help?'

'I would like to speak to the prime minister, please.'

'Do you have business with the prime minister?'

'He asked me to call him when I came to parliament, so I'm calling.'

'Do you want seats for question time?'

Tucker twirled around, confused, eyes scanning the lobby. 'No, I don't want to go to question time. I need to speak to the prime minister.'

'I'm sorry, sir; the prime minister is busy right now. What is this regarding?'

'The bank foreclosing me.'

'Should you not be speaking to your bank, sir?'

Tucker drew a deep breath, then with a lower tone said, 'I have spoken to my bank and they have said I will lose my farm next week. The prime minister promised no farms would be lost; I want to ask him to help me.'

'Just one moment, sir.'

Tucker waited as music played.

'I'm sorry, sir; we can't help you right now, so close to question time. Could you ring back after question time? I will then connect you with the prime minister's principal private secretary, who will be most capable of helping you.'

'I have to wait?'

'Yes sir, but ring back after question time; we shall sort it for you.'

'What do I do in the meantime?'

'Have a coffee in the Terrace café, or perhaps watch question time.'

'I'll call back.' Tucker shoved his phone into his jeans before returning to the information attendant. 'Excuse me, where do I get to see question time?'

'Straight up those stairs, sir, and around to your right. There is security there and you'll need to check your phone into the cloakroom, and maybe your hat. Check with security.'

Tucker bounced up the marble stairs and walked as directed to find a long queue waiting by a security station. He walked past the crowd and up to the security ropes.

'Hi, I want to go see question time. Do I need to check my phone?'

'Sir, you can do that over at the cloakroom. Your hat will be fine but get rid of all metal you may wear, as this sucker goes off like a Christmas tree if it detects anything.'

Tucker glanced over to the cloakroom to see yet another queue. He trudged over to join the line. It surprised him how promptly he moved to the front, dropping his phone and belt into the blue tray in return for a numbered slip of paper. He then joined the waiting queue. At fifteen minutes to two o'clock, the line began meandering to the security station. When he stepped through, the metal detector sounded. Two security guards came to his side, asking if he had any metal as they waved a wand over him, stopping at his watch, then the metal studs of his jeans. He was thankful he wasn't wearing his steel-capped boots. The guards waved him on, and as he passed the security, he noticed the bin full of water bottles with various amounts of liquid still in them. Nothing ever allowed through it seems.

He joined yet another queue, waiting for further instructions as they neared another security station. They provided a sheet of information listing the members and where they sat in the House of Representatives' chamber, along with a list of dos and don'ts to make sure gallery spectators did not disrupt proceedings.

Eventually, they directed Tucker to a side entry door, two attendants showing him where to sit. He walked down the steep stairs in the gallery high above the open chamber below. He sat in a centre seat on the front row, then leaned forward to study the half full chamber. A security attendant rebuked him, telling him to not lean on the front balustrade.

As it neared two o'clock, the chamber became active, with politicians taking assigned seats and ministers filing through doors. As the speaker took her seat, the prime minister entered the chamber with an arm full of files, walking to the central parliamentary table separating the government and opposition members.

'Order.' The speaker interrupted a member of the opposition who was reading a speech. 'It being two o'clock, debate is interrupted and will be resumed at a later time in accordance with the orders of the day. Questions without notice? Does anyone have questions?'

Meredith Bruce stepped to the despatch box.

'I call the leader of the opposition.'

'Thank you, Speaker. I direct my question to the prime minister. Prime Minister, your former foreign minister, now backbencher, the member for Moncrieff, has said he is the best person to lead the government. Will you give him the opportunity to test his support with a vote of your party and end this chaos and uncertainty plaguing your government?'

Christopher Hughes, the manager of government business, moved to the government's despatch box. 'Speaker, on a point of order, this question has nothing to do with government business, therefore I ask that you rule it out of order.'

Everett Menzies, who had been attorney general in the Gerrard government and was now opposition manager of business, came to the box. 'Speaker, on the point of order, the news today is full of conjecture about the uncertainty of the government's credibility with leadership speculation. We must have confidence in the government and who leads us. Therefore, this is of vital public interest. I would suggest that the House and the country would be keen to know with certainty who the prime minister will be next week.'

The speaker nodded. 'I accept the point that this speculation is of public interest and will allow the question. I call the prime minister.'

Stanley took a deep breath as he stood, then moved to the despatch box. Staff expected the question and briefed him on what to say.

'Speaker, I thank the honourable member for her question.' Stanley paused, glancing at Bruce. 'I find it interesting she has the temerity to ask such a question when it is clear the member for Moncrieff and I have a long-established friendship. We have worked together for many years in developing policy and providing leadership, not only for our party but also the country.' He turned and smiled towards Harper, who also smiled, holding up his thumb.

Government members responded, 'Hear, hear!'

Stanley resumed speaking as Harper continued to smile through gritted teeth.

'I say temerity, Speaker, because the leader of the opposition is trying to cover up the biggest scandal of the day.'

'Tell us,' a government backbencher interjected. 'What is it?'

'It seems members haven't heard the startling news, Madam Speaker. Let me advise the House that the former prime minister, Andrew Gerrard, will stand for parliament again, we assume in his former seat of Melbourne, won so decisively by the current independent member.' Stanley nodded towards Jaya Rukhmani, who smiled and nodded back. 'It seems at four o'clock this afternoon, the former prime minister will announce his intention to seek re-election, suggesting he will return as the elected prime minister.'

'Hear, hear!' the government members chanted with raucous laughter.

'Order,' the speaker said.

Stanley continued. 'I am sure the leader of the opposition would welcome Mr Gerrard's return to the parliament to lead his party, which can only mean one thing.'

'Tell us what,' came a call from the backbench. 'Tell us.'

'The leader of the opposition is now playing second fiddle to a man again. The same man, according to a recent article in the Hancock media, provided mentoring and patronage to the leader of the opposition. The question that should be asked is this: shall the leader of the opposition step aside for Andrew Gerrard to resume his role as leader, even though he is not in the parliament? Or can it be, Madam Speaker, that he is already controlling their strategy, including writing their questions? I ask you, Madam Speaker, do we have an opposition in the House, or is it in a hotel somewhere waiting for the pronouncement at the four o'clock media conference?' Stanley resumed his seat to great laughter from the government benches. The opposition remained stoic, none looking comfortable.

The news surprised Jaya Rukhmani, who had heard no gossip or formal announcements. She wrote a note to Meredith Bruce. *Is it true?* She beckoned an attendant by using her call button and had her note delivered to Bruce, who swivelled in her chair, nodding back to Jaya.

Jaya then scribbled another note to Barton Messenger. *What does Gerrard mean for Melbourne?*

A few minutes later she received his reply. *We will definitely run a candidate.*

Bruce was now at the despatch box again.

'My question is to the treasurer. Earlier this week the prime minister made a statement that farmers will have the protection of government from the big corporate bankers. Can farmers struggling in the regions hear the treasurer outline what efforts he has made towards ensuring the government's message?'

Messenger had prepared for the question, coming without notes to the despatch box.

'I thank the leader of the opposition for her question, or is it Andrew Gerrard's question?'

The chamber erupted with shouting.

'Order.'

'The prime minister has spoken of the urgent need for protection of our farmers, and the rural communities afflicted by this severe drought. It is this government's intention to protect our farmers. They advised us that overzealous bankers are claiming they are at risk of unsecured monies borrowed for recurrent expenditure rather than capital borrowings.'

Tucker paid particular attention to the treasurer, glancing over to Rukhmani to watch her reaction. She looked distracted by other matters as she scribbled on her pad.

'Our farmers feed us. They give the raw materials for our everyday lives, and we need to make sure we protect them until it rains. Until we have strong rains to break the drought, we will need everyone, and that means all those who manage money in our rural districts, to ensure they offer relief for our hard-working agriculture industry. Please feel assured, Speaker, we do not endorse anyone being taken advantage of during this troublesome time.' Messenger resumed his seat.

Tucker tightened his face and nodded, pleased with what he heard, still wondering why his banker was forcing him to sell his herd.

'I call the member for Cowan.'

'Thank you, Speaker. I direct my question to the prime minister, following on from the treasurer's response to the earlier question.' The government backbencher paused for a moment. 'Prime Minister, what assurances have you received from the major banks in the management of their lending practices? Have they guaranteed they will stop pressuring farmers and other small business operators during this period of drought?'

'The prime minister,' the speaker said.

'I thank the honourable member for the question, and I acknowledge the representations made to me from rural and regional members of the House. Drought is not a partisan issue, and I thank those opposite for treating the crisis with respect. Before making the statement earlier this week, I met and toured many of the stricken communities in affected regions. I learned of their stress and worries over the management of their lending portfolios. I learned of their concerns about the practices of some banks in threatening foreclosure. I spoke with many hundreds of hard-working farmers and their families.'

It pleased Tucker that the prime minister had been listening.

'I then took those concerns to each of the banks, talking to their board of directors and their senior management, and they have assured me they will not be foreclosing on any farm or small business in the drought affected areas.'

Tucker's eyes widened, and his jaw dropped.

'I've been told that if any overzealous local managers are foreclosing, then they will be moved from the region.'

'Bullshit!'

The prime minister stopped and glanced up to the gallery behind him to focus on the man in a large cattleman's hat standing leaning over the parapet, glaring down upon him. Members of parliament were also staring up, as were the media from their gallery above the speaker's chair.

The speaker moved to the edge of her chair, peering into the gallery. 'Order! Order in the gallery. Attendants, please remove the demonstrator.'

Attendants moved towards Tucker.

'If that's true, why is the bank chasing me and my family off my farm next week?' Tucker shouted as attendants squeezed past the spectators sitting in the same row. 'You promised me, but they're throwing me off my family farm next week.'

As the attendants grappled with Tucker, he shouted again. 'You won't even see me. I tried an hour ago. You're full of bullshit.'

Seizing an opportunity, Christopher Hughes was at once to Stanley's side. 'Offer to see him.'

'What?'

'Call on the speaker to have him removed and shown to your office.'

'Why?'

'Optics. Good press.' Hughes resumed his seat.

'Madam Speaker if I may.'

'Prime Minister?'

'It seems obvious the demonstrator is in crisis and wants to see me. Can I ask the security attendants to transfer him to my office? I will then meet with him after question time to figure out if the government can help his plight.'

The clerk moved to attend the speaker and recommend an action to her, then stepped away.

'As the visitor is being escorted from the House, I ask security attendants to move him to the ministerial wing under tight security. Have him wait for the completion of question time so the prime minister can meet with him.'

The prime minister resumed his seat and question time continued as if nothing had happened.

CHAPTER FIFTY-THREE

The chamber transformed into a working mode when the prime minister asked that further questions be placed on the notice paper. The clerk announced the next item on the notice paper, Christopher Hughes presenting papers. Meredith Bruce headed for Jaya Rukhmani, leaned in, and suggested they should have a coffee. Jaya agreed, and the two left the chamber by the central doors leading out to Members' Hall. They strolled past the reflection pool towards Aussies Café, purchased lattes and settled in at a quiet table by the window.

'I hear you're getting nervous with the government's shenanigans over the leadership.'

'Are you ready to serve?' Jaya smiled.

'Always.'

'Not too young? Not too inexperienced?'

'I'm a former minister, so no, I'm not inexperienced.'

Jaya took a sip of coffee, studying her.

'I'm told you have committed to Stanley,' Bruce said.

'I don't want a change of leadership, not in his first term. Christ, we had all that crap years ago. Do you remember?'

'Well before my time,' said Bruce. 'But that shouldn't stop a government tossing out a terrible prime minister.'

'What's this story about Gerrard coming back?'

Bruce peeked about her, checking to see if anyone was listening to their conversation. 'I don't have a clue, quite frankly. I haven't spoken to him since the election.'

Jaya paused for a moment, before leaning forward and asking, 'Are the rumours true?'

'About what?' Bruce avoided her gaze.

Jaya sipped her coffee, peering at Bruce over the rim of the glass before placing it down on the table. She grinned then said, 'Sisters in this place should stay together, supporting each other, don't you reckon?'

'Not sure I follow.'

'It's in our best interests to keep Gerrard out of the parliament, is it not?'

Bruce didn't respond. With her fingers, she twirled her glass in the saucer, watching it, thinking about the conversation.

'Politics is hard. It doesn't need misogynistic bastards like Gerrard to be running the joint again,' Jaya added.

She could see Bruce deliberating, so sat quietly, waiting for her opportunity.

Bruce looked up and smiled, lifting her coffee. 'He can't lead the party if he isn't in the parliament,' she said, nodding.

'Messenger sent me a note during QT; they will run a candidate if Gerrard runs.'

'Were they not going to run, anyway?'

'Yes, they were, but given I threatened them with changing my support to you they backed off a bit.'

Bruce grinned. 'You manipulative little devil.'

'Oh, look. I came here wanting to do things, although I have found that opportunity doesn't exist for independent members. I want to leverage a small amount of my power without selling my soul.'

'You know if Gerrard runs, he'll want to win, and if the government runs a candidate, you are likely to lose.' Bruce didn't hold back in her sharp assessment.

'I want to know if the rumours are true for you.'

Bruce hesitated. 'What do you want to know?'

Jaya hesitated too. They both knew what she was alluding to, but neither wanted to confirm their thinking.

'Were there ever Me-too allegations against Gerrard?'

'Why would you want to know that?'

'I have learned from spending time here that we have to do whatever it takes to get things done.' Jaya paused. 'I want to make sure Gerrard doesn't have any chance of winning the election; that has to be good for you.'

DOOMED

Bruce eyed Jaya, nodding acknowledgement for a woman who had learnt much in her short time in parliament.

'You know what, Jaya?' She dropped her head and then reconnected a steely gaze. 'If you don't want Gerrard to run against you, then I would make sure there is no reason he would want to come back into the parliament.'

'How do I do that?'

'Make me prime minister.'

CHAPTER FIFTY-FOUR

They marched Brian Tucker to the prime minister's suite surrounded by six security attendants, who directed him to the side entrance used by media wanting information or a quote from a spokesperson. They showed him into a meeting room with two security staff standing outside. A sympathetic staffer brewed him a mug of tea, rustling up sweet biscuits for him, one chocolate. He decided against calling Kathy and took a few sips of the black tea, ignoring the biscuits.

Thirty minutes after question time, a staffer member invited Tucker to follow her. She led him, with security staff close behind, to the prime minister's formal office. As they announced him, Stanley strode to shake his hand, directing him to sit on the leather couch. He also pointed to Messenger to sit in a nearby chair.

'Now Mr Tucker, I have had one of my staff check my diary notes and it seems we met some weeks ago.'

'Yeah, it was at a CWA morning tea.' He glanced at Messenger. 'I also had a chat with the treasurer and a journalist.'

'What was the outcome of our chat?'

'You said you would help the farmers.'

'And, we have,' Messenger said.

Tucker glared at him with a grimace. 'You told me you would call me. You didn't. You also said you would talk to the banks. You didn't.'

'We have spoken to the banks; they assured us they would take no action, which we announced. I then didn't consider it a priority to contact you.'

'Nice word, priority.' Tucker sneered. 'Except my bank manager this very morning told me they will come to take possession of my farm next Thursday unless I reduce my borrowings.'

'Can you do that?' Stanley asked.

Tucker glimpsed at him, cocking his jaw. 'Well, if I could, I sure as hell wouldn't be here.'

'You want me to talk to your bank?' Stanley asked.

Tucker tightened his bottom lip, then nodded. 'Yeah, that would be nice.' He squinted at both politicians with a wry smile. 'I'm expecting that won't happen, and so this moron of a relief manager will come to my farm, shutting me and my family down.'

'What do you mean, shut you down?' Stanley asked.

Tucker shook his head. 'It means after more than a hundred years they will force my family off the farm and my children will have no future...' He paused for a moment, dropping his head. Stanley peeked at Messenger as Tucker continued. 'I will not have a future and it will be impossible for me to support my family.'

Messenger responded, 'Mr Tucker, that sounds a little dramatic. Are you sure the bank will do that?'

Tucker glanced up at Messenger. 'No matter what I say to them, no matter what I do, they still demand their money. My herd is starving. I've been culling numbers for weeks. If I cull any further, or sell off my prime breeders, then it will take years to build the herd and my flock again, costing a fortune. They are coming for me, and I walk away with nothing.'

'Would you like water?' Stanley asked.

Tucker shook his still bowed head, rubbing his forehead.

'Mr Tucker, this is what I'm going to do.' Stanley stood, showing the meeting was over. Tucker took the cue. 'I will ring your bank manager. I will also ring her head office advising them I do not want any action taken on you. I will not let them take your farm, so rest easy. Go home, look after your family; I'll make sure this will be fine for you.'

'What makes you so sure?'

'I'm the prime minister.' Stanley grasped his hand, placing his free hand over the grip, shaking it. 'And whilst I am prime minister, I will not have any Australian suffer any foreclosure. You have my word.'

Tucker gazed at him, engaging his eyes. 'Thank you.'

Messenger sat after Tucker left, waiting for the prime minister.

DOOMED

'Do you reckon this is just a one off?' Stanley asked as he returned.

'I think there is more in it than we know.'

'You think he's not telling us the truth.'

'Yes, of course he is, but the bank branch is acting contrary to policy.'

'Just a couple of calls will solve it. I'll get onto it,' Stanley said.

'You've got a lot on with Harper jumping up and down; do you want me to do it?'

'No, I said I would do it.'

Messenger nodded, hoping Stanley would get it done before next Tuesday, just in case.

CHAPTER FIFTY-FIVE

Andrew Gerrard was never one to be a politically wilting petal. His thirty-year parliamentary career had been brash, and he was often at the centre of controversy. He had manipulated the numbers to secure the opposition leader's role just at the right time, because eighteen months later he was elected prime minister, promising to give the electorate a new Australia, one in which we all Australians could be proud.

He lowered taxes for most Australians, except those who earned too much. He insisted on increasing funding for education and health. He sought a community mandate for the nation to become a republic but was soundly rejected at the plebiscite. He reacted by evicting the governor general from the two properties set aside for her, and reduced her budget by saying, If the King wants a representative, then he can pay for it.

He was brash and loud, taking no prisoners in parliamentary debate and ridiculing opposition, be it in parliament, the media, or even his own party. He flaunted his power for almost twenty years, using his position to get whatever he wanted. His rumoured philandering was legendary, although never confirmed, and he often promoted women if they met his lustful criteria. Hardly anyone spoke against him. Those who did found themselves at the bottom of the access list. A politician would never cross him for fear of his acid tongue and his retribution.

The cocky former prime minister had been the long-term member for Melbourne, yet seldom visited his electorate. He owned no real estate in the city, let alone his electorate. His disdain for the daily grind of politics had ended at the last election when he lost his seat to Jaya

Rukhmani, delivering her the pivotal vote in the parliament and the balance of power.

He hated it.

After spending three years in exile in France, pandering to his wife's needs, he came to the view that he could not afford it, so needed to return to politics. Not just to the parliament or government, he expected to come back as prime minister. He still had deals to be done, especially his agreement with the Indonesian President to provide him with a financial legacy. He could see that Stanley was struggling, so if ever there was a time for him to make a remarkable return, now was it.

Gerrard considered Meredith Bruce a casual dalliance, without the ticker to be prime minister. If the party were to lose the next election under her leadership, then they might just be exiled in opposition for a generation.

As expected, Stanley was proving to be useless, so now if he could win his seat then his numbers would deliver the leadership. Hopefully voters could see that a vote for the party would mean they could have Andrew Gerrard back as prime minister, and all would return to normal.

That was the plan.

Never one to be respectful or timid with any political move, Gerrard beckoned the media to come listen to his plan, assembling them by the front gate of the prime minister's precinct in Kirribilli. It was an outrageous gesture, one Gerrard liked. He had often conducted media conferences from the same spot during his years as prime minister, so he hoped the recognition factor would help his announcement.

'Thank you for coming.'

Gerrard stood tall, commanding the moment. He was ramrod straight, dressed in his finest Italian suit, accented by a French silk tie.

'I have called you here today to discuss my concerns for Australia under the leadership of the current government. I remain concerned about their do-nothing approach to important policy. The electorate elected a change in government with the barest of margins, but I detect a strong mood to return to what was. I stand ready to facilitate that new goal.

'I've learned a lot during my leave from the parliament.' Gerrard was not referring to notes, a skill none of the current leaders had. 'The Australian people wanted to send me a message; I received it loud and clear. I have learned humility. I apologise for any grievance I may have caused to allow your distrust of my government to grow.'

Cassandra Rogers was standing in front and centre of the media pack, smiling as she listened, taking notes. She didn't believe a word he was saying.

'The Stanley government is in chaos. Decisions being made do not help the Australian people. One only has to refer to the drought relief package that just doesn't seem to get through to those who need it most. The riot earlier this week is a direct reflection and consequence of how poorly this government is performing. It is time for us to return to stability.

'I believe Australians do not want their government dithering and powerless to carry out urgent reforms. I cannot stand idly by and allow the destruction of our once great economic performance. I cannot allow decisions to be made which hurt our working families. I cannot allow industries to be closed, as suggested by the prime minister; a prime minister who has little respect within international forums and zero respect within his own party.

'For this reason, I am standing again for prime minister. Over the next two years, I will place before the Australian people a manifesto of policy with them as the central tenet to make sure they feel confident and secure with their next government and their next prime minister. I will argue every day for a fair go for all Australians, not just those born here. My government will offer increased expenditure into services that affect them, and I assure all Australians, I will not be providing benefits to the top end of town.

'It is time for all of us to make a stand and say no to the crisis and chaos of the current government. Allow me, as your prime minister, to elevate the debate on policy that affects you and your family.

'I am running for prime minister so that we can make Australia great again.' Gerrard smiled; the slogan never lost its appeal. 'Questions?'

Cass spoke. 'Mr Gerrard, you will notice I am using the epithet mister, as you are not prime minister, you are not leader of the opposition; heck, you're not even in the parliament...'

Gerrard interrupted. 'What's your point?'

'My point is, under what authority do you make these statements?'

'My authority is the power of the people.' Gerrard connected with the cameras. 'Those Australians who voted for me for twenty years to lead them. Those Australians who voted for me at the last election, but denied my leadership because of a wicked, spurious campaign, run by Rukhmani and her agents, who terrorised and frightened voters leading up to election day in the electorate.

'I speak for those Australians who remain shocked at the chaos of this government and the way we now portray politics in Australia. We need a change, so I am running to make sure Australians get the government they need and deserve.'

Gerrard ignored Cass's follow up question and did not allow her to ask another over the next ten minutes. He then closed the media conference. Once clear of journalists, he made his way to Cass, who was standing to the side.

'Hi Cassie. Long time no see.'

She smiled. 'Andrew, how have you been?'

'Too many croissants and wine, I'm afraid.' He stood before her with a wry smile, stroking his chin with his thumb. 'You look gorgeous, as always.'

'Still the same old Andrew Gerrard, thinking with the wrong head.'

'Don't be like that; we had our good times.'

'More like your good times,' Cass said.

'I recall you liked it.'

'Andrew, why are you doing this? Surely Bruce can win.'

'She won't; she doesn't have the ticker.'

'She may surprise you.'

'Once I beat the Indian, she won't have the numbers to survive a challenge from me, even if she is prime minister elect.'

'You win Melbourne, and the party wins the election. You reckon you are prime minister again?'

Gerrard didn't respond, just cocking his head like an all-knowing kid, grinning.

'What makes you think you can knock off Rukhmani?'

'She's only in there because of default. I didn't bother to run a campaign last time. This time I have more than a mill to do the job.'

'She won't be that easy.'

'Of course, she will,' Gerrard scoffed. 'She has no support, no money, and this time the good voters of Melbourne will see her for who she is.'

'That's a little racist, don't you think?'

Gerrard scoffed again. 'Just because they didn't see her last time, doesn't mean they won't this time. It will be a black or white decision.' He laughed.

'Times have changed; I suggest you ease up on that type of provocative language.'

'A joke is still a joke.'

'Not anymore.' Cass began moving away, keen to return to her Sydney office.

'I hear your boss Tony Hancock is up for an appointment?'

'So, I hear.'

'I wouldn't be packing my bags if I were him.'

'Not your decision.'

Gerrard tapped his nose with his finger. 'He owes me, big time, and I suspect he knows my network.'

'You and he are like little kids in the sandpit.'

'Didn't stop you from playing with us, now did it?'

'Get stuffed, Gerrard.'

'Don't be like that, Cassie.'

She moved away.

'Hey nice arse, sure you don't want dinner?'

Cass kept walking, giving him a finger.

'Tony, it's Cassandra.'

'Hi Cass, what can I do for you?'

'Gerrard is coming for you.'

'What makes you say that?'

'Your appointment to LA is on his radar.'

Hancock didn't respond.

'It seems he thinks you owe him. Once back in the parliament, he'll collect his dues by sacking you.'

Hancock exhaled heavily. 'Well, best we make sure he doesn't return.'

'Unless you have dirt on him, I suspect he'll be making a triumphal return at the next election, which may be sooner than we think.'

'What do you know?'

'There'll be a change of prime minister, maybe even two by next week's end.'

'Stanley to go; who else?'

'Rukhmani has said she will only support Stanley. If they get rid of him, she may switch support to Meredith Bruce.'

'That doesn't mean an early election,' Hancock said.

'If Meredith runs as prime minister at an election, then Gerrard cannot claim he will become PM. She could go early to increase her margin, leveraging the leadership chaos of the government.'

'What do you think will happen?'

'There is one sure way to keep Gerrard out of the parliament, and that's if Bruce becomes prime minister.'

CHAPTER FIFTY-SIX

Cass was lucky to get a ticket on the last flight back to Canberra. She wasn't looking forward to humping it back with others in a car. She wanted to catch up with Christopher Hughes to find out what his plans were, given the Gerrard announcement. The complexity of the leadership of the government was becoming fraught with possibilities. Just a week ago Hughes had been talking about knifing Stanley and manipulating Stavloukas, unsettling the stability of the party room and forcing a leadership challenge. Now the dynamics had shifted, his strategy had changed.

She asked the Uber driver to drop her off at the top of the street, so she could walk to Hughes' house. It was late. The air was warm on her face, and she thought about a swim. A smirk crossed her face as she remembered the last time, and the little-boy comedic excitement of Hughes as he joined her in the pool. She had teased him, but also warned him she wouldn't weaken to his boyish charm by providing what he wanted, although she didn't mind him ogling.

As she neared his house, the front door opened. Hughes and another man stepped out on to the portico. She backed into the darkness by a tree to watch. She could pick up random words, but it was proving difficult to hear what they were talking about, so she moved closer. It seemed friendly, and the men were reinforcing an agreement by enthusiastically shaking hands. She watched as one man left the property for a parked car on the opposite side of the street, under a bright streetlight. It was not until he turned, returning a wave that she identified him. This revelation surprised her but didn't shock her.

The car moved off.

Cass waited five minutes or thereabouts before stepping away from the tree and walking up the path to the front door. She gave it a thump with her foot, as the wooden ridges would have hurt her hand. Within moments, the door swung open. Hughes seemed surprised to see her, but bowed and waved her in. She strolled through to the living room and plonked herself at the stone kitchen bench.

'Would you like a wine, or have you come for a whine?'

'I see you were entertaining tonight.' Cassandra made it obvious she was examining the remnants of dinner. 'Anyone I know, or indeed, should know?'

Hughes slid a glass of Chardonnay to her, smiling in response.

'I have other guests who enjoy coming here, and they offer excellent company, as opposed to the hard work you force on me.'

'You can't always get what you want.'

'But I get what I need.'

'What do you need, Hughesie?'

Hughes moved to the couch, flopping into the soft leather, and leaving Cass at the bench. She watched, then joined him.

'I saw Gerrard at his media conference today,' she said.

'What's he thinking? No one will vote for him; the punters were happy to see the back of him.'

'I wouldn't bet on it. His announcement changes everything for you and Bruce.'

'It doesn't affect us.'

'You know, Chris, for someone so clever, I don't think you're terribly smart.'

Hughes took a mouthful of wine and leaned forward. He reached for a piece of cheese from the platter still on the coffee table, taking the opportunity to move closer to her.

'The plan is to have Stanley boned next week. Don't quote me, but I don't suspect he will be a candidate for the leadership.' He popped his second piece of cheese onto a cracker, then into his mouth, smiling. 'Gerrard will have nothing to do with it.'

Cass smiled as he inched further towards her, feigning a move to a more comfortable position. His head flopped back onto a cushion, and she dropped her hand, trailing a finger across his forehead, pushing back his hair.

'Such a cocky sod, always getting what you want.' She smiled as he looked up at her. 'You have no idea what's going on, do you?'

'We have a new prime minister next week, as per plan.'

Cass chortled with a sigh. 'With all of your planning to knife the prime minister, setting up Stavloukas, pushing for Harper, ensuring Stanley missteps, you still don't get what's going on around you.'

'Wait up?' Hughes held up his hand. 'Stanley is making his own mistakes.'

'I saw you with Stanley when the farmer was screaming out in question time. Did you plan that?'

'Noooo.' Hughes smiled. 'That has helped, but it wasn't me.'

'I wouldn't put it past you to have organised the riot the other day.'

Hughes stopped smiling and slitted a glare. 'That's very Machiavellian of you.'

Cass paused for a moment before taking a sip of wine. 'Do you have any links to the mob that came to riot?'

'No.' Hughes smiled, wary of the journalist. 'Why would you ask?'

'Oh, I don't know.' Cass leaned back into the cushion in the lounge's corner. 'I would think it odd that a senior minister of the Stanley government would have a private dinner with a union leader responsible for a parliamentary riot just days ago, wouldn't you?'

Hughes took a nervous swipe of wine. 'When I say you are too clever by half, what I'm saying is, you may owe me big time.' He eyed her, then sat up, moving forward on the lounge, and placing his glass on the table. 'I've said you will know what's going on when it happens.'

'Yes, but I don't think that's enough.'

'What do you want?'

'Another glass of wine would be great.' Cass held out her empty glass. Hughes snatched it, moving to the kitchen bench for a refill.

'You mentioned Gerrard may affect the leadership coup. How do you mean?' Hughes called from the bench.

'Bruce doesn't want Andrew Gerrard in the parliament, agreed?'

'Obviously.'

'What would stop him?'

'Scandal.'

'You're thinking with blinkers,' Cass said, as she took the over-filled glass from him with two hands. 'Think… Gerrard says he will run to win back government.'

Hughes considered the question as he returned to the lounge, back into his corner.

'I suppose if Bruce was already prime minister, he wouldn't have the gravitas to claim he would win government.'

'You see? You're not so dumb after all.' Cass laughed, teasing him.

'Big problem with your theory. We are the government, not Bruce.'

Cass took a large mouthful; she leaned forward, placing her glass on the table, then struggled out of the lounge to stand before him. 'If you change leader next week, what could happen?'

Hughes shook his head, gazing up at her, bemused by the question.

'Jaya Rukhmani, the candidate Gerrard will run against, and defeat, may support her little mate Meredith Bruce, solving both their problems.'

The penny dropped for Hughes as he watched her unbuckle her belt.

'If you change leader, you may change government.'

'She would never do that.'

'You, more than anyone, should know.' Cass turned and slid her cargo pants down, kicking off her shoes. 'In politics, you never say never. I'm going for a swim.'

CHAPTER FIFTY-SEVEN

Christopher Hughes had been pumping his legs on the stationary exercise bike for the last fifteen minutes, increasing his tempo as he watched the television reporting the chaos in Canberra. Barton Messenger climbed on the unit beside him and increased his own tempo. He checked back to the screen once he was in rhythm.

'Anything interesting this morning?' Messenger asked.

'Same ol' dross. I'm waiting to see what Cassandra Rogers has to say.'

'She on our side, or Harper's?'

Hughes didn't answer as he pumped his knees.

'What do you think will happen?' Messenger asked.

'I think we are okay with the numbers, but Jimmy is working hard to raise his.'

'Stavloukas in play?'

'I hope she is.' Hughes flicked a finger across his dripping brow. 'She'll take numbers from Jim, leaving the numbers firmly with Pete.'

'Will there be a formal challenge next week, do you reckon?'

'Pete will not spill, so there will need to be a petition from two members to bring it on. I'm not sure anyone is brave enough to do that.' Hughes had other plans.

'What do you think of Gerrard?' Messenger asked, increasing his revs.

'He has to win his seat first, and that's not a given.'

'If we run a candidate, we could win.'

'Just so long as the Indian doesn't get re-elected.'

'Jaya.'

'Yeah, whatever.' Hughes was dismissive. 'We don't need independents declaring they may support the opposition.'

'She hasn't said that.'

'If she does, then we should go to an election before Bruce claims government.'

'That sounds drastic.' Messenger said, unsure whether forcing an early election was a good idea.

'Look,' Hughes dropped his tempo, 'the only way Bruce could keep Gerrard out of the parliament is if she were prime minister. She could seduce the Indian to support her. They both win-win.'

'Jaya suggested that move only if we drop Peter.'

'She's not one of us, though, is she?'

'If she were?'

'Things change, numbers change, and Stanley could be in trouble.' Hughes peeked at Messenger over his shoulder. 'We could be in trouble.'

'Pete's safe; we don't need Jaya in the party to change that,' Messenger said.

'Whilst she remains an independent and that Sword of Damocles is hanging above our head, she has the power. Chaos reigns.'

Messenger slowed, glancing over to Hughes. 'While she is an independent, Peter remains prime minister.'

'It's only good for her and Bruce, not for us. We need to have the power, not an independent. She can shift to Bruce, then we're stuffed.'

Messenger considered the statement, confused by it. He thought if Jaya had the power, it was a good thing for Stanley, but Hughes was insisting it wasn't.

'Ah, here she is. Christ, look at those legs.'

Cassandra Rogers was sitting on the edge of the breakfast show couch on the stage set up outside the parliament on Federation Hill. The Hancock Television producers thought it would make great television to have the show moved to Canberra for an outside broadcast, given that a dark cloud of leadership speculation had descended upon the parliament. Wardrobe insisted she got out of her workwear and into an outfit more suitable for the genre of the program, rather than the drab nature of politics. She didn't mind but thought her frock a little short.

'Nothing will happen today,' Cass responded to a question from the host. 'Marginal seat members are already back in their electorates.

Safe seat members are still in bed in their Canberra accommodation, and ministers? Well, they are no doubt having secret meetings trying to count numbers.'

'What's the process from here?'

'The government has a party room meeting next Tuesday; that is the likely time for a challenge for the leadership.' Cass switched her look into the camera and began her analysis. 'James Harper, the former leader of the party, has said he may stand for the leadership if they spill the position. But there's no guarantee the party will seek a resolution to the chaos.'

'How do they force a vote?'

'A petition signed by at least two members, non-ministerial members, I might add, will need to be presented to the party room meeting, calling on a spill of all positions. They then have a vote to confirm the spill, then they seek candidates for the position of prime minister, and the deputy.'

'What do you expect will happen?' the host asked.

'I think there will be a spill motion, but I am not sure if that will succeed.' Cass worked the camera again. 'If they spill the leadership positions, there will be at least three candidates. Ginni Stavloukas, James Harper, and of course, Peter Stanley. As for the deputy, I suspect a female will be elected.'

'Messenger gone?'

'He's young; he has time to make a return, but on this occasion, he's a political dead man walking.'

The analysis surprised Messenger.

'I wouldn't believe anything she is saying,' Hughes said.

The host then asked another question about Andrew Gerrard.

'Yes, we have political ambition all over the parliament at the moment, don't we?' Cass grinned. 'Former Prime Minister Gerrard is not even in the parliament, yet he is claiming he is the leader of the opposition, and once re-elected, he will resume his position as prime minister, which is an extraordinary development.'

'The Gerrard juggernaut is about to descend upon us once again?'

'I wouldn't be so sure about that,' Cass said, confident in her words. 'There is much that remains unanswered by Gerrard. For instance, the manner in which he conducted business. How he applied patronage to those who favoured him, and the many trade arrangements he dealt with. I will report more on that Monday.'

'We look forward to that, thank you. Cassandra Rogers, Hancock Media's chief political correspondent.'

'What's she got on Gerrard?' Messenger asked, stepping off the bike.

Hughes was slowing his cycling, cooling down. 'Beats me, but I'm sure it'll be a juicy story.' He got off the bike, wiping the seat and draping the towel over his wet shoulders. 'Let's catch up with Pete, in an hour, if you have the time.'

'I'll be there.'

Thirty minutes later, as Messenger strolled back to his office from the gym, passing Aussies and Members' Hall, he called Wilson Campbell, the excitable former deputy leader he had replaced three years earlier.

'What's this story I'm a dead man walking?'

Campbell enjoyed his reputation for never holding back when talking with colleagues, never wanting to play the game of political subterfuge. 'You haven't got the numbers, Bart.'

'Who has?'

'Ginni is telling colleagues she will drop out of the leadership vote if they promise her the deputy's job.'

'We don't want that,' Messenger said.

'Tell me about it.'

'What do I have to do to win?'

'Call your colleagues. Try to get them to think long term. You are the future; we can't kill you off just yet.'

'What do you think about Pete's chances?'

'Frankly, his only chance is to not have a vote.'

'What's the chance of that happening?'

'Zero.'

Messenger hesitated as he reached the ministerial wing. 'So, a vote is dead-set on for Tuesday?'

'We will have a new prime minister Tuesday.'

'Thanks Wilson, take care.' Messenger exhaled, almost sighing as he turned into his office. His chief of staff, Julia Haworth, was arranging files on his desk when he entered.

'What's up boss? You look as if you've seen a ghost.'

Messenger mocked a laugh. 'That's because my career is dead.'

She straightened, studying her boss as he flopped into his chair, leaning back, and gazing towards the ceiling.

'Why?'

'If we have a leadership spill next week, they're likely to choose one of the leadership candidates to be the new deputy, which means I'm out.'

Julia considered the issue for a moment, then suggested, 'So, why not be a candidate?'

Messenger didn't respond, waving her away.

As she was leaving, she stopped in the doorway. 'It's not just your job, boss. It's all of us here who put the effort in for you. So why not fight for us? Rather than accept what others have in mind for you, why not fight?'

His eyes followed her as he reflected on what she had said. *She may be right.*

CHAPTER FIFTY-EIGHT

Christopher Hughes was already in the prime minister's office, but there was no sign of the PM as a staffer ushered Messenger into the room. Hughes glanced up from his newspaper, waving Messenger to sit in the leather lounge.

'Where is he?'

'On his way; something to do with his wife in Perth. Although nothing could be that important to override the issues we have before us.'

Messenger squirmed. 'I think his wife is on her last legs.'

Hughes continued reading his newspaper. 'So is he unless he gets more focus.'

Messenger shook his head, content to wait for the prime minister, who rushed through the door five minutes later.

'Sorry I'm late boys.' Stanley went to his desk, checking a string of message slips before removing his jacket and slinging it over the back of his chair. He walked over to the lounge, taking a seat in a hard chair opposite his colleagues. 'Tell me, what's going on?'

Hughes folded his newspaper away as he said, 'You're cooked, I'm afraid.'

'Thanks for the confidence,' Stanley said.

'Confidence doesn't beat numbers. My last count has you at forty-five.'

'Geezus, who's missing?'

'Tom is at the UN. We have three in the UK, on a CPA delegation, and one or two not answering phones.'

'What do the others have?'

'Sixty. I would think James has the bulk of that vote. So, second preferences may come into play. If they do, then you may fall over the line. But if it's head-to-head only, then I suspect James may have them all.'

Stanley glared at him, then crossed his gaze to Messenger, who shrugged his shoulders.

'Well, that can't be good.' Stanley gave a wry chuckle. 'Can we turn it around?'

Hughes tossed his feet onto the marble table before him, leaning back into the couch. 'I think we need to get on the front foot.'

'Which is what?'

'Rather than have James demand a party meeting to discuss the leadership, challenge him by asking for a petition to be signed by at least fifty-five members.'

'They can do that with just two,' Messenger said.

'They can, but let's flush them out.' Hughes began outlining his plan.

Stanley stood and moved back to his desk, pushing a button on the desk phone before asking, 'Coffee?' Both colleagues shook their heads. 'Can I get a latte please, Adam? Thanks.'

Hughes persisted. 'You suggest you may organise a meeting of the party to discuss leadership, then remind the media you won a recent vote. Tell them it should be up to the challengers to come up with at least fifty percent of the party room to trigger another vote.'

'What good would that do?' Stanley asked as he resumed his seat.

'Flush the traitors out,' Hughes said, smashing his fist into the palm of his hand.

'If they don't need to sign, why would they do it?' Messenger asked.

Hughes sat forward. 'Because Pete says at a press conference today, he will only allow a spill of the leadership positions if fifty percent of the party wants it. If they do, then they will need to put their name to the petition.'

'If they do, they get exposed.' Messenger now understood.

'Correct.'

'They won't do it.' Stanley shook his head.

'Then you will not be forced into a leadership challenge.'

Stanley raised his eyebrows in surprise, dragging the corner of his mouth down and nodding. 'Good one.'

DOOMED

'What happens if they get fifty percent to call on a spill?' Messenger asked.

No one answered, pausing for a moment to consider the question.

'I suppose,' Stanley mused, 'I will then need to call a spill. If that gets up, then I resign and don't stand.'

Hughes didn't answer, masking his delight.

Messenger did. 'That would be the honourable thing to do.'

Stanley crossed his legs, nodding, gazing towards the floor. 'That means we have to put the effort into exposing those who want a change of leadership.'

'Let's put it this way,' Hughes said. 'You won't have the humiliation of losing a vote as it now stands. If you push them to expose themselves, then they may just change their minds and stay in the shadows.'

'It's a risk,' Stanley responded as he rubbed his chin.

'An enormous risk,' Messenger said. 'I wouldn't do it.'

'How else do I kill off friggin' Harper?' Stanley demanded.

Messenger could say nothing, knowing there was no other obvious alternative.

'Do you have any dirt on him?' Hughes asked.

'Nope, he's like a sanitised sock. Clean and ready for action.' Stanley smiled. 'Although, there is talk he set me up during the last campaign. Nothing proven, just speculation.'

'I've got nothing,' said Messenger, shrugging, when Hughes switched his gaze to him.

Hughes sat back, cooling his excitement. He was now one step closer to becoming prime minister. He just manipulated Stanley from the leadership contest next week. He only needed fifty-five colleagues to sign a petition and the contest would be on without the prime minister's supporters still hanging on for a miracle.

A staffer brought in the coffee, the crestfallen Stanley sipping it, staring at nothing in particular as he realised he was about to lose his job.

'If there is nothing more we can do here, I have several things I have to do before Tuesday. It seems my numbers for the deputy have loosened.' Messenger gave a smile of angst to Hughes, who shrugged, as if suggesting he could do nothing to help. 'Let's hope they do not complete the petition.'

'You'll be fine, Bart; trust me,' Stanley said, standing to shake his hand. 'This will blow over; the party will come to you in time.'

'Yeah, sure.' Messenger remained unconvinced that a Machiavellian life was what he wanted. 'Pete, can I just remind you about the farmer?'

'He's on my to-do list.'

'Let me know any developments please, Chris.'

Hughes nodded.

As Messenger left, Stanley commented, 'The kid will be an outstanding leader one day.'

Hughes didn't respond, as he thought Messenger's future would not even be on the front bench when he won the leadership next week. He didn't need an ambitious competitor in cabinet leaking what they said. This prompted him to think of Cassandra Rogers. He made a move to leave so he could make a call.

CHAPTER FIFTY-NINE

Stanley strode out into the courtyard to face the media. The wood panelled doors were now wide open, with Australian flags on stand-alone poles lining the backdrop. The prime minister's notes were on the lectern, the waiting media already ensconced behind the thick red ropes dangling between brass poles. He adjusted the microphone, glanced about the crowd of interested faces, paused for a few moments to allow equipment to be switched on, then began his fight to keep his job.

'The Australian people are tired of governments playing politics when they should focus on serving them, delivering good government.'

Stanley was not reading from his notes; he didn't need to.

'It would amaze them that a serving first term prime minister, who faced a leadership challenge just a few short weeks ago and won the ballot with a significant majority, is now again under threat. I wanted to return the country to good government, announcing several initiatives, and many Australians have found the time to contact me about them to let me know the country is on track and I am listening to what voters want.

'Indeed, we are establishing a significant drought package, ensuring our farmers and regional businesses are not forced into financial arrangements that inhibit their livelihoods.'

Stanley remembered the farmer and scribbled a reminder on the first page of his notes.

'I don't want to linger on the government's policy and its implementation; what I want to do is address the idea that there remains leadership instability and a willingness among some to test the numbers again.

'I have advised James Harper that should he wish another go to win party room confidence, then he should present a letter seeking such a meeting with a majority of the current party room, which as it stands at the moment, is fifty-three. There are several members away from the country, so of those who can attend Mr Harper should secure that amount, fifty-three signatories.

'If I receive that letter with the prescribed number of signatories, I will ask the party room for a vote to spill all leadership positions. The party room has already given me a majority, so Mr Harper will need to provide a majority of members seeking a spill, and they will need to put their names to it.'

Stanley referred to his notes, shifting two pages from the top of the pile.

'This will be a historical moment, and it's important that members who wish to alter history place their names to it. So, when I receive the letter, it is my intention to invite a ballot to spill the leadership.' Stanley paused for a moment. 'If they carry the motion to spill the leadership, I will consider that result as a vote of no confidence in my leadership. I will then not nominate in a subsequent ballot for leader.

'I must say, and I want to be as open and transparent as possible here, that there is a minority in the party room, supported by some within the media, particularly from Hancock Media, who have sought to intimidate and bully others to force them to seek a change in the leadership. Many people have described it, both within and outside of the parliament, as madness. As you all know, this government has had strong results since its election; we are ensuring our election promises are being met.

'I remain saddened by my friend Jim Harper, who feels the need to drive his ambition to lead the government. I would have preferred that we could discuss these matters within cabinet.' Stanley scanned about the throng of media. 'I am happy to take questions and ask that you don't all shout at once.'

The media pack shouted in unison.

It was difficult for the prime minister to name who to ask first but caught the recognisable face of Cassandra Rogers in front and pointed to her.

'Prime Minister, you mentioned that there have been bullies forcing the party to resolve the leadership crisis. I wonder if you could identify who these bullies might be?'

Stanley took a deep breath, smiling before saying, 'Throughout my career, I have resisted bullies, and it seems reasonable to suggest we have various forms of political bullying, not only in the parliament but also in the media. I note with interest that former Prime Minister Andrew Gerrard, who bullied his way through almost twenty years of running this country, is again trying to bully his way back into the parliament. He is demanding the leadership of the opposition, although he is not in the parliament. I am surprised by the support of the media towards this idea, given the uncertainty and troubles he had at the end of his term as prime minister.' Stanley paused for a moment. 'Within my party it seems the only way to stop the bullying is to give into it. We have seen the media succumb to the fake news, which has been leaked by some within the government with hidden agendas. I have never given in to bullies, and I do not intend to start now.'

Cass pushed again for a response. 'Do you trust those you are closest to?'

This caused Stanley to pause and glance at her with a querying shake of his head.

'In my line of work, I trust everyone, and no one. I place my personal feelings aside, working with those who want to work for the betterment of the nation.'

The prime minister broke off the media conference, packing up his papers.

'I am hopeful we will resolve these matters next week, and I look forward to that meeting. Thank you all for coming.'

He turned on his heel, ignoring the shouted questions, walking back into his suite, then into his office, where his principal private secretary was waiting for him.

'That went well, Prime Minister.'

'Am I being set up, Jacqui?' Stanley asked as he tossed his notes on his desk.

'Who by?'

'Who's closest to me?'

'Christopher Hughes.'

Stanley nodded, his clenched hands resting on his hips as he considered the response while gazing out the window at the departing media.

CHAPTER SIXTY

Jaya Rukhmani returned to Melbourne after parliament adjourned. She was enjoying sitting with her senior staffer, Robert Wong, at a café in Little Collins Street, evaluating the events of the week, and where they would be politically. They weren't optimistic following the announcement by Andrew Gerrard that he was going to run again. They assumed it would be much harder running as an independent against the all-powerful former prime minister.

'What do we need to kill the fatted goose?' Wong asked, stirring his cappuccino, deep in thought about the prospects of winning.

Jaya was sitting cross-legged, observing the hustling people rushing past, her head resting in her hand and her elbow on the table. She sighed, turning to her loyal staffer. 'What chance do we have?'

'If it was a two-horse race, then we are last.'

'Why so gloomy?' Jaya asked.

'We have zero resources. If we were against the Greens or some other minor party, or even the government, we might have a chance, but we have no chance this time against Gerrard.'

'Why do you think?'

'He's in opposition. He will be more active,' Wong said, thumbing his chin. 'He'll run an anti-government campaign. He'll have heaps of cash, and he'll have a greater name recognition than us.'

'What you are saying is: if he runs, we are gone?'

'I thought I already said that.'

'So, we stop him from running.'

'How do we do that, professor?'

Jaya sat for a moment, bouncing her foot, the weight of reality shrouding her.

'I suppose we can make Meredith Bruce prime minister.' She checked around to see if others could hear, then smiled at her second-favourite former student.

Wong thought about it. 'If we do, there is no guarantee we win.'

Jaya exhaled, blowing out her cheeks. 'Geezus, Robbie, is there any scenario which allows us to win?'

'If we had resources we might; that means we become a government member.'

Jaya thought about the statement.

'Which party?'

Wong smiled. 'Whichever one stops Gerrard from running.'

She considered it for a moment.

'So, if I understand you… You are suggesting we hand Meredith the government benches, then join her party.'

'Something like that.'

'Interesting.' Jaya nodded with a smile. She then dragged her phone from her bag and texted Messenger, suggesting dinner on the weekend.

The reply came: Come to my place. I'll cook.

She smiled as she replied that she would be over at seven.

'You and him got something going on?' Wong asked.

'Who's him?'

'Your favourite former student.'

'Maybe.' Jaya grinned, blushing. Not that Wong would have noticed.

CHAPTER SIXTY-ONE

From under a doona, Cassandra Rogers twitched, emerging from her drunken coma. She stretched hard, especially her back, before curling up again, hoping for more sleep. Her bedsit was dark. She hoped it wasn't time to get up to face the world, a world she often regretted dealing with. Political intrigue was an exciting game, but she questioned whether she had become a player instead of a reporter. Her Stanley articles were truthful, but she wondered if some truth should stay private.

She rushed her tongue about her mouth; it was dry, and her throat needed lubricating. A glass of water was on the side table, so she thrust out a hand, searching for it; a mouthful would help. Once she found it, she raised her head. A throbbing pain thrust itself into consciousness for the first time. She groaned as she rolled over, sitting up on an elbow to drink the water. What started as a mouthful emptied the large glass. Once done, she flopped back into her pillows.

'What have I done?'

Cass draped a soothing hand over her forehead, trying to remember what had happened the previous night. She couldn't remember. How she got home to bed was anyone's guess. Lord knows where her car might be. Hopefully, it wasn't outside. Her fingers began searching for the phone, first on the bed, then under a pillow and on the bedside table; finally, she checked over the side of the bed, hoping to see a shape.

Nothing.

There was nothing else for it. She needed to get up.

Flicking back the doona, she sat up, which didn't help. She wasn't feeling good, and there was trouble brewing within her. Feeling the immediate need to fix it, she made a dash for the bathroom, making it just in time to rid herself of the exuberance from hours earlier. Thankfully, her hair was tied back.

When she had recovered and cleaned herself by splashing cold water over her face several times, she staggered back into her room, tugging open the curtains and squinting against the bright sunlight. She moved to her kitchenette, almost stumbling, needing the bench to give steadying support. She took a glass from the drying rack, filled with water, downing it, then refilling it and staggering back to bed. As she lay down, her head swirled, forcing another dash to the bathroom.

She found her phone amongst strewn clothes and fell back into bed. It was some time before she felt she could look at it. Her headache thumped even more as she scrolled through the calls she made last night. At least ten were made way too late to her children in Western Australia. She couldn't remember calling or who she would have spoken to, but noted that each of the calls, bar one, was very short. She also had several missed calls from the same number. She suspected she may have a little explaining to do to her former husband.

As she lay trying to piece together what might have happened, she recalled a dinner with Meredith Bruce, with perhaps one or two bottles of wine consumed. Well, maybe four. They had both entertained each other by telling stories about sacrifices and interesting challenges they had faced progressing their careers in a maze of men more interested in them than their work. They compared horror stories, laughing at the clumsiness of men unable to cope with assertive women, but still boyishly stupid in trying it on at every opportunity. Bruce laughed when Cass disclosed she had stopped going to parliamentary booze-ups because she tired of the adventurous hands that seemed to be everywhere with free alcohol.

'Why is it men always think you are up for it?' Cass had asked Bruce.

'I think it's because they think they're always ready for it, then you have to be.'

'Do they ever think of anything else?'

'Yes, of course they do.' Bruce laughed. 'But only in between their carnal thoughts, which pop into their heads at a rapid rate. I realise, no matter their age, they all think with the wrong head.'

They both cackled acknowledgement of these thoughts to be facts, ordering another bottle of Chardonnay.

Cass was grasping the idea that she might have been naughty with her dinner companion. Trying to ignore the messages the body aches were sending about overindulgence, she was still to recall political conversations and how she left the dinner, figuring she would talk sometime over the weekend with her boozy mate, the leader of the opposition.

She switched her attention to news and her twitter feeds, catching up on overnight political shenanigans.

The prime minister's challenge to the Harper troops to provide a disclosed group of leadership dissidents was proving successful, as there was yet to be any confirmation of a petition calling for a leadership spill doing the rounds of any government member. The strategy to expose the malcontents might work for Stanley.

Cass mused over whether to contact Hughes.

She decided against making the call. She didn't want to be linked to him if he was still in Canberra. She smiled at the thought of her last skinny dip and the obvious, embarrassing reaction that her boldness caused him. Best to steer clear of him for a few days, at least.

Hancock had told her to make the stories happen. She had done so but wondered if it was enough. She scrolled through recent calls, prodding a connection to Hancock.

'Cassie, what a surprise. How can I help?'

'Tony, I'm working on a few lines for stories next week. I'm wondering if you had decided on the television hosting role yet?'

'Why do you keep asking about this?'

'You promised me, and you are yet to make an announcement.'

'I always said, get me the stories, and if you do, you'll be added to the list.'

Cass rubbed her temple with her fingers, her eyes closed. 'You said, just a few days ago, you would decide shortly.'

'And I will.'

'What are you waiting for?'

'My appointment to LA.'

'Gerrard will stymie that, even if I can get it for you from Hughes.' Cass regretted mentioning Hughes.

'What's Hughes got to do with it?'

'He's going to be appointed prime minister on Tuesday.'

Hancock didn't respond for a few moments.

'Hughes is your source?'

'He will sign off your appointment on Wednesday, but only if I ask him.'

'I need Gerrard out of the way.'

'Bruce and I reckon we have a solution.'

'What's that?' Hancock was sceptical.

'Bruce will be prime minister by Thursday if the government change leaders on Tuesday.' It chuffed Cass that she was an insider. 'Hughes will win the leadership, then sign your appointment; the following day he'll lose his job.'

'Bullshit, that won't happen.'

'Jaya Rukhmani will deliver Bruce to the government benches. Gerrard is no more, and you get to keep your appointment.'

'You're crazy,' Hancock said. 'You won't be able to manage that.'

'Jaya has already committed herself to supporting Bruce,' Cass said. 'Sisters are doing it for themselves.'

'If you pull that off, I'll give you the job.'

'No, Tony.' Cass pushed back on her frivolity. 'No matter what happens, you promised me. I expect you to deliver this week.'

'We'll see.' Hancock finished the call.

CHAPTER SIXTY-TWO

Messenger opened his front door to a smiling Jaya, stepping aside to allow her to enter. As she passed, she pecked his cheek. He was hungry for more, wrapping her in his arms; she responded lovingly.

As they separated, he asked, 'Can I take your coat.' He offered his hand, then stopped her. 'No, wait. The last time you were here there wasn't much to you.'

Jaya smiled as she slipped off her white topcoat, revealing a traditional Karnataka saree.

'I thought I would come casual tonight.'

Far from casual, the rich red silk wrapped around her blouse and petticoat, shaping her figure. The pleated pallu draping over her left shoulder. She mixed gold with silver bangles, which jingled as she passed over her coat to a gob-smacked Messenger.

'You look beautiful.'

'Thank you, handsome; let's hope your dinner matches my effort.'

'I feel underdressed.' Messenger glanced down at his sloppy-joe sweatpants and slip-ons. 'Let me get the meal into the oven and I'll go change.'

'Can I watch?'

Messenger gave a sly smile. 'Nooooo, pour us some wine. It's already in the lounge.'

Ten minutes later they were on the soft couch, ensconced amongst the cushions and chatting about the week from political hell.

'What do you think will happen?' Jaya asked.

Messenger sipped his wine. 'I hope nothing comes of the petition and we can go on with little more trouble.'

'Stanley is gone, surely?'

'He can get it back,' Messenger said, but with little confidence. 'If he goes, so do I.'

'They'll keep you on as deputy. They'd be mad to make a change.'

'Haven't got the numbers, I'm afraid.'

Jaya frowned, wincing her face. 'Really? Why?'

'Ginni Stavloukas is making a run for the leader. They have suggested to her that if she doesn't, she can have the deputy's job.'

'No one can promise that.' Jaya shook her head. 'A party elects its leaders; it's not a prize to give someone for being good.'

'You'd think that, but she has the numbers; this means I'm out, and that could mean I'm out of the ministry.'

'Rubbish. They can't do that.'

'A leader can do anything in our party. They pick the ministry they want, and that could mean I'm gone.'

'Why would they do that?'

'Apparently, I'm a threat to them.'

'Why? Because you are young and handsome and would increase their vote.'

Messenger checked his watch. 'Something like that.' He untangled himself from the lounge to check on the meal.

'What are we having?'

'I've got a nice cut of beef. I thought we can have a variety of vegetables to go with it.'

'Beef?' Jaya questioned from the lounge as he walked into the kitchen. 'You know cows are sacred in India, don't you?'

Messenger stopped before opening the oven, feeling embarrassed. 'Oh, sorry Jaya, I should have asked. Never mind, we can step out to a restaurant on the waterfront.'

Jaya turned to face him with a sad look on her face, making him feel more stressed, but then transitioned into a broad smile. 'You are a dopey man, aren't you? I'm an Aussie girl and I eat Aussie things, including meat.'

'Funny ha, ha,' Messenger said as he slunk back into the kitchen.

Two hours later, as they finished their second bottle of wine after a sumptuous meal, they headed back into the lounge, and Jaya lay with her head resting in his lap.

'I've been thinking about what you said earlier.' She flicked her eyes up to him.

'Giving it away?'

'No, not having the numbers. How do you know you don't have the numbers?'

'The numbers man told me.'

'You believe them?'

'No reason not to.' Messenger recalled his discussion with Wilson Campbell.

'So why not count them yourself?'

'If Ginni is proposing to be deputy, and is doing a deal, then there is no point.'

'You know it doesn't matter, don't you?'

'Why?'

'If you blokes change the prime minister, I have no deal with Harper. So, I could change my support.'

'There's been talk.'

'I figure, if I can keep Gerrard from running against me, then it would be worth my while to support Meredith.'

Messenger didn't reply. He ran a finger across her forehead, prompting her to close her eyes. He then ran his hand back through her thick, wiry hair. She moved her head in unison.

'Mind you if I had a reason not to support Meredith, I couldn't, could I?'

'Like what?'

Jaya sat up, turning to face Messenger. 'If you were prime minister, I could never vote against my favourite student, now, could I?'

'What are you suggesting?'

'Run for the leadership if they force Stanley to have a spill.'

'That's the second time that's been suggested to me.'

'Have you tested the numbers?'

'Harper has the support, and if Ginni changes her position, then he would have it unopposed.'

'Are you sure?' Jaya asked.

'How do you mean?'

'No one else will put their hand up?'

'The only one with the gravitas to stand is Chris Hughes.' Messenger glanced over to her. 'He's been working the numbers for Stanley.'

'Whose idea was the petition?'

'Hughes.'

Jaya ran her tongue across her teeth as she smiled. 'I thought I taught you better than this.'

'What do you mean?'

'Beware the one who stands behind, encouraging you to step forward.'

Messenger thought about her comment for a moment. 'Nah, he wouldn't.'

'Why don't you test the waters, ask a few folks for a vote? You never know.'

Messenger didn't respond, draining his glass as Jaya stood up from the lounge.

'Now take me to bed.'

Messenger glanced up as she moved into a few dance moves made popular in Bollywood, hands snaking above her head.

'Are you always this forward to your students?'

'Only the handsome ones who should be prime minister.'

CHAPTER SIXTY-THREE

The fly screen door squeaked as she slowly pushed it open, banging shut as the tentative child let go. Another forgotten chore yet to be done. The tot crept to the edge of the wooden veranda, concerned for her father, who sat on the stone steps, a long-neck beer dangling from his fingers, gazing out at nothing in particular. The sun was long gone, yet the warmth of the day still hung around. The perfect temperature for those who hated the heat and resented the cold. She took a seat next to her dad, peeking up at him, hoping to gain his attention. She dropped her curly-haired head to her arm resting on her tucked-up knee and waited.

'Annie? Where are you?' A mother's call came from deep within the homestead. She sat up and glanced at the door.

'I'm outside, Mummy.'

Her mother came to the wire door and spoke in a hushed tone. 'Come, leave your dad.'

'He's been crying again.'

The innocent comment prompted her father to brush his cheeks.

'Annabelle,' her mother pleaded with urgency. 'Please come; time for bed.'

The child thought it inevitable, so didn't resist, standing and placing a consoling hand on his shoulder. 'Love you, Daddy.'

Tucker nodded but said nothing as she headed off to bed.

He was onto his fourth beer but was slowing down, knowing it was doing nothing for him other than creating a grumpy mood in the morning. His drinking had increased over recent weeks as he waited for a response to the financial crisis he was facing. Droughts come and go, but no money meant no prospects, and he couldn't fathom a solution to his problems. The prime minister had promised to get the bank's foot off his throat, but he was yet to hear from him. If you couldn't trust the leader of the country, then who could you put your faith in?

A little while later, Kathy Tucker stood at the wire door, keeping her distance. 'You coming in soon, hon?'

Tucker didn't answer.

'You okay?'

'I'm fine,' Tucker said.

She knew not to push it any further, heading off to go to the comfort of bed.

Tucker stood and stretched, shrugging off a chill, before walking towards his paddocks. His kelpies sensed he was moving, and scrambled from their haven under the veranda, falling in behind him. He was spending more time these days wandering the paddocks, searching for something; checking his dams, hoping the water level had increased; walking past the covered pits of carcasses, checking his breeders. Kathy considered it aimless and wondered why he would do it, suspecting there might be mounting worries he never spoke about.

Tucker's thoughts focused on the future. He now had greater clarity following his meeting with the prime minister. The future would be okay because the prime minister promised it would be. But he still hadn't received a call.

CHAPTER SIXTY-FOUR

The prime minister made a few calls, assembling those he believed to be his closest advisers in the windowless cabinet room to discuss options before the party meeting scheduled for the following morning. Five ministers joined Stanley. Three sat opposite at the long oval table. Hughes positioned at one end, near the door. Messenger took his usual seat beside Stanley, who sat in front of the Australian flag.

The room had changed little since Andrew Gerrard refurnished it years earlier. The overpriced etchings of native wildlife still festooned the walls. Australian classic literature filled the few shelves. It was a stark place, meant for decisions affecting the country, not a place for smiles and joviality. The mood in the room reflected the décor. No one was keen to talk. Few wanted to share genuine feelings.

The media could sense political blood. They had been running stories since Stanley challenged those who wanted him gone to name themselves by signing the leadership spill petition. It was an unprecedented move. Many in the party complained about the tactic, wanting the prime minister to do the right thing and resign.

The media took part in any political assassination, quoting off-the-record comments from backbenchers and hysterical briefings from anonymous ministers. This created a perception of chaos within government so the prime minister would be blamed, killing off his leadership.

Sure, there were questions about the lack of direction by the government and the reluctance of the prime minister to make decisions, but the chaos claims were unsubstantiated. They did it for ratings, but they did it for themselves, building their own brand.

A political killing was the main game, always.

A prime minister's scalp was the cherry on top for many seasoned journalists, none more so than Cassandra Rogers, who appeared to have impeccable sources, given the accuracy of her claims.

Stanley was sitting forward at the table, his elbows resting on the large leather pad designating the leader's seat. He clasped his hands together, chin resting on his thumbs as he flicked his eyes about his colleagues.

'How sure are we they don't have the numbers?'

No one answered.

'How many do they have?' Stanley asked.

'They have around thirty,' Hughes said.

'Will they get to fifty-three?' asked Jack Stevenson.

'If they get to forty, I'm done anyway,' Stanley said.

'I'll do another ring around and figure out if any colleagues are getting nervous,' Messenger said.

'What's the Greek doing?' Hughes asked.

'She spoke to me this morning and said she would not run if I offered her the deputy's job,' Stanley said.

Messenger shifted in his seat as others glanced over to him.

'What do we do?' Stevenson asked.

'I'm sorry to have to say this to you, Bart, but we may thrust you onto the altar of sacrifice,' Hughes said.

'Can it be a vote, rather than Ginni being the only nomination?' Messenger asked.

Hughes narrowed his eyes, sniggering behind his hand and squeezing his nose as he gazed over at Messenger.

'There's nothing to stop you from standing against her, but I can't guarantee you the numbers,' Stanley said.

'I'm just cast aside, is that it?'

'Your time will come, Bart,' Hughes said. 'To save Pete, we need a sacrifice.'

'She doesn't want the treasury portfolio, so you get to keep your job,' Stevenson said.

'Big deal.'

'Don't be like that,' Stanley said.

DOOMED

'She doesn't have the numbers, Bart; you'll be okay,' Stevenson said. 'Just stand up and nominate when nominations are called.'

'Will I be the only one?' Messenger asked, glancing at Hughes. Hughes nodded.

'So, you have no plans?' Stanley asked.

Hughes skewed his mouth. 'I have zero plans to run for deputy.'

The reality of this innocent statement hung in the air for a moment as no one spoke.

'What do we do if they get the numbers?' Helen Cavanaugh asked.

'I call for a spill motion and step aside,' Stanley said. 'If they get the numbers, then my days as leader are finished.'

No one responded.

CHAPTER SIXTY-FIVE

When the parliament was first constructed, the mediation room had been an undertaking by architects to give parliamentarians somewhere to get away from the stress of the day and meditate or pray. Christians sought it out for a prayer meeting, but as their numbers grew, it became far too small. Other faith-based politicians used it for their quiet times. It's often said that power is the ultimate aphrodisiac, so if a clandestine meeting during the day was needed, this was the perfect place.

The windowless room was soundproof, the only access via a lift from the senate side of Members' Hall. The lift opened onto a small alcove containing two doors: one leading to the meditation room and the other to a fire escape. The trap for novice players was to be caught in the alcove, so the fire escape stairs were often the escape route for those not wanting to be seen.

Christopher Hughes stepped from the lift, hoping no one was waiting. The alcove was empty. He secreted himself into the meditation room, sitting on the large leather ottoman fixed to the floor to await his associate. As he waited, he flicked through his messages, occasionally tapping an answer, but mostly forwarding them to a staff member.

A light tap on the door brought him to his feet to unlock and then open the door. James Harper entered.

'Such a Machiavellian thing to be doing,' said Harper as he circled the small room.

'How's the count?' Hughes asked.

'I have it at thirty-three, but it's stalling.'

'Will you get fifty-five?'

Harper paused for a moment, considering the question. 'I reckon there's a chance. But I need something to get doubtful folks over the line.'

'If they aren't falling over themselves to sign now, what will get them to change their minds?'

'We need public support for a change of leaders.'

Hughes shook his head. 'I've got Hancock Media editorialising for change; what more do we need?'

A thin smile rushed across Harper's lips, as if he knew there was more to the story. 'Yes, Cassie Rogers is doing rather well, isn't she?'

Hughes smirked.

'What I need is someone close to Pete to pull the pin,' Harper said.

Hughes dropped his head, averting Harper's gaze.

'What about you, Chris? Is it time for you to nail your flag to the mast?'

Hughes was leaning in a corner of the room and shoved himself off to pace the floor, thinking through strategy.

'Perhaps if we have several ministers go to the prime minister and resign, then declare their position, that might get others over the line,' he said.

'Not you?' Harper smiled, his eyes narrowing.

'Not yet.'

'If it's going to happen, it has to happen before lunch, so their announcements can hit the midday news bulletins.'

'Who would you suggest?' Hughes asked.

'Can you get Helen and Stevo over the line?'

'They'll never leave him.'

'They will if they're offered something in my new ministry.'

'You reckon self-interest will convince them?'

Harper laughed.

'Can we afford to give them something?' Hughes asked.

'Can we not?'

Hughes kept pacing; hands thrust deep into trouser pockets. 'If you get Wilson to do it, then I reckon you can get the other twenty to sign the petition.'

'You reckon he'd do that for me?'

DOOMED

'Promise him the trade portfolio and he will drop his trousers in the chamber.' Hughes chuckled.

'That'd be great. Fifty-five signatures. Pete calls the spill, stepping aside, and I'm the only nomination.' Harper dropped his head back, peering along his nose to gauge Hughes' response. 'I win the leadership unopposed.'

Hughes stopped pacing for a moment. 'I hear Messenger is doing the numbers.'

'For deputy?'

'If you say so.' Hughes turned. 'He may run for leader to block the Greek's run for deputy. He's not happy.'

'I don't want him as my deputy.'

'Nor do I.' Hughes stifled the irony with a chuffed sniff and thin smile. 'I'm not sure of his plans, but I thought I would tell you he is talking to people.'

'It shouldn't be a problem,' Harper said, moving to the door.

'Get the ministers out in the media and I'll do the rest.' Hughes didn't follow him to the door.

'I'll buzz you if there is anyone outside.' Harper cracked the door and left, heading for the fire escape.

A few moments later, a message came through that it was all clear, so Hughes stepped out into the alcove and pushed the elevator button. When the doors slid open, a journalist and a parliamentary officer came out as Hughes walked in. No one spoke.

Forty-five minutes later, after visiting the prime minister, the finance minister Helen Cavanaugh led Jack Stevenson and Wilson Campbell to a crowded media pack in the courtyard, by the ministerial wing. She settled in front of the cameras. Her colleagues stood on either side, grim faces, mouths turned down, furrowed brows knotted above the bridge of their nose.

'Just fifteen minutes ago, we met with the prime minister to tell him it is our sad and troubling view that he has lost the confidence of the party room. It is our judgement that he no longer enjoys the support of a majority of members.'

The senator had gained a tough political reputation but struggled with what she had to say.

'We recommended to him it was in the best interests of the government for him to spill the leadership at tomorrow's party room meeting, allowing the transition to a new leader. We explained that this troubling view had come about because many colleagues who supported him at the recent vote for leader had approached us, advising that they were now changing their support towards a new leader.

'We offered our resignations, advising the prime minister that others will also submit their resignations during the day unless he allows a spill of all leadership positions to be taken at tomorrow's meeting. The prime minister did not accept our resignations, and we remain part of his cabinet.

'These are tough times for everyone in the party. It was with regret that we took this action, but we believe there is no alternative. We encouraged the prime minister to ignore his call for a petition of members, allowing a spill motion to be taken. If the spill motion is accepted, then we recommend the prime minister to take it as a vote of no confidence in his leadership and to step aside so that transition to a new leadership team can be made.' Cavanaugh stopped talking, stepping back to allow Stevenson to speak.

'As Helen has told you, we met with the prime minister and tendered our resignations, offering him our collective judgement that it was imperative to stop the uncertainty of leadership within the government, and that we should spill the leadership, transitioning to a new leadership team. We have taken soundings from our colleagues, and we conveyed their advice that they will transfer support from the prime minister. In those circumstances, I believe there should be a leadership spill at the party room meeting tomorrow, so these matters can be resolved.' Stevenson nodded and stepped back, prompting Campbell to step forward.

'It became clear to me this morning, before meeting with the prime minister, that there had been a significant shift of support away from him. I conveyed this advice to him at the earlier meeting. We must settle this uncertainty. My recommendation to him was that we can only do this at the party room meeting tomorrow.'

Cavanaugh stepped forward to end the media conference, suggesting that there would be no questions out of respect for Prime Minister Stanley, and they would say nothing further.

Watching on the live broadcast on television, Christopher Hughes guffawed. 'Self-interested morons.'

CHAPTER SIXTY-SIX

'Do you think it's wise to meet like this?' Jaya asked Messenger as she sat at his usual table, out of the way against a window in the small café area outside Aussie's coffee shop. It was a busy thoroughfare and the place to meet to plot and scheme.

Messenger had invited her, and she was at the stage in their relationship when she couldn't resist the chance to see him.

'Who's going to think we are planning anything if we are meeting out in the open like this?' He peeked over his shoulder to check if anyone was listening as he tipped a sachet of raw sugar into his latte.

'Are we planning something?' Jaya smiled. 'Dinner perhaps?'

Messenger grinned. Although he tried to resist, she attracted him with her wily charms. 'Do you think we should get together?'

'As in getting together?' She smiled, then lowered her voice. 'Or getting together.'

'Stop it.' Messenger smiled, checking out the nearby tables.

'You love it, Bart. I know you do, and it's time to enjoy yourself.'

Messenger nodded, as if agreeing to a wise pronouncement, and took a sip of his latte. 'Socially, I agree, but I'm more worried politically.'

'What, we can't be friends?' Jaya used her fingers, showing inverted commas. 'Because we aren't on the same side, we can't be friends?'

'We are friends.'

'Close friends?'

'Jaya, please.' Messenger checked over his shoulder. 'You're making me nervous.'

She smiled. 'You are so cute.'

'Have your coffee.'

She took a sip. 'Not as good as Melbourne.'

'I agree, but we mustn't complain, lest we become coffee snobs.'

'Argh.' Jaya screwed her face. 'It tastes burnt.'

Messenger smiled.

'So, do you have the numbers?' Jaya asked.

'Nope.'

'Shame.' She took another quick sip of coffee. 'What about Stanley?'

'They haven't got the numbers for a petition. I'm not sure what will happen.'

Jaya eyed him, thinking through alternatives.

'What would happen to you if I went with Meredith?'

'Why would you do that?'

'I told you.' She scrunched her face. 'If I can keep Gerrard out of the election, then that's good for me.'

'You reckon he won't stand if Bruce is prime minister?'

'What would be the point? He wants to be the prime minister. That can only happen if they go to an election in opposition.'

Messenger sat for a few moments, watching colleagues walk to the café to order coffee. He noticed Meredith Bruce and Cassandra Rogers in an animated discussion at a table further along the corridor. He smiled and waved acknowledgement to a few colleagues as they queued for coffee.

'To answer your question, I suspect we will have a new leadership group. I'll be on the front bench in opposition. Thanks very much.'

'How else do you suggest I save myself?'

Messenger didn't have an answer. If he was honest, he would prefer her out of parliament. He liked her, but their political conflict of interest lingered.

'Jaya,' he said, pausing for a moment and watching her. 'If the petition gets up, then stuff is going to well and truly hit the fan. I'm out of a job, and I may well not be treasurer. If you support the opposition, then my career is over.'

'That is so unfair.'

'It's the ugliness of politics; when there's blood in the water, the sharks come to feed.'

'You are going to blame me for losing government, and by extension your career?' She pushed away her unfinished coffee, standing. 'You wouldn't be in this position if you didn't have a dud as leader. I told you to run.' She looked down at him. 'Now it's my turn.'

Messenger didn't watch her go. He just stared into her vacant chair, thinking through the angst that was building in him. He sat forward, knotting his hands in front of his face, and wringing them. He had a choice. To let events manage him or manage the events. He'll make a few calls, but this time for himself, rather than his leader.

'That's interesting,' Cassandra Rogers observed as Rukhmani stormed off.

'What is?' Bruce scanned the cafe.

'Is that the government being denied a vote or something more sinister?'

Bruce now saw the member for Melbourne brushing past queueing patrons, then looked back to a disconsolate Messenger.

'I'd hate to admit to it, and hope it goes no further, but I quite fancy the treasurer.'

Cass laughed out loud. 'Doesn't the ministry have a bonking ban?'

'Only with their staff.'

They both laughed, adding to amiable discussion over coffee. They were enjoying their growing relationship. Bruce always mindful that Rogers was after a story. In the past, she had provided sensitive information to make sure she got her message into the media.

'What's Rukhmani's position if the leadership changes?' Cass asked.

Bruce gnawed at her bottom lip, shaking her head. 'Your guess is as good as mine. She wants to stop Gerrard from standing. I've told her that the only way to stop him is to install me as prime minister.'

'What are you expecting to happen?'

'God only knows with that rabble.' Bruce took a sip of espresso, washing it over her tongue, kicking it to the back of her throat. 'Geez, that's good.'

'Who do you reckon will be prime minister after tomorrow?'

'It doesn't matter. Their chaos is what's giving Gerrard the leg up he needs. He'll just use the change of leadership to highlight his years as a stable leader. Fuck him!'

'I thought you had?' Cass said with a cheeky grin.

The colleagues burst into laughter again, disturbing others sitting in quiet conversation.

'You're so mean.'

Cass continued grinning, then hardened her gaze. 'If you take Gerrard out of the equation, who don't you want opposite you in the chamber?'

Bruce focused. 'They're all stale white blokes past their peak competence. Harper would be much tougher than Stanley.'

'What about Hughes?'

'He's not running. I heard he's doing the numbers for Stanley.'

Cass smiled. 'Why do you think Stanley is doing so poorly?'

'Really?' Bruce raised her brows, pursing her lips at the suggestion. 'That old snake. Now that would change the dynamics. I would suspect he would be better than Harper, but very beatable. Is Ginni running?'

'She's done a deal to be deputy no matter who wins.'

'Messenger is gone?' The news surprised Bruce.

'What are you going to do if Rukhmani doesn't come over to you?'

'I haven't considered it. In fact, I'm not counting on it.'

Cass gazed at her. 'What? You're just going to give Gerrard a free kick with the change of prime minister?'

'What can I do?'

'Expose him to be the charlatan he is. Hancock will support you.'

'The Mercantiles owe me, I reckon,' Bruce said.

'If you kill Gerrard off, they will.'

A hovering group of staff interrupted their discussion, prompting them to check the television above them. Someone increased the volume for the media conference. Senator Cavanaugh was speaking. Muffled murmurings amongst those watching were not distinguishable. Cass took a pad from her bag, scribbling a few notes as Stevenson stepped forward.

Bruce leaned over and whispered, 'That's killed Stanley; there's no going back now.'

Cass nodded, continuing to watch as Campbell stepped forward.

DOOMED

Then it was over. The gathering went about their business as if nothing had happened, as if it was to be expected.

'Cavanaugh was his strongest supporter,' Bruce said, before tossing back the rest of her coffee, swirling for the caffeine hit.

'They are struggling to get the petition numbers. She isn't smart enough to do this by herself. She must be on a promise.'

'Game on.' Bruce smiled as she collected her things from the table.

'Good luck with it,' Cass said, as Bruce stood, preparing to leave. 'It's not them you have to worry about if Rukhmani doesn't step over the line. It's Gerrard.'

'Don't I know it. See you.' She squeezed Cass' shoulder as she stepped off.

Cass watched her go, considering what to do. She sensed that Christopher Hughes' fingerprints were on the three ministers' announcement. *Why else would they be, one minute resolute with Stanley and the next recommending a transition?* She smiled at the thought that they weren't recommending a transition to Harper.

Rather than cross to the Representatives' wing through the marble foyer of Parliament House, she took the long way and cut through the courtyard that was accessible from any of many heavy glass doors near the Members' Hall. A media pack had already set up, waiting for any politician to come and give a view. The anxiety and excitement levels of a leadership challenge lifted the spirits of those closeted by the daily humdrum of politics. The media was now leading the charge for stories. Killing season was what the Canberra media gallery hoped for, often playing their part in creating it. Just like Cass.

She pushed through a heavy door by the chamber and walked along the green carpeted corridor to Rukhmani's office.

'Is Jaya in?' Cass asked Robert Wong, who was going through the in-tray by the door.

'She's on the phone at the moment. I'll check to see how long she'll be.'

Cass smiled at the ploy.

A few moments later, Jaya opened the sealed door to her office, asking Cass to join her. She offered a drink, which was declined, before dismissing Wong.

'What brings you to this lonely corner?'

'I've come to see the most powerful person in the parliament.'

Jaya shrugged a laugh. 'I wouldn't have thought so.'

'Tomorrow you decide who will be the prime minister. I want to know what your plans are.'

'Stanley is prime minister, and I support him.' Jaya hadn't warmed to Rogers since being done over.

'If he loses a vote?'

'Then we shall see.'

The reluctance to talk miffed Cass and she tried another tack. 'I reckon it's time for fresh blood and having Harper as prime minister is like having Gerrard back in the parliament.'

Jaya didn't respond.

'I mean we just keep getting lumbered with old white men. I don't think they represent the electorate.'

'You want me to support Meredith?'

'Let's put it this way. We don't need Gerrard back in the parliament.'

'I agree with that.'

'What would you say if they elected Hughes leader?'

Jaya was cautious. 'On the record he is no different to Harper. Off the record, he is better than Harper.'

'Messenger?'

'He's not running, from what I hear.'

'If he was?'

'Well, at least he's not an old fogey.'

'You like him?'

'What are you asking?'

Cass smiled. 'For leader, do you like him?'

'I would make that decision when I am faced with it.'

'I noticed you had words at Aussie's.'

'Nothing to see here, Cass.'

'I've just spoken to Rukhmani. You may need to do some work with her.'

'Who's she going to support?' Hughes said.

'She won't support Harper and may swing to Bruce; she's undecided. You need to offer her something to get her over the line.'

'What's her issue?'

'I reckon the drought is her main issue, but what she really needs is Gerrard out of the way.'

'Easier said than done.'

'Oh, come on, Hughesie. You know how to cut them down.'

'Are you prepared to talk about the dirt file we have on him?'

'Only if someone went on the record,' Cass said.

'Would Hancock support the story?'

'If he got the LA gig, yes.'

'And if he doesn't?'

'You assured me.'

'Just saying, if I can't work a miracle?'

'Then feel assured, he'll support Bruce and Gerrard.'

'After all we have done together?'

'Listen here, Hughesie. We have done nothing together; my work is to report you morons.' Cass stopped walking for a moment. 'I'm betting Rukhmani is going over to Bruce. That means, if you want to be prime minister, you better satisfy her, otherwise she'll move her vote. I can assure you.'

'Leave it with me.' Hughes left the call.

Cass smiled as she pushed her phone into her jeans. 'Chaos.'

CHAPTER SIXTY-SEVEN

The House of Representatives assembled at two o'clock for question time. The speaker called for questions without notice. Meredith Bruce stood at the despatch box to ask the prime minister whether he retained the confidence of his ministers, but the prime minister was yet to arrive in the chamber. She asked anyway. Barton Messenger stood to take the question.

'Point of order, Madam Speaker.' Bruce was on her feet.

'Leader of the opposition on a point of order?'

'My question was to the prime minister. We have not heard of ministerial arrangements, so we expect the prime minister to answer, not his apprentice. Could you please arrange a call to the prime minister's office to wake him and end this chaos?'

The opposition benches erupted in laughter. The government benches didn't respond.

'There is no point of order; I call the deputy prime minister.'

'Thank you, Speaker. The House is aware of the many issues facing the country at the moment. The prime minister is delayed and will be with us soon.'

'Sleeping, more likely,' came a call from opposition benches.

'Crying himself to sleep,' a wag shouted.

Laughter erupted.

'Order.'

Messenger ignored the interjections. 'In the meantime, I will answer questions on his behalf, as I have done in the past. Madam Speaker, the opposition leader, asks if our prime minister has the confidence of his ministry and the brief answer is... of course he does.'

'Hear, hear.' The government backbench was now engaged.

'This, of course, is in stark contrast to the leader of the opposition, who is also not in the chamber.'

An opposition member was quick to her feet opposite, ignoring Bruce's wave down.

'The member for Stirling on a point of order?'

'As usual, Madam Speaker, the government cannot see and remains blinded to the fact that the leader of the opposition is at the table.'

Bruce winced, knowing what was to come.

'There is no point of order; the deputy prime minister.'

'The member for Stirling claims we are blind. She cannot have read the news: the leader of the opposition, one Andrew Gerrard, is somewhere in Australia sunning himself, preparing for a return to the parliament, claiming he is the rightful leader.'

The racket behind him became much louder, supporting his answer.

'In fact, I see the former leader of the opposition at the table cringing at the very idea that Andrew Gerrard will be back to take her place. And this will be no different to the favours Gerrard provided her when he promoted her to the front bench. There were others with greater merit, but he promoted the member for Reid ahead of others. I can assure you, Madam Speaker, we on this side of the House do not subscribe to the rumours floating about of members opposite being favoured by the then prime minister in his usual nefarious way.'

The opposition erupted from the slight.

Everett Menzies, the opposition's shadow attorney general, rushed to the despatch box.

'The deputy prime minister will resume his seat. Manager of opposition business on a point of order?'

'Madam Speaker, the deputy prime minister has impugned the leader of the opposition, smearing her reputation in the most horrendous manner. I ask him to withdraw, and if he were a gentleman, he would apologise.'

Messenger responded when the speaker directed him but didn't apologise to the scowling Bruce.

'Madam Speaker, as I was saying, before being interrupted by an over-sensitive opposition, I have news for Andrew Gerrard, the leader of the opposition, in waiting. He needs to first win a seat. He will have formidable opposition in Melbourne if he expects the current member to roll over and allow him a win. She beat him last time,' Messenger glanced to Jaya, 'and, I'm told she will do it again.'

'Hear, hear.'

'Now let's end this conversation about confidence and the amorous reputation of the former prime minister. Let's discuss policy and government action that is making Australia a prosperous place instead of the wasteland Andrew Gerrard led us to.' Messenger sat in the prime minister's chair, smiling at Bruce, as a government backbencher rose to ask the next question.

Question time continued its vocal contest for the next hour. The rancour obvious. The frustration of the opposition and their lessening respect for the government's answers to questions about the drought and plans for the Kirkpatrick mine increased noise levels.

Meanwhile, government staff tried to locate the prime minister. No one in his office knew where he was. His security unit confirmed he had not left the parliament. His phone remained on his desk along with his pager. An anxious head of security brought together a small team to sweep the building to locate him.

Officers searched every office; rooms rarely used were unlocked and checked, even in the meditation room. They made a public address announcement asking the prime minister to respond and contact his office. They swept public areas, although Stanley had not swiped his card to signify that he was leaving a secured area. Two burly federal police officers fronted the Members' and Guests' dining room, on level two, where several invited guests were still enjoying a late lunch. Staff were asked if they had seen the prime minister, and officers checked the bathrooms. The lights to the Members' only cafe on a secured mezzanine section overlooking the dining room were dim, but the officers checked anyway.

Peter Stanley had arrived for lunch at midday, helping himself twice to the buffet. He ordered a bottle of red wine, enjoying a rare opportunity to lunch with colleagues. They cracked jokes, extolling humorous anecdotes about earlier elections and parliamentary personalities. The bells calling members to question time emptied the room, but the prime minister lingered to finish his wine.

He was now asleep in the corner, which a quick glance into the room would have missed.

A federal police officer shook his shoulder. Stanley jolted up, perplexed.

'Prime Minister are you okay?' the officer asked as the other reported the find to the central search coordinating base.

'What's the time?'

'It's almost three, sir.'

'Oh hell, I'm late.'

Stanley stood, reassuring the officers he was okay, and fled the dining area, rushing to question time, the officers scurrying behind him. He took the elevator from the second floor to the formal foyer of the chamber. As he burst from the elevator, attendants opened the doors for him to pass. Messenger was speaking as he entered the chamber. A rousing cheer from the opposition erupted.

Messenger continued to answer the opposition's question about the drought, reminding members that the government had instructed the banks to take no action on foreclosures and the drought was the concern of all Australians, not just the farmers. The prime minister ignored the caterwauling and took his seat, pulling files from the top of the table and burying his head in the notes.

A government member stood. The speaker formally recognised him, and he asked the defence minister a question. Messenger sat down next to Stanley.

'What number are we up to?' the prime minister asked.

'This is our eighth. Where have you been?'

'Let's not worry about that now. Is there anything I should know?'

Messenger glared at Stanley as he continued to check his notes.

'Yes, we're getting flogged.'

'Anything specific?'

'You and the drought.'

'What else is new?' Stanley glanced up, scanning the opposition benches for a moment, judging their mood. 'They look angry.'

'May have a reason to be, boss.' Messenger checked over Stanley's shoulder, seeing James Harper approaching from the backbench aisle. 'Heads up, Harper is coming.'

Stanley turned as Harper arrived, leaning into the prime minister and removing two pieces of paper from his jacket's inside pocket.

'You wanted fifty-three; here are fifty-eight. The last ten signed just now, while we waited for you.' He passed the pages and withdrew.

Stanley opened the sheets, studying the list of names and signatures.

'It's the petition,' Stanley said, as he shared the list with Messenger.

Messenger didn't respond as Hughes came to the table, leaning over their shoulders to see what was on the paper.

'How do you want to handle the rest of question time?' Hughes asked.

'Let's do the drought question, then I'll close it.'

Messenger frowned. 'Are you sure you want to take one more from them?'

'If I'm going to talk about the drought, then I have to.'

Hughes moved away. Messenger returned to his usual seat on the front bench as the defence minister completed his answer. Stanley checked the petition to see if it recorded the minister; it did.

Meredith Bruce moved, seeking the call.

'Madam Speaker, I address my question to the prime minister. Can the prime minister confirm he retains the confidence of his party as leader? Can the prime minister agree that thirty-eight of his colleagues who voted against his leadership plus all those who sit opposite do not want him as prime minister of Australia? And, given you have received notice of a petition seeking a leadership spill from the member for Moncrieff, just now, will you not agree that you have lost the confidence of the majority in this party and this chamber?'

'I call the prime minister.'

Stanley didn't move.

'Prime Minister?' the speaker queried.

Stanley gazed at her, before pushing himself from his chair, moving to the despatch box and staring at it, filling his lungs. The chamber fell silent as parliamentarians watched him. Some in the media gallery high above the speaker were taking notes or tapping keyboards; most fascinated by the drama being played out below them.

'Madam Speaker, I thank the honourable member for her question. You may recall just last week the former prime minister, Andrew Gerrard, announced he was standing for re-election and that he expected to be leader once he had regained his seat of Melbourne. He claimed he would also be prime minister again. Therefore, the current incumbent is wasting her time.'

Bruce shook her head, wincing, wishing she could rid Gerrard from her life. He had once been helpful for her career, but now she was on her own and would have a prime minister's scalp on her belt.

'These facts diminish the authority of the current temporary leader of the opposition, and she remains irrelevant with regard to the current parliament. Confidence and respect are something the opposition parties know little about, and this government...' Stanley paused. 'My government... will continue to offer Australians the opportunities they want. Australians will continue to retain the confidence my government brings them.'

Stanley finished to a rousing cheer from his government members, smiling as he sat, thinking that half of them would vote against him tomorrow.

Bruce was quick to her feet.

'I seek leave to move the following motion... that this House has lost confidence in the prime minister.'

'Is leave granted?'

Hughes shook his head.

'Leave is not granted,' the speaker said

Bruce then read from a prepared note. 'I move that so much of standing orders be suspended as would prevent the Leader of the Opposition from moving this motion forthwith: that this House has lost confidence in the prime minister.' She signed the paper and passed the note to the clerks sitting to her right below the speaker's chair.

'Madam Speaker, today we have a prime minister in name only. A prime minister who couldn't bother to front up to question time and offer the Australian people confidence that their prime minister is in control. We have heard media reports that the government is planning a spill of leadership tomorrow following an election for their leader just a short while ago. This is unacceptable and shows that the government is in utter disarray and in chaos.

'The parliament needs to vote on this motion for no confidence in the prime minister because we have seen little action on the major policy events happening in and around Australia.'

Christopher Hughes moved to the despatch box, and the speaker called upon him, forcing Bruce to sit.

'I move that the member be no longer heard.'

The speaker sat forward in her chair. 'The question is that the member is no longer heard. All those in favour say aye, the contrary no. I think the ayes, have it?'

'The noes have it.' A cry came from the opposition backbench.

'The noes have it; division required?'

Meredith Bruce counselled her team to be silent.

'The ayes have it.'

'Is the motion proposed by the opposition leader seconded?'

Everett Menzies came to the despatch box, hoping to get words out before being shut down by Hughes.

'Well, thirty-eight government members have the back of the prime minister. They have his back in their sights. They have knives in their hands, and they are advancing. This government is doomed…'

'I move that the member be no longer heard.'

The speaker completed the protocol of calling a vote, then put the substantive motion.

'The question is that the House has lost confidence in the prime minister. All those in favour say aye, the contrary no.' She waited for the shouts to finish. 'I think the noes have it.'

The opposition benches erupted and called for a division.

'Division required? Ring the bells.'

The clerk turned the hourglass timer for five minutes; the bells throughout the parliament rang and a small green light flashed at the bottom left of all two thousand seven hundred parliamentary clocks.

After five minutes, the speaker instructed, 'Lock the doors.'

Attendants closed, then locked the doors to stop any late arrivals entering.

'Order! The question is that the House has lost confidence in the prime minister.

'Those in favour will pass to the right of the chair, the noes to pass to the left. I appoint the members for Stirling and Cook as tellers for the ayes, and members for Forrest and Blair tellers for the noes.'

Members then went to their places. The opposition switched

sides of the chamber and government members passed them as they converged on the opposite side.

'Members will take a seat as soon as possible.'

Jaya Rukhmani was yet to move.

If she voted with the opposition on this confidence motion, she would vote to install Meredith Bruce as prime minister. Those with a keen interest in the result were watching her. Her head was down reading papers. She stood and moved to the centre aisle between the voting blocks, prompting the speaker to instruct her to sit.

'The member for Melbourne will take a seat.' Bruce smiled at her; Messenger didn't look. Jaya then took a seat to vote no.

After five long minutes, the speaker stood.

'Order. The result of the division is ayes seventy-two, noes seventy-three. The question is determined in the negative. Members will resume their normal seats.'

Stanley scooted around to the government side of the chamber to the despatch box.

'I ask that all further questions be placed on the notice paper.'

This was the cue for the parliament to resume normal business.

The speaker stood and announced, 'I have received a letter from the honourable member for Port Adelaide proposing that a definite matter of public importance be submitted to the House for discussion, namely: the Government's chaos and division on drought policy, which is forcing Australian farmers to be in danger of losing their farms. I call upon those members who approve of the proposed discussion to rise in their places.'

More than the required number of opposition members rose.

'Hear, hear.'

The shadow minister for water presented his speech on the perilous times ahead for the nation's farmers and rural communities if the parliament did not act to quell the growing incidence of climate change. As he did, the chamber emptied of members as they went about their business, leaving just a few opposition members to listen and support the member.

As Christopher Hughes passed Jaya on the way out, he stopped. 'Thank you for your support today, Jaya.' He gave her a cheesy smile.

'I promised to vote for Stanley on any confidence motion,' Jaya replied, then paused, opening up into a smile. 'That doesn't mean I will support you after tomorrow.'

Hughes didn't respond; he just nodded and walked off to the corridor leading towards the Members' Hall. He caught up with Messenger, who was dawdling back to his office.

'We need to talk about the Indian.'

Messenger shook his head. 'Her name is Jaya.'

'Whatever,' Hughes said. 'If we change the leader tomorrow, there is no guarantee she will vote for the new one.'

'You mean Harper, don't you?'

'Of course.' Hughes squirmed. 'I'm just thinking of contingencies,' he said as they strolled over the echoing wooden floor past the newspaper library. 'If we change leaders, she just said she may vote for the other mob on a confidence motion. Then we're stuffed.'

'So then why change leaders?'

'You're asking this question after that performance?'

'He has a lot on his plate and got held up.'

'James has the numbers for a spill, so it's on.'

'If we change leader, we may well lose government. It makes little sense to kill the government just for a change of leader.'

They walked until they hit the grey carpet, then stopped, as Hughes needed to branch away.

'If the Indian was on our side, then we wouldn't have a problem.'

'What are you saying?'

'If she re-joined the party, then we would have the numbers.'

'She would never come back; she hates us.'

'If we give her an offer she can't refuse?'

Messenger thought through the idea. 'She has said she wants to run again, and according to the polls she would have a better chance if she was a member of the party.'

'You're mates; why not have a chat with her?'

'There would be no problem if we didn't change the leader.'

'You know, and I know, that's just not going to happen. Not after today.'

CHAPTER SIXTY-EIGHT

Cassandra Rogers made her way to the opposition leader's office and was waiting at reception to speak with Meredith Bruce when Jaya entered.

'Not happy with Meredith to be PM?'

'It's not that.' Jaya felt embarrassed. 'I promised Stanley.'

Just as Jaya finished explaining, Bruce came out of her office.

'Ah ladies, come in. Nice to see you.' She stepped aside, allowing the women to enter touching Cass' elbow as she passed. 'Please sit down.' She pointed towards her lounge area.

'Meredith, I just wanted to explain the vote.' Jaya started but cut off with a wave of the hand from Bruce.

'No need to explain; I understand. You promised Stanley, so I would have expected you to do it. I just wanted to test what they would do. They didn't disappoint when they guillotined the speakers.'

'Thanks for being so understanding.'

'Think nothing of it.' Bruce waved her hand again. 'What will you do when you face another vote tomorrow?'

'Depends on who's leader.'

Cass took a note. Jaya saw her. 'This is off the record, Cassandra, please,' she said.

'You've come a long way in a few days.'

'Once bitten.' Jaya smiled.

'Who needs to be leader for you to vote against them?' Bruce asked.

'Harper or Hughes.'

Bruce crossed her legs, stroking her chin. 'Is there anyone else likely to get up?'

Cass and Jaya both shook their heads, uncertain whether others might have the numbers.

'Messenger?' Bruce asked.

'He hasn't got the numbers and is likely to be dumped as deputy,' Cass said with confidence.

'It's only ever about the numbers.' Bruce was considering something else on her mind and turned to Jaya. 'Do you think you can beat Gerrard?'

'It'll be difficult. Recent polling says my profile needs a lift,' Jaya said.

'So, the only way for you to survive is if he doesn't stand?' Bruce suggested.

'Basically.'

'Well, you had better consider your future if you want to stay in the parliament.'

Jaya took the hint, standing to leave. 'Meredith, once again, I'm sorry.'

'Don't even think about it,' Bruce assured her. 'Put your mind on what might happen tomorrow. Do what's right for you.' She stood, leading Jaya to the door and smiling as she left.

'You think she'll support you tomorrow?' Cass asked once the door closed.

'Oh, look, she may. But I will not count on it.' Bruce resumed her seat. 'She's nice, Jaya, but I don't trust her.'

'Then what's the Gerrard plan?'

'If he gets back in, then my career is over.'

'Then why let him bowl in and take what he thinks is his?' Cass sat back, resting a Doc Marten on the brass and marble coffee table. 'I hate these power crazed cockheads who think they can do and say whatever they want to keep us under control. I've had enough.'

'That sounds personal, Cass; having man problems?'

Cass scoffed as she turned away. 'Why is it you never hear about women in power using their position to undermine others, using their sexuality to get their way?' she asked.

'We're wired different, I guess.'

Cass stared at Bruce. 'Why is it the sisters seem to succumb to the wiles of these powerful men, when they should just say no?'

'It's the imbalance,' Bruce said. 'Generally, and I emphasise I am generalising, sisters think their talent needs a patron, and to get one, they let them have their way.'

Cass pouted her bottom lip, turning the corners of her mouth down as she nodded agreement. 'Are we going to let Andrew Gerrard get his way again?'

'What can we do?'

'Expose him, and indeed others, like Tony Hancock.'

'That's a little radical, wouldn't you think?'

'I have a sleaze sheet on three very handy randy misogynists. It could form the core Me-too story and a great headline. Using Gerrard as the focal point in the article, though, would be excellent and kill off his comeback.'

Bruce shifted in her seat. 'Do you have any volunteers? There must be a heap of them.'

'I'm sure there are. I'm certain they would come forward once exposed, but we need an initial admission.'

'Why are you looking at me like that?'

'I would like you to do it.'

Bruce didn't respond, scoffing at the thought. 'What makes you think he Me-tooed me?'

'The discussion in the chamber today,' Cass said. 'Certain pointers you have raised at our dinners. I reckon you are as ambitious as me, and like me, you would have done anything to get ahead.'

Bruce laughed, turning away. 'That's ridiculous.'

'Is it?' Cass probed her further. 'You tell your story, and I will guarantee we run hard on it. We will set up a podcast, seeking stories from other victims. I have to drive the revelation, basing it on his bad habits when he was prime minister.'

'Can you promise me it won't be libellous and come back on me?'

'I can if you use parliamentary privilege.'

Bruce stood up, pacing the floor, before settling into the chair at her desk.

'Let me think about it.'

'If we get it on the public record, then there will be no recourse to you. I would expect it will mean the end of Gerrard.'

'Let me think about it.'

Cass took her cue and said goodbye, leaving Bruce to mull over the proposition. As she worked her way back to the media gallery on the second floor, she called Christopher Hughes.

'If you win tomorrow, you won't be prime minister for very long. The Indian will never support you.' Cass smiled as she gave the news.

'Serious? How do you know?' Hughes asked.

'She just told me during a meeting with Bruce.'

'Are they planning something?'

'They were strategising and cooking up plans for tomorrow. I would be on your toes if I were you.'

'Fancy another swim?'

'No thanks.' Cass ended the call. 'Cockhead.'

CHAPTER SIXTY-NINE

Jaya raised her hand when she recognised Barton Messenger moving through the outside tables of the Kingston Hotel. The Kingo was a pub for locals, and she enjoyed cooking steak on the Steakhouse grill. The beer was cold and unpretentious compared to other establishments catering for the political crowd. It was also a short walking distance to her serviced apartment in Gibbs Street, but she was hoping to stay at the Hyatt tonight.

'Can I get you a drink?' Messenger leaned in, kissing her on the cheek. 'A wine perhaps?'

'I'll have a schooner of draught if you don't mind.' Jaya grinned.

'A beer?' Messenger asked, suspiciously. 'I always thought you were a Chardonnay girl.'

'I am, but given we're at the Kingo, I thought I would join in the fun.'

'Fair enough.' Messenger moved away into the bar, soon returning with a schooner for Jaya and a Stella Artois glass for himself.

'Here's cheers, gorgeous,' he said, clinking his glass as he took his chair at the metal table under the awnings in the paved outdoor area. 'How was your day?'

'Are you kidding me? It was dreadful.' Jaya gulped a large mouthful. 'I feel so stressed by it all.'

'They will bring on another tomorrow; how will you vote?'

'I don't know.'

'Will you support James Harper if he gets up?'

'You know Hughes is running, don't you?'

'He's supporting Stanley.'

'And when he doesn't have to?'

Messenger shrugged. 'It's all up in the air at the moment. All I know is that the petition is signed, and I'm about to lose my job.'

Jaya took another generous mouthful of beer. 'You know?' she said, leaning back in her chair, 'I wouldn't put it past him to have set up this whole thing.'

Messenger ignored the jibe. 'Do you think I should run?'

'Yes, I do. I've said it before, and I will say it again. The government needs you to lead it. No, scratch that. The country needs you to step up.'

'Will you vote against me?'

'Of course not, silly.'

'Then why vote against someone else like Harper, or Hughes, for that matter?'

'I need to beat Gerrard.'

'Then why not re-join the party?'

'You've got to be joking.'

'No, I'm not.' Messenger smiled. 'We would welcome you with open arms.'

Jaya didn't respond. She took another drink, then another. Then she gazed at Messenger and asked, 'What's in it for me?'

The response surprised Messenger, distorting his face. 'So, you are interested?'

'If you folks fund my campaign, then I could be.'

'Christopher is keen to open discussion with you.'

'Wait.' Jaya placed her glass on the table. 'Hughes has sent you as an emissary?'

'We are just trying to figure out what you're thinking with a change of leadership.' Messenger shrugged, trying to minimise Jaya's unexpected rush of anxiety.

She crossed her arms, tapping her foot, not happy with the setup. 'Is this why you suggested having a drink this evening?'

Messenger didn't respond

Jaya's face tightened. 'So, it was?'

'I said nothing.'

'You didn't have to; your face gives you away.'

'Jaya, please, this is the business of politics,' Messenger said. 'I said this weeks ago. You can't complain about it now.'

DOOMED

Jaya glanced about her before settling her gaze on a group of people preparing to leave.

'I don't like this Machiavellian stuff. I just want to be a good federal member of parliament and do my job.'

'No one likes leadership challenges, but when they come, everyone gets tarnished.'

'Your troubles have nothing to do with me.'

'They will if you vote down a new leader.'

'Oh, for heaven's sake.' Jaya wanted to move on. 'Let's eat and get out of here.'

Messenger finished his beer. 'I'm going back to the House; the prime minister wants to meet with me.'

'That'd be right.'

'Don't be like this.'

'Like what?' The comment hurt Jaya. 'Not enjoying being played?'

Messenger shook his head as he got up and left without saying another word. A white commonwealth car was waiting.

Although the parliament's chambers had closed for the evening, there were plenty of people wandering the corridors. To get ahead, ambitious politicians often stayed back to keep up with the constant legislative and policy workload demanded of them. Some stayed back to carouse, claiming they were networking. Some called constituents, and others called local party members to make sure they retained the confidence of delegates who voted on their preselection. Tonight, government members were listening to the pitch of James Harper advocates or the covert operatives of Christopher Hughes. No one was talking up the prime minister's chances.

Messenger walked from the House of Representatives' security entrance through the darkened carpeted corridors to the ministerial wing, stopping on the way at the whips' office to check likely numbers for the meeting tomorrow.

'We are preparing ballot papers for the spill motion and at least two sets for the leadership,' said the whip.

'Are you preparing deputy leader ballot papers?' Messenger asked.

'We have not been told to do so. Which means no ballot or no contest. What are you hearing?'

'I'll be contesting, I can assure you.'

'Good lad; that's what we like to hear.'

Messenger kept striding through the corridors, past the opposition leader's office and through the glass connecting corridor with its wooden floors to the central ministerial core, then around to the prime minister's office. As he entered, Maurice Roussett was sitting at the prime minister's desk finishing a call.

The prime minister and Hughes were both sitting on the leather couch, slips of paper strewn across the coffee table along with two tumblers generously splashed with whiskey, an almost empty bottle before them.

'Thomson is a no,' Roussett said to Hughes, before punching in another number and rocking back in the chair, a foot on the desk.

'He's a no to what?' Messenger asked as he took a seat in a rigid chair opposite.

'We only have to convince five petition signers to change their vote to not have a spill,' Hughes replied. 'Try Ronaldson next,' he said to Roussett, who made a note.

Messenger sat for a moment to consider the task before them, then asked the prime minister, 'What do we do if they win the motion for the spill? Will you step aside?'

'It'll be a vote of no confidence, so I must,' Stanley said.

'Then what?'

'We call for nominations,' Hughes said.

'And who will that be?'

'Well,' Stanley paused for a moment. 'James for starters.'

'Unopposed?'

Stanley gazed at Messenger, screwing his lips as if thinking.

'One of you, I would expect.'

'Who?' Messenger asked, glancing at Hughes, still with his head down working the numbers. 'Will they get your votes?'

'My votes are all over the place at the moment; some are on the petition, so there is no certainty James has the majority.'

'Let me ask again.' Messenger sat forward, resting his elbows on his knees. 'Who should be the next prime minister?'

Stanley looked over to Hughes, who stopped reading, picking up his tumbler and glancing back at the prime minister.

'You two have been very supportive, so work it out between yourselves.'

Hughes flicked a glance towards Messenger, who did the same to him; neither spoke.

'Ronaldson is a no,' said Roussett after a pause.

'Damn. Mickey has always been one of mine,' said Stanley.

'Have you spoken to the Indian?' Hughes asked Messenger.

'Her name is Jaya, and I would mark her down as a no.'

Hughes held the tumbler to his lips, pausing for a moment, then sipping.

'She implied she will not support Harper,' Messenger added.

'What about anyone else?'

'She didn't say, but I got the distinct impression she would only support Pete.'

'Implied or said?' Hughes asked.

'The only vote I can guarantee for me, and I can't use her,' Stanley lamented.

'Implied,' said Messenger. 'I asked her about joining the party. She would need guarantees of significant support to fight against Gerrard.'

'If Gerrard wasn't there?' Hughes quizzed.

'Then she still may join, but I got no concrete statement from her.'

'We need her,' Hughes said.

'Why?' Stanley asked.

'If this goes against you tomorrow, Pete,' Messenger said, 'we need to secure the government by ensuring Jaya doesn't use her vote against us in a vote of confidence. Chris suggested inviting her back into the party.'

'Would she be eligible for the party vote tomorrow if she did?' No one responded.

Eventually Hughes spoke. 'I suppose if she signs the right papers and is approved by national office before the meeting at twelve, then yes, she could very well join us.'

'That's a vote for me then.'

Hughes nodded, chuckling. He didn't care; he already had his numbers.

Cass was in her cubicle in the media gallery, wrestling with a story about misogyny in politics and the ruthless use of power to get whatever a political operative wanted or perhaps needed.

She considered politicians to be just ordinary people doing extraordinary things. It seduced many of them who then used this power to cajole whoever felt intimidated or vulnerable. She knew the irony was that politicians didn't appreciate their power was a passing gift. They lamely assumed personality and style were the reasons they appeared so attractive. Her phone buzzed.

'I wasn't expecting you to pick up,' Hughes said.

'No, I don't want a swim.'

'We need Gerrard gone, and quickly.'

'That won't be easy. We need to mount a case.'

'Those statements I got you. Were they any good?'

'Terrific.' Cass was not enthusiastic. 'They aren't silver bullets; they seem sketchy.'

'You said you were a victim.'

'I will not kiss-and-tell like that just for you.'

'What do you want?' Hughes asked.

'I told you. I want my show.'

Hughes didn't respond to this and changed tack. 'If we get rid of Gerrard, we have Rukhmani.'

'You're kidding,' Cass said, shaking her head as she realised what he was saying. 'I can't work miracles before the vote tomorrow.'

'Write something for the paper tomorrow, then talk about it on the breakfast shows.'

'Can't be done.'

'We need the Indian to know we have her back, but we need to do that from government, not opposition.'

'So, tell her yourself,' Cass said.

'I can't.'

'Why, surely she will listen to you?'
'I just can't.'
'Have you crossed swords over policy or something?'
Hughes didn't reply.
'Chris, you're going to have to trust me on this if you want me to swing her. What's the story?'
'I'm not happy about this.'
'Tell me.'
'We had a Me-too moment.'
Cass shrieked with shock, then laughter. 'You are kidding me? You dead set moron. Can't you ever keep your dick in your pants?'

CHAPTER SEVENTY

'Do you trust him?' Messenger asked Stanley again about Hughes' methods and support after their colleague had left the office for the evening.

'No, not really, but he has been very supportive.'

'Just like Brutus.'

'If you're worried about him, why not put your hand up for the job?'

'I was considering it, but I don't have the numbers.'

'Do you have enough to beat Harper on a three-way vote against Chris?'

'It would be tight because my supporters are voting for Harper no matter the other candidate.'

'Will they come to you if you nominated?'

'They could; why?'

'Because I could swing them against Chris if James wasn't the other candidate.'

'Do you think I can do the job?' Messenger asked.

'Better than those two, let me tell you. You've been a great deputy, but Chris is happy to throw you under the bus as deputy, and I'm not happy about that. You may even lose your front bench status.'

Messenger felt a buzz in his stomach that moved to his shoulders as he contemplated what his colleagues had said. If he could find the numbers to get ahead of Harper, he could then transfer Stanley's numbers away from Hughes to get over the line. He could be the prime minister in less than twenty-four hours.

'Lieberman is a no,' Roussett announced, still at the desk.

Stanley glumly looked at Messenger and sighed. 'It's over for me, and that's a good thing. My mind is on my family at the moment. This job is killing me.'

'You took us to an election victory, Pete; never forget that.'

'Maybe things would be different if we had our own majority,' Stanley said.

Messenger didn't respond. It was time to contact his numbers man and ask for an effort to get support.

'Have you contacted the bank the farmer asked you about?'

Stanley clicked his fingers at his memory lapse. 'No, but I will do it tomorrow.'

'Do you want me to do it?'

'No, I promised him, so I'll speak to the bank and call him.'

'Okay, I'll leave you to it.' Messenger stood. 'I have my own calls to make.'

'Thank you, Bart. You're a good man.'

'Okay, we can do it, just.' Wilson Campbell was delivering the news, referring to his list. 'It's going to be tight; you may be down one or two votes. But we can do it. It may come down to what they had for breakfast.'

'Would James beat Chris if I wasn't in it?' Messenger asked.

'It would be tight, but with you in the mix the numbers go crazy.'

'What's the support for Hughes?'

'Solid, but when I throw you into the contest, then I get slippage.'

'What do you think I should do?' Messenger gnawed at his lip.

'I can guarantee you have lost the deputy's role, so you have nothing to lose.'

'Is it too early for me?'

'You're young, but you also have a solid reputation, Bart,' Campbell said. 'If you don't do it now, you may never get another opportunity.'

'How certain are you with the numbers?'

'You may need one or two, so if I were you, I would try to get them.'

'Haven't we hounded them enough?' Messenger scratched his head.

'They have, but you need at least one.'

'Thanks, Willy; you are a champ.'

'Thank me tomorrow if we get you elected. Let me know if you change your mind.'

'See you in the morning.'

Messenger asked his driver to wait ten minutes, just in case, but no longer, as he got out of the white commonwealth car. She was on the second-floor level, room 216 of the Adina apartments, a large modern heritage-style complex where many politicians and staffers stayed. Some shared; others chose self-catering rather than the expense and privilege of the five-star hotels that Messenger preferred.

He cut through the underground carpark to the stair-well near her door, bouncing up the stairs. He didn't know if it would please her to see him; he hadn't bothered to call, and indeed, he was taking a risk, as she sometimes shared with Robert Wong.

It was late; the lights were still blazing. He placed his ear near the door to listen for talking before he gently rapped a knock. Jaya came to the door after the second, more solid thump. He could see movement behind the door viewer and heard the chain drop against the metal as the door opened. She moved straight into his arms and kissed him.

'I'm sorry, darling. I didn't mean it,' Jaya struggled to say as Messenger reciprocated. 'Come in before we're seen.'

They untangled themselves, moving into the lounge. Jaya grabbed him tight. Her satin and silk robe felt good to touch.

'Would you like a drink? I was just on my way to bed.'

'A wine would be great.' Messenger broke away, sprawling into the lounge chair by the door leading to the balcony.

'It's so nice to see you.' Jaya dragged an open bottle of Chardonnay from the refrigerator, collected two glasses and moved over to the lounge. 'What's happening? Why are you here?'

'I'm one vote from being prime minister.' Messenger sat stone faced.

'Shut the hell up!' Jaya stopped dead, her mouth dropping open. 'Are you serious?' she asked as she flopped into the lounge.

'If I can get ahead of Harper tomorrow, I can knock off Hughes.'

'Hughes is running?'

'They implied it this evening.'

'There is no way that creep will ever be prime minister.'

Her response stunned Messenger. 'Not sure what that's about.' He leaned forward and picked up his glass, clinking a toast with her. 'Anyway, I'm close, but I have to get past Harper.'

'Are you sure Hughes will run?'

'He hasn't declared, but everyone expects him to, including Stanley.'

'The prime minister is happy he is being shafted by him?'

'There's no evidence Hughes has worked against him, but since Stanley will not run if there is a spill, it doesn't matter who does.'

'Who do you need to convince? Can I help?'

'Yes, you can.'

'Who do you want me to call?'

'I want you to vote for me.'

'Of course, that's a given. I would never vote against you in a no-confidence motion.'

'No, it's not that vote I am talking about.'

'What then?' Jaya shook her head, confused, sipping her wine.

'I would like you to come to the party meeting tomorrow and vote for me.'

The comment rattled Jaya, and she shifted awkwardly on the couch. 'I already told you, I wouldn't join the party to stop any censure motions.'

'It's a vote for me that I am asking for.'

Jaya gazed at him, not recognising her feelings. She would do almost anything for him but re-joining the party might be a step too far.

'My team says I am a vote or two short. I thought I could use your support and in return we crank up your campaign in Melbourne.'

Jaya gnawed her bottom lip, thinking through options. 'You know this is not helping us, don't you?'

'What do you mean?'

'This may send a wedge through us?'

Messenger considered the response, then turned away from her. 'I don't support that view.'

'You think we can continue, do you?'

Messenger gazed at her, placing his glass on the table before him, then fell to his knees to hug her. 'I want us to continue, absolutely.'

'In secret?'

'No.' He kissed her.

Jaya shook her head. 'You don't think you have a conflict?'

'Yes, I do, but it's declared if it's public.'

Jaya placed her hands on his cheeks and drew him close to kiss.

After an extended embrace, Messenger resumed his seat, holding her hand.

'What do you reckon?'

Jaya dropped her eyes and sighed. 'Hold that thought.' She stood, then moved away to the bedroom. 'I need to make a call.' She collected her phone, closing the door behind her.

Messenger watched her go then flopped back into the chair, bewildered. Ten minutes later, Jaya returned from the bedroom, looking sheepish.

He smiled and asked, 'What's the story?'

'What's in it for me?'

Messenger wasn't expecting the question. 'How do you mean?'

'If I do this, and you become prime minister, what's in it for me?'

Messenger had heard the question before from colleagues willing to sell their vote. 'A funded campaign; not enough?' He tried to stay calm.

'I will do this, but I want a portfolio.'

He laughed out loud.

Jaya now seemed embarrassed, but just as determined. 'I know it will cause a lot of crap.'

'Ya think?' He spoke across her.

'If you want my vote, then I want a portfolio.'

Messenger looked back at her and smiled. 'Which one?'

'Trade.'

'Why?'

'Because the growth of India and the region is important. I think I have something to contribute. I'm better than most of your front bench; you have even said that. So, I don't see a problem.'

Messenger agreed with her but didn't show it. His face didn't etch one emotion. 'And us?'

'We keep doing what we're doing, and in time if we are serious, we go public.'

Messenger smiled; his eyes brightened.

'And if I can't deliver?'

'Hmm, good question.'

'Why don't we compromise?' he suggested. 'Why don't I appoint you to chair the Foreign Affairs and Trade parliamentary committee, and if I am re-elected, and you win your seat, then I promote you?'

Jaya tapped a message into her phone. It pinged back at once. She looked at it, smiled, then sighed.

'I want it in writing.'

'You don't trust me?'

'Of course, I do, but Robert doesn't.'

'Deal.'

Messenger leaned over, offering his hand. Jaya took it; she shook it, and still holding it, stood up, dragging him to her.

CHAPTER SEVENTY-ONE

Tony Hancock was viewing the high-rating national breakfast program on his network as he enjoyed a cup of tea in bed. Newspapers strewn across his covers, with headlines driving a change of leadership for the government. He agreed with his covert business group, the Mercantiles. They considered Prime Minister Stanley a liability and wanted him gone, and they had assigned Hancock to do the job. He wanted Stanley gone because the prime minister was yet to give approval for his appointment as trade commissioner to Los Angeles.

Tamara O'Byrne sashayed in, passing him a plate of toast before slipping into bed beside him. She gave him plenty of room, as she understood he was working.

Hancock was waiting for the program to cross to the nation's capital and give an update on the leadership crisis. He had driven his key journalist Cass Rogers to get the leadership stories and felt guilty he was making promises he could never keep.

'Thanks for the toast, gorgeous.'

'Pleasure, treasure.' O'Byrne snuggled into the abundance of pillows. 'What time do you think you'll be going to the office?'

'Why?'

'I might get a lift with you.'

'Is that a good idea, do you reckon?'

'I have no problem unless you do. Do you have a problem being seen with me, darling?'

Hancock hesitated for a moment, then smiled. 'Not at all. I just thought with the announcement about the show being made, it might help you if there was no link to me.'

'We are a couple or we're not.'

'It's not that easy, hon; we have reputations to protect. Now let me watch my program,' he said.

'You know I don't want this job, don't you?'

'We are here because you told me you wanted the job.'

'Yes, but now I am here, I don't need it.'

Hancock bit his bottom lip as he continued watching, thinking he might have created something bigger than he had been expecting. He was thankful when the host asked Cass her first question.

'Canberra is in turmoil this morning as both sides of politics struggle with their own scandals.' Cass was in the Canberra studio holding papers before her, which Hancock thought unusual. 'The government will discuss leadership challenges in the party room from noon, when it is likely a new leader will emerge, and Australia will have its third prime minister in three years. This chaos has affected the money markets, plunging them to two-year lows, and policy has been on the back burner for days, if not weeks.'

Hancock smiled.

'Issues like the drought and the foreign workers' legislation are yet to be completed. Farmers are feeling the pinch. The government has promised the world, yet they are still to deliver anything. You may recall my interview with Brian Tucker last week, after his parliamentary protest. As late as this morning, he is yet to hear from the prime minister.'

The host directed her to the opposition.

'They are having their own challenges, with calls for Andrew Gerrard to re-enter the parliament as leader. We hear that a scandal reaching the leadership echelons of the party will be exposed as early as today, or perhaps tomorrow.'

The host cut in. 'What is the scandal that will come out?'

'I can't confirm anything now. The discussions I have had show that it could be a Me-too moment, which is the worst thing that could happen to the opposition, given the government is losing control.'

'Me-too?' The revelation stunned the host. 'How strong is the information you are getting?'

'From a victim.'

'A victim? Which means there could be more than one?'

'Yes, that's right.' Cass frowned to make sure her face implied her story was a serious matter, although she had no facts.

'Are we talking politicians?'

'Yes, senior politicians in the opposition.'

'Is that fair? We can't name anyone, but by not doing so, we have just suggested that all the opposition parliamentarians could be involved, or none?'

'Is it fair? I think the story is of national importance and we should discuss the matter.'

'But Cass, it's our parliament you are talking about.'

'I know what goes on around here behind closed doors, believe me. It's a boys-club and many privileged politicians take advantage of their position, be they at the top of the tree or at the bottom. I know, for instance, from personal experience, how harassment works, and I can tell you it is as rife within the media as it is in the parliament.'

'Whoa, wait. You are implying you are also a victim.'

'I didn't say that. I said I know from personal experience about the harassment within parliament and the media, including Hancock Media.'

Hancock jolted forward, stretching for his phone, stabbing, and scrolling before prodding the number of the show's producer.

'It's Tony; cut her off.' There was a slight pause. 'Cut her off now or leave your desk.'

The television displayed a lost transmission screen, then after a few moments went to commercials. He knew it wouldn't be long before the crisis would come his way and considered who to contact first, Rogers or his corporate affairs lawyer.

'What's wrong, hon? What's happened?'

'I have to go; see yourself out when you're ready. I'll let the concierge know you will leave later and to arrange a limousine for you.'

'Anything I can do?'

'Let's have lunch.'

Cass took the call, as she knew she would have to. Her red Docs rested on her desk, and she was leaning back on the legs of her chair. She'd already spoken to a wild Meredith Bruce and now she was ready for Hancock.

'You told me to get the stories, so I have the stories and I'm ready to publish.'

'What are you trying to do by bringing the network into it?'

'There is a culture of harassment within the network, and you know that.' Cass said. 'Hell, you're the worst offender.'

'Why raise this now?'

'Why raise this now?' Cass said, sarcasm in her tone. 'Why raise this now? Hmm, maybe because I am yet to be appointed to replace Nicholls. Maybe because I sacrificed my family for your network. Maybe because the network has a toxic male culture that suppresses women, and maybe it's time to clean it up. You can either fix the problem or be part of the problem. Either way, I am on a mission to be rewarded for the years I have given you. On top of that, I am determined to stop this casting couch mentality the place has.'

'You've got nothing.'

'Really?' Cass held a transcriber close to the mouthpiece, pushing the play button.

Hancock didn't respond when the recording finished.

'You want to hear it again?'

'What are you planning to do?'

Cass smiled. 'The first thing I plan to do is bring down the government if that sleaze ball Hughes becomes prime minister. I have received a statement by a politician confirming an incident like my experience with him at his house in Canberra. We can both describe him as huge if you know what I mean. But that's not all. I have him linked to the construction union, doing a deal to destabilise the community. The evidence has him starting the parliament riot.'

'You are kidding?'

'No, I'm not.' Cass took her feet off the desk and straightened. 'He has been hitting on me for years and I've had enough. He needs to be brought down a peg or two, and this will be the first story on my new program. I will then do solid follow-up stories on blokes in power who have given women hell.' She paused for effect. 'You decide if you want to be part of the program, Tony.'

DOOMED

'What about Gerrard?'

'He'll be my second story as soon as my contact speaks in the parliament about her experiences to protect herself from him.'

'You're going to destroy the joint.'

'That's the plan, and you can either be part of it or not. You can get the credit for it or not; that's up to you, but, and here's the kicker: I want a five-year contract, with two five-year options, signed in front of me by Thursday. So, you have two days to make it happen.'

Hancock didn't respond. Cass could hear his rapid breathing, then deep breaths.

'You bitch.'

'Yeah, you're right I am.' Cass said with contempt. 'But I'm not a patch on you and what you have made me do over the journey. After all these years, this is my bonus, so get it done, otherwise you're done.' She pushed the call end button and dropped her phone onto the desk, then leaned back into her chair and kicked her feet up on the desk. She locked her fingers behind her head and smiled, gazing at the ceiling in satisfaction.

'One down, two to go.

CHAPTER SEVENTY-TWO

Frankie Hughes remained ambitious for her husband. She enjoyed the celebrity of politics, without the incendiary activities necessary for success. Now she was hours from relocating to the prime minister's residence at the Kirribilli compound, already sketching out plans for an early catch-up with the girls. Her husband did what he had to do, including betrayal, but she knew that if she ever complained she would never have the life she coveted, so she accepted his behaviour, ignoring the gossip.

Hughes asked his wife to travel to Canberra, which he seldom did. This time was different, as a photograph of the elected prime minister hugging his wife would be wonderful media, dispelling any talk of marriage troubles. He loved her, considering her an asset throughout his career. He didn't mind her alternative life and her international travel, showcasing herself amongst the societal influences of Sydney. He enjoyed her company, but also enjoyed his time away from her. It was perfect for both.

Frankie stayed close to the politics, understanding the significance of what was about to happen. Taking down a first term prime minister was such a drastic, desperate tactic, but she agreed Stanley had to go. She just hoped the party would call upon Christopher to lead them so that she would become the nation's first lady.

The couple perched themselves around the marble kitchen bench at their Canberra home, watching the breakfast program and considering Cassandra Rogers' provocative comments, implying the government had skeletons that should concern them.

'Is she talking about you?' Frankie was unafraid to call her husband out when she considered he might have transgressed.

'I wouldn't have thought so.'

'Where does she get most of her information from?'

'To be honest with you,' Hughes sipped his tea, 'this challenge would not be happening without input from me.'

'Do I need to be concerned?'

'Not at all. She has been here a few times for a drink and a light supper, but you can relax; nothing untoward happened between us.'

'Do you have the numbers?' Frankie asked for the first time, forking small pieces of chopped fruit into her mouth.

'I believe so.'

'What could go wrong?'

'A third candidate may split the vote. So long as I'm in the last two I should win; with a significant margin, I might add.'

'This is good, darling. What time do you want me there?'

'Come in around twelve. The party meets then; it should be over by one. We can do media together, then have lunch.'

'Do you want me to stay overnight?' She raised her glass of juice, then sipped it, studying her husband.

'That'd be nice, but I suspect I will be very busy setting up jobs and getting commissions sorted. Maybe you can catch a flight home after the swearing in.'

Frankie brushed off any negative thoughts, looking forward to getting back to Sydney. She would have plenty to do preparing for the relocation.

'Does James know you're nominating?'

'Maybe; I don't know. I suspect there may be chatter, but he hasn't challenged me about it, so I think not.'

'If you pull this off, darling, it will be the pinnacle of all our plans. I'm so proud of you.'

'We'll be having Christmas at Admiralty House this year.'

Frankie smiled at her husband, raising her glass again and gazing over the rim. 'I can assure you, we shall do a lot of things at Admiralty House, my love.'

DOOMED

Ginni Stavloukas was the only one missing when the cabinet met at ten to discuss policy decisions and legislation. She was still working on the numbers for her challenge to become deputy prime minister. She hadn't taken Christopher Hughes' assurances that the work Messenger was doing to shore up his numbers was a waste of time. Nothing in politics is what it seems, and she had learned not to trust anyone.

Prime Minister Stanley acknowledged when he started the meeting that this was likely to be the last meeting of his government's cabinet, hoping the assembled ministers would continue to respond to the agenda. Ministers who made earlier statements were a little shy to look at the prime minister.

'Prime Minister, I can report that government funding is being distributed to agencies who are managing the drought relief, and we have farmers receiving funds,' Messenger said. 'Our plan is to meet with banks later this week, to find out if they have stopped foreclosing, and report if they have any rogue bank managers causing a stir out bush.' He glanced to the PM. 'Have you contacted the Tuckers and their bank?'

Stanley shifted in his chair. 'I am planning to do that prior to the party meeting.'

Messenger shook his head, disappointed.

Stanley moved on. 'What is the status of the foreign workers' legislation? Are you able to handle this, Christopher?' He nodded to Hughes, who then moved closer to the table.

His adviser Krakos had briefed him, and he advised the cabinet the union movement was at peace with the amended legislation. He had negotiated a settlement, finalising it at a meeting earlier that morning. He expected Garrick Higgins, the union secretary, to make a statement before midday, a statement he wrote.

Stanley closed his folder. 'Colleagues, I just want to say a few things about today's meeting.' He clasped his hands before him, leaning on his forearms. 'Thank you for your support since I have been leader. I think it is fair to say, I never expected to be elected.' Hughes drew in his bottom lip and bit down hard. 'But I have tried my best. Several of you have expressed that my best isn't good enough, and now we are forced to change a first term prime minister. History says the new leader will have their work cut out for them.'

Hughes dropped back in his chair, swinging it sideways, backwards and forwards, and observed the response of his colleagues.

'The challenges we have faced together have been significant,' Stanley continued. 'I am proud we have worked well as a team. Some of you may consider that the government has not performed well, but I am happy. We secured government, then delivered for the Australian people. Whatever happens, I remain supportive of the government, and will serve out my time in whatever capacity the new leadership team thinks fit.'

Stanley stopped speaking. Messenger took his cue to lean forward and speak. 'Thank you, Prime Minister. It is with sadness we find ourselves in this position, brought about by a cabal of colleagues who believe James Harper will be a better prime minister. I, for one, have appreciated your support and guidance in the early days of government. I can assure you; we all work for the betterment of our nation.'

'Hear, hear.' Several colleagues assented.

Messenger paused for a moment, breathing to relieve a sudden dose of anxiety. 'It seems my position is also under threat; already a deal has been done to secure the role for Ginni Stavloukas. Whether my re-election happens, well, we'll just have to wait and see. I would hope we recognise my endeavours within cabinet, and I will be re-elected. Suffice to say, I thank you all for the courtesy and confidence in me you have provided. I look forward to working with you in the next ministry.'

Hughes sat forward. 'I must say on behalf of the team, we thank you, Prime Minister, and you, Barton, for your service, and we hope the party room meeting works out for everyone.'

Stanley smiled. 'Is there a candidate other than James?' He stared at Hughes. 'Has anyone got the support of the independent, like I have?'

No one spoke.

Messenger glanced to Hughes for a response, but there was nothing. No formal announcement of a nomination. Still true to Stanley to the end, or so he thought.

The prime minister stood, swept up his things, then strode off to his office, leaving the others having a quiet chat as they sauntered away.

CHAPTER SEVENTY-THREE

'Is everyone ready?' Cass steadied her earpiece with a finger, waiting for a cue from the Sydney studios. She was about to break into normal programming to announce startling political news. 'Count me in.'

A countdown from five brought her into the national news broadcast.

'Good morning from Canberra. Just one hour before the government's party room meeting, when the prime minister is expected to resign after losing a motion to declare all leadership positions vacant, I can announce a Hancock Media exclusive. The independent member for Melbourne, Jaya Rukhmani, in what appears to be a calculated move, has joined the Conservative Party, sitting on the backbench for the government. In what we can only describe as an unprecedented situation, Ms Rukhmani will now be entitled to attend the party room meeting and vote in the election for a new prime minister.

'With me to explain this development is the member for Melbourne, Ms Rukhmani.

'Jaya, can you please let us know what has made you decide to join the government, ignoring the wishes of your electors in the last election who voted for an independent member?'

'We are facing tough times with the likely change of prime minister. I promised to support Peter Stanley as an independent, but now I would like to make sure greater government stability by casting my vote with the government.'

'Will you still support Peter Stanley when you enter the party room to vote?'

'I have always said I will vote for ethics and integrity. Peter Stanley has shown that to me since his government was formed. I will continue to support him, but if he is no longer in the race for leadership, then I will consider other candidates.'

'Observers have linked you to Barton Messenger; will you support him?'

'In what way am I linked to Mr Messenger?'

'Some in the party suggest you are close.'

'Who?' Jaya tightened her lips. 'Who in the party suggests we are close?'

'Senior figures.'

'Do you have a name?'

'I can't reveal my sources.'

'You make a spurious claim about me and my ethics, with no evidence,' Jaya said, frowning. 'When challenged, you cannot offer any substantive information to confirm your claim.'

'All I asked was, will you support anyone else?'

'No, you didn't. You tried to link me with the treasurer.'

'What is your answer?'

'To what question?'

'Will you support others if Peter Stanley is not in the race for leader?'

'Of course.'

'Have promises been made to you?'

'In what way, promises?'

'Have you any assurances that you will receive benefits if you vote a certain way?'

Jaya hesitated and then smiled. 'You are a piece of work, aren't you? I offer this exclusive interview and already you have me linked with the treasurer and now you are suggesting I have taken a bribe to vote a certain way.'

'It's not what I am saying at all. I'm just trying to understand why you would decide to join the government during a leadership challenge. Why not yesterday, why not next week, why right now?'

'My electors have sent me to Canberra to make sure we have good government. I am attempting to do just that by re-joining the party, which pre-selected me for the seat of Melbourne.'

'Is this an attempt to head off Andrew Gerrard?'

'Andrew Gerrard will need to run his own campaign without me. Let me just say this. Meredith Bruce is an effective leader of the opposition. She does not deserve the omnipotent presence of Andrew Gerrard destabilising her. He has already had his go; it's time for someone else.'

'So why not just vote for the opposition when they move a no confidence motion?'

'I want stable government, not instability, which seems to be your desire.'

Cass turned to the camera. 'Well, there you have it. The independent member for Melbourne is joining the government and will attend the party room meeting scheduled for midday today.'

Meredith Bruce watched the interview and was too shocked to move once normal programming resumed. She had just lost the potential vote that could have made her prime minister, and she now wondered what else she could do to stop Gerrard imposing himself on the parliament and the party and stealing the leadership from her. Her telephone sounded soon after the interview. She recognised the number.

'You were a tad harsh on our sister, Cass.'

'What does she think she is doing, going to the government? What happens to Gerrard now?'

'It's now up to me, I suppose. I just need to fight him off.'

'You've done that before,' Cass joked.

'Not enough though.'

'Have you had any second thoughts about exposing him?'

'Yes.'

'And?'

'I'm still considering it,' Meredith said.

'When?'

'How much detail do I need to give?'

'Just raise it under privilege and let me do the rest.'

'You won't use me?'

'Just your quotes.'

'Will this be good for me?'

'Who's to say? I can promise you one thing: it'll stop Gerrard. Stop him dead in his tracks.'

'Promise me,' Meredith said. 'I'm a little frightened of what might happen.'

'I have Hancock on side, but if we are to do it, I need to drop the story tomorrow. Then I'll follow up next week with a more comprehensive story.'

'What does that mean?'

'It means, despite the government's issues, you need to go into the chamber and speak. You've got to do it before question time today, otherwise it'll be lost.'

Bruce inhaled, bringing a thumb to her mouth, and gnawing the nail. 'You're not making this easy for me.'

'You want him gone?'

'Yes, of course.'

'Then you have to act. The sooner the better.'

Bruce didn't respond at once. She hoped Cass would speak, but she too was silent.

'Okay, let me think about it. Leave it with me.'

'I'm here to help; take care,' Cass said.

She dropped her phone onto papers, leaned back in her chair and rubbed her eyes with the heels of her palms. She stretched away the anxiety. Then she smiled.

'That's two.'

The buzz of the parliament created stress as political staff rushed through the carpeted corridors, facing the prospect of a new prime minister. No one knew the state of the numbers, because unless a politician confirmed their vote, they could vote anyway they pleased in a secret ballot. This uncertainty made the number-crunchers nervous. Candidates thought they could believe their numbers people, but they were always at the mercy of changing politics, the dark art.

Christopher Hughes dressed in his finest Italian suit, his shiny black shoes almost mirror-like and his hair in place; he smiled as he wandered about the corridors talking to supporters and confirming they remained tight. When he reached Barton Messenger's office, he ignored the staffer at the reception, heading straight into the treasurer's office without knocking.

Messenger was at his desk, hand in his ruffled hair, a pen tapping an excel spreadsheet. He glanced up, smiling, and tugging a sheet of paper over his notes.

'I just wanted to thank you for getting the Indian to re-join the party,' Hughes began. 'It will help me. Or indeed, whoever we choose as leader,' he corrected himself. 'You're mitigating any potential confidence motions in the chamber, which is a brilliant effort.'

'Her name is Jaya.'

'Yeah, whatever.' Hughes dismissed the correction.

'If you continue to disrespect her, she may not support us.'

'I am not interested in being nice to her.' Hughes flopped into a chair. 'I'm sure she will benefit from being a member of the party. So well done.'

'Jaya has said she wants help with her campaign against Gerrard; are we able to support her?'

'So long as we keep her vote, then we will support her.'

'I'll let her know.'

'I've been thinking we should do something for you.'

'Keeping my job would be great.'

'Deputy or treasurer?'

'Either; both.'

'I'll talk to the team and see what we can do.' Hughes stood, moving away. 'Well done. I appreciate it.'

Messenger didn't say goodbye as Hughes left, leaving the door wide open. He sniffed a chuckle as he thought about the looming meeting. His adviser Julia Haworth strode in with a pile of papers to be signed, pausing before placing them in front of him.

'Anything I should know about?' she asked.

'Hughes is already making prime ministerial decisions.'

'What do you expect? He's a creep.'

'Not what you should say about a senior minister.'

'Woe betide he gets the vote today.'

'He has the numbers, so I am told,' Messenger said.

'How can he have certain numbers when he has been organising for Stanley?'

'He can because he plays the game pretty well.'

Julia said nothing for a moment. 'Are you in the race?'

'I'll be close. I'm hoping for the sympathy vote for the deputy.'

She turned to leave. 'You underestimate yourself too much, boss.'

CHAPTER SEVENTY-FOUR

Members were already in attendance in the party room, taking their usual chair, chatting with colleagues, and laughing at the witticisms and corny anecdotes. It was only when the prime minister strode in, tailed by his deputy, that silence shrouded the room. Messenger noticed Jaya amongst a group of senators and returned her smile.

'Colleagues, there is no point in discussing any other matter than the petition which is before me,' Stanley began. 'The petition is seeking to put forward a spill motion for all leadership positions and is signed by fifty-five of our colleagues.' He scanned about the room, specifically to those he trusted, yet had signed the petition. 'Some in the media describe it as a suicide note for the government. I would hope this does not happen.'

'Hear, hear,' several members responded.

'The government I led has been an effective one. We achieved much, especially in economic and social reform, but it is also fair to say we have had our challenges. Having a drought doesn't help policy development, nor our balance of payments, for that matter. The cabinet worked together, resolving many of the challenges facing the nation. The political reality is that a minority in the party room believe we should not have changed leaders three years ago. They keep alive an idea that we should return to the previous leadership. Indeed, many of you have complained about the intimidation and bullying to force colleagues to get to the position where we are today. Remarkably, a government leading in the polls is subjected to a leadership challenge.'

Stanley placed the fingers of his right hand into the side pocket of his jacket, which was buttoned in front, statesman like.

'We went through a leadership challenge just a few short weeks ago. Yet many in this room did not accept the result. So here we are today to resolve the leadership issue again. I will say this before proceeding.' Stanley paused, scanning the room, his gaze coming to rest on James Harper. 'Whatever the result, I hope it is our wish we support the prime minister and allow him, or her,' members now considered whether Stavloukas had a change of heart, 'to lead the party and this government effectively until the next election, when, hopefully, we will be successful.'

Stanley glanced about again and saw Jaya Rukhmani.

'I especially wish to thank Jaya Rukhmani for her decision to re-join the party. I am certain she will contribute significantly to policy and politics in the future. I have appreciated her support of me in the House.'

Jaya smiled and nodded an acknowledgement to Stanley.

'It is now my formal duty to move a motion to spill the leadership of the party. All those in favour, say, aye.'

A loud response from the room.

'To the contrary, no.'

There was no response, which didn't surprise anyone.

'Given that resounding response,' Stanley took a deep breath, sadness rushing through him, 'I will take it as a vote of no confidence in the leadership. Therefore, I declare all positions vacant. I call upon the whips to prepare for an election for all positions.'

The whips stood and moved to the front of the room with the ballot boxes and papers ready if required to conduct a vote.

'We will now conduct a ballot if required for the position of leader and prime minister. Are there any nominations?' Stanley asked.

Harper was quickly on his feet, looking confident. His plan with Hughes had brought him one step closer to reaching his ambition. His wife was waiting in his office, and she would be his first call.

'James Harper,' Stanley declared with little enthusiasm. 'Is there any other nomination?'

There was a slight pause and members looked about. Harper was not expecting any other nomination. Hughes, using the timing of a dramatic actor, rose from his place. A sudden buzz of murmuring rushed through the room. Harper swivelled to face him, astonished by his colleague's nomination. Hughes shrugged his shoulders, smiling towards Messenger.

DOOMED

'Christopher Hughes.' Stanley wasn't surprised, secretly hoping there would be a contest. 'Anyone else like to nominate?'

Messenger was gazing at his hands clasped on the table in front of him. He looked up, seeing Jaya's smiling face, and felt his confidence grow. It was now or never.

'Anyone else?'

Messenger took a deep breath and rose to stand in his place next to Stanley.

'Barton Messenger; anyone else?' asked Stanley, scanning about the room and hoping for no further nominations. 'No? Whips, please distribute the voting slips.'

Stanley resumed his seat, as did the nominees, as whips passed a yellow slip to all one hundred and six members and senators in the room. Once done, Stanley took to his feet to instruct that only a single name was to be written clearly on the paper: that of the person they would prefer to be their leader. The paper was then to be placed in the ballot box.

Some members showed their vote to colleagues; others scratched a name secretively before rushing to fold the slip of paper. Stanley showed his vote to Messenger, who smiled.

'You'll do a good job, Barton.'

'Thanks, Prime Minister.'

'No longer, my boy; no longer.'

Stanley then stood to explain further procedure.

'The whips will now tally the votes; they will remove the candidate with the lowest number of votes before the second ballot. If any of the candidates wish to scrutineer the count, they can have a colleague do so.'

The crazy, brave confidence of the candidates meant that none of them asked for scrutineers.

'This shouldn't take long,' Stanley said as he sat.

But it did.

It was twenty minutes before the chief whip came into the room to announce the result.

'Senators and members, if I could have your attention. The result was very close. In order of nomination: James Harper, thirty-four; Christopher Hughes, thirty-seven.' Members began calculating the arithmetic. 'Barton Messenger, thirty-five.'

The room erupted with loud voices questioning the result.

'Recount.' Harper was on his feet.

'I declare Christopher Hughes and Barton Messenger to go to the second round.'

'Recount, I said,' Harper almost shouted.

Stanley gazed at Harper. He considered whether he should accept the request, given the way Harper had undermined him and forced this meeting. He decided Harper could squirm a little longer.

'Whips: recount required, and this time no doubt scrutineers will be used.'

The whips marched off to the office opposite the party room, followed by two delegated scrutineers for Harper and Hughes.

Stanley sat and leaned into Messenger. 'This is exciting; did you think you would have those numbers?'

'I knew I needed one more to get over the line.' Messenger smiled.

Stanley glanced over to a smiling Jaya, then back to Messenger. 'Yes, son. I think you will do very, very well.'

The whips counted the slips of paper and confirmed that all were there. They then went through each one carefully, placing them in one of three piles. Occasionally a scrutineer would ask them to slow the count, and in two cases they questioned whether a name was Hughes or Harper. Once they had the piles, they then counted each one twice, confirming the original count.

The chief whip returned to the party room, announcing the result again. Harper was not happy, not only with losing the ballot but also because Hughes had hoodwinked him. He passed on his displeasure to his key supporters.

The whips distributed a light blue voting slip for the second ballot, and members and senators followed the earlier voting procedure. Once collected, Hughes sent a scrutineer to observe the count, which didn't take long.

'Senators and members, the result for a leader, with twelve abstentions, was fifty-five votes, coincidentally the same number that signed the petition for the leadership spill, for Barton Messenger, thirty-nine for Christopher Hughes. I declare Barton Messenger to be the duly elected leader.'

The party room erupted in spontaneous applause, with most members standing.

Hughes didn't stand, wishing he were elsewhere. Harper grudgingly stood and clapped his new leader, the whippet-smart lad from Melbourne.

Peter Stanley clapped as he stepped to the side, then backed away to a spare chair amongst the members.

Messenger stood and glanced to Jaya, who cheekily blew him a kiss. 'Colleagues, I'm surprised by your confidence, and I assure you, I will work every day to make sure that voters return the government at the next election. I will seek your advice, your collegial efforts, and your friendship during my leadership of the party. I'm first amongst equals and I will make sure I never forget that. I am standing on your shoulders, and I will fight for you every day.'

The members clapped again, even more so as they recognised they had made the right decision.

'The position of deputy now has to be determined, and I can tell you that you should make your vote count. I have no right to influence your choice, but with someone so young in the principal job, it may be an opportunity to offer wisdom and experience to the role. I ask those who nominate to reflect upon that assessment before they do. This is a time for growth, so make your decision count. I now call for nominations for the role of deputy leader and deputy prime minister.'

Ginni Stavloukas wasted little time rising to her feet.

Twenty-five minutes later, after three rounds of votes, the chief whip stood before the party room to announce the result.

'With a significant majority, I declare James Harper to be deputy leader with seventy-eight votes. Wilson Campbell, twenty-eight votes.'

'Please congratulate James and thank Wilson for his contribution,' said Messenger, as Hughes, who had had enough, strode from the room.

'You're kidding me,' Cass giggled as she listened. 'What was the vote?'

Jaya explained the one vote margin in the first round, then the eventual result, including the results for the deputy.

'This is a terrific result.'

'You see, there was no reason to go for my throat this morning,' Jaya said.

'You were the difference though.'

'My vote helped Barton get over the line. I wasn't the difference; the other thirty-four votes supported him.'

'Yeah, but without your vote, he would not have got it.'

'Maybe, but at least Hughes failed.'

'How did he take it?'

'Badly.'

'I must call him.' Cass smiled.

'He deserves it.'

'Why are you so viral on him?'

'He once invited me to his Canberra home on the pretext of discussing trade policy.'

'Don't tell me,' Cass interrupted. 'He invited you for a swim?'

'No, it wasn't as friendly as that.'

'What?'

'All I will say is that he had a go at me.'

'Are you prepared to say something about it?'

'Like what?'

'I'm preparing an article for tomorrow about Me-too in high places. I can discuss Hughes if you would like me to?'

'I'll pass on that. I'm over it.'

'I'm also doing a television special on it in about a week, if you change your mind.'

'Unlikely. I'm just glad he isn't the prime minister. Talk soon.'

Cass smiled as she dropped her phone from her ear, pushing the end call button. She shook her head and focused on her story.

'That's three.'

CHAPTER SEVENTY-FIVE

The speaker for the House of Representatives took the chair at 2 p.m., acknowledged the country of the indigenous peoples and read prayers. Messenger was quick to the despatch box.

'Madam Speaker, I seek your indulgence to make a brief statement.'

'The prime minister may proceed.'

'I wish to advise the House that earlier today the federal parliamentary Conservative Party elected me, the member for Gellibrand, as leader and the honourable member for Moncrieff, as deputy leader. As a result, I was sworn in as prime minister prior to question time, and the member for Moncrieff sworn in as treasurer. For the information of the House, I will consider new ministerial arrangements during the next few days and will inform the House when appointments have been made. In the meantime, we will follow current arrangements. I'd also like to place on record the thanks of this House, and indeed the parliament, for the committed service of former Prime Minister Stanley. I have extended sincere best wishes to him, and I don't intend to prolong that matter here today in the House.'

Meredith Bruce stood at the despatch box on her side of the chamber. 'On indulgence, Speaker. I wish to congratulate the Prime Minister for his promotion to this high office. It's a special privilege to be elected prime minister, and I wish him well. I also want to put on record our acknowledgement and thanks to former Prime Minister Stanley, and whilst we didn't always see eye to eye, he served his country well.'

'Questions without notice; are there questions?' the speaker asked.

Bruce was back to the despatch box.

'My question is to the prime minister. Peter Stanley was prime minister this morning. He no longer is. Why?'

Messenger was ready for the question.

'I thank the honourable member for her question. We in this party are equals. We are pre-selected by party members who then ask us to provide leadership; elected members do so by electing one of their own to lead them. The leader is first amongst equals and serves at the pleasure of the party and its elected members. This is in stark contrast to the system of the opposition party where a former prime minister, who is not even elected to this chamber, can bestow upon himself the role of leader, and in his mind become the next prime minister. I am struck why the leader of the opposition has not denounced this announcement as inappropriate and out of order.'

Bruce watched Messenger, reflecting on his comment.

'General Stormin' Norman Schwarzkopf once said, when placed in command, take charge. This is my intention; what is the leader of the opposition's intention? Will she ever take charge?'

Bruce dropped her head. She doodled on her pad, disengaging from question time. Various questions about the economy, foreign workers, the union riot, national security, and aged care were asked and answered until the last question from the member for Mallee was given the call.

'My question is to the prime minister. Can the prime minister update the House on how the government is helping farmers and rural communities to cope with the devastating effects of drought?'

The speaker called the prime minister.

'Madam Speaker, I thank the member for Mallee for her question. As the House would know, the drought is having a catastrophic impact in New South Wales. We also know the devastating effects it is having in Queensland and Victoria after many years. The challenge we have is everyone's in Australia, and we must work together to make sure our hard-working farmers and rural communities are not left isolated by the government or indeed all Australians.

'During my recent visit to farming districts I observed farmers exhausted and almost at the end of their tether. But I also saw their grit to overcome their disappointments, providing hope to their communities. I spoke with Brian Tucker, whose family has worked the land of Tucker Farm for generations. Only a few short years ago pasture was up to their knees; now he trucks in water and feed for his stock. Yet he knows that the pasture will return; he just needs support.

'Madam Speaker, in this country we look after our mates, and our mates are doing it tough. So, the government has started the biggest drought relief package ever instigated. This package will give direct financial assistance and charitable support when required, and we have directed the banks to take a rest from their over-enthusiasm in their management of farm loans.

'My government will look after our farming communities. We will make sure that help for all farming communities will be available for those needing it. We will make sure that feed and water will get to where needed, and we shall do so until those rural towns and communities recover.'

The chamber provided a collective vote of support. 'Hear, hear.'

'I ask that further questions be placed on the notice paper.'

Bruce was quick to her feet.

'Madam Speaker, I seek to make a brief statement on indulgence.'

'The leader of the opposition on indulgence.'

'Thank you, Speaker.' Bruce paused for a moment, anxious about what she was about to say. As Messenger packed up, beginning to leave, she said, 'The prime minister may wish to stay and listen to my statement.'

He turned and smiled, deciding to resume his seat.

'During my career, I've always tried to do my best, whether in the parliament or in the courtroom, to progress the status of women, providing a notion of hope for the future within the community. Equality before the law is a given, but there is never equality before the powerful who would misuse their power, no matter who they are. I have always stood for what I believed to be right, calling out behaviour I believed unacceptable.

'It requires many within the abuse spectrum to overcome daily struggles and challenges in their workplace. Whether it is verbal, mental, emotional, or even physical abuse, I want to acknowledge that many women feel shame when mistreated by men, or indeed women, with power. Many of the abused, particularly women, have to face fear every day to just keep their jobs, and yet still feel good about ourselves.

'Life, and indeed a career, can throw ugly things at us, yet the resilience many of us have shown to mitigate the predators amongst us provides a brighter sunrise to overcome those dark and ugly nights. I am sure many of us have raged against those in power who would do us harm through nuance, gesture, joke, or comment. When challenged, there is denial from the abuser and often gas-lighting towards the accuser, condemning them for misunderstanding normal workplace protocols and behaviour.'

The chamber was silent. Messenger unsure where the statement was heading.

'What I know, Madam Speaker, is that speaking truth is the most powerful tool we all have. And I'm proud and inspired by all women who have felt powerful enough to speak up and share their personal stories about those who have abused them. I want all women, young or old, to be brave and call out poor, unacceptable, misogynistic, predatory behaviour when it happens, ensuring we rid ourselves of the ugly and the evil among us who cannot distinguish between right and wrong.

'So today, I want to acknowledge my gratitude to those women who have walked before me in exposing those abusers who have never been called out. Those women who have endured years of abuse, and often assault. These were the powerless, with little choice other than to resist those who abused them as best they could, as they had bills to pay. I am grateful for their bravery and their inspiration to all women to stand up, to speak up and be counted, no matter who they are, or what they do.

'Following their leadership, I wish to reveal that I am a victim of abuse and I proclaim… Me-too.'

Messenger sat forward in his chair as if moving to support his colleague.

'I can declare that as a new minister in the previous government, Andrew Gerrard convinced me that my career would be enhanced if I was to surrender to the demands of the then prime minister for sex.

'I can disclose I have a recording of the former prime minister confirming that my position in the government was due only to the satisfaction of his lecherous desires with me and that if I wanted to stay a minister in his government, I needed to be available to him day or night. I have recorded evidence, now held by my lawyer, of the former prime minister threatening me with dismissal unless I succumbed to his demands, be they here in parliament or at his residence in Sydney.

'Madam Speaker, I disclose this information today to allow the Australian public to know that Andrew Gerrard is a sexual predator and is not a fit and proper person to represent any electorate in this august parliament. I would recommend to Mr Gerrard that he rethink his demand to be elected prime minister. I also ask that if there are others who have succumbed to Andrew Gerrard's demands in the past, then please let me know and I will report them within the protection of this chamber until he has apologised for his behaviour and announced his unconditional retirement from politics.

'I seek leave to table a transcript of a conversation between myself and the former prime minister poolside at the Sydney residence, which will in part confirm my disclosure.'

'Is leave granted?' the speaker asked.

Messenger had gripped his mouth as he watched Bruce. He nodded consent.

'Leave is granted.'

'Let me finish by saying this: whilst I am a victim of harassment, power and sexual abuse from the former prime minister, I decided not to be a victim. I will continue to develop progressive policy, to speak for those needing a voice, and I will always fight for justice for those who find it hard to get any within our society. I thank the House.' Bruce sat, glancing over to Messenger.

Messenger was quick to the despatch box. 'Madam Speaker, on indulgence.'

The speaker granted leave.

'It is not often there is a moment in history that changes the culture of an organisation, or indeed society. Madam Speaker, I believe we may have just witnessed such a moment. I will carefully consider the words of the opposition leader and I will determine if the government should respond. I thank her for her authenticity and her honesty. The rawness of the message could not have been easy for her, and I have great admiration for her.'

She nodded a thank you as Messenger resumed his seat and the chamber went on with procedure.

In the press gallery watching the speech was Cassandra Rogers, who fist pumped as she strode back to her workstation.

'Yes!'

CHAPTER SEVENTY-SIX

Brian Tucker read the news about the new prime minister's drought relief package over a cup of tea in Barellan after coming to town for supplies. He felt good. The government had acted, and the stress of worry lingering around him could disappear. He could concentrate on rebuilding his herd and flock once the rains came.

Tucker ignored the feature story about the former Prime Minister Gerrard, as it convinced him all politicians were crooked. Stanley never contacted him as he promised, which confirmed his assessment. They were morons. With the drought package now revealed in the national newspaper, it assured him the new prime minister might differ from the others. Process takes time, he knew that, but it pleased him to be now out of it. The news made him happier than he had felt for some time.

As he was about to leave the general store, the owner, Harry Mulligan, approached him. They'd been at school together, played on the same football team, and attended each other's weddings.

'Brian, I don't want to raise it, but I must.'

'Raise what?'

'Your slate is very heavy.'

'When it rains, Harry; you know that.'

'I need something, mate. My bank is killing me.'

'Which one?'

'The Rural.'

Tucker snorted in disgust. 'She's a bitch, that one.'

'Says she'll close me down by the end of the month unless I get some cash to her.'

'How much do you need?'

'If you can give me fifty percent, that'll help.'

'I wasn't planning on visiting Wagga for a few days, but I'll slip over there now and have a chat. The government is supporting us so the money will follow soon enough.' Tucker slapped the paper.

'Mate, I need something today or tomorrow.'

'Harry, leave it with me. I promise.'

'You're a champ, Tuck. I knew you'd understand.'

'I'll sort her out today and get money to you, I promise.'

'That's great. Hey, let's catch up on the weekend. Why don't you and the family come over Satdee for a barbeque?'

'Sounds great; we'll be there.'

'Say hello to Kathy for me.'

'Will do. Stop worrying, Harry. If I can get through this, then anyone can.'

Tucker placed the groceries and a bag of hardware supplies on the back seat. He secured the paint and solvents in the back tray of his ute and headed off to Wagga Wagga, figuring he would be there before the bank closed, and back home before dark.

He normally parked in front of the bank, but today it seemed the streets were busy, so he secured a park outside a strip of shops. He checked out the flowers in a bucket on the footpath outside the florist and bought a bunch for Kathy, placing them in the passenger seat out of direct sunlight before heading to the bank.

There were only a few people in the bank. They attended to his demand to see the manager, with staff ushering him into the familiar office.

Sophie Papadopoulos secured the door, asking if Tucker would like a drink. He declined, keen to complete the discussion that had worried him over the last few weeks.

'Mr Tucker, nothing like shaving it close to a deadline.'

'What do you mean?'

'Well, following our discussions you need to offer the bank a substantial drawdown on your borrowings before 4 p.m. today. It being 3.45 p.m., I suspect it is a close shave.'

'I don't understand. The government announced no action will be taken against farmers and has directed banks to back off. These are the new prime minister's actual words, not mine.'

'So why are you here?'

'To get money.'

Papadopoulos shook her head, lost for words. 'You want money?'

'I need to pay bills. In particular, the Barellan co-op, which you have threatened to close this week.'

'I have no money to give you.'

'What do you mean you have no money? Like, you have no money here?'

'I have no money at all for you. In fact, I want money from you, today, or we come and foreclose tomorrow.'

'You what?'

'Mr Tucker, you are aware of our terms. The bank has carried you for way too long as it is. You enjoyed our credit; now it is time to pay some of it down.'

'We are no different to anyone else.'

'You are very different from everyone else. They pay their bills; you don't. The bank must take action.'

'The bank or you?'

'I am the bank.'

Tucker didn't respond, his throat dry as he tried to gulp. He felt a dull ache deep in his gut, like a rushing out of his soul.

'Mr Tucker, we have tried to explain the urgency of this case. We have tried to manage your needs, but you have left us with little choice. We must act tomorrow.'

'You're foreclosing?' Tucker almost whispered the question.

'We are taking back our security.'

'I don't understand.' Tucker was a little distant. 'The government has provided the funds. Why is that not good enough?'

Papadopoulos sighed, agitated with the conversation. 'We have no record or advice that the government will secure funds; therefore, we have to act.'

Tucker's face tightened; his jaw gnarled to a sneer. 'You take my farm; you take my family.'

'Your family has nothing to do with the bank, Mr Tucker.'

Tucker stood. 'My family has everything to do with the bank.'

'Please stay calm, Mr Tucker.'

'Calm! You want me to stay calm?' he shouted. 'Where do you think we go when your thugs come for the keys tomorrow?'

'Mr Tucker.' Papadopoulos' anxiety increased, and she checked past him, waving to a male staffer. 'You've ignored us. You have taken advantage, and now you have to accept the result.'

Tucker began snorting like a bull; he was becoming hazy, wondering what to do. Two bank staff entered the office and stood to one side of the desk.

'We will sell the farm, the stock and machinery. If there is any surplus, once our loans and fees have been cleared, we will reimburse you.'

'It will rain soon, for heaven's sake.'

'It may do, Mr Tucker, but this has nothing to do with our arrangements. Now can I suggest you go home and prepare for our visit to reclaim our property tomorrow?'

The two staffers stepped closer as Tucker surveyed his options. He bowed his head, turned, and left.

As he headed back to his vehicle, Tucker's body responded to the news, and he buckled over, grabbing his knees to steady himself. His face contorted as he fought back tears. A concerned woman stopped and asked if he was okay. He waved her away. When he got back to his truck, he leaned against the front guard, wondering what to do. He thought back to his meeting with the prime minister and the promises made. He tugged out his phone and called the government.

'Good afternoon, Parliament House.'

'Could I speak to the prime minister, please?'

'One moment.'

'Prime minister's office.'

'Can I speak to Mr Messenger, please?'

'Who is calling?'

'Brian Tucker, from Tucker Farm.'

'Mr Tucker, the prime minister, is in a cabinet meeting. Would you like to leave a message, or talk to someone else?'

Tucker thought about what to do. 'Please ask him to call me; it's very important. I met with him, and Mr Stanley, last week.'

'I remember, sir.'

'It's vital I speak to him before five this evening.'

'I'll do my best, Mr Tucker.'

'Thank you.'

Tucker's mind was racing across various topics as he waited for the call, tapping his fingers on the steering wheel. Tempted him to go to the hotel for a brandy, he waited, thinking about what to say once the prime minister called.

It was five-fifty before he decided what he should do.

The prime minister hadn't called, and he figured out he was on his own. All the work he had done for the community and his farm meant nothing. It had all been a waste of time, and the lectures about family that his father had driven into him amounted to nothing. That left no one to help. If the prime minister didn't bother calling, why would anyone else want to help him? 'Bastards.'

He thought about his visit to the parliament and the manner they treated him. He thought about the journalist and the chair of the inquiry. He thought about the dismissive nature of the bank and the politicians, and his effort over the years to make the community a better place.

As he stared through his windscreen, he noticed that the chemist next door to the florist was still open. He stepped from his vehicle and wandered in, searching through shelves for specific items he thought he could use in the plan he was hatching. There needed to be a reckoning, and he wanted to be prepared for tomorrow.

He found what he was searching for in the personal hygiene rack. He scanned through the scant offering, wondering how to use the item he wanted and reading instructions on the packaging. After studying various brands and checking for use, he took the stoma bag with the adhesive protection layers to the front desk and swiped seventy-five dollars onto his cash card, hoping there were enough funds to cover the purchase.

He pitched the chemist's bag onto the front seat, started the engine and drove off, ignoring any traffic and focusing on heading back home and what he had before him. As he left the main street, he tossed the bouquet from the vehicle.

CHAPTER SEVENTY-SEVEN

The prime minister's limousine swooped into the driveway of Adina Apartments and stopped by the front entrance. A security officer scampered from the front seat, opening the back door to allow Messenger to exit. He moved swiftly through the complex to the familiar room; the officer maintaining a respectable distance. He tapped the door, and within moments it swung open with a smiling Jaya Rukhmani already relaxing in bed wear.

'Come in.'

'Put some clothes on; I need you to see something.' He stayed in the doorway.

'Formal or informal?'

'Relaxing.'

'That doesn't help.'

'Your exercise clothes would be good, but a pair of trousers would be better.'

'Where are we going?'

'You will see soon enough, now get moving.'

Jaya wasn't happy with the sudden pressure to get dressed and dithered for a moment as she changed her top three times, trying to match her black jeans. She pushed and pulled her thick hair, and in the end left it out and loose. She shrugged on her leather jacket as she slipped on her heels. One last check in the mirror and she joined Messenger.

'This is Patrick,' Messenger said, waving a hand at his security officer. 'He has the evening shift.'

'Hello, Patrick.' Jaya smiled.

'Ma'am.' Patrick strode off back to the waiting car, with the prime minister and Jaya following.

'Where are you taking me?'

'You'll see; be patient.' Messenger smiled, taking, and squeezing her hand.

The leather seats were warm as they jumped into the back of the BMW. It took off once Patrick was back in the front passenger seat, and when it hit Giles Street, another car joined in behind as the convoy departed the area, reaching Canberra Avenue, turning right, and motoring past Manuka Oval. The procession moved left into State Circle, increasing its speed when it entered Adelaide Avenue. Jaya had little idea where she was as her surroundings rushed past. She just squeezed Barton's hand and kept watching out the window, conscious there were two burly strangers sitting in the front.

The kilometres ticked over until the BMW exited the highway, just past the Kent Street overpass, then swept through a bend, over Yarra Glen, then right into the dimly lit street leading past the Royal Canberra Golf Club. The cars sped through the manned security gates and stopped at the portico of a grand white house.

'What is this? Where are we?' Jaya asked as she stared at several people waiting for the vehicle to stop.

'This is Yarralumla.'

'Say what?'

'I've just moved in and thought we could have supper together.'

'Welcome, Prime Minister,' a well-dressed man said as he opened the door and stepped back to give Messenger room to get out of the car. Jaya scooted across the seat and exited the same door.

'Hello, Edward, nice to see you again,' Messenger said.

Edward bowed, then said, 'Welcome, Ms Rukhmani, nice to see you.'

The courtesy intimidated Jaya, and she didn't know what to say or do, so she said nothing and smiled.

'We will meet with staff in the morning, but these ladies will look after you this evening. This is Elizabeth and Jane.'

'Hello, nice to meet you.' Messenger shook their hands. He then followed Edward's direction to enter the house. Jaya followed, thankful at least that she wasn't wearing her gym gear. Edward showed them into a small lounge, and they checked about, a little bemused by the experience. They glanced at each other before turning to see Edward waiting for instructions.

'Prime Minister, this is your home, so treat it as if it were, and not a museum.'

'That might be a little difficult to do.'

'Your suite is upstairs, and I shall show you that once you are ready. We also have visitors' chambers if required.' He smiled at Jaya. 'Just use the internal communication system to order anything you want, including food. We are here to serve you.'

'I can do most things,' Messenger said.

'That may be, sir, but they charge us with the responsibility of serving the prime minister of Australia, so please allow us to do our job.'

Messenger considered himself well chided.

'I am sure you have much to talk about, so I shall leave you. There is wine in the ice bucket over on the sideboard and a small plate of bites. If you would like a hot drink or more food, then perhaps push seven on the telephone and we shall provide whatever you need.'

'Thank you, Edward.' Jaya walked to him and held out her hand. 'We appreciate your help.'

'A pleasure, madam.'

'Yes, thank you Edward. I'll call you if we need anything,' Messenger added. When the door closed, they looked at each other.

Jaya began prowling the room, checking out the curios and paintings.

'Who would have thought a professor of politics and her student would ever stand in the house of the prime minister of Australia?' Messenger said.

'Why am I here?'

'I was told I could move in this evening and thought I would like to share the moment with you.'

Jaya studied her student. 'I always thought you would go far, you know that?'

'I'm here because of you; the least I could do was share the moment with you.'

Messenger backed away to the sideboard, pouring two glasses of chardonnay as Jaya tucked herself in to the corner of the soft cushioned couch.

'I also wanted to say to you that, as expected, I could not convince my colleagues to promote you,' Messenger said, as he approached her with the wine. 'But I will announce you as the new chair of the Foreign Affairs and Trade committee when I announce the new ministry and committee chairs tomorrow.'

Jaya flushed with excitement, stretching up to take her glass, then clicked his. 'Thank you.'

'I know it's not what you want, but things will change if we win the next election.'

'I don't know if I can wait that long.'

Messenger frowned. 'Now hang on, Jaya. I can't just sack an experienced minister; you'll just have to bide your time.'

'I wasn't talking about that, silly.' Jaya stretched over to Messenger and kissed his cheek. 'I was talking about us.'

CHAPTER SEVENTY-EIGHT

The response to her feature article on the misuse of power in the corridors of parliament dominated social media all day. It encouraged a fresh wave of women to step forward, talking about their experiences. It exposed politicians other than Andrew Gerrard for inappropriate behaviour, and the vitriol was out of control. Cassandra Rogers received confidential emails from former staffers naming former and current serving members and senators as predators. She received photographs supporting claims, and several public servants serving in overseas embassies had given up their experiences. What surprised Cass even more was the claim they did not limit it to powerful men.

In the article, she had encouraged victims to call out the behaviour by sending their experiences, no matter the circumstance. She received emails about leaders in the community, but a constant stream of stories exposing all levels of society were also arriving. From over seven hundred emails, it seemed whoever had power seemed to misuse it.

The stories were not just about sexual predators; the sadness also came from tales of workplace humiliation, bullying, and the intimidation caused by anyone insensitive to the protocols of decent humanity. *How was it that people are taken advantage of when they were just doing their job?* It did not prepare Cass to deal with the volume of contacts, all seeking her help to expose the cretins who had ruined and dimmed a bright light.

She couldn't help them all yet felt compelled to do something. She could not come up with a plan, and a feeling of hopelessness set in. A fog of sorrow and frustration sent her home, via a bottle shop, and now she lay on her couch with a doona cocooning her in comfort as she finished her second slug of cheap brandy. Seeking another charge, she stretched over to the bag of ice she had bought along with the brandy, filled the glass, then poured herself a generous splash of elixir.

She snuggled back into the doona, holding the glass on her chest, and putting her phone by her head on the thick arm of the couch. She studied the ceiling, thinking through the events of recent weeks. She questioned whether she had done the right thing in writing the stories, setting up other stories, and pushing the politics. For what? A promotion?

She glanced over at a shelf at a photo of her children. Had the never-ending wish to get the promotion she coveted been worth it? She was now the announced new host of the national show to replace Nicholls. The money didn't matter; she was going to get less than Nicholls anyway, so why had she pushed and shoved her way to get the appointment? Was she proving Tony Hancock wrong? She had given up her family and now they treated her as a distant relative, someone to talk to every once in a while. Was it worth it?

She took another sip, which wasn't enough, so she washed done a greater mouthful; it burned the back of the throat, gagging her. It startled her when her phone vibrated.

'Cass, it's Meredith.'

She sat up, putting her glass on the table. 'What's wrong?' Bruce's tone made her feel anxious.

'I'm feeling lonely and thought I would call.'

'Where are you?'

'In my office, at the House. Where are you?'

'Three nips into a bottle of brandy at my Canberra place,' Cass chuckled. 'Do you want to come over?'

'Tempting, but no thanks.'

'What's wrong, hon? You sound down.'

Bruce didn't respond for a moment, then said, 'Politics, who would have thought it would be so stressful?'

'Not the glamazon life you thought it would be?'

'It's harder in opposition.'

'What's up?'

'They have dragged me through the mud with this Gerrard thing.'

'Who's doing that to you, the government?'

'No,' Bruce scoffed. 'They've been very supportive, especially Jaya. No, it's my side. I think there may be a challenge afoot.'

'You're kidding; why?'

'Sending us into a losing spiral when we had the other side in the sights.'

'Is Gerrard behind it?'

'Don't know; don't care, quite frankly.'

'Will you survive?'

'I think I have the numbers stitched up, but the Victorians are after blood. They want this woman to bleed.'

Cass snorted at the ridiculousness of it. 'You already do.'

'That's men for you; no damn idea.'

Cass became serious for a moment. 'Have you heard from Gerrard?'

'He's gone to ground. His lawyers have been in touch for a transcript of the tapes.'

'Will you release them?'

'Not unless they force me.'

'Are you okay?'

'Look, I'm fine. I just need to talk to genuine people rather than patronising politicians and their eunuchs.'

'Are you regretting it?'

'Not at all.' Bruce sniffed. 'I wanted him gone, so sometimes you need to do things you don't want to. But you see...' she paused for a moment, 'that's the problem with girls; they let the blokes do what they want and hope they won't get hurt by it, but in reality, it damages them. Although I took advantage of what Gerrard gave me, I think my willingness to get ahead damaged me.'

'I know what you mean.'

'It's not that we can't get ahead on talent; the blokes just want their pound of flesh to help us.'

'Guilty.'

'What are you saying?'

'They promoted me to host the national current affairs show this evening.'

'What? That's fantastic news; well done.'

'Took over twenty years. Cost me my husband...' Cass's voice wobbled. 'I lost my babies, and I had to say yes too often to get to the right office. Now I am questioning if it was worth it.'

'At least you did it, and now look at you.'

'Ethically I'm challenged by it all, though.'

'You got there,' Bruce said.

'I killed Stanley with the fake news about his wife. I used the farmer who was in the parliament the other day to get to the PM, which caused the farmer grief. I used leaked material to kill off other challengers to Hughes.'

'Wait up,' Bruce interrupted. 'You were working for Hughes?'

'Hancock wanted stories, so I invented them based on what Hughes was telling me.'

'Why was Hughes using you?'

'He wanted me. So, I played him and then set him up to fail.'

'How?'

'My little friend Jaya was putty in my hands.'

'You used her to work with me, knowing she would screw Hughes?'

'You see what I mean?' Cass sniffed. 'I will do anything to get what I want.'

'Hmm,' Bruce murmured. 'But you made it,' she said, then sparked up. 'That's gotta be good for everyone, surely?'

'Yes, but at what price, Meredith, at what price?'

'I faced my demons because of you.'

'Yes, and now look at the trouble you're in.'

'No trouble I can't handle. Sisters will look at us and think they can do it as well.'

'Let's just hope they don't have to do what we did to get ahead.'

'How much brandy have you got left?'

'I've only had a couple.'

'See you soon; let's celebrate.'

'What? Why?'

'I want to get rid of this black mass that's sitting in me, and I reckon you might just be the person to give it to.' Bruce laughed. 'Besides, you owe me a few wonderful stories, so let's plan for me to be your first guest.'

Cass laughed. 'Then come and we can talk about the future.'

'Sisters! Yes. See you soon.'

CHAPTER SEVENTY-NINE

The spiralling smoke was noticeable as the two black Toyota Hilux Invincibles came over the rise just before nine. From this distance, it was difficult to identify: a fire was just starting or ending. Either way, the senior security officer made a call to the local first responders to attend. He then called the police to give them a heads up on what they were about to find. The trucks came to a stop near the barn. The men disembarked, gazing towards what was once a family homestead, now a burnt-out rubble.

The bank had briefed them that trouble could occur. It normally did when they were called to evict emotional people who failed to pay debt. The security officers were used to it and came prepared to tether troublemakers until police arrived. Sometimes guns were pointed at them, but more often than not the property owner complied.

All eight men dressed in black tactical overalls, caps and jackets emblazoned with a yellow security firm logo. Two went off to check sheds while the others fanned out, searching for any sign of life.

'Not good, skip; look at this.' An officer was pointing to two dogs at the base of the front stone stairs, their throats cut.

They made another call to the police, updating them and advising that they could expect a tragedy, and to send an investigative team from Wagga. The police instructed them to secure the property and wait for their team, who were on their way, one by road, the other by helicopter.

The commander issued instructions, returning to his vehicle to begin a report, and ensuring he didn't forget important information. As he wrote, a tap on the roof of the vehicle disturbed him. He looked up, scanning the area. Seeing nothing, he focused back on his pad.

The noise happened again, followed by another and then another. He glanced up through the windscreen and a drop of water trickled down the screen. The glass covered with droplets as the intensity increased. The rain dumped its load for more than an hour and only eased when police arrived.

Cass was feeling a little seedy when she dropped her bag on her desk, so she strolled to the kitchenette for a water and a cup of tea. As she passed the editor's office, Peter Cleaver yelled, summoning her. She entered, knowing it would be full of cigarette smug and the stink of tobacco, which she was in no mood to contend with.

'What do you think of your farmer mate?' Cleaver asked, blowing smoke to the ceiling.

'What farmer mate?'

'The one who was in here last week causing a stir.'

'What about him?'

'He's missing. Fire destroyed his farm, and his family confirmed inside.'

The news hit hard. She placed her hands on her hips, then on her knees as she bent, trying to breathe.

'You okay?'

'When did this happen?'

'Overnight. They've found bodies, but his truck is missing so they suspect him.'

'Why?'

'It seems the bank was coming to foreclose today and remove them from the property.'

Cass straightened and brushed a tear from her cheek. 'What do you want me to do?'

'Instead of heading back to Sydney, Hancock wants you to handle the politics here.'

'No issue; I'll get the background. He is well known around here.'

'Link him to Messenger if you can. He and Stanley met him last week. See if they failed to do anything that could have stopped this tragedy.'

'Maybe we need to talk to someone from the bank?'

'They deny any issue at head office.'

'What about the local branch?'

'I'll get someone out there this morning. Wagga, isn't it?'

'I'd reckon.' Cass moved away. 'Why the hell would he do that?'

'Who knows? Just do whatever you can to get the story.'

Cass nodded, moving off back to her desk.

'Do whatever I can to get the story.' She dropped into her chair, bursting into tears.

The prime minister was at his desk early, broadening his comprehension of the issues across all portfolios so he could speak with authority on any matter affecting the government and the nation. He wanted to lead question time for the rest of the sitting period so the media would offer a comforting image of the new prime minister. He instructed his media staff to use every opportunity to have him on radio and television to relay the message that he was in charge. Although supportive of Peter Stanley, he saw how the former PM had struggled with detail, which limited his decisions. This would not happen to him.

There was a knock on his door and a head poked around with a smiling Stanley asking to enter. Messenger waved him into a seat.

'I've come to see how you're settling in,' Stanley said, beaming.

Messenger stood, pleased to see Stanley, as he wanted to speak with him. He had decided on his new ministry, and his former mentor was not in it.

'Pete, thanks for dropping by. How is Alison?'

'All things considered; she is doing okay.'

'Has the prognosis changed?'

Stanley glanced at Messenger, then out of the window. 'One day at a time, Bart. One day at a time.'

'I'm sorry about all the stress that this has caused you and no doubt your wife over the last few weeks.'

'You had nothing to do with it, so don't worry.' Stanley smiled, wanting to change the topic. 'What job are you giving me?'

Messenger paused for a moment, gnawing his bottom lip, and thinking what he might say. 'I have nothing for you in the parliamentary team.'

Stanley gazed at the prime minister; his face reacted as if he had smelt something acrid, then he said, 'You're dumping me?'

'Yes, I am.'

'Why?'

'Two reasons.' Messenger thumbed his forefinger. 'I think it's time you dedicated whatever time left to your wife. And second, I consider it's best for the make-up of the ministry if you aren't there. There remains much to do, and I suspect there may be resentment still in the team.'

'Not from me.'

'Of course, but maybe to you.'

'They'll get over it.'

'This is the point; I don't think they will. So, I've made this decision.'

'Kick me while I'm down; yeah, nice one.'

'Pete, it has nothing to do with kicking you.' Messenger squirmed. 'I want you to take a break from the responsibility of a ministry and spend quality time with Alison.'

'I have no say?'

'No, you don't.'

'So, what happens when she goes?'

'I'll consider that when it comes up.' Messenger tugged the chair closer to his desk. 'I'm considering the next diplomatic appointments due in twelve months, and if you are available, I would like to offer you a role.'

'In a shit hole I suspect.'

'How does High Commissioner sound?'

'London?'

Messenger nodded.

Stanley squeezed a smile. 'I suppose I could be interested. When's it due?'

'Before the next election.'

Messenger's new chief of staff entered the office, interrupting the discussion without waiting for permission.

'Prime Minister, there has been a significant development out west,' Allan Hyatt advised.

'What have they done now?' Messenger queried, smiling at Stanley.

'No sir, not WA. Out back of Wagga. There's been an incident at Tucker Farm.'

Both politicians knew who Hyatt was talking about.

'The police have established a major crime scene and they have a call out for Brian Tucker.'

'What's happened?'

'Too early to tell but there appear to be three bodies.'

Messenger leaned back in his chair; his jaw dropped open, and he looked towards Stanley.

'Did you call his bank?'

'No, I didn't.'

CHAPTER EIGHTY

The rain caught up with Brian Tucker as he was crossing the border into the Australian Capital Territory. It bucketed down, upsetting him as he planted the accelerator, increasing his speed to a dangerous level. He screamed at the water smashing his windscreen. The wipers flicked off water at speed, but they weren't fast enough to provide enough vision, so he eased. He had one last job to do.

The final two hours from Yass had been watchful for him, looking out for police or any other authority instructed to keep a watch out for his Mercedes utility. He had swapped licence plates with Kathy's car to reduce suspicion. His intention was to park at the old parliament house, hiking the kilometre to the parliament. He wanted to let the politicians know how he felt; wanted them to share his grief.

The long drive on country highways strengthened his plan for retribution. He had packed his Sunday best clothes and would change into them. Hopefully, the rain would have eased by then. He didn't want to meet the politicians bedraggled. The plan was to enter the House and see the new prime minister, to let Messenger know what his actions had done to his family.

Tucker parked his vehicle outside the National Archives building in a bay closest to Federation Mall, near trees to protect him from prying eyes that might wonder what he was up to. He stepped out of the cabin; the smell of rain still strong in the air. He wondered if his farm would have got a heavy dump. He opened the doors of the vehicle on the passenger side to offer privacy and prepared himself. Once his trousers were on, he rummaged through the plastic chemist bag, opening the stoma kit. He read the instructions and prepared his skin by giving it a quick wipe with the antiseptic patch provided. He adhered the first tab near his umbilicus, pushing it hard to make sure there were zero adhesion issues. He then attached a protective seal to the tab ready for the colostomy bag to be attached.

Once he was ready to attach the bag, he dropped small sponges he had cut from a kitchen dish sponge into the bag. They were soft and pliable, which he considered would be handy if asked about them. He then poured liquid into the bag. Enough for what he wanted to do; not enough to raise suspicion. He tucked his business shirt in, then fastened his trousers and belt. He completed his ensemble by tying a silk tie and tugging on a jacket. He ran cream through his hair, brushing it into a business executive's shape and style. He closed the doors and checked out his reflection, considering himself respectable enough for an unassuming visit to the parliament.

Before leaving, he tossed his keys on the front seat, placing a book of matches in his silk tie. He checked the truck to see if it was secure and left for the parliament.

Tucker had no problem going through the first security checkpoint at the public front door. He was careful to keep his face shielded from security cameras, gazing down as much as possible as he passed through the scanners. Once in the front entrance hall, he decided he should begin queueing for question time. He wanted to see the new prime minister and hoped the security officers would not recognise him from a week earlier. He checked his phone and ensured there were no other items like metallic pens that would set off the security scanner.

He joined the queue thirty minutes before question time, expecting a wait of twenty minutes before he would move through security. He tried hard to look inconspicuous by gazing out the window. Anxiety was building as he thought through scenarios he might face at the scanner. It was a slow crawl before he reached the eight security officers working through the spectators, keen to watch the parliamentary show that was question time. The entertaining theatre of the chamber was in high demand. School children filed through without challenge. Then it was Tucker's turn to walk through the scanner after emptying his pockets of assorted items to mitigate any suspicion from security officers.

'Step right through, sir,' an officer instructed as Tucker stalled.

He stepped through, and as he expected, the scanner picked up the liquid container he was carrying.

'Sir, step to one side, please,' another officer directed.

'Are you carrying any liquid, sir?' The officer waved a wand over him.

'No, I'm not.'

The officer waved the wand, and it sparked as it passed over his attached stoma. 'What do you have there, sir?'

'It's my colostomy bag.'

'What's that, sir?'

'I've had bowel surgery and my waste comes out into the bag.'

The officer empathised, seeking greater understanding. 'Please stand behind the screen, sir.' He directed Tucker behind a screen with a corridor maze for privacy. 'Tony, can you please join us?' He waved to a colleague.

'Tony, this gentleman has a colostomy bag that has set off the scanner; we just need to check it.'

'Sure. Sir, could you please show us the device?'

Tucker tugged out his shirt, unbuttoning it and revealing the top of the device.

'Please excuse this intrusion, sir.' An officer leaned in and checked closer. 'Could you undo your trousers, sir?'

Tucker complied, and the officer manipulated and took the weight of the malleable bag.

'It feels very liquid, sir. Is that normal?'

'Very normal. I make extraction before the shit firms.'

'There are soft lumps amongst it, so that makes sense.' The officer was squeezing it, sharing a look of weird wonder. 'How often do you empty it?'

'Twice a day.'

'Due soon?'

'Five or six this evening.'

The officer straightened. 'That's fine, sir; you can dress now.'

The other officer studied him. 'You look nervous, sir. Are you okay?'

'Not every day you drop ya daks in front of the police.'

They laughed.

'Not police, sir, just security.'

The officers led Tucker back out into the security space, guiding him through to the second station and explaining to colleagues that he was fine to go through. He then followed directions to the public gallery behind the government.

'Sit over there, sir.' An attendant directed him to a seat he did not want.

Tucker went down the steps, complying with the direction, but then walked past the allocated space to the front row and scooted along until he was behind the prime minister. He checked back towards the attendant with a querying shrug. The attendant waved him away, busy with the next spectators keen for a seat.

A minister was standing at the despatch box answering a question, with opposition backbenchers giving her a hard time. Tucker sat forward, looking over the parapet, watching the prime minister working through papers before him. He scanned the front bench, then the backbenches, trying to see Peter Stanley, but he could not pick him out. He then scanned the media gallery to his left, observing familiar faces, including the woman who had interviewed him.

Tucker checked over his shoulder, speculating whether anyone could see what he planned to do. There were interested spectators of the chamber behind him, but they were more interested in the affairs of state than in him. Now was the time to act. Maintaining a gaze into the chamber, Tucker rummaged under his shirt, pushing, and pulling at the seal until it loosened and fell away from the tab. He then dragged the bag from his trousers, placing it under his seat so as not to attract attention. He was now ready. He checked the clock and waited for the right opportunity, anxiety increasing his perspiration. He yanked out his hanky, dabbing his brow, then blowing his nose, checking about for any suspicious movement towards him.

As he waited, a group of visitors filed into the seats beside him, chatting about proceedings. Tucker was becoming more nervous, wanting to act before the end of question time. Another ten minutes.

'My question is to the prime minister; can the prime minister give an update to the House of the government's drought relief package? And can he inform the House if farmers are receiving benefits yet?' A government backbencher asked the question Tucker was hoping for.

Cassandra Rogers, sitting in the media gallery, was also waiting for the question, having been advised by the prime minister's office that it would be asked when she enquired about the prime minister's response to the tragedy at Tucker Farm. She tapped her pen against her pad, waiting for Messenger's answer. She glanced over at the backbench members. Most were working on their social media devices, ignoring the prime minister, but not Jaya Rukhmani, who seemed more than interested in the answer. Cass made a note to call her and ask why.

'I call the prime minister.'

'Thank you, Speaker, and I thank the honourable member for his question. I can report to the House that we have had significant rainfall along the east coast throughout the day.'

'Hear, hear.'

'These rains, as members would know, are important, and we have recorded four hundred and fifty mils in the drought affected regions. But the drought is yet to be broken. We will need another three or four similar downpours over the next three months to make sure that the drought is broken. While the rainfall is welcome, and has been widespread, which is very encouraging for our farmers and our rural communities, we still need patience. Key farming indicators such as soil moisture, farm dam levels, ponds along waterways and pasture health have diminished over the past few years. This means that whilst there is hope, we need to remain supportive of the rural family.'

'Huh,' Tucker said too emphatically, attracting a glance from Cass, who didn't recognise him.

'Even when the drought ends, farmers will face more challenges that the Australian community will need to support. The pastures are dead, and there is little chance of crops being planted this season unless we have more rain. Those farmers who carry stock, many of whom forced to sell or destroy them, will need to restock their farms, and this will be an expensive process.'

'Ya got that right,' Tucker said louder, promoting Messenger to pause and glance over his shoulder at the interjector.

'Order. The gallery will please be quiet,' the speaker advised.

Tucker shifted in his seat, checking around, but could not see any attendants interested in him, so he gazed over the parapet once more.

'Madam Speaker, the sad acceptance is that the drought doesn't stop if it rains. The recovery could take years, and debt may hinder farmers. Many may have psychological wounds from the battles they have with nature, their creditors, and their banks. Of course, there is always the worry that another drought is just around the corner, so we cannot underestimate the emotional toll.'

Tucker dropped his head into his hands as if not wanting to hear what the prime minister was saying.

'Today, for instance, police advised us of the tragedy of a great Australian farming family whose heritage to the land and agriculture history goes back more than a hundred years. I'm advised tragedy has devastated Tucker Farm, with the death of Mrs Kathleen Tucker and her two daughters, Fiona and Annabelle, and the razing of the heritage-listed homestead. Police are investigating, and we hope we will find Mr Brian Tucker, as the community has not seen him since yesterday.'

Tucker wiped his face of tears.

'The government has worked hard to provide funds for farmers. We have advanced cash to various regions for feed and water to be trucked in to aid with the care of the stock, and as we work with communities, we hope our support will aid in their mental health associated with the stress they are facing.'

Tucker took a deep breath and reached under the seat for his bag.

'My government has instructed all banks to make sure they do not add to the pressure of the farming community by forcing debt repayment. I have asked them to cease the former credit management direction of forced foreclosures. I have spoken to all banks, and I have received written assurances they will not act, as they have accepted the government's guarantee on their loan book.'

Tucker, with head bowed, was muttering to himself, and a woman leaned over and touched his arm.

'Sir, are you okay?'

This stirred him into action, and he rose to his feet, shouting. 'Bullshit!'

The House now focused on the man as he stood in the public gallery, glaring at the prime minister.

Tucker pointed down to Messenger. 'You speak rubbish, and you tell lies.'

The Speaker reacted. 'Order; attendants remove the interjector.'

'You promised me and my family nothing would happen,' Tucker yelled with an accusing finger at Messenger.

Cass recognised who was yelling and called down to the prime minister. 'Bart, it's Brian Tucker.'

Messenger heard Cass's call and stood to address Tucker.

'Order.'

'Mr Tucker, this is not the place for this discussion.'

'Yeah? Why the hell not?' Tucker saw two attendants squeezing through shocked spectators, trying to get to him. He climbed up on top of the thin parapet. Screams and gasps came from the public gallery as they watched. 'Don't come any closer or I'll jump.' The politicians below remained seated and silent, watching.

The attendants stalled for a moment, looking at the speaker.

'Be careful,' she advised, and they slowed their approach.

Tucker faced the chamber, wobbling on the small ledge.

'You promised me, and you didn't deliver. Now I have lost everything because of you.'

'Mr Tucker, let us talk about this. You know we can't achieve anything here. Let's go talk in my office.'

'Like we did last week when Stanley promised me they would not foreclose my farm? He lied, and so did you. You all lie.' Tucker waved one hand across the chamber, the other clutching his bag.

The speaker waved security to the floor below to break his fall if he jumped or fell.

Cass was awe struck and hadn't moved, shocked by what she was witnessing. Tucker was on her level, and she could see he was fraught. She stood and called to him.

'Brian? Brian?'

Tucker looked towards her.

'Don't do this; let's talk. I'll get your story out. We can change what's happened.'

'Fake news, lady,' he shrieked. 'We can't change nothing. They came to my farm today, and it's gone. Everything is gone. Everything.' He sunk his head.

The two attendants in the gallery began ushering spectators away from Tucker to give more space and make sure of their safety. Tucker checked around him to see what was going on and almost toppled over, startling more gasps from the public gallery opposite and a scream from a politician.

'Tucker let's be reasonable and talk about this together,' Messenger appeased, his hands wide open.

'You killed my family, you and your lies, the lot of you.'

The farmer held the bag high and poured solvent over the top of his head. It dripped and poured over his clothes.

'What are you doing? Don't do this,' Cass wailed.

'You bastards took it all.'

'Order, attendants move in and take control,' the speaker demanded.

'Tucker, this is not the way,' Messenger said, now making his way through the chamber to just below him.

Politicians were standing and moving away from their seats, clearing the area below him, staring up and wondering what he might do. They didn't know what to do. Others left the chamber, keen to get away from the drama.

More attendants moved closer, waiting for the right moment to grab the madman.

'Keep back! Keep back or I'll jump. I warn you.'

The politicians and the public in the gallery became alarmed as they suspected what they might be about to witness. Many covered their faces, others gnawed on a fist; some yelled for Tucker to stop, others yelled to the staff to do something.

Tucker withdrew his small book of matches from his tie, tearing a match from the folder and striking it.

'Stop him!' Cass cried.

'Tucker, don't,' Messenger appealed.

'It's too late. I'm doomed, and so are all of you, you morons.'

Tucker threw away one dud match, ripping another from the folder and igniting it. He then held it to his face and his head exploded into a ball of flame, which consumed his upper body.

'Doomed!'

He held out his hands as the flames whooshed. He stood staring up into the ceiling with his arms out as if crucified, then after the flames engulfed him, swan dived into the chamber, landing with a thud on the backbench seats. Those that could screamed or despairingly yelled. The attendants did their best to put out the flames, one taking off his jacket and smothering, while another came rushing into the chamber with an extinguisher and stifled the flames, exposing a charred, black, and red corpse.

It struck Messenger dumb. His shoulders hunched as he wandered back to his chair and flopped down. He dropped his head into his hands, wiping away tears. There were loud, distressing sobs from many in the gallery. Others were filing out, keen to get away.

Cass flopped into her seat, staring at the sunlight streaming in from the skylights. She felt sick that the only thing she could think of was whether she should report the incident. A tear streaked down her cheek, then another. A shudder ran through her as she fought to stop her body from convulsing.

As staff surrounded Tucker's body, Messenger stood, beginning the trek back to his office. He seemed almost catatonic. There would be briefings for him and the media to prepare. He ignored the chaos around Tucker as he passed. Jaya stopped him as he got to the brass door. She stood in front of him, blocking his way. He gazed at her, not acknowledging who it was, unresponsive. All feeling had drained from him. His face had dropped, and it was difficult to recognise him.

'Bart, are you okay?'

Messenger glanced at her. 'Tell me it wasn't me.' He frowned, his eyes frightened and watering. 'Tell me I didn't do this.'

Jaya held his hand and touched his face, cupping it with her other hand and smiling.

'You did not do this.'

Messenger turned and checked back into the chamber, then lifted his eyes and saw Cassandra Rogers. He shook his head, and she nodded in response.

'It's not our fault, Prime Minister,' Cass whispered, her body collapsing into heavy sobbing.

Messenger turned away, squeezing Jaya's hand, a tear trickling. 'What am I to do?'

CHAPTER EIGHTY-ONE

The Red Goose brassiere perched above the sand dunes of Cottesloe Beach offered panoramic views of the Indian Ocean, the white fine sand beach extending to the north and the breakwater to the south. On a clear day, clients could see Rottnest Island. The perfect place for a late brunch. The hoi pollie of Perth descended on the most popular beach to frolic. Most sat on the balcony to watch over children while they enjoyed a wine tipple or a meal.

The remnants of the smashed avocado Cassandra Rogers enjoyed were now cleared, and she cherished the sun as she read the Hancock Sunday paper. The news of the federal election the previous day covered over ten of the first pages with features further towards the centre. She checked over the rail at her children and watched as Christian cut a wave. She smiled at how well he was doing.

The electorate returned the Messenger Government with a significant majority. The front-page displayed a photograph of the prime minister, with arms raised in victory above his head, holding the hand of his beaming fiancé.

'They are a great couple,' she said, showing the page to Meredith Bruce.

Bruce was about to sip her latte and peered at the photograph. 'He is a smart man, that one.'

'Do you miss it?' Cass asked.

'I have my down times,' Bruce said, finishing her coffee. 'But I have no regrets retiring. What about you?'

Cass glanced out over the water again. 'Nope.'

'How did Jaya go?'

Cass searched the results. 'She went to preferences, but now has a four percent margin.'

'You reckon she will stay in the parliament?'

'I would, would you?' Cass asked.

'No conflict being married to the prime minister?'

'They will be a power couple and I suspect very useful for them politically.'

'He was her student, wasn't he?' Bruce asked.

'He was, and yet no scandal.'

'Good luck to them.'

Cass returned to her newspaper as Bruce glanced about, spotting a familiar face entering the brasserie. 'Don't look now but Peter Stanley just walked in.'

Cass crumpled her paper and glanced to the door and waved. 'He's our local member. Well, he was until yesterday.'

Stanley acknowledged the wave and wandered through the tables to the balcony to speak with them.

'Are you by yourself, Peter?' Cass asked.

'As a matter of fact, I am.'

'Why not join us?' Cass suggested, folding her newspaper. 'We have already eaten, and we are about to order another coffee.'

'That would be lovely,' Stanley replied, sitting in a spare chair. 'What do you think of the result?'

'Messenger has done really well,' Cass said. 'His policies were clear, and he ran a solid campaign. The bullshit with Harper done and dusted, and they worked as a united team.'

'I agree, it was an excellent decision to elect him as leader.'

Bruce smiled. 'Could have been you.'

'No.' Stanley grimaced. 'I now realise I was over-promoted. I had way too much going on with my personal life, which killed my time in the chair.'

Cass nodded, gnawing her lip. 'You won an election.'

'Only just and only with the help of Rukhmani,' Stanley declared, smiling. 'She has done well, hasn't she?'

'Minister, I heard,' Bruce said.

'Good enough to be in cabinet,' Stanley said. 'But I reckon that won't happen because of her relationship with Bart. She'll be given a junior portfolio, I reckon.'

A waiter took their order and refilled the water glasses.

'What's your plans, Peter?' Cass asked.

'On the record, off the record, or background?'

Cass laughed out loud, disturbing others nearby. 'I don't do that anymore.'

'How are you enjoying it?' Stanley asked.

'I was just saying to Meredith that it's the best decision I ever made moving here.'

'Just as well, the television program didn't last long once Nicholls left,' Stanley said.

'Nothing to do with the dolly-bird they appointed after Cass?' Bruce asked.

'Maybe, but it lost its way after you retired,' Stanley said, glancing at Rogers. 'Only weeks after you pulled the pin?'

'Something like that,' Cass said, checking on her children. 'My kids needed me more than Hancock did.'

'So, what are you planning for yourself now, Peter?' Bruce asked.

'You don't know?' He peaked at her, and she shrugged. 'I'm off to London as High Commissioner at the end of the month.'

'Oh, that's great news,' Bruce said. 'Well done.'

'Thanks,' he said as he leaned back to allow the waiter to serve. 'What are you up to these days?' Stanley asked after they waited for the waiter to leave.

'I'm practicing commercial law in the city,' Bruce said. 'Once that Gerard kerfuffle ran its course, I moved here.'

'Involved in the local branch?'

'Shit, no!' Bruce exclaimed. 'Those days are well and truly over.'

Cass eyed Stanley as they talked. She then reached out and touched his arm. 'I am genuinely sorry for the way I treated you during those last days. I feel really embarrassed.'

'It's all good, Cassandra,' Stanley placed his hand over hers. 'All good.' He nodded and smiled. 'It allowed me more time with Alison before she passed, so I'm grateful.'

Cass smiled, leaving her hand as she regarded him for a moment. 'We're getting married in two weeks. Do you want to come?'

ENJOY THE READ?

Consider leaving a review on Amazon or Goodreads.
I would be very grateful if you did.
If you would like to communicate with me then please do.
I always respond and enjoy chatting about future projects
If you would like to be added to my Advanced Readers list, then please let me know
readers@richardevans-author.com

ACKNOWLEDGEMENTS

Motor neurone disease (MND) affects the nerves called motor neurones in the brain and spinal cord. These nerves tell muscles what to do. It is an insidious disease and at this time there is no cure. It afflicts many and does not show any preference as to who it chooses. My cousin Lyne lost her much loved husband Robert Howell to the disease without warning and quickly. Others taken include politicians: I served with one, Peter Cleeland the former member for McEwan, who left his family and friends way too young.

A group of dedicated folks have worked for over ten years and raised more than a million dollars for research into MND as a dedication to their dear friend Michael Rodger, another taken too early. I want to recognise Louise Mogg, Stephen Giles, Georgia Rodger, Alannah Giles, Georgie Ross and Russell Higgins for their efforts every year.

In 2021, I donated my portfolio of titles to the MND Charity Ball and Auction. Part of that auction prize was having a character named after the winner within Doomed. The package was purchased by Jill Hedin for her husband Garrick Higgins, and he appears in the story as the union representative negotiating covert deals. Thank you for Jill and Garrick for your support of MND.

I must acknowledge and thank the Member for Watson, the Honourable Tony Burke for inspiring the title of this book. I am not sure the reason I was watching parliament on 21 August 2018, but the eloquent Mr Burke rose to speak on a no confidence motion against the prime minister, Malcolm Turnbull. As he began his speech he said, *'There is no-one in this chamber who has a record of anything they claim being a high point of principle ultimately being DOOMED the way this Prime Minister does.'* He then listed a number of points ending with the exclamation - DOOMED. And that dear reader is where the title came from. Thanks Tony.

Patty Kavadias, Trish Stewart, and Anne and Michael Keaney have again provided valuable feedback as has former colleague Phil and Cate Barresi, and Deborah Daly. Michael Tate provided insight regarding geographic consistencies, and Greg and Anthea Pelgrave provide continued support. Denise and Paul Tyrrell also provide substantial support, and I remain grateful for their promotional efforts.

I thank my colleagues at Yarraville writer's group for their willingness to provide suggestions and support. I also acknowledge the splendid work the Australian Society of Authors do to support novelists needing a kindly word. Their Literary Speed dating allowed me to present the full manuscript read by several publishers. I encourage you to join your local writers' group and even join your representative body to increase the voice of authors.

I also acknowledge the good folk of Williamstown who make the village the best kept secret in Melbourne and remain interested in the work I am doing.

The team at 852 Press have been enthusiastic for the Democracy Trilogy and I thank them for their efforts in bringing it all together with their team of designers, editors and support personnel.

On 19 August 1996, the Australian national parliament was subjected to an attempt to storm it by radical unionists who were part of a much larger peaceful group demonstrating against the government. Was it an insurrection? I suspect those resisting the angry mob thought so, especially those who were injured. I drew upon my personal experience of this event within Doomed as I was there in the foyer of the parliament on that day when it happened, assisting parliament staff to repel the mob until I was directed by security away from the scene. Within the book in Chapter 47, I have drawn upon the grave addresses to national parliament of Prime Minister Howard, Speaker Halverson, Opposition Leader Beazley, and ALP Senator Faulkner. Indeed, I incorporated selected quotes from their Hansard parliamentary addresses concerning the 1996 riot as responses by the fictional characters. I wanted to reference their words because we should never forget that black day for democracy in Australia.

It is vital to have strong family support when working on writing projects and I wish to acknowledge mine for their insight, humour, and advice during this project. Julia, Anthony, Kaitlyn, and Taylor bring much pride to me.

DOOMED

Finally, let me acknowledge the many folks I have met during my political and business career who have all helped shape my imagination, my creativity and in some cases the stories I draw upon when writing about politics. The journey has been a pleasure to share with you.

ABOUT THE AUTHOR

As a political insider, Richard Evans served as a federal member of parliament for Cowan in Western Australia during the turbulent 1990s. He now specialises in writing political thrillers, writing about the exotic characters in the mysterious world of the Australian Parliament. He lives above a pub, opposite a church in the historic bayside village of Williamstown, overlooking the grand international city of Melbourne.

For more information about his other books, or to contact Richard please visit:

www.richardevans-author.com

EPISODE 1 DEMOCRACY TRILOGY

A plane crash begins a sequence of events which leads corrupt Prime Minister Andrew Gerrard, after a long political career, to rush through legislation designed to secure his ill-gotten gains for his retirement. Stalwart – and soon retired – Clerk of the Parliament, Gordon O'Brien, sets out to foil the Prime Minister's plan with the help of investigative journalist, Anita Devlin.

O'Brien, a stickler for correct parliamentary process is concerned by the rush to legislation and becomes aware of various incidents, which by themselves would mean little but collectively shape a conspiracy to defraud the government.

The Clerk anticipates there is a potential fraud upon the government being enacted, he has run out of time and now must act. He forces the Speaker to resign, and O'Brien takes her place, causing the parliament to prorogue, imposing a general election, preventing the fraud.

For a **FREE COPY** of Deceit and to join the advanced readers team is now available from the following link:
www.richardevans-author.com

EPISODE 2 DEMOCRACY TRILOGY

The Mercantiles, a long-established, clandestine group of high-tax-paying business owners have grown frustrated by Prime Minister Andrew Gerrard's failure to meet promises, and decide the nation needs a change of government at the upcoming election. They call upon experienced and ruthless political operative Jonathan Wolff to organise their election campaign and defeat the prime minister.

Realising he cannot win the election his way, Wolff initiates an explosive campaign designed to remove the prime minister by defeating him in his own electorate using an independent candidate.

Investigative journalist Anita Devlin is appointed by her editor to promote the Stanley campaign as the publishing owner, unknown to her, is a member of the Mercantiles. She discovers the nefarious Wolff strategically working the campaign, and endeavours to expose his influence and manipulation.

**For more information and purchasing options visit
852 Press.com.au**

She wants her culture and country back. Independence was never ceded, and she will do whatever it takes to get it back, including the ultimate sacrifice. When government peace talks stop, revolution begins.

Revolutionary leader, Nellie Millergoorra, campaigns for an aboriginal homeland to preserve indigenous culture by advocating the prohibition of mining in Arnhem Land using a United Nations declaration to convince a disrespectful government to sign a treaty. Nellie will do whatever it takes to finally gain independence and end government regulation over her people.

When there is no agreement, she recruits mercenary special forces to inflame community chaos establishing an explosive aboriginal revolutionary movement.

In a surprising confrontation with a reluctant prime minister, who is threatened with an ultimatum he can't ignore, Millergoorra negotiates a treaty whilst facing her own battle for survival.

Forgotten People is gripping political thriller featuring surprising plot twists, compelling characters, and a kick-arse female heroine.

**For more information and purchasing options visit
852 Press.com.au**

He's the nation's chief law maker. His daughter is fighting for her life in intensive care, a victim of a terrible crime. Will he ignore the prime minister's demands and his own laws to save her? Or will politics and the Catholic Church prevent him from doing his job?

Treasurer, Parker Osborne, initiates a covert plan, in partnership with Vatican emissary, Cardinal Rosseau, to guarantee proposed euthanasia legislation is destined for failure in the national parliament triggering a leadership challenge.

In a surprising development, the prime minister makes a decision which changes everything.

The Kill Bill is a gripping political thriller featuring emotional and surprising plot twists, convincing characters, and exposes the black-art of politics that will have you questioning the ethics of assisted dying. If you like fast-paced, page-turning thrillers that draw you into the story then Richard Evans' fourth book will not disappoint you.

Buy The Kill Bill today and learn how the black arts of politics really works.

For more information and purchasing options visit
852 Press.com.au

Printed in the USA
CPSIA information can be obtained
at www.ICGtesting.com
LVHW020924150923
758207LV00005B/476

9 780648 932864